DEADLY
CURE

DEADLY CURE

WILLIAM CUTRER, M.D.

SANDRA GLAHN

kregel
PUBLICATIONS

Deadly Cure

© 2001 by William Cutrer and Sandra Glahn

Published by Kregel Publications, a division of Kregel, Inc., P.O. Box 2607, Grand Rapids, MI 49501. For more information about Kregel Publications, visit our Web site: www.kregel.com.

Library of Congress Cataloging-in-Publication Data
Cutrer, William.
Deadly cure / by William Cutrer & Sandra Glahn.
    p.   cm.
    1. Genetic engineering—Fiction. 2. Medical ethics—Fiction. 3. Physicians—Fiction. I. Glahn, Sandra. II. Title.
PS3553.U848 D4   2001   813'.54—dc21   2001033756

ISBN 0-8254-2385-6

Printed in the United States of America

1 2 3 4 5 / 05 04 03 02 01

To Bob Cutrer and Alexandra Glahn—
infusers of life,
having fine minds
and creative potential
waiting to be fully explored.

And to all who value life from the first cell to the final farewell.

Authors' Note

IN THIS, OUR FOURTH COLLABORATIVE WORK—and our second work of fiction—we have endeavored to write an engaging drama set in the context of real-life ethical dilemmas. The rapid advance of scientific knowledge and the legalities of research relating to life and death, love and loss, cloning and stem cell research have enormous ramifications that require careful consideration.

While the plot and characters of *Deadly Cure* are fictional, the techniques portrayed in this story are as real as today's headlines. As a continuation of *Lethal Harvest,* this book includes an invented disease and a few fictional technological procedures, but the research portrayed here (and its potential for good or ill) is both accurate and ongoing.

> *Precious in the sight of the Lord is the death of His saints.*
> —Psalm 116:15

Acknowledgments

THOSE WHO WRITE SUCH BOOKS AS THIS, drawing on the process of years of education, medicine, ministry—and just plain living—owe a debt of gratitude to the many people who have significantly influenced their lives. To all our family, friends, professors, patients, and readers, we express our heartfelt gratitude. Nevertheless, several individuals deserve special recognition.

Sandi would like to express her love and appreciation for Gary, her husband and greatest encourager, a partner in every sense and the embodiment of *hesed,* personified in various characters within this work.

Bill would like to thank Jane, his wife, for her faithful love and tireless devotion to the ministry they share. Gifted by God in so many ways, she is a precious treasure indeed. Also, a deep debt of gratitude is owed to Dr. Danny Akin, mentor and friend, along with colleagues at Baylor Hospital in Dallas for their inspiration and encouragement through the years of medical practice.

We are thankful for those who have given generously of their time to read and provide feedback on parts of the manuscript, including Virginia Swint, Kelley Mathews, Jennie Snow, and

Kathy Rhine. We are also grateful to Dennis Hillman at Kregel, who has been a friend and a brother.

In Lethal Harvest . . .

MALPRACTICE? CARLOS RIVERA HAS FILED suit against Dr. Lucas Morgan and his fertility clinic. The prominent Mexican official claims that the wrong fertilized ova were implanted in his wife, Leigh.

Luc's embryologist, Dr. Tim Sullivan, keeps painstaking records. Surely no such mistake could have happened. Yet after Dr. Sullivan disappears and is presumed drowned in a freak car accident, Luc and his partner, Dr. Ben McKay, find evidence of irregularities.

Ben, who has cut back his medical practice to devote himself to chaplaincy work, comforts Tim's widow, Marnie. She begins to understand God's love as she and Ben work together to puzzle out the mysteries of Tim's secret research and help one another to heal wounds of the past. Some wounds may be beyond healing. The beautiful twin girls born to Carlos and Leigh Rivera from egg cells used in Tim's experiments have a seemingly impossible genetic makeup and a deadly form of leukemia.

The thread of clues takes Luc, Marnie, and Ben into ever more disturbing territory. Tim has been working feverishly toward a breakthrough in the treatment of akenosis, a genetic neurological disease that is destroying the health of the president of the United States. They find out that Tim Sullivan, the president's nephew, was a victim of this deadly family heritage.

As the three friends delve into Dr. Sullivan's work, they get close to uncovering the truth—perhaps too close. Powerful people have a stake in keeping secret the details of Tim Sullivan's life and death. A bomb blast destroys the fertility clinic and almost kills Luc. Then Marnie receives a frightening e-mail from a Dr. Allan Brown, a scientist who appears to have cracked the code on most of the treatment problems related to akenosis. Dr. Brown is seeing amazing results in his experimental treatment of akenosis sufferers.

As she communicates with Dr. Brown, Marnie learns that her husband is alive.

Torn between loyalty to her new Christian faith and her curiosity about her husband's unethical medical breakthroughs, Marnie turns to Ben. Together they confront Tim, a brilliant but out-of-control scientist who has tested the new treatment on himself. As his patients begin to die, Tim turns to Marnie and Ben for help in facing his own mortality.

Chapter One

"WHAT'S THAT NOISE?" DR. BEN MCKAY cringed as he walked with the obstetrics resident from the emercency room to Labor and Delivery.

Fred shook his head. "Don't know. Sounds like one of those old 'baruga' car horns."

"You're too young to remember those."

"Oh, and what are you? Forty? That's not exactly ancient."

The sound persisted and grew louder, then quit as the men approached the L&D unit, located next to the maternity entrance. A woman dressed in black leather and high-heeled boots slammed through the door screaming, "Help! Someone help me! She's having a baby! She's having a baby—in my *car!*"

My turn again, thought Ben, the obstetrics attending physician on "walk-in" call. All OB specialists associated with the Northern Virginia hospital took a turn each month as "doc in the box." As such, they cared for everyone who showed up at the hospital without a personal physician.

Ben picked up his pace. "Go grab a nurse and a precip pack," he told Fred. "I'll see what's up."

Fred nodded, then hustled through the L&D door barking, "Got a delivery on the dock. Get an OB pack!"

Ben followed the hysterical woman—clearly a "lady of the

evening"—out to her car. He fiddled with the door handle on the Chevy. A model from the seventies, the car had rusting chrome and a patchwork of fenders and hood in several shades of blue. When the door finally jerked opened, Ben was met with a scream: "It's coming! It's coming!"

"It's all right." Ben tried to calm her with his voice. "I'm a doctor, and we can help you. Let's just see what's—"

Another contraction gripped the woman. She took her hands from between her legs and clamped them onto Ben's forearms, digging her long nails into his flesh. Ben ignored his own pain and worked to find the baby's head. There it was—the tiny head, already delivered.

Assessing the situation, Ben eased his fingers below the baby's ears and found the neck. Two loops of umbilical cord encircled it.

The woman continued to scream and squeeze Ben's arms as he gently slid the cord, one loop at a time, over the infant's head. Then he guided the baby, starting with the upper shoulder, with gentle downward traction.

Though the woman writhed, kicked, and called Ben a combination of unflattering names, he elevated the infant, freeing the posterior shoulder. Out came the rest of the tiny boy with a gush of water and blood.

"Just breathe, ma'am. The baby's out. Please try to relax."

Ben shifted his position in the tight quarters. With one hand on the baby's chest, he felt a pulse but detected no respiratory effort. *I wonder how much the cord impaired his oxygen supply.* He wiped the infant's face with his thumb and bent over him to puff a few breaths into his mouth.

Ben heard clattering and looked up to see Fred arrive on the dock with a gurney. With him was Maryann, the OB nurse. They had with them the OB pack containing instruments, sponges, cord clamps, and scissors—all the necessities for a rapid delivery.

"How're we doing?" Fred asked. As a first-year resident, he still got excited about obstetrical cases.

"Baby boy," Ben said. "About five pounds. Just now starting to breathe." At that, the new arrival uttered a little cry. Soon his whimpers escalated to a robust scream.

The mother, however, had sunk back into the seat and lay in silence.

Ben spoke in a lowered voice. "How're you doing, Mom?"

She responded with emphatic profanity followed by unintelligible syllables.

Ben looked at the mother's friend and motioned to the patient with his thumb. "What's going on? Has she taken something? Is she on anything?" He smelled no alcohol, but the mother's odd behavior troubled him.

"She took some stuff for the pain. I gotta go." The driver of the vehicle lit a cigarette, turned to get in, then looked back at Ben. She swore. "You really made a mess of my car."

Ben shrugged.

"I gotta go, man. Can you put a move on it?"

Ben swiftly clamped the umbilical cord in two places, then cut between the clamps. He handed the baby to Maryann, who wrapped him in a blanket and headed for the nursery. With considerable difficulty, Ben and Fred lifted the woman out of the back seat and onto the gurney.

Ben turned toward the driver and called out, "Does your friend have any previous pregnancies or medical conditions?"

"I don't know nothin'. I just brang her here." With obstetrical pads and sponges still in the back seat, she fired up the engine, slapped her car in reverse, then squealed out of the lot. Speeding away, she blasted her horn, filling the night with "Ba-ROO-ga."

Ben blinked against the bright lights as he wheeled the patient into the hospital toward the L&D admission desk. She offered no resistance as she lapsed in and out of consciousness.

Looking down, Ben noticed that he was covered with blood, meconium, and amniotic fluid. *What a night!* He glanced at the clock on the wall. *Four-thirty.* He looked at Fred. "I'll go change while you deliver the placenta and repair any tears. Shouldn't be too tough."

"Got it covered." Fred waved Ben in the direction of the doctor's locker room and headed down the hall with the patient.

As Ben passed the nurses' station, the charge nurse looked him over and chuckled. "Birthing room's not good enough for you anymore, eh? Gotta go with the 'Birthing Buick'?"

Ben smiled. "Chevy, actually—old Impala."

Ben walked into the doctors' lounge and glanced in the mirror. Blood was smeared all over his scrubs, hands, even some on his face. *Gee, forgot how much "fun" this was.* Having worked a long, busy shift, he sat down and rested his elbows on his knees, trying to muster up some energy. Finally, he stripped off his scrubs and noticed that the blood had soaked through to his skin. *Better shower before pulling on new blues.*

The hot water stung his arms, and he looked down with alarm. The woman's fierce grip had actually gouged through the skin in several places along his forearms. Ben inspected the wounds to see how deeply she had cut him. *They ought to give us combat pay for "walk-in" call.*

The shower restored some of his energy, and ten minutes later he pulled on fresh scrubs. Fred bounded through the door.

"Hey, doc. How ya doin'?" Fred asked.

"Fine. But really tired of emergencies. Everything go okay?"

"Sure. The placenta was sitting there when we got back, and it took only two stitches to fix a small tear."

"No abnormal bleeding?"

"Nope, she's fine—but a bit snookered. You should've seen her arms. Track marks everywhere. Definitely a junkie. I drew all the labs, drug tox screens. And Maryann said the baby was fine—but they're gonna put him on narcotic withdrawal. Watch for a couple days, just in case."

"Did you get an HIV test in the labs?" Ben tried to sound casual.

"You bet," Fred replied. "I order that on all walk-ins. You never know . . ."

"Good job." Ben stood. "You're right. You never know."

Justin Norwood, age seventeen, of Austin, Texas, checked in at Doctor's Medical and Surgical Hospital in Louisville, Kentucky. Suffering from an inoperable brain tumor, he'd been experiencing increasing seizure activity for eleven months. Still, no one expected him to die—not for at least another year anyway. Yet two weeks after his shot of Genevex's Viragen 828, sores covered his mouth, eyes, and ears, and he had slipped into a coma.

At seven-thirty that morning, Justin's mother entered his private room, followed by the chaplain, her husband, and Dr. David West. Justin lay unconscious, as he had for seven days, caged in by raised bed rails. Mrs. Norwood recoiled slightly at the smell of glycerin and hibiclens soap. After surveying the room, she pulled up the only chair and seated herself next to her son. She held a tissue to her chin and used it to dab at her eyes.

Justin's cowboy hat lay at his side, and his mother reached out to caress its edges. On Justin's left, the ventilator that was keeping him alive made its rhythmic suck-whoosh. Monitors mounted on the wall to the right fed wires to his body.

After fifteen minutes of weeping and good-byes, the parents nodded to Dr. West.

He raised his eyebrows, as if to ask, "Are you sure?"

They nodded in unison again.

The physician flipped the switch on the ventilator, and its bellows ceased delivering oxygen to the unconscious patient.

After a few sobs and a long period of silence, the mother asked, "Is he? . . ."

Dr. West stepped forward and lifted Justin's wrist, holding it for many seconds, checking for a pulse. Then he laid down the wrist and put on his stethoscope. Placing the instrument on Justin's chest, he listened for the minute that spans eternity. "Yes. He's gone now. Peacefully. No pain at all. I'm very sorry for your loss."

Once the family had left, Dr. West went straight to the hospital administrator's office. "We'll have to send a report to NIH," he told her. "A lot of people are going to be upset about this."

The administrator chewed her pencil. "I hate to think what the informed-consent lawyers will try."

"Yeah. His parents are already claiming they had no idea. They come all the way up here from Texas to get cutting-edge treatment and two weeks later their kid's dead."

"They signed the forms."

"I know. But now the kid's old man claims he's read more specific disclaimers before getting his teeth cleaned."

"What have you got for me, Harrison?"

The surgeon general of the United States asked the question without rising to greet his visitor. He motioned abruptly to a chair. "Sit down. It's been far too long since we talked."

"Yes, sir," Dr. Steven Harrison answered flatly.

"And we have some important business to talk about, don't we?"

Harrison nodded as he sat. "Appreciate the opportunity to be here." His tone suggested he didn't.

"Well?"

Harrison shrugged. "What exactly do you want to know?"

"Stop stalling." The surgeon general tapped his fingers together. "I've waited long enough for a status report on your research. I want it *now*. The president's symptoms are rapidly becoming more severe. I'm not sure how much longer we can cover for him."

"Yes, sir. Well, we're exploring three promising fronts." Harrison paused.

"Go on. . . ."

"There's the viral vector work. We're hoping to insert the corrective gene sequence into the cells that way. We've accessed the lab protocol from the Human Genome Project and pinpointed that abnormal sequence in akenosis. It's a tiny abnormality of the Y chromosome. Only a few nucleotide pairs are aberrant. Plus there's the possibility of breakthroughs in other genetic based abnormalities. . . ."

"What have you *got*, Harrison?"

"We have the corrected sequence. We just need a reliable viral probe, something we can trust to deliver it. We have trials underway at several centers. Personally, I think this is our best chance."

"What about those cloned cells you were raving about?"

"We've . . . run into some problems."

"Problems?"

"As you know, Dr. Sullivan, the president's nephew, had some success working with a pure cell line cloned from maternal eggs. But the human trials—"

"Often the treatment with cloned human eggs was fatal."

Harrison nodded. "But the cell line showed remarkable promise. It was able to precisely copy normal healthy tissues and aggregate at the site of injury. I think Sullivan just pushed the human trials too quickly. We're trying to duplicate his work, or obtain some of his special cell culture to pursue this line further."

"You're still trying to *obtain* the cells? What have you been waiting for? Harrison, perhaps I've not made it clear—we're out of time. The president's disease—akenosis—is causing his mental and physical condition to deteriorate rapidly. You mentioned *three* lines of research? Viral vectors, cloned eggs—that's two."

"We're also testing tissue cultures of specific cell types. In the case of the president's disease, the problem is primarily related to the myelin sheath in nerve cells, so we're growing healthy nerve cells in the lab with the hope that we can successfully transplant them. The process has worked for heart, pancreas, and kidney patients. But we haven't had any success in neurological transplants—not yet, anyway. Still, if we can unlock this mystery, we can reconnect transected spinal cords and perhaps reverse many neurological syndromes."

"Harrison, I'm not interested in 'many neurological syndromes.' We have a president who's dying from an inherited disorder. He knows it; we know it. And *you* promised to come through. The president's nephew was our brightest researcher and now he's dead—because of decisions you authorized."

"That's not . . ."

The surgeon general gestured with his hands, silencing Harrison. "Actually, you've promised to deliver on a number of occasions."

"Yes, sir."

"And the best you can do is sit here cowering and talking about reversing neurological syndromes? I suggest you return to your lab and start doing your job. No excuses, no explanations. Get it done! Press all three research protocols to the limit. I don't have to tell you how important this research is to the world—or at least to your country—and . . ." the surgeon general paused, "to your career."

⟋⟍e∂⟋⟍

The ring of the phone in the call room jarred Ben out of sleep. He waved around in the darkness until he picked up the phone. "Yeah?"

"It's nine A.M., doctor. You asked for a wake-up."

"Thanks. Appreciate it." Ben was always polite to the staff, even after only three hours' sleep. Stirring the cobwebs from his brain, he mumbled, "G'bye."

Still lying in bed, he noted his own elevated heartbeat and altered breathing. *Thank God—it was just a dream.* But with the dream, the hidden fear that haunts physicians resurfaced—the danger of contracting a serious disease in the line of duty.

Swinging his legs over the side of the bed, he rubbed his eyes. Ben McKay stood six-foot-one, with dark brown eyes that matched the color of his hair. His strikingly handsome looks matched a happy temperament. When relaxed, his lips naturally turned up at the edges, presenting the world around him with a disarming warmth. But at the same time his eyes mirrored a wistful sadness, a trace of past hurt.

High-risk calls were the part of medicine Ben hadn't missed. Yet now that he'd returned to full practice after six-years, he had to take his turn treating the "walk-ins." He dragged himself to his feet and shuffled down to the doctors' lounge to shave.

Suddenly, Ben remembered that the marks on his arms were real. He stopped and stared down at them. *Better not tell Marnie until I know something for sure; no need to upset her.*

Later, as Ben dressed, tightening his tie, he glanced at his watch. He calculated that he had just enough time to grab a bagel at the doctors' café. Then he'd head over to the new clinic to walk through the punch list with the contractor. He returned to the call room and dialed the admissions desk at L&D.

"This is Dr. McKay," Ben said after the ward clerk answered the phone.

"Yes, doctor?"

"Could you give me the room numbers for last night's walk-ins? We had a Ms. Jordan, Ms. Greene, and a lady that delivered at about five A.M. on the dock."

"You mean the Chevy?"

"Yeah," Ben chuckled. "That's the one."

"We have her down as a 'Jane Doe.' She refuses to give her name. No ID on her. She just went upstairs to seven-oh-four. Not exactly a candidate for Miss Congeniality, is she."

"No," Ben laughed. "More like 'Miss Demeanor.' Guess I'll swing by and see how she is, unless—are any residents there to cover it?"

"No. Dr. Landon's in the back. The rest are upstairs making rounds."

"I'll catch up with them on the ward." Ben hung up and suppressed a yawn. *Breakfast will have to wait.*

Exiting the doctors' elevator, Ben saw the house staff—the chief of OB and several of the first-, second-, and third-year residents. They stood in a white-coated cluster around the nurses' station, reviewing charts and considering the various patients' treatment plans.

"Dr. McKay," came the chief's greeting as he spied Ben approaching. "I hear you had quite a night!" All the residents turned toward him. Fred had spread the story of the hooker, and Ben had been the subject of lively banter over breakfast.

"Yep. Fred and I stayed pretty busy."

"Is it true that you offer an oil change with every delivery?" the chief quipped.

"We're a full-service operation," Ben retorted. "But we don't do windows."

Looking as exhausted as first-year residents always do, Fred chimed in. "If you're looking for our car lady, she's still pretty gorked."

"But is she doing all right otherwise?" Ben worked to keep his voice steady.

"She's fine. Foul-mouthed, but fine. And the baby's doing great, too—no problem. Your Chevy mama wants to stay another day. I'm guessing she likes the free ride, complete with room service. But the nurses are already asking if we can get her out of here."

"And the labs? Anything turn up?"

Fred found the patient's chart and thumbed through it. "Doesn't look like we have the results on anything much yet," he told Ben. "She's real anemic, but we don't have the drug screen back yet, and of course it'll be at least tomorrow before we have the other stuff . . . nothing back on the hepatitis screen or HIV . . . I'll make a note to check on 'em and give you a call, Dr. McKay."

Chapter Two

"*Buenas noches, señor,*" the maitre d' bowed in the presence of Carlos Rivera. "*Señora* Rivera," he nodded his recognition to the mayor's wife.

The tall, slender woman smiled and nodded in return. "Good evening."

In deference to her response, the maitre d' dropped into English. "This way, please." Leigh followed him, and the mayor trailed behind, stopping momentarily at one of the tables to greet a city official.

"Will this be acceptable?" the maitre d' asked, presenting a table by an expansive window.

Carlos nodded and sat across from his wife. Before them, western Mexico's Mountains of Sinaloa stood in massive silhouette against the setting sun. The nearest peak hid enough of the sun's vanishing rays that the lights of the city below already twinkled. The mayor took his wife's hands. "Five years. Happy anniversary. And that blue dress—you look magnificent tonight."

Leigh smiled slightly. "Thank you, Carlos. It's so good to have something to celebrate. With the twins so sick, it's been easy to live mostly at the hospital. I know I've neglected you."

Carlos dismissed his wife's apology with a gesture. "They are improving. Perhaps they will be home soon. Then we can put this behind us." He leaned forward to look into his wife's eyes. "It is you who must forgive me . . . for ever doubting you."

"Of course I have forgiven you." Leigh glanced down, unable to hold his gaze. "But it hurt deeply that you didn't believe me . . . in my love for you."

"It is true. But to look at them is to know that there is not a trace of my blood in them. And you—look at you, my California girl. Blonde. Blue eyes. Our *niñas* look just like you . . . so beautiful. Can you blame me for being suspicious when everywhere we go men cannot take their eyes off you?"

"Oh, Carlos."

The mayor shook his head, making it clear he was not just flattering. "I am sorry. You *know* I am sorry I doubted. But what was I to think? The genetic tests proved they were not mine. How could I even guess that they had *no* biological father—that someone had *cloned* you? That all of their blood came from *you?* Cloning your eggs—it still seems impossible. Your eggs—used for an *experiment?*" Carlos looked away and grew quiet.

He felt the calming touch of his wife's hand on his. Carlos was a powerful and passionate man, and that passion could escalate quickly to rage. He turned to look at Leigh but spoke through clenched teeth. "Those doctors—they do not know who they are dealing with."

Will Boralis pulled into Marnie's driveway as she was just backing out to go meet Ben at the health club. Both rolled down their windows.

"Hey, Dad. What's up?"

"Just coming to get rid of that jungle you call a flower bed," he murmured gruffly.

"Good luck. It's a wreck for sure." Marnie was unconvinced by his tone, knowing that, while he fussed, he really loved doing her gardening.

"Where are you off to?"

"Playing racquetball with Ben."

Will raised his eyebrows. "You've sure been seeing him a lot since he got back from his gig in Romania. How do you run a business?"

Marnie chuckled. "That's a perq of being a publicist, Dad—flexible hours. As long as I've got a personal organizer, a fax, and a laptop, I can work around my social life."

"Must be nice. You know, in my day we worked. . . ."

"Really, Dad, I need to get going. Don't want to keep him waiting."

"Suit yourself. How long you gonna be gone?"

"Just a few hours."

"All right. Have a good time, honey. Emily's out of school at three?" Marnie's daughter, a first grader, occupied much of her grandfather's time.

"Yeah, but I'll be home by then. I sure appreciate the yard work."

Will softened. "Aw, well, I wouldn't do it for just anybody, you know."

"Nice place," Marnie said as she took in the expansive plush green carpet and upscale décor of the exclusive Arlington Heights Sports Club.

"I've reserved court seven. We've got it for an hour," Ben told her.

"Starting when?"

"In ten minutes."

"Great. Where can I change?"

Ben pointed the way, then he entered the men's area. A wooden locker bore a brass nameplate etched with his name. Minutes later, he emerged in gym shorts and a Dallas Cowboys T-shirt. He stationed himself outside court seven, waiting for Marnie.

He didn't have to wait long. As she walked toward him, Ben tried not to stare, but it was hard to take his eyes off her— tanned skin, long dark hair pulled back with a pink hair band, pink sleeveless tank top, and black Spandex shorts. *She's stunning.*

"A Cowboys shirt in Redskin territory?" Marnie raised her eyebrows.

"I like to live dangerously."

"By the looks of your arm, you're not kidding."

"Oh, that? Yeah, a patient scratched me during a tough delivery. Apparently, she didn't like my bedside manner." Ben did his best to laugh it off.

"Nice patient."

Marnie pulled the cover off her racquet and slid her wrist through the loop, so it wouldn't go flying when her hands perspired. Then Ben guided her through the door that doubled as part of the back wall of the raquetball court. The club had just been through a multimillion-dollar renovation, and it still smelled of varnish. Ben opened a trap door, and they placed their water bottles, keys, wallets, and Ben's beeper in the small storage area.

After a few gentle stretches, they were ready. When Ben opened a new can of balls, the whoosh of the vacuum seal echoed in the enclosed court. He bounced a few of the balls with his racquet. "Want to warm up a bit?" he asked.

"Sure."

"You said you've played a little?"

"Uh-huh, a little, but it's been a long time."

Ben stroked one of the balls off the middle of the front wall.

It rebounded directly to Marnie, who returned it smoothly to the center of the wall. After a few shots like that, Ben was taking notice. "Nice backhand and footwork." She had always seemed too delicate to be very athletic, but now he noticed her well-toned arms and legs.

"Thanks," she said without missing a step.

Ben hit a few angle shots, but Marnie gracefully repositioned to play the caroms, effortlessly stroking the ball back to the middle of the front wall.

"About ready?" Ben asked

"Let's give it a go." She smiled broadly.

Ben bounced the ball to her. "Why don't you serve first? Want to keep score or just hit for fun?"

"We can keep score. Just remember, it's been a long time, so be nice."

He walked toward the plexiglass back wall. "I'll be nice. Before Luc got hurt in the clinic bombing, he and I hung out here a lot."

"How's he doing?"

"As my business partner he'll be back soon. But it'll be awhile before he's back to being my racquetball partner—and I miss the competition." Ben bent his knees slightly, leaning forward, ready to play.

"Score's zip–zip," Marnie said, bouncing the ball in front of her as she stood in the serving box. She rocked back, bounced the ball off the floor, and whistled a low smash off the front wall. It barely cleared the service line, hugging the backhand wall.

Ben stood frozen in his stance as the serve blew past him to the back corner. *Lucky shot!*

"You miss the competition, you say." Casually retrieving the bounce off the back wall, Marnie walked back to the server's line. "One–zip."

Ben inched a bit toward his backhand side and readied himself for the next one.

Marnie bounced the black rubber ball twice, drew back her racquet and—smack. The shot was almost identical to the first, low and fast into the front wall, rebounding down the backhand wall. Ben's lunge fell just short.

"Two-zip."

Ben clenched his teeth; he was not used to being aced. "Nice one," he forced himself to say. He hitched up his shorts, tightened his grip, and slid even farther into the backhand corner to receive her next serve.

Marnie bounced the ball steadily, drew back her racquet again, and ripped the serve into the left corner of the front wall. The ball caromed off the side wall, screaming cross court into the forehand side. Ben was hopelessly out of position, and the ball headed into the corner.

"I thought you said you played 'a little,'" he said. He was being hustled.

"Right—a little . . . every day of my life in college."

Ben's look warned her not to toy with him. "You got me. I just assumed you didn't play." He was growing more intense.

"You assumed wrong." It was Marnie's turn to shoot a look.

"All right," Ben said. "Sorry for the male stereotype stuff. You've had your fun. *Now* let's play."

"Long as you don't hold back because I'm a woman—seeing as how you miss the competition and all." Marnie was laughing now.

"I'm not worried yet."

"On with the game, then," she said playfully. "I believe that's three-zip. Did you say *you* have played before?" She teased.

"Just serve the ball. I'm all over it."

She served again. This time Ben was indeed ready, and the game was on.

In another minute, it was Ben's turn to lean over to serve.

"Nice glutes," Marnie said.

Ben looked shocked.

"Oh, c'mon, Ben. It's trash talk, doncha know. A little intimidation."

He smiled slightly and took the remark as progress. It had been awkward for Marnie to relate to a former chaplain. She had once wounded him unintentionally by saying she considered them a "third gender."

He served hard, and again they jumped into motion. He had power and court savvy, was able to occupy space and make it difficult for Marnie to move as she needed. But Marnie had a remarkable touch and made creative shots that left Ben standing flatfooted or slamming headlong into the wall.

For the next thirty minutes the only sounds were balls or bodies hitting the wall or each other, and an occasional "nice shot" or "interference" when one impeded the other's route to the shot. Ben eventually noticed their audience. A few of his friends, with towels draped over their shoulders, stood behind the glass walls, watching from the running track that circled the courts. "We've got a crowd."

Marnie shrugged.

"They never stopped to watch Luc and me play."

"Are there many women players?" Marnie asked, catching her breath between points.

"None like you," Ben said. "Beautiful, articulate, and athletic—is there anything you can't do?"

"You do *so* exaggerate." Marnie smiled. "It's your serve."

Marnie won the game by the narrowest of margins.

Seeing that he had lost, Ben's friends ragged on him from the gallery. "Hey, old man, you're toast—burnt toast! Whipped by a woman—wearing pink!"

They played again; this time Ben won by three points. He did not even try to tone down his elation as he pulled her into a quick hug. "I can't wait to set you up to play Luc when he's back in action. You'll kill him."

"Whatever." Marnie chuckled.

As Ben prepared for the tie-breaking third game, he noticed that some of her fragrance had rubbed off on him.

Both competed intensely, hoping to win again before their time ran out. The score was 10-12 in Ben's favor when his beeper went off. By the time he'd returned the call, their court time had expired.

"Great game," he said. "Sorry it had to end so abruptly."

"No problem. But don't think you won just because you were ahead."

"Wouldn't think of it." Ben smiled and stood looking at her. "You were incredible. I can't wait to do this again."

"I'd love to."

"Got time for the hot tub?" He could feel the jolt of testosterone from their fierce competition.

"Sure."

Ben made it to the water first. He was thinking about how the chlorine in the water stung his injured arm—until Marnie appeared in a bathing suit. He had never seen her in one. He gave her an appreciative glance as she approached, then he quickly looked away. *Wow.*

"How's the temp, Ben?"

"You've probably had hotter bubble baths. Probably not even a hundred degrees."

Marnie stepped in and sat down. "They must not be in a hurry to move people out then."

"Guess not."

"Ahhh." Marnie leaned back, letting the water engulf her neck up to her hairline. She closed her eyes. "I'm certainly in no hurry."

Ben wondered if she'd said that because of the warm water or the company. He found a jet for his lower back and sat, barely touching Marnie. He reached for her hand and interlocked her fingers with his. Her eyes opened only long enough to complement her smile. After a few moments' silence, she spoke again. "I've played a lot of racquetball but never with a guy who drew a crowd."

"They were watching *you* kicking my bu—uh, my *nice* glutes."

Marnie giggled. "Thanks, but it wasn't me they were watching; it was *us*," she insisted.

Ben leaned back and relaxed. "*Us*. I like the sound of *us*."

Marnie, her eyes still closed, ran her fingers lightly over his forearm. As she did so, a thought caused Ben stabbing pain. *What if I've got HIV? She's already lost one spouse. Couldn't put her through that again. And it'll be six months before I know for sure.* He gently removed her hand from his arm and scooted over so she had room to rest it on the seat between them.

Marnie looked at Ben, a question in her eyes.

Ben shook his head slightly.

"Did I do something wrong?"

Ben saw the hurt. "No. You're fine."

She studied his expression.

"I mean it. You're fine."

Just then a senior couple who had finished swimming laps descended the stairs into the hot tub.

"How's the water?" they asked.

"Temperature's a little cool here," Marnie answered, glancing at Ben as she spoke.

Their privacy interrupted, Ben and Marnie soon headed for the locker rooms.

Chapter Three

MARNIE WAS FINISHING UP IN the locker room when her cell phone rang. She looked at the caller ID but didn't recognize the number.

"Hello?"

"Honey, I've got bad news," a panting voice told her.

"Who is this?"

"Ruth Ann, your neighbor."

"What . . . what is it?"

"I had to call nine-one-one for your father. Looks like he's had a heart attack."

"Is he alive? Is he all right?"

"The ambulance just left with him."

"Was he conscious?"

"Yes, he was able to tell me your number while the paramedics worked on him. He collapsed out on the lawn. And he seemed to be in pain."

"Thanks, Ruth Ann. I'm on my way. Wait—where is he?"

"I didn't think to ask where they were taking him. Oh, dear!"

Marnie stifled a groan. "That's all right. I'll find out. Gotta go." She clicked off the phone, grabbed her gym bag, and rushed out to find Ben. He was waiting for her at the club's café.

"Dad's had a heart attack!"

"What?!"

"A heart attack. The neighbor just called me. He was conscious, in a lot of pain. But she forgot to ask where they were taking him. Ben, I don't know where he is! I should've been there. I should've been helping him out there—it's *my* yard." She began to cry. "We'll have to call all the emergency rooms. He was doing some yard work for *me*," she said hoarsely.

"Marnie, let me have your phone for a second. What's your address?"

She answered him as she handed the phone to him, and he punched in some numbers.

"Yes, this is Chaplain McKay. You just sent a unit to forty-seven-eighteen Ninth Street to pick up an elderly gentleman—possible heart problem?

"Forty-seven sixteen? Yeah . . . probably called from next door . . . yes . . . yes, I see . . .

"Unit seven-fourteen? And where are they en route? . . . Doctor's Hospital. . . . Thanks so much for your help."

Marnie stared in amazement.

"Chaplain's line. It goes straight to nine-one-one dispatch. Even though I'm back to practicing medicine, they don't mind if I use it. Let's go. I'll drive." As they walked briskly to his car, Ben phoned the receptionist at the clinic where he'd been practicing until the new clinic's grand reopening. "Lisa? Dr. McKay here. I need you to get me the number to the physicians' ER at Doctor's Hospital."

He turned to Marnie, "Help me remember this number."

She fumbled in her purse for a pen and wrote it down as he called it out.

"Thanks, Lisa," he said. He punched in the numbers Marnie had just written. After identifying himself, he asked for the triage doctor.

While he was on hold, Marnie reached the passenger's side of his car. Ben fumbled with his key and then opened the door for her. He got in the driver's seat and reached for his seatbelt before speaking on the phone again. "Hey, Sam—Ben McKay here. I understand you have a patient, Will Boralis, just arrived in unit seven-fourteen. Can you give me a status report?"

Ben held on for a minute, then said, "Thanks. And would you page Dr. Rosenthal—have him ring me at . . ." He turned to Marnie, "What's this cell number?"

After he had finished, Marnie asked, "Is Dad okay?"

"Doc says he's looking good, breathing easy, making a fuss."

"That's Dad."

"I still have chaplain privileges at Doctors' and a cardiologist buddy who consults there."

"Thanks for comin'," Will said, looking up at Ben.

"How are you doing?"

"Feeling pretty important. I have my own private OB/Gyn."

Ben laughed. "How do you feel?"

"Actually, a lot better. But then, with enough morphine, I'm guessing everybody says that."

"I see it hasn't dampened your mood any," Ben smiled. "What happened?"

"I was moving some plants in the yard. Thought it was just indigestion. Good thing the neighbors were around to see me collapse on the lawn. It was pretty scary." He lay silently for a moment and then asked, "Is Marnie around?"

"Uh-huh. In the waiting room. I'll bet I could sneak her in if you're up for it."

"Ahh, I hate to cause a fuss." Will sounded unconvincing. "Appreciate your coming. Sorry to mess up your racquetball game."

"We were finished anyway. You should've told me she was an ace."

"All-Conference in college."

Will smiled at Ben's pained expression.

"Anything you need before I go get Marnie?" Ben asked.

"No, but thanks."

After a few quick phone calls, Ben returned to the ER waiting room for Marnie. As he approached, Marnie stood and searched his face, her eyes full of questions.

"He's going to be fine," he assured her. "Want to see him?"

"Can I?"

Ben glanced over each shoulder then leaned closer to Marnie and whispered, "With the right friends, sure."

He ushered her back through the ER to her father.

Minutes later, a nurse poked her head around the curtain and spoke to Ben and Marnie. "We'll let you know when he's ready for transfer to coronary care. He should be up there in an hour or so."

"Thanks," Marnie said.

Ben inclined his head toward the exit. "Your dad needs rest and quiet now."

Marnie gently brushed her hand across the stubble on her father's cheek and wiped her eyes. Then Ben escorted her out.

Back in the empty waiting room, Marnie swallowed hard, then sobbed tears of relief. "First I lost Mom . . . then Tim. . . . I was so afraid Dad was next."

Ben held her as she cried, fighting back his own tears. *And I may be next. . . .*

Finally, she pulled away. "What else can you tell me?" she asked, looking up at him.

"Early test results say it doesn't look like a heart attack," he said in a soothing voice. "At least, if it was, there's no significant damage. Your dad may need some exercise and diet modification—probably won't be eating any more of your Suicide Fettuccine Alfredo. But that just leaves more for me. EKG shows the acute changes are reverting to normal, which is typical with angina. He's feeling better, probably thanks to a combination of nitroglycerine, oxygen, and morphine. His first cardiac labs look normal. They'll repeat them in twenty-four hours to see if they're elevating. And just to be sure we've got all the bases covered, I called my cardio buddy, Dr. Rosenthal. He'll check the test results right away. If your dad is still at immediate risk, he can do an emergency angiogram/angioplasty, even this afternoon."

"What?"

"If your dad has any damage or deterioration, Dr. Rosenthal can get right in there with his balloons and stints and save any heart muscle that's in jeopardy."

"When did you get all *this* set up?" Marnie asked, clearly grateful for his initiative.

Ben smiled, "Hey, what are friends for?"

Marnie threw her arms around Ben and rested her cheek on his. "You're the best. How can I thank you?"

Ben returned her embrace and squeezed his eyes tightly shut, filled both with pleasure and pain by her spontaneous outburst of affection.

"Let me arrange for someone to pick up Emily. Looks like I'll be here a while."

"Good idea."

Just as Marnie was clicking off her cell phone a few minutes later, Ben saw Bob King through the picture windows.

"Look—we've got company."

"It's Bob! How did he know?" She looked at Ben.

"I called him from the phone in ER." Bob was on staff at Cherrydale Church, where Marnie and Ben attended. A kindly gentleman in his sixties, he often rode with police officers. It was he, in fact, who had broken the news to Marnie that her husband's car had disappeared into the Potomac.

Marnie rushed to greet him. Ben had stood as they approached, and the two men exchanged a hearty handshake.

"Appreciate your coming," Ben said.

"An honor to walk with you through tough times—and you've certainly had plenty of them," he said looking at Marnie.

The three friends sat together, and Bob was brought up to date on Will's condition. Then Ben stood to leave.

"I've got to get back to the office."

Marnie's look into Ben's eyes said more than the catch in her voice as she spoke. "Thank you, Ben."

Chapter Four

DR. WEST WALKED INTO HIS OFFICE and leaned across his desk to pick up the phone. He had to call Dr. Steven Harrison, the surgeon general's appointee for special research. Harrison had a personal interest in Dr. West's work.

"Doctor Harrison, this is Dr. West in Louisville, Kentucky. You asked me to keep you informed on the Genevex therapy in the Norwood case—the malignant glioma . . . right. Um . . . he's, well . . . he has expired. . . .

"Yes, sir, three days ago. I wanted to wait for the post report before contacting you. . . . I'm afraid so. His condition went rapidly downhill. . . .

"There was definitely a brief period of improvement, but his seizures returned. Temperatures continued to spike over a hundred and six. . . .

"Uh-huh. In the end he stopped making any respiratory effort on his own. EEG was flat. . . .

"Yes, of course, that risk is always present, but . . .

"Yes, we used Viragen 828. . . . The post CT scans demonstrated massive destruction throughout the brain. . . . Correct, sir. The cause of death was herpes encephalitis. . . .

"Sir? . . .

"The president will never go for *what* now? The president of what, sir?"

Once they were alone in the waiting area, Bob King turned to Marnie, "I guess you're pretty familiar with the hospital scene."

"Not so much. Tim specialized in embryology, so his patient care was limited to humans tinier than the head of a pin."

Bob chuckled.

Marnie continued. "Most of his work took place in the lab."

"I see. Well, I'm sorry—again—for your loss and all you've been through in the past year." Bob paused, carefully considering his next words. "I know Ben was a great support, and it seemed that you two were an item. But then things seemed to cool off."

Marnie pursed her lips, then looked around the empty room before speaking. "Actually, I've been thinking I should to talk to you. You don't know the half of it."

"What do you mean?"

Marnie motioned toward the corner of the room farthest from the door. When they were seated, she spoke in a hushed tone. "Bob, this is confidential."

"Of course," he said and drew closer.

"Even my own father doesn't know—but you're my pastor." She took a deep breath and continued. "Tim didn't die by drowning; he died from self-administered gene therapy."

Bob stared at her.

"But—but I thought . . ."

Marnie nodded. "I know. But the truth is, Tim had been working on some experiments to cure a genetic disease. He had early symptoms of the disease himself. But his research involved human embryos, which at the time was taboo."

"And it's not now?"

"That's right. It was illegal then; the laws have changed a bit, so most of what he did is allowed now. Anyway, a court case threatened to uncover his work, so he opted to disappear. But he was still alive, with a new identity, continuing his research. He went by the name Dr. Allen Brown."

"The *Washington Post* said—"

"He drowned in the accident, and they found his body months later."

Bob nodded.

"Ben and Luc Morgan—Ben's other partner—helped me do some nosing around. We got too close to learning the truth. So Tim contacted me to stop us. He told me that my life was in danger unless I left it alone."

Bob leaned back, trying to digest the magnitude of what he was hearing. "I had no idea. . . ."

"No one did. At the time we had to keep it secret. Tim convinced himself that his experimental gene therapy would work. He injected himself with it. He died a few weeks later. A massive brain hemorrhage."

"So the news about the body being found in the Potomac?"

"They released that story the morning after he actually died."

Bob shook his head. "Wow."

Marnie continued. "Anyway, nobody would admit what had happened, since the truth . . ." Marnie looked around again, "could've hurt the president."

Bob's eyes grew wide. "The president . . . of the United States? Is that why the clinic was blown up?"

Marnie nodded. "I got the impression from Tim that the explosion was a warning. Actually, I think whoever did it meant to kill Luc, too."

Bob looked at her thoughtfully. "*That's* why you and Ben suddenly broke off your romance. You'd found out your husband was still alive. And there I was, encouraging him to get together with you."

"You couldn't have known."

Bob looked down at his hands. "And after you'd been through all *that,* Ben left for a few months in Romania." Bob looked back at Marnie. "Was that good or bad?"

Marnie shrugged. "He'd made the promise to help at the hospital there. I think he did the right thing to go, even though it was tough. Everyone thought Tim had been dead for six months, but Ben knew I'd really just lost him. He said he didn't want to complicate my grief process. But what a roller coaster! I needed time to sort through my feelings about a lot of things—including Ben. But he was the only one who knew what really had happened, so it was hard to have him gone."

"And he's a man of honor, so he kept his word to the Romanians."

Marnie smiled and nodded. "You've known Ben for a long time. Once he says he will or won't do something, he sticks to it, even if it kills him."

Bob nodded.

"While he was in Romania setting up the clinic, we kept in touch daily by e-mail. But I'm sure glad he's back."

"No doubt." Bob shook his head slowly and placed a gentle hand on Marnie's shoulder. "I'm so sorry . . . so sorry for all you've been through. . . . And now this." He motioned toward the ER.

Leigh Rivera eased around a loaded serving cart in the spacious but bustling kitchen of her hacienda in Culiacán, Sinaloa, Mexico. "Is everything set?" she asked, glancing around at the orderly chaos. "Maria, you always amaze me. If there's anyone who can throw a fiesta, it's you!"

"Ah, *señora, gracias!*" Maria cocked her head to one side. "I am so happy for you and the mayor that your *niñas* are coming home today. And welcome home to you! You can stop living at the hospital. Just look at you—they don't feed you right!" She wrapped the slender blonde American in her large arms. "It will be so good to have you back here. I thank God, who is good." She crossed herself.

Leigh's blue eyes looked gratefully down into Maria's. "Thank you. Yes, it's a wonderful day. It's been so many months since . . ." Leigh lowered her voice, "since that horrible night when they got so sick. What would I have done without your help?"

The cook looked at the floor and wiped a tear with her apron. "It was nothing, *señora*."

"I have to show you something, Maria." Leigh handed her the gown and plastic gloves she had been holding. "You'll need to wear these when you touch the babies. They're much better, but they're still very sick."

Maria looked alarmed. "*Señora,* may I ask—is that the reason for all the construction here? They are still very sick? The mayor tells me so little."

"Yes. The babies still need a lot of medical equipment. Tonight our guests will be able to see them only through the glass. But, Maria, don't be sad. At least our little girls will be home!"

By eleven that night, the Riveras' "Welcome Home" celebration had kicked into full swing. The impressive guest list indicated just how well-connected the mayor was. Several couples at the table had stood to dance, leaving Carlos Rivera alone with his thoughts. Amid the laughter, food, and music, he watched his wife from across the room. Despite her exhaustion, Leigh positively glowed—she was so thrilled to have her children home at last.

Carlos, too, was glad to have them back, but he still felt angry that they were ill. More than that, he felt recurring bouts of rage that the twins carried the proud Rivera name, but nothing else from his family. They were totally "hers" instead of "theirs." It mattered not at all that the implantation of experimental embryos in his wife's body was not deliberate. The late Dr. Sullivan had performed unauthorized cloning experiments with her eggs, and his partner had accidentally transferred the wrong embryos into Leigh's uterus during an *in vitro* fertilization cycle. The afternoon's mail had not helped his mood on that score.

His assistant jarred him out of his thoughts with, "Good evening, *señor.*"

"Good evening, Ramon," the mayor smiled.

"It is a wonderful party."

Carlos nodded his acknowledgment and motioned for Ramon to join him at the table. The first assistant, a discreet, good-looking bachelor, had gained Carlos's trust in the past few months. Now seemed like an ideal time to tell Ramon even more.

Carlos lowered his dark eyes. "Ramon, I want to talk to you about something."

Ramon said nothing, but he leaned in, giving Carlos his undivided attention.

"Today, I received a letter by courier from my attorney establishing the settlement from Dr. Luc Morgan in Virginia. The doctor told me on the phone six months ago that I would be satisfied with the terms. But he lied. I am not pleased; he is not to be trusted."

Ramon leaned in even more closely as the beat of the music grew louder.

"The letter claims the doctor cannot pay beyond his insurance policy limit, but that amount—a mere two million U.S. dollars—is only half what I demanded. I have already rejected this. We need a fair settlement."

Upon hearing the amount, Ramon remained cool, but his eyes grew wide.

Carlos continued. "Dr. Morgan promised to set up a trust fund for the babies." He seethed as he added, "The babies are sick because of his dead partner's experiments! But the letter I received today sounded like an ultimatum—no trust fund until there is a settlement. His attorney is mistaken if he thinks I will agree." Carlos took a drink and remained silent for a moment. His assistant waited patiently.

"Ramon, the clinic in Virginia has our remaining embryos, so we must proceed carefully. My wife and I want more children. We must not jeopardize anything. We will get satisfaction eventually."

The band announced a ten-minute break, and couples from his table began returning to their chairs. Carlos lowered his voice. "But for now, we play the game—we just play it skillfully." He ended abruptly with, "We will finish this later."

The next morning, Ramon tried to reach Luc, but the clinic was closed. A message directed him to call Ben's beeper number. Ben returned the call from the hospital clinic.

"Yes, Mr. Gomez, I'm Dr. Morgan's partner. He's at home recovering from some injuries. What can we do for you?" Ben asked.

Ramon asked a few vague questions. How much did this doctor know about Carlos Rivera? Ben quickly assured him that he was familiar with the case.

"Mr. Rivera wishes for Dr. Morgan to send his frozen embryos to Mexico," Ramon informed him.

"We're fully willing to do that, sir," Ben assured him. "Actually, we don't have the embryos here—although, they'll be sent to our new clinic soon. However, we have another proposition for you. Instead of our sending the embryos to Mexico, we'd like to invite the Riveras, as guests of the clinic, to come to Washington for an embryo transfer."

Ramon was suspicious. "I do not wish to sound bold, but why should we trust you?"

Ben spoke gently. "If Mr. Rivera wants us to send the embryos, we will. But we also want him to consider that our success rates are better than those in Culiacán right now. We want to give the embryos the best possible chance of survival."

Over the next ten minutes, Ben tried to assure Ramon that Luc and he were looking out for the Riveras' best interests. Finally, Ramon put Ben on hold. When he came back on the line, he told Ben, "Dr. McKay, the mayor invites you and Dr. Morgan to come to Culiacán to view our medical resources. Perhaps you could then advise us on conforming to international standards. And perhaps you could bring the embryos with you when you come."

"I'll talk with Dr. Morgan about the possibility. I appreciate the invitation," Ben said. "But I'd suggest that we not bring the embryos that way—the transport medium won't remain stable for long if the facilities aren't adequate. We need to see the clinic first."

Chapter Five

THE NEXT MORNING, BEN EASED HIMSELF into a living room chair in Luc's home. "I had an interesting conversation with Carlos Rivera's assistant yesterday afternoon," he told his partner.

"Good news about the settlement?"

"No. Sorry. Rivera wanted us to send their embryos to Culiacán. I countered with an invitation that he and his wife come here for a transfer instead. Then he invited us to come scope out their clinic in hopes of doing it there."

"So how did you leave it? I can't travel."

"I told him I'd talk to you."

"What do you think?"

"A little diplomacy could help in the court case."

"As far as I know, a settlement is in the works, . . . but, hey, it couldn't hurt."

"I've been wanting to go down there with a mission team. Maybe I can do both at once. I'd really like to go. In fact, last night I got permission from our denominational agency in Mexico to take a team to work with a little church in Culiacán, if you agree, buddy."

Luc was all smiles. "Sounds like a good sign. You're more diplomatic than I am, and you know Spanish. The only sentence I know in Spanish is 'Where's the bathroom?'"

Ben laughed. *"Donde está el baño?"*

"Sí," Luc said. "Whatever it takes to make Carlos Rivera more amiable. And I agree about the embryos. It's too risky to take them until we know what sort of facilities they have."

"This is Dr. McKay," Ben spoke into the phone, "calling about a Jane Doe, a 'walk-in' I delivered on the third of March. Ran an HIV and drug screen. Got the screen back—waiting on the HIV. Any results yet?"

"I'll check, doctor."

Ben cradled the phone on his shoulder and untwisted a metal paper clip while he waited. After a minute, the lab attendant returned.

"Do you have her admit number?"

"Oh, of course. Sure. Sorry. Let's see here." Ben checked the record in front of him. "It's one-zero-zero-five-four-three-dash-six-four-six."

Ben waited through the long pause.

"Yes, doctor. That test came back HIV-positive."

"And the Western Blot?" his voice shook as he asked about the follow-up study that confirms the initial screen.

"Yes, sir, it's a positive, too. And the note says that Public Health has been notified."

"Good. Thank you." Ben gently hung up the phone, conscious that he'd remember this moment for the rest of his life—however short that might be. He felt a little faint. But, after a full minute staring at his desk pad, he stood to attend to the next waiting patient.

"Dr. Harrison, this is Dr. Rex Beard." Dr. Beard shuffled through papers with one hand while he held the phone in the other. "I'm responding to your request for an update."

"Thank you, doctor. What have you got?"

"Pretty good news, actually. The most promising is Alison Ward. She's a patient here in Oregon at Salem Memorial Hospital. Thirty-seven years old with multiple brain tumors. Otherwise in good health."

"Let me get my note pad. . . . All right, please continue," Harrison said.

"She presented with interesting symptoms. Headaches. Tingling in her left knee and in her jawbone. A burning sensation in her right thumb. Lost sight in her left visual field. Initially, some metallic smells and tastes gave the clue that helped with her diagnosis."

"And the therapy? I presume that's why you're calling."

"Yes, Dr. Harrison. She received a shot of Genevex's herpes simplex viral vector with the TK gene. At ninety-six hours we started chemo to destroy the altered tumor cells, sparing the normal brain cells."

"And? . . ."

"It's amazing. She's experienced rapid improvement. Her sight has been restored, and her medical team is just ecstatic. It looks really promising."

"Is she your only test case?"

"No, sir. She's one of seven with surgically inaccessible brain tumors. Actually, she has too many tumors to make surgery practical. Of the seven subjects, four have improved and three remain unchanged."

Ben waited in the office of Dr. Mark McLaughlin, a specialist in infectious diseases. *Sure feels weird to be on this side of the desk.*

In a few minutes, Dr. McLaughlin entered. Ben stood to shake his hand.

"Good to see you, Ben, though I'm sorry about the circumstances."

"Thanks for working me in on short notice."

They both sat, and Dr. McLaughlin thumbed through Ben's file. "So, you were being the Good Samaritan and didn't have a chance to double glove? Bummer."

"Yeah, fortunately the guy who was helping me did, though he didn't get scratched up like I did."

"A real appreciative patient, eh?"

"She didn't call me anything I'd never heard. She had a pretty limited vocabulary."

Dr. McLaughlin smiled sympathetically. "I know the type. You risk your life to help them, and they cuss you out."

"Basically."

Dr. McLaughlin shifted to a more serious tone. "You know the routine, Ben. We draw blood once a month for six months. If they're all clean, you're off the hook. Because of the exposure, you might want to take oral meds now. I would, if I were you."

"Will that obscure the test results?" Ben asked.

"Not really. We can still make the diagnosis, but if you did contract HIV, the meds could make a huge impact on your survival and symptom-free interval."

Survival. The word sliced through Ben. He'd used it often enough, but it had never applied to *his* future.

His doctor noticed. "Yeah. It's a bad deal. But the odds are still with you, even with the scratches and the blood exposure. The likelihood of infection is probably only 10 or 20 percent. Let's look on the positive side. Incidentally, did the patient have any other positives?"

"Don't know. I took the gammaglobulin for Hep A and have been vaccinated for Hep B, so I should be in good shape there. She came up negative on those."

"Good. Sounds like we've got the bases pretty well covered, then."

"Beyond living and dying, another key concern is a relationship I'm in."

"Well, you're certainly at risk. You need to use protection. I recommend—"

"Sorry. I wasn't clear. The relationship isn't physical in that way. I was just thinking out loud."

"Does she know about this?"

"No."

"I see."

"Everything with us is sort of on hold for now. I have to see how this is going to turn out. She's already lost one husband, and I wouldn't want to put her through that again."

Dr. McLaughlin looked down solemnly. After thinking for a few seconds he said quietly, "Let me start you on the meds."

It was Saturday morning. The fear was still in the background, but Ben awoke with a vague sense of pleasant anticipation. It went beyond the dream he'd just had about Marnie. Still too groggy to know why, he just knew it promised to be a decent day.

He opened one eye and glanced at the digital clock. *I've got ten more minutes.* He had awakened before the alarm. In a few moments he was lucid enough to remember: *Today's the day.*

The grand opening of the new clinic was scheduled for ten that morning. At last, Luc had recovered from the burns and broken femur caused by the explosion in the last clinic. The occupational therapist had given him the green light to return to full practice. Ben had resigned his position as hospital chaplain when he resumed full-time medical practice. He had been seeing patients at the hospital's clinic, which allowed for the opportunity to do work-ups and minor procedures. But he was eager to get back to doing more of the high-tech procedures—*in vitro* fertilization and ovarian hyperstimulations.

Now, after all the months of blueprints, hassling with contractors, and hiring new staff, Ben and Luc would be practicing medicine together full time again. It had been six years since personal tragedy had caused Ben to resign full-time practice. It was time to come back.

He lay on his bed praying, asking God to spare his life and to help him and Luc touch the lives of hurting people through their new clinic.

Ninety minutes later, Ben backed his Explorer out of the driveway and headed to the Northern Virginia Center for the Enhancement of Fertility, or Novacef. As he pulled into his freshly marked parking spot behind the building, he noticed Luc's car—a green Jaguar—parked in its space. *Guess he's champing at the bit, too! Hope he enjoyed his disability leave, because his nights "on call" will be back soon—like, starting tonight.*

Ben locked his car with a beep and walked to the back door. He punched in the security code and entered the clinic. "Mmmm." He inhaled deeply the smell of new paint, wood, and furniture mingled with the catered brunch. Before even seeing the tables heaped with food, he knew he'd find bacon and sausage.

Looking around for Luc, he found the place empty. *Where is he?* He peeked out the front door and saw no one, then leaned down to pick up the *Washington Post* that had been delivered. After closing the door, he tucked the paper under his arm and stood in the waiting room, his arms folded and a broad smile on his face. For a few minutes he watched brightly colored fish circling rock formations in the saltwater tank in the center of the room.

Ben looked through the window into the business office from the reception area. *Beautiful.* Silent computer terminal screens waited to be filled with medical histories and billing information. The charting area featured the latest—a rolling system of files. Already patient charts had been transferred from the hospital clinic where Ben had been working. Obviously, the new staff had already been busy getting everything organized for Monday's opening.

Some five hundred dignitaries, doctors, nurses, and friends had received invitations to the event. Ben and Luc had scheduled it for that Saturday from ten until four, so nurses from various shifts could drop in, and doctors could come by after rounds.

Ben walked back to his wood-paneled office. He ran his fingertips over his cherry desk, credenza, and the desktop computer. He picked up and studied the phone. Yes, it was set up to receive his laptop modem line. *Everything's just great.* Even his reference books smelled new, since his own library had burned in the fire that followed the bombing. *Good thing they gave us a generous insurance settlement!*

He walked around and sat at his desk, folded his hands, and propped up his feet. Since he had more than an hour before visitors arrived, he unfolded the paper and turned to the sports page. Then he flipped back through the national and regional news. A page-three medical article caught his attention.

Salem, Ore.—One of the first test subjects to receive a dramatic experimental gene therapy died Friday from complications following a stroke at Salem Memorial Hospital.

Doctors in the experimental clinical trials report that Alison Ward, 38, lost consciousness suddenly and quickly succumbed to massive bleeding in her brain stem. Ward was being treated for multiple brain tumors.

In a brief statement to reporters, Dr. Rex Beard related that the gene therapy was initially successful, obliterating tumors and restoring the patient's eyesight.

"In this case, the gene therapy worked," Dr. Beard insisted. "However, the chemotherapy, while destroying the tumor, also caused a massive brain stem hemorrhage. A certain amount of risk always accompanies this sort of therapy. Our condolences go to her family."

Hmm. Ben shook his head slowly. *Massive brain hemorrhage. Just like Tim Sullivan and his human guinea pigs.*

Of the six other patients in the trial, three are reported to have improved.

Ward's husband confirmed that his wife had signed liability releases in which she accepted the risks involved.

"It looked safe. The doctors presented it as being safe. Since it would benefit everybody, I encouraged her to do this. We were misled," Mark Ward complained.

Test subjects were given the herpes simplex virus—the virus that causes the common cold sore—as a "viral vector." A viral vector acts as a vehicle to carry specially engineered DNA to the cancer site. Using such viruses to "infect" the cancer cells, researchers use genetic material to deposit healthy DNA within the tumor cells. The carrying virus can be neutralized to prevent it from causing its usual illness.

In the case of Ms. Ward, the herpes virus transplanted a corrective gene that would make cancer cells highly sensitive to the chemotherapy drug ganciclovir. The tumor was "painted" with the gene, which the chemotherapy readily attacked, killing the tumor.

The tests are being conducted by the genetic research laboratory Genevex, and . . .

The story continued several pages away, and Ben searched for several seconds.

. . . the pharmaceutical company issued a statement: "The failure in this case is not related to failure of Genevex's technique in genetic engineering. It was, unfortunately, working too well, leading to the unusual complication that took the patient's life."

Investigators will make a full report to members of the U.S. Senate's Health, Education, Labor, and Pensions public health subcommittee. Members of this committee have been assigned to oversee gene therapy clinical trials to determine whether there is a need for more vigorous government supervision.

Too bad. Gene therapy looks so promising, but it's still not ready for primetime.

"Ahem."

Ben was startled out of his reverie and jumped up to clap Luc on the back. "Hey, where've you been, buddy?"

Luc's eyes gleamed. "We got a shipment this morning from UT Southwestern—the Riveras' embryos and Tim's LG cell line."

Ben smiled. "Ahh, the infamous cloned Leigh genes?"

"Uh-huh. I was back in the lab—making sure the refrigerator is as tight as Fort Knox."

"Good idea—we don't need any repeat performances of the last tragedy. So are you ready for this?"

"Sure am! You know I've been reading journals and doing phone consults, but I can't wait to get back to patient care. And it'll be great to have you as my partner, delivering babies again. You made a great chaplain, and you probably helped a lot of people after what you went through losing Juli—" Luc quickly changed direction. "But I'm glad you're back full-time."

"Thanks," Ben smiled, wearing a faraway expression. Then a mischievous smile flashed across his face. "And I'm glad you're healed from all your injuries—because *you're* on call tonight and tomorrow."

After a mother-daughter breakfast, Marnie dropped off Emily at home, where she and her grandfather could look after each other. Will was still officially convalescing, but already he was beginning to feel more like his healthy, irritating self. She headed to the clinic. Once there, she peeked her head in the front door. "Hi. I'm a little early," she told Ben, who was standing in the reception area.

"Great! Come on in! I'll give you the early-bird tour."

Surveying the surroundings, Marnie nodded her approval. "Wow, this looks classy!"

"Glad you like it," Ben grinned. "Come on, let me show you around."

When they got to his office, she noticed that her own picture was displayed prominently on his desk. Ben looked down at her brown eyes and saw them sparkle. "Is that to ward off women who want to marry a good-looking, single doctor?" she asked.

Ben smiled. "No way. It's to announce to the world what a lucky guy I am. Of course, most people will think it's my teenage daughter—or maybe they'll think it's the picture that came with the frame."

Marnie chuckled. "Yeah, right." She sat in his leather chair, admired his computer, and eyed the books on his shelves.

"How's your dad?" Ben asked.

"Much better. He's home now. I guess he'll live with us for a while. He needs to eat some healthy cooking."

Ben nodded thoughtfully. "Sounds good."

"That whole deal scared us all, but it looks like we'll have a happy ending. Thanks again for your help, doctor."

"Any time." He returned her smile and nodded toward the reception area. "Come on. It's about time to shake hands and kiss babies . . . or is that shake babies and kiss hands?"

"I hope not!" Marnie exclaimed. She hopped up and followed him out. They passed Luc's office. In the next office, a diminutive woman of about thirty-three years was shelving books.

"Hello, Dr. Pak," Ben said.

"Hello, Dr. McKay. I'm just arranging things."

"Dr. Pak, let me introduce Marnie Sullivan. Marnie, this is Dr. Courtney Pak, our new embryologist."

Marnie extended her hand "Pleased to meet you."

Courtney sized up Marnie, then shook her hand. They all stood for a moment in awkward silence.

"We're taking the grand tour," Ben said.

"Yes, the place is lovely," Marnie added. "Really nice."

Courtney, apparently eager to keep working, nodded and turned back to the boxes. Taking the hint, Ben and Marnie excused themselves and continued down the hall.

"So, tell me about her." Marnie said.

"We took advantage of a great opportunity. She trained at the Smith Clinic for Reproductive Technology in Norfolk. She was their best—the top candidate. There's virtually *nothing* she can't do with a microscope and the tools of the trade. She can do ICSI, ROSNI, assisted hatching. She's so good with the eggs. By reputation she has incredible credentials, and—"

"So how did you get her, if she's so good?"

"Hey, she wants to work with the best!" Ben puffed out his chest and grinned broadly.

Marnie smiled and shook her head.

"Truth is, she got passed over for the staff position at the clinic. She was in line to become the teaching professor, but she's a bit naïve about the politics of medical staff appointments. So, at the last minute they gave the job to a slightly less-qualified but better-connected candidate. There she was—her relatives back in Taiwan, no family here, no close friends, and now no position. She heard about Luc and called. We set up the interview, and voilà! We have a new embryologist—the slickest egg doc around! And she was even 'reasonable.'"

"What's her belief system?" Marnie asked.

"Her family practices Buddhism. She said that she hasn't had the time—or inclination—for religion. We talked at length, and she's willing to work within our ethical guidelines. She's meticulous in her work."

"Sounds as if you like her a lot."

"She has a good heart and great skills. It'll be interesting to see how it all turns out."

Chapter Six

Dr. Steven Harrison, perusing his *Wall Street Journal*, was interrupted by the voice of his assistant, Dana.

"Dr. Harrison?"

"Yes?"

"Sorry to buzz in, doctor, but Mr. Groves says he needs to talk to you immediately."

"Of course." He thought for a moment. "I'll take it now, thank you." He pressed the blinking light on his phone and drew a deep breath, knowing that the next few moments with the senior assistant to the U.S. president would be like a root canal without anesthesia.

"Yes, Mr. Groves," he said brightly. "Harrison here."

"You'd better have something to tell me," Groves snarled. "And it better be today."

"I'm sorry. Our best project looks too risky to try on the president. But we have several ongoing studies in different avenues. I'm optimistic about a solution, and I think we're getting very—"

"Enough!" Groves broke in. "I've heard this before. You've got nothing yet, right?"

"We're close. But I can't recommend a trial of therapy with anything at the moment because—"

"You're out of moments, doctor. President Sullivan, on the recommendation of his medical advisors, will announce that he's stepping down from the presidency. He can't run the country. We can't wait on you any longer."

Harrison, his mind racing for something positive to say, simply muttered, "I understand."

"I'm not sure you do, doctor."

With a click, Dr. Harrison sat holding a dead phone line. He had expected the call. He had even expected the axe to fall before long, but that hadn't made the descending blade any easier to watch.

Even if we can't find a cure for the president, surely there's a lot of money to be made here. As he reflected on the past year, he kept coming back to Tim Sullivan's work in Dallas. With Dr. Sullivan's LG cell line, developed from fusing two human eggs, he'd seen dramatic improvement in so many Parkinson's disease patients, only to see them revert to their previous levels of functioning. Harrison had lied to the surgeon general when he said his researchers were still exploring this option. It had seemed too risky. *The horrific deaths of all the akenosis patients, the ones with the same condition as the president. . . . And the MS patients—so close and yet so far. Still, in terms of other diseases, maybe Dr. Sullivan was on the right track. What did he have? Was it the pure cell line? What if we used umbilical cord cells? So much potential.*

He glanced back at his *Wall Street Journal* and the biomedical research companies that he'd been following. Some of them were part of his personal portfolio. A few were intimately involved in his search for a "presidential therapy," although none knew about that particular application of their research.

This ol' rat has more than one hole to crawl into. Before the crash, I'll make sure I don't burn.

≈❧≈

A week after the clinic opened, Luc arrived home from work at nine P.M. His wife was cleaning up the kitchen, and the noise from the dishwasher prevented her from hearing the garage door opening. He sneaked up behind her and grabbed her. "I've got you alone, and your parents don't know it!"

Janelle gasped. "Luc! You just about gave me a heart attack!" She laughed, gave him a hug, and planted a kiss on his lips. "Glad you're home."

"Me, too. Where are the boys?"

"One's doing homework; the other two should show up any minute from ball practice."

Luc headed back to the bedroom to change. He took his wallet out of his pocket, and moving the stack of mail on his dresser to lay it down, he saw a return address that caught his eye. *Brock Gaylan, M.D., New Orleans.* Janelle always sorted out the junk and left his personal mail where he'd remember to read it. *That name . . . I can't exactly place it, but it sounds familiar. I wonder if he got my name through the Christian Medical Association's placement service.*

Luc opened the letter.

Dear Dr. Morgan,

This may seem like a long shot, but allow me to reintroduce myself. We met two years ago at the national meeting of the Society for Assisted Reproductive Technologists in Palm Springs. I played in your foursome.

I think I remember him—one of the presenters. Did some solid work with anti-embryo antibody diagnosis and therapy. Certainly well credentialed. I remember the course. He was a big, redheaded guy. He had a wicked slice but was generally affable and sharp. Luc read on.

I heard at the last regional meeting about the bombing, and I'm sorry about your injuries. I also heard about

the new clinic, which brings me to my purpose in writing. Without going into all the details, I am seeking a
position out of the state. My first choice would be the
Washington, D.C., metro area, as I was stationed there in
the military and later received training at the Fairfax Ge-
netics Clinic.

I enjoyed the camaraderie on the golf course and wondered if perhaps we could work together. Are you fully
staffed now that the clinic is ready to open?

Luc didn't waste any time changing his clothes and heading
to his home office to make the call. *Willing to leave New Orleans?
Interesting . . . Brock's on Central Time. If he's really a workaholic,
he'll still be there.* He dialed.

"Brock Gaylan?"

"Yes?"

"Luc Morgan in Virginia."

"Hello! I didn't expect to hear from you so soon."

"Well, as it happens, we *would* like to add another doc here."

"No kiddin'?"

"Yeah, in fact, I thought you might have known we had an
opening because we've had our feelers out. We just hired a
terrific egg wizard from the Smith clinic."

"You lured someone away from Smith?"

"Hey, don't sound so surprised!"

"Sorry—mostly I'm impressed, though I really shouldn't be
surprised. Your last egg guy, Tim Sullivan, was no slouch either."

Luc changed the subject. "So, when were you thinking of
moving?"

"Four to six weeks would be ideal, but I'm flexible."

"Then when would be the best time to come to D.C. so we can
discuss it? We can show you around the clinic, talk about options,
and make sure your golf game is still good enough to qualify you."

"Uh-oh," Brock said with a laugh.

~e❧~

Dr. Harrison pressed the record button and began dictating. "Dana, I need this letter on my official letterhead." He flipped through his Rolodex, stopping on the card for the Texas medical school, and read aloud the address. "This is to Dr. G-a-l-e T-a-n-n-i-n-g—that's a male, not a female. Here's the body of the letter:

"This is a matter of utmost national consequence and nothing short of absolute confidentiality will be acceptable. Last fall, when researcher Dr. T—" Harrison smirked. *Tim Sullivan would be "Allan Brown" to him.* . . . "Last fall, when researcher Dr. Allan Brown died, he instructed a colleague to provide you with all his notes on neurological stem cell research. Because the project had government involvement and funding, it is imperative that I obtain complete copies of all the research, including notes, files, and computer disks. Most importantly, I will need a sample of the pure cell line Dr. Brown developed."

He completed the letter, turned off the dictation machine, and punched a button on the intercom. Dana's voice greeted him. "Yes, doctor?"

"I've just dictated a letter in response to the call from Mr. Groves. I need you to drop everything and help me get it out."

"Of course, doctor. . . . Was Mr. Groves really from the president's staff?" Dana was new and did not know better than to ask such questions. She still was awed by "official conversations."

"Yes. He needs my help on a project. Get me the letter to proof ASAP." Harrison had the cool confidence of a man all too familiar with political gamesmanship. "When you finish, bring it in immediately for my signature—and then overnight it."

Harrison had been watching, with intense interest, the rise and fall of the biotech stocks, including Genevex. Now the timing was perfect. Genevex stock was plummeting, along with the majority of the sector. The bad public relations generated by deaths associated with their gene therapy product had put additional pressure on the fledgling pharmaceutical company. More than half of its capitalization had been lost in a month.

He pressed the intercom button again. "Dana?"

"Yes, sir?"

"I need you to place a call to Mr. Richard Collier, CEO of Genevex Corporation in Boston. You'll have to look up the number. But tell him that I need to talk to him—now."

"Yes, sir."

Harrison punched out on the intercom, knowing that Dana would represent him in dramatic fashion as being associated with the surgeon general's office. She loved official protocol and was tenacious about getting through.

In a matter of minutes he saw the blinking line and heard Dana's voice. "Dr. Harrison, Mr. Collier on line one."

He intentionally waited a full minute to pick up the line. "Mr. Collier, it's so good to finally speak with you. As my assistant surely told you, I'm Dr. Steven Harrison."

"Yes, doctor. What can I do for you?" Collier said.

"I serve the federal government in a research capacity—appointed by the surgeon general. It's been part of my responsibility to investigate deaths associated with gene therapy."

Collier coughed nervously.

"Your company has been in the news lately, no doubt much more than you would like."

"Yes, sir, it has. But as all of our reports have shown, you'll see that it wasn't the fault of Genevex."

"No need to be defensive. I'm not calling to criticize. I'm actually calling to offer my assistance."

"What sort of assistance?" Collier sounded surprised.

"I have access to research that I believe could drastically reverse the trend in your company's profit picture. If I may be direct, sir, we could be talking millions, if not billions."

"I see." Collier was tentative. "And what sort of research might that be?"

"I've been working with viral vectors to try to prevent transplanted organs from being rejected. In the past year, I've overseen a particularly interesting project that has given me exclusive access to research that could change the future of your company."

"Go on."

"We've developed a pure cell line, which we could combine with your company's assorted 'gene patches' instead of using viruses. As you've seen, viral vectors can have unpredictable results. Perhaps this very special cell line could be used as a more predictable carrier of specific gene sequences."

Collier was quiet, so Harrison forged ahead.

"You can certainly appreciate the vast market potential. Thousands upon thousands of people with transplants—kidney, liver, heart, lungs—all these people require expensive and dangerous antirejection medicine. And even at that, their bodies may still reject the organs. This cell line could change all that. Using Genevex technology, we could either defeat the rejection phenomena in the host by splicing in a gene, or we could make cloned transplantable organs that are not recognized by the host immune system—you know, make the body think the new organ is its own tissue. All the transplant patients will look to Genevex technology." Harrison leaned back in his chair and awaited a response.

"Must be a very interesting special cell line. Tell me more about it."

"Not so fast. First, I have some questions for you."

"What sort of questions?"

With shrewd probing, Dr. Harrison inquired about parts of Genevex's therapies to which only a high-ranking official involved in overseeing their gene therapy would have access. He designed his questions simply to reveal how much he already knew, not to seek more information. He went on to discuss his own research with organ rejection therapies—in the process establishing yet more credibility with Collier. By the time Harrison was asking pointed questions about Genevex's financial holdings, Collier's skepticism had turned to hope.

"So having heard all that, do you have any questions for me now?" Harrison asked.

"Yes. I'm curious to know more about the makeup of this pure cell line. What exactly is it?"

"I'm not at liberty to discuss the specifics of the special cell line right now, but it has been developed under the auspices of the U.S. government."

"And what are *your* terms in this deal?" Collier sounded nervous.

"I'll stay in my government position for the time being, but I can consult with Genevex on this project for a fee. I want direct involvement in the company's daily operations and an agreement that Genevex will purchase, staff, and give me oversight of a facility in Dallas that's already equipped for this type of research. And, of course, equitable percentages of profits." Harrison knew Collier had no other options. Genevex was headed for bankruptcy if a major breakthrough didn't happen overnight, and the high-risk gamble he was offering was probably the only hope they'd had in months.

For the next forty-five minutes the two men worked though a tentative plan of agreement, pending the formality of a personal interview.

When they had finished, Harrison was satisfied that he had skillfully chosen his words, texturing the conversation with statements that convinced Collier he could pull off the greatest medical coup of the decade. And Harrison, for the most part, believed his own sales pitch. He was sure he could turn Genevex into the next pharmaceutical superpower.

A few days later, Dr. Harrison spent the day at Genevex headquarters in Boston interviewing with Richard Collier. That night they celebrated Harrison's new position and their renewed confidence that the pharmaceutical company was about to become a household name. Harrison emerged from his lavish suite near Copley Plaza to meet Collier in the hotel bar for a drink.

Genevex's CEO, a slender sandy-haired man, seemed almost giddy. "What a day this has been!" he said as he shook Harrison's hand heartily. More reserved, Harrison studied this man he had so easily manipulated.

"So, tell me something, Harrison," Collier said. "Now that the deal is sealed, when do I hear the full story on this cell line you have?"

"Now's as good a time as any. But we'd better go up to my suite to discuss it." Collier picked up the tab, and the men carried their drinks with them.

Harrison led the way to his suite on the tenth floor. The men settled comfortably into the living room chairs by a panoramic window overlooking Boston. Harrison began. "As you know, the surgeon general appointed me to handle some special research projects. My top priority was to work with a researcher who was related to the president. I can't tell you exactly how, but I will tell you that his research focused on trying to cure the president of a disease that will lead to his resignation in the near future."

Collier sat forward.

"He combined the chromosomes from a patient's egg and added them to the chromosomes of another egg from the same woman. The nucleus of one egg actually acted as sperm when combined with the other egg—it contributed genetic material. He managed to stimulate the egg cell to replicate and divide."

"Amazing. Egg plus egg equals—what?"

"A cell line of pure chromosomes from a single X of the mother, along with all the maternal chromosomes in that egg. With a precise charge of electricity, the DNA aligned. The resulting DNA sequence is not precisely the mother's, but it is extremely close."

"That *is* remarkable."

"Once our researcher had the pure cell line, he figured that the stem cells—which are able to develop into any cell line in the human body—should be able to recognize disease and mature into the proper cell line to affect permanent healing. Having created a cell line that survived in the laboratory, both in mice and in chimps, he graduated to human subjects."

"Good night! How did he get approval to do that? We can't seem to get anything past the government."

"It wasn't legal. Let's just say it was—'approved.'"

Chapter Seven

"Dr. Harrison," Dana said through the intercom. "There's a delivery here that I think will interest you. It's from Dr. Tanning in Dallas. Do you want me to open it for you? It's marked confidential."

"No, thanks. Bring it right in!"

"It's pretty heavy."

"Then I'll come get it." Seconds later, he walked briskly to Dana's desk. He picked up the archive box, took it into his office, and shut the door. Then he cut the strapping tape with his gold letter opener. Inside, he found file folders with patient names and a stack of computer printouts with research notes on them. *"Allan Brown" sure kept great records. Gotta hand it to him for that,* he thought as he looked through everything Tanning had sent. *No doubt they'll send the cell line to my lab.*

As Harrison was closing the box, he spotted a letter from Tanning attached to the outside pocket of the address label. He read it and then threw it down on the desk with a curse. *What do you mean you don't have any cell line left? . . . Why couldn't you get it to replicate?*

He stared out his window. Then he picked up the letter and reread it, focusing on the words that made him feel ill: "The other half of the cell line was sent to the new clinic of Drs. Ben

McKay and Luc Morgan at their request, along with the remaining Rivera embryos."

*Why did I wait so long? This will be harder than I thought.
Still . . . it can be done.*

He spent a moment plotting how to get the cell line and
then reread the note. *Remaining embryos? Are they part of the
special cell line from Mrs. Rivera? Or are these embryos from
both Riveras? Do the Riveras even know about this? Maybe they
could get me what I need!*

Marnie was in her home office at eleven-thirty in the morning. After sending a press release for a software company, she
logged on to check her e-mail. The phone rang.

"Are you watching the news, Marno?" Luc's wife, Janelle,
asked.

"No. Why?"

"I think you'd better turn it on."

Even as Marnie was asking why, she spun around in the
chair and clicked on the remote. Her desktop television lit up
to reveal President Sullivan giving a speech.

". . . My decision in doing so comes out of a desire to put
the needs of America first in the face of my declining health."

"He's not *resigning* is he?" she asked Janelle.

"Yes. He is."

Marnie put Janelle on the speaker phone and sat back in shock,
watching President Sullivan speak of the country's need for a
fully functioning president, of his gratitude, of the difficulties of
his own long fight against the debilitating neurological disease
that had already claimed his brother's life. *Not to mention my
husband's life, but we can't mention that, now can we?*

The resignation speech drifted into a recitation of administration accomplishments; of the importance of peace in the Middle

East; of the president's feeling of kinship with every citizen. His final request was for the prayers of his fellow American.

Marnie looked at the photo on the wall to her right. How long had it been since she had posed there, with one arm around President Calvin Sullivan and the other around her late husband, Tim Sullivan, the president's nephew?

"This is the scene Tim gambled his life to avoid." Her voice trembled; it was so hard to say the words.

"I know. And I'm so sorry," Janelle responded. "I'm calling Luc. They probably don't know yet up at the clinic. Want me to ask Ben to call you?"

"That would be nice, thanks."

Five minutes later, Marnie saw Ben's name on the caller ID. She picked it up with, "Hi, Ben."

"Hey, babe . . . you holding up?"

"Yeah."

"Kind of opens some old wounds though, huh?"

"Yeah. Feeling some raw pain here, for sure. Thanks for calling."

"Got any lunch plans, Marn?"

"Not feeling too hungry at the moment. Sorry."

"I didn't mean food as much as the company."

"That would be nice."

Fifteen minutes later, Ben met Marnie at the doctors' entrance so she could avoid facing patients in the lobby. Neither said a word—their eyes said it all. He led her by the hand back to his office, shut their door, and wrapped her in an embrace. At that, she sobbed in his arms.

"When will it ever end?" she asked. "I keep thinking I'm better, and I'm healing, and then . . . bam. Something happens, and it all comes back. Still, I shouldn't be surprised. Tim *told* me his uncle was going downhill. And now I feel so selfish. Tim was trying to prevent all this, and all I did was blast him."

"Marnie, remember? Tim deserted you to do illegal research—

took a new identity and everything? And it wasn't like he gave
you a choice."

When Dr. Courtney Pak saw Ben and Marnie emerging from
his office twenty minutes later, she could tell Marnie had been
crying. She pulled aside Bonnie, one of the office workers. "Is
something wrong with Dr. Ben's friend?"

"What do you mean?"

"I saw them leaving his office just now. Her eyes were as red
as tomatoes."

Bonnie had worked at the old clinic, having signed on with
Luc fresh out of nursing school. She took great pride in her
role as the office information center. "Most likely she's upset
about the president resigning. Marnie—that's her name—she
was married to Dr. Tim Sullivan, President Sullivan's nephew.
He was the clinic's embryologist. He died when his car went
into the Potomac. They didn't find his body for months." She
lowered her voice. "*I* think his death may have been tied to the
clinic in some way. I mean, somebody tried to bomb Dr. Luc
later."

Courtney was taken aback.

Bonnie pressed on. "But anyway, I think it's just great. I
mean, she loses her husband, and Dr. Ben lost his wife. She's
the best thing that's happened to him in six years."

"Wait." Courtney held up her hands to slow down the
firestorm of information. "Dr. Ben was *married?*"

"Yeah. His wife got a blood clot at the end of her pregnancy. He lost her and the baby in delivery. Because of that, he
quit delivering babies until just recently."

Three months after Ben's run-in with the prostitute, he had a blood sample drawn at his office and sent over to the lab. His instructions said to send the results to Dr. McLaughlin.

A few days later, Mark called. "We're clear. So far so good. Check back again in a month, all right?"

Marnie and Janelle emerged from the women's locker room at the Arlington Heights Country Club and made their way to the workout area. After her racquetball game with Ben, Marnie had joined the club, determined to whip herself into better shape so she would not be beaten again. Three times a week, Marnie and Janelle met for a twenty-four-minute bike ride while their kids were at school.

"What's up?" Marnie asked as she slid her feet into the straps and began to pedal. "You don't seem yourself today."

Janelle did the same. "I think I have the baby blues. My boys are eleven, eight, and six. I'm supposed to be thrilled that my youngest starts all-day school in a few months. But instead of looking forward to it, I'm dreading it. I know I'm a little over forty, and maybe I'm crazy, but I've been pining for another baby. After I nearly lost Luc . . . it's changed my perspective on some things. You must think I'm crazy."

"No way. That's not crazy. Not at all!" Marnie said. "What does Luc say?"

"I haven't mentioned it. His standard response to anything like that is, 'I just want you to be happy.'"

"Nothing wrong with *that* answer."

Janelle shook her head. "It's just one of those longings I have that'll never be satisfied, I guess." She looked over at Marnie, who bore a compassionate expression. Then she looked away. "Listen to me going on like this! I have a great husband

and three kids. You have no husband and one kid, and I'm telling you about my longings. Sorry."

Marnie shook her head. "We all have longings, 'Nelle. You're entitled to yours, too."

"Yeah, but I'll bet mine are nothing like yours."

"I'm not sure there's much point in comparing. Pain is pain."

Janelle shrugged and nodded. "Yeah, I guess maybe you're right. I'm glad you see it that way."

For several minutes, the only sound was deep breathing. Then Janelle spoke again. "So, . . . how *are* things going with Ben?"

"From my perspective or his?"

"Yours. Though I hope there's not a big difference between the two."

"I think there may be." Marnie looked down at her feet.

"How so?"

"It's just that he seems to be pulling back from me lately."

Janelle glanced over and read the unspoken hurt on her friend's face. "But he acts so goofy around you. Can't you see it?"

"You haven't spent much time with us lately. He's different now. Something has changed. When he first got back from Romania he was so warm, but now . . ."

"He's crazy about you! If anything, *you've* been the one who's cool about this relationship."

Marnie shook her head. "Maybe I'm a good actress, then. I just wish I could get him to open up." Marnie turned her head away to wipe clouded eyes. She regained control and continued. "I've always been the kind of woman who knows what I want and goes after it. But when it comes to Ben . . ." She shook her head. "One day I think we're serious; the next, I'm not so sure. He's a mystery. The Lord's going to have to perform a miracle for things to work out between us."

"Hmmm. Maybe Ben's got cold feet."

Marnie shook her head. "Really hard to say. He's been pretty distant. He's so capable, so in control of himself—almost too much. He knows how to give, but I wonder if he knows how to receive. But, then, he did ask me to go on the Culiacán trip."

Janelle nodded.

"I took that as a good sign, though I guess since I went with the team to Kiev last year I'm a missions-trip veteran. Anyway, I'm hoping our time in Culiacán will help me get some direction. I have no idea whether we have a future—or not."

Chapter Eight

"You've lost that lovin' feelin',
   "wo-o, that lovin' . . ."
   Uaah. Ben fumbled for the switch on the clock radio. *Five a.m. oldies,* he muttered to himself. *Glad I don't have to get up this early all the time.* He swung out of bed, rubbing his eyes. As the new chairman of the Medical Records Committee, Ben had arranged to meet with the chart review group at six for their monthly mandatory meeting.

The Records Committee was serious business. Each doctor practicing at the hospital had to complete charts in a timely manner, both for legal documentation and to enable the hospital to file for reimbursement. Violators paid stiff penalties for failure to submit careful, timely records. The committee put habitual offenders on the "A" list, meaning they couldn't admit patients for elective surgery until they submitted completed charts—a strong incentive for busy surgeons.

Ben arrived at the conference room adjacent to the cafeteria. He followed the other five members of the committee through the breakfast buffet line, provided courtesy of the hospital. Ben piled on the eggs, biscuits, and gravy, figuring he might not see food again until evening. At the end of the line, waiting for them, stood Ms. Mathews behind a cart stacked with problematic charts.

"Well, Tina," Ben said smiling, "what've you got for us today?"

"The usual. A few missing signatures, consent forms, and a bunch of charts without history-and-physicals by the time of discharge."

"By the time of discharge? They're supposed to be on there within twenty-four hours!"

"Yes, Dr. McKay. But not everyone keeps up like you do. And then . . ." She hesitated. "Then there's the usual stack of Sudderth charts."

"Again?" Ben asked.

She nodded.

"I'll have to talk with him. What've you got from him this time?"

"About twenty-five—all delinquent in some form or fashion."

"Really? Doesn't he have the residents do the charts?" Ben asked.

"Oh yeah. He apparently pays them to do all the history-and-physicals, but they sometimes wait until the patient has been discharged, and the chart gets bounced before they fill in the blanks."

"How do they do an exam after the patient has gone home?" Ben asked.

"Indeed, Dr. Mac. How *do* they do that? Must be very astute physicians, doncha think?"

Ben sighed and handed out the charts to the committee, keeping Travis Sudderth's huge stack for himself. Dr. Sudderth was a fellow OB/Gyn, so the procedures and codes would all look familiar.

"Wow. He does a lot of surgery, doesn't he?" Ben asked no one in particular. The others on the committee, engrossed in charts, didn't seem to hear him. He looked back through his stack. *Sudderth sure does a lot of hysterectomies and D&Cs for relatively benign causes.* Ben flipped to the pathology reports and found that not one of these patients had anything significant to justify their operations.

Once all the physicians had set aside their charts, they conferred. When they finished, Ben told Tina, "Send the standard 'letters of encouragement' to these staff physicians, but send Dr. Sudderth an official letter that I—as chair of medical records—need to speak with him to clarify some of these things."

The committee adjourned, and Ben headed toward the office. On his way he passed one of his old doctor friends. "Hey, McKay, I hear you got stuck chairing medical records."

"Yeah," Ben grunted.

"Gee, welcome back. I had that duty once."

"Want it again?"

"No thanks! Been there, done that, ate the donuts."

"Yeah, it's a real joy."

"Just watch out for Sudderth, or you'll find yourself losing sleep."

"Thanks for the tip."

At 7:15 A.M. the physician sat down across from the couple in the out-patient center's waiting area. He had arrived early for his first surgery at the center, eager to wear the surgeon's gloves again. He had a few extra minutes to talk with his first case of the day, so he extended his hand to greet the husband. "Mr. Wills, I'm Dr. Brock Gaylen."

"Hey, call me Jeff. Nice to meet you, doctor. My wife's told me all about you. We're grateful."

Brock looked at Debbie Wills, an obese woman in her mid-thirties. She looked quite different from when he'd seen her at their last appointment. The center had instructed her to check in for surgery without make-up and nail polish. "You ready?" he asked.

She nodded. "A neighbor's got the kids covered. I'm so glad you didn't say what my last doctor said."

"What's that?"

"That I should quit trying and be happy I have two kids. I just feel like our family is incomplete."

Jeff patted his wife's knee, and Brock smiled.

"Do you really think I'll be able to go home this afternoon?" she asked.

"Absolutely. Sure."

"Okay. Well, would you mind explaining to Jeff what's happening here. I tried, but it all seems pretty complicated."

Jeff nodded. "If you don't mind."

"Sure. Not at all." Brock leaned forward, rested his elbows on his knees, and lowered his voice to the soothing tone he used with anxious patients. "When I ordered the usual infertility work-up on your wife, I found a slight shadow on her hysterosalpingog—the, uh, the x-ray test where we inject dye through the uterus and tubes to see if the tubes are open. So we'll be doing an operative hysteroscopy with a standby laparoscopy to find out what that shadow is. That's the complicated way of saying I need to get inside to take a look. I don't expect any problems, and this may give us another piece to the puzzle."

Not long after his conversation with Jeff and Debbie Wills, Brock stood in the surgical suite, holding Mrs. Wills's hand while the anesthesia put her to sleep. Someone clicked on the Mozart CD he had brought. Then, after the prep, the drapes, and the stirrups, Brock glanced forward to look at the sleeping patient's face.

"A problem, doctor?" one of the nurses asked.

"No. I always like to start my surgeries with a reminder that there's a real person there. In this case, she's someone's daughter, wife, mother. Life is precious."

One of the nurses gave another the "thumb's up" signal behind his back.

"All right—let's get started," he said. He did a pelvic exam and told one of the nurses. "Everything feels normal. No masses, no evidence of adhesions."

She wrote down everything he said, then added, "Tubbo here is looking good."

Dr. Gaylen looked up. He spoke evenly but firmly. "Nurse, when you're working my shift, you treat the patient with dignity. No rude remarks. We have no idea how much the brain picks up in its unconscious state, . . . but even if it's nothing, we're dealing with a human being here. Try to remember that."

"Yes, sir."

He returned to his work, his attitude remaining cheerful despite the reprimand. "Speculum in the vagina. Visualize the cervix. Because of her two previous vaginal deliveries, I think I can get the scope through without any dilation." He sounded the uterus to nine centimeters, which was normal for her thirty-five years and the fact that she'd birthed two children. Then he gently inserted the hysteroscope, using generous amounts of fluid.

After a moment of exploration, he spoke again. "The initial look is good." He hooked up the TV camera to the scope. By doing so, he could sit up comfortably, and everyone in the room could see what he was viewing through the tiny fiberoptic scope at the top of the instrument that he held. "Ahhh, very nice. Uterine lining lovely and pink, even though she's been on a GnRH analog to decrease the estrogen. But hey. What have we here? A tiny punching bag?"

The room fell momentarily quiet again except for the sound of the patient's breathing and pulse rate.

"Upper left by the tubal opening, we've got a small fibroid." Silence again. "Bingo. We've also got a broad-based fibroid on the back wall of the uterus pushing into the uterine cavity. I'll bet that's what I saw on the HSG. But ten-to-one it's the tiny one that's causing her fertility problems. Let me have the re-sectoscope." The surgical nurse handed him a thin metal loop attached at the end of a telescope.

He easily snagged the small fibroid, shaving it off. "Now for your sister," he said as though speaking to the mass. Then he added, "Uh-oh. You want to bleed, eh?"

A short time later Brock left the surgical suite and found Jeff Wills. "I found two small fibroids," he told the nervous hus-band. "We had a bit of bleeding on the larger of the two, but I used a combination of laser and electricity to coagulate the bleeder. I had to leave a bit of it in place, but I'm optimistic."

A little over a week after the records meeting, Ben crossed the street to Doctors' Building Number Three. Entering the reception area on the sixth floor, he couldn't help but notice two triple-matted Piranese engravings of Roman architecture in gold-gilded frames. *Very elegant—and expensive.*

"Good morning, I'm Dr. Ben McKay, and I'd like to have a word with Dr. Sudderth," he told the receptionist.

"Is he expecting you, doctor?"

"Probably not. I sent him a letter, but I didn't hear back from him. This will take only a minute. It's about hospital charting information."

"Certainly, doctor. Let me see if he's in with a patient. Would you like to wait here or back in his office?"

Ben looked around and eyed the full waiting room. "I'd prefer to wait in his office until he's available, thank you."

The receptionist guided him back and motioned for Ben to have a seat. He studied the large, well-appointed room as he waited.

After six or seven minutes, Dr. Travis Sudderth popped in. Ben immediately noticed his silk suit. A watch that looked like a Rolex peaked out from a cuff. "Dr. McKay—good to see you. I was meaning to get back to you on that medical records thing. Getting after the residents. Supposed to have all that done so I'm not bothered. Gotta keep to schedule."

Ben was taken aback by his rapid speech. Sudderth seemed nervous and didn't make eye contact. "Great to hear you're working on it. But I'm troubled by the fact that some of your patients apparently aren't getting a history-and-physical until after discharge."

"Oh—you know the hospital rules. I do the exams here in the office. Redundant to do another when they're admitted for elective surgery. My patients are generally healthy. Waste of time and money. With all the outpatients and the short-stay policy, I get 'em in and out fast. Medical records transcription crew can't keep up with me. You know I do more Gyn cases than anyone else, so the hospital better keep me happy, 'cause I keep the registers rolling, if you catch my drift." At this he turned his eyes to Ben, with the slightest hint of threat.

Bloodshot. Pupils tightly constricted. Sort of unusual. Obviously I'm getting nowhere here. "Dr. Sudderth—" Ben started.

"Call me Travis."

"Okay, Travis. We all have to follow hospital policy for medical liability protection and for the administration of the place. My job on the records committee is to keep you off 'the list' so no one has to restrict your privileges. Just want to keep things going smoothly."

"Got it," Travis said tersely. "Anything else? I have a full schedule—patients to see. . . ."

"So I noticed," Ben said, remembering the full waiting area. He turned to leave, then stopped. "One more thing."

"Yeah?" Travis edged toward the door.

"I looked through the path reports on a number of your cases and, frankly, there isn't much pathology to justify some of that surgery."

"You know you can't pick up everything on path!" Travis insisted, growing defiant. "You wanna know why I do the most surgical cases here? Because I'm the best surgeon. The *best*. When you do high volume like I do, some cases are less dramatic than others, but I have good outcomes and very satisfied patients."

"That's true," Ben replied. Dr. Sudderth had some of the most loyal patients around. "I just wanted to inform you of my impressions and encourage you to get your charts done on time. Otherwise, you know they'll restrict your privileges."

"Sure they will," Dr. Sudderth replied sarcastically. "Sure. Like they always do. As long as I'm filling beds and keeping the ORs busy, they'll find a way for me. Thanks for your time, doctor." He held the office door open for Ben to leave.

As Ben crossed in front of him to exit the office, he reconfirmed the red eyes and detected the faintest sweet smell, mostly hidden by the doctor's cologne, but unmistakable nevertheless.

He's been near some marijuana. Real near.

"Just one more shot, doc," the beaming father told Ben as he held the newborn daughter. The camera flashed. "Fantastic! All done. Thanks so much."

"My pleasure!"

Ben handed the child back to her mother. It had been a normal delivery—first child for Kim and Danny Murphy. They had come to Ben in the middle of a tough pregnancy, concerned that they were not getting the attention their high-risk pregnancy needed. Ben had spent several late nights with them when Kim had threatened preterm labor. But she'd made it to term, and tonight they celebrated.

"How can we ever thank you?" Danny grabbed Ben's hand.

"Seeing this sight is thanks enough," Ben beamed, looking at the mother holding her child.

"Listen, we have a box at the stadium. If you're a Redskins fan, we'd love to have you join us some time."

"Appreciate the generous offer. But actually, I'm a diehard Cowboys fan," Ben insisted.

"Don't you know you're in Redskin territory?" Kim teased.

"Haven't you heard that the Cowboys are America's team?" Ben shot back without hesitating.

A few minutes later, Ben sat, basking in the afterglow of a satisfying delivery, sipping on a Sprite before heading home. He propped his feet on the desk and tipped back in the chair. Sitting near the nurse's station below the row of TV screens, he casually scanned status reports for patients in each room. Earlier in the evening he'd sat there monitoring Kim Murphy's contraction pattern. Now he'd returned to finish off his drink.

"Yes, yes, I know. I've called twice before," he heard Karen, the ward clerk say. She raised her voice. "But we have an emergency! We need to find Dr. Sudderth right away. I know you said he checked out, and he's here at the hospital. But he isn't answering the phone or his pager or the overhead page. . . .

"I know, but he isn't answering . . .

"Right. Thank you. Yes, please page him again. It's urgent!"

Ben called over, "Karen? What's going on?"

"Dr. Sudderth has disappeared again. He's the on-call doc and is supposed to be here in the L&D wing, but I can't find him. The resident has a lady down in the ER who's in shock or something, and we need to send another doctor down there right away since he can't operate alone."

"Who's the resident, Karen? I'll call down to ER."

"Casey, the third-year. . . ."

"Got it. I'll call right now."

A moment later, Ben walked up to Karen's desk. "Since my

patient has already delivered and is doing fine, I'll go down to ER to help out."

"Thanks, Dr. McKay. Thanks a lot."

About an hour later, Ben and Casey walked into L&D after having performed the emergency surgery—a laparotomy for a ruptured tubal pregnancy.

"Glad we could save the tube," Casey said.

"Yes, but it always makes me sad that there's no way to save the baby in an ectopic pregnancy."

Casey nodded thoughtfully.

"That patient had some serious blood loss. Good pick-up on that diagnosis," said Ben. As they started to pass Karen's desk, Ben stopped and asked, "Did Dr. Sudderth ever call in?"

"Yeah. You won't believe it. He claimed he was asleep in the back, in the residents' quarters. Said he didn't hear his page—insisted it wasn't working."

"And the phone?" Ben asked skeptically.

"Claims he never heard it until just now," Karen replied.

"Oh, really?" Ben said, unable to avoid sharing Karen's tone of sarcasm.

"Yep. Of course, it's always like this when the studly Dr. Sudderth has ER call." Karen's voice trailed off.

Ben raised his eyebrows at this remark. "Which room is he in? It's only nine o'clock!"

"He's in six—the one with the TV-VCR."

"Of course."

"Probably watching porn films, or adding another nurse to his collection of scores."

"I see. Well, let me drop by and tell him about his new patient—the one we just operated on," Ben said.

"You tell him, Dr. McKay!" Karen grinned with satisfaction.

Ben went back to the doctors' locker-room where they had scrubs, showers, and facilities for the long hours on call. He rapped gently on call room six. "Dr. Sudderth? Travis?"

The door opened slowly. Travis Sudderth looked like he'd been run over by a crash of rhinos. Hospital policy prohibited smoking, but the room reeked of cigar tobacco. Ben could see that Travis was on something else as well—alcohol, or perhaps a touch of cocaine.

Chapter Nine

"HEY, I HEAR YOU HAD AN INTERESTING NIGHT," Luc called out the next morning when Ben passed by his office door.

Ben stopped and leaned in. "How'd you hear?"

"Breakfast at the docs' café. You were the talk of the place."

Ben entered Luc's office and sat down in one of the Queen Anne chairs. "*What* did you hear?"

"That you nailed Sudds . . . called the chief of staff. . . . He sent the chief of OB to deal with it. You covered the ER for the residents."

"Amazing. Sometimes gossip is actually accurate!"

Brock, the new partner, poked his head in the door. "Hmm, sounds juicy in here."

"Oh, there's more!" Luc continued, motioning for Brock to join them. "Chief of OB came in and found Sudds in terrible shape, so he threatened to test him for drug use and have him busted, dismissed from the staff, license revoked."

"Ow. Also true," Ben said. "Word travels fast. No privacy in this place for anybody!"

"Apparently not. Talk about your midnight train to Georgia. They say Sudds checked himself into the doctor detox clinic in Atlanta this morning," Luc added.

"Right. And I have to coordinate coverage for him."

"Bummer!" both doctors said in unison.

"Yeah, bummer for all of us."

"Is Sudds the lady-killer I keep hearing about?" Brock asked.

"That's the story," Luc said.

"The one who brings women to the call rooms?"

"So we've heard."

"I heard his last woman was a real moon howler," Brock said in his New Orleans drawl, shaking his head. "I guess after enough Tequila everybody's a glamour shot. Ben, does this mean you're gonna inherit Travis Sudderth's Porsche and all his girlfriends while he's gone?"

"Yeah, right."

While Will and Emily played Uno, Marnie pulled her rolling carry-on from her bedroom into the entryway. Then she lugged out two full suitcases, setting them down with an "Ugh!"

"Need some help with that?" her father asked, looking up.

"Naw. I am woman; hear me . . . whine."

"Suit yourself," Will said. Looking back at Emily he said, "Draw two."

His granddaughter grumbled loudly and then complied.

"There's a lasagna in the freezer. Don't forget to turn off the slow cooker on tonight's pot roast," Marnie told her father.

He grunted his acknowledgment. "Sure you don't need me to take you to the airport?"

"No thanks, Dad. Not this time."

"All right. Got your ticket? Money? Passport? When I traveled with the government, they trained us to ask ourselves that at every stop."

"I have everything I need. Thanks."

"Well, don't worry about us. We'll be great, won't we?" He glanced over at Emily, who looked unsure.

"Why do you have to go, Mommy?" she grumbled. "I wanna go, too."

Marnie bent down to plant a kiss on her daughter's head, then tousled her hair. "I love you, Sweetie, and I'll miss you. I'll call you every other night, okay?"

Will looked up at Marnie. "We'll be just great; don't worry about us. I hope you have a good time."

"Thanks, Dad." Suddenly deep in thought, Marnie returned to her bedroom to straighten it up. She knew her dad wanted her to have a good week with Ben, mostly so her mood would improve. She didn't want to tell him that Ben's affections had cooled in the last month, even more than before. *Dad would want to know what has made Ben withdraw. I wish I knew the answer.*

Ben and Marnie rode to the airport in the front seat, with Ben's friend Bill in the back. The guys talked about sports, news, and weather, while Marnie rode in silence.

As team leader for the short-term mission, Ben made sure he arrived first. Bill had asked to borrow Ben's car for the week, so he helped the couple unload their luggage, then left them alone at the ticket gate. Marnie looked for some sign of warmth, but trip details consumed all of Ben's attention.

Later, when the team boarded, Marnie sat wedged between two athletic builds, but sitting in a snug seat next to Ben suited her fine. Once she settled in, the guy on her right reached over to shake her hand. "I'm Scott Robins, the new youth pastor."

They chatted until after takeoff and then Marnie looked over at Ben and smiled. "Thanks for saving me the best seat in the house." Ben had handled purchasing the tickets for the team, and he'd obviously arranged the seating. But she immediately regretted wearing her heart on her sleeve.

He answered her quietly so only Marnie could hear him. "You had me concerned. I thought you might talk to your other seatmate the entire time, and I was going to have to spend the flight pouting."

Marnie glowed. "You have my undivided attention. Something you want to discuss?"

"No. Just wanted you here . . . with *me*." He leaned back and closed his eyes in satisfaction.

"You're a mystery, Ben McKay."

Carlos and Ramon waited at the airport terminal for the arrival of the twelve-member mission team. Carlos had asked Ramon to arrange for a bus to transport everyone to the Hotel Real de Culiacán.

"You look puzzled, Ramon," the mayor observed.

"It is nothing."

"Tell me."

Ramon hesitated. "I am curious, señor. Why do you show so much kindness to a man you are suing? How can you trust him?"

Carlos gave his assistant a sly smile. "The suit is against Dr. Morgan, and it was Dr. Sullivan's fault. So while Dr. McKay was their partner, he was not actually involved. Yet, he seems to be the key to resolving everything. He seems to have influence with Dr. Morgan, and he has offered to help us—to do the embryo transfers for free and even to fly Leigh and me to Washington. I need his expertise to bring our embryos here. And besides . . ." Carlos looked around to be sure no one else was within earshot, "there are things I can find out about him and Dr. Sullivan's widow if they are here."

"Dr. Sullivan's widow is coming, too?"

Carlos nodded. "Did I not tell you? She and Dr. McKay are . . . involved, yes?"

"Interesting."

"Is it not? Victor has done his homework, you see." Again Carlos had an evil grin.

"So—what 'other things' do you plan to find out?"

"You will see, Ramon." Carlos motioned to the gate. "Here they are now."

A group of passengers on the other side of old metal detectors filed in from the tarmac and began searching for their bags. Carlos found his way to Ben and began the introductions. Once the group had their bags, the mayor moved them quickly through customs and out to the bus.

"I would like to invite you and your lady friend to join me in my limousine," Carlos told Ben, watching carefully for a reaction.

Marnie blushed and looked at Ben. Before he could answer, Carlos added, "We can stop at the hotel and get everyone registered, and then the bus will take everyone to Emanuel Baptist, where you will work this week."

Ben and Marnie conferred for a moment, and it was decided that she would stay with the team and Ben would go with the dignitaries. Soon, Ramon slid into the front seat next to the limo driver, while Carlos sat in the back with Ben. "One day while you are here," Carlos told Ben, "I will need to take you on a tour of our hospital." Then in flawless English he bragged about his large, modern city, gloating over his accomplishments since becoming mayor.

"Dr. Luc, phone call for you on line three," Lisa said. "It's a Dr. Steven Harrison with the surgeon general's office. He needs to talk to you about important government business relating to Tim Sullivan."

Luc looked up with alarm in his eyes. The combination of

Tim's name and government business sent a cold shiver through him. He still had vague suspicions of possible government involvement in the previous clinic's bombing.

"Thanks," he said, and headed back to his office. He shut the door and punched line one. "This is Dr. Morgan."

"Hello. This is Steven Harrison. We spoke briefly during the investigation of Dr. Sullivan's research. I was his advisor."

"Yes, I remember."

"And I'm working on biological studies similar to his—on stem cells and tissue cultures."

Luc sighed with relief. The call was just about research. "I see. And what can I do for you?"

"We're doing some important studies using stem cells, trying to stimulate organ growth in mice. We can already reproduce functional skin and some blood cell lines from the stem cells. We're on the brink of curing some major diseases, and it's truly—well, it's just thrilling, really. Unfortunately, we're still experiencing only about a three percent survival rate on the clones. Generating a pure cell line from which to predictably derive good cultures has proved elusive. Dr. Sullivan, as meticulous as he was at record keeping, accomplished some things I've been unable to replicate, particularly that egg-egg division and growth."

He paused, then continued. "He somehow made a breakthrough that I can't seem to repeat. To generate functional tissue cultures for transplantation, we need to discover what exactly he developed. We're missing the journals from the last week of Dr. Sullivan's studies, and I wondered if they might give us some clue. So if you could get those to me, and . . ." he added casually, "I was also wondering if you have any more biological material?"

There was nothing odd about this request. Although Tim had done illegal human cloning, some of his research held enormous potential for the treatment of disease. Luc fell silent for a long time before speaking again. "Well, I guess, . . . yes, perhaps it would be a fitting solution to the dilemma of what to do with Tim's life's work. Can't say I ever understood fully what he was able to accomplish, but he was a genius as a researcher. I'd hate for his efforts to be wasted. My partner, Ben McKay, is out of town at the moment, and I'd prefer to discuss it first with him. But I can't think of any reason why he'd object."

"Of course," said Dr. Harrison, the excitement in his voice clearly evident. "When will he be back?"

"At the end of the week, if all goes as planned."

"Oh," Harrison sounded deflated. "I'm at a very critical stage of my work. Would it be possible to have at least a small sample now? I'm pretty sure I can stimulate the culture to grow if we can just get even a tiny bit."

"I suppose so. I can authorize the release of one sample and then talk with Ben about sending more when he gets back."

"Wonderful! I'll have my representative there this afternoon with the appropriate transport device. Thank you so much, Dr. Morgan. We stand at the threshold of some remarkable discoveries. Dr. Sullivan was well ahead of his time—truly the leader in this field."

Several hours later, Luc and Courtney Pak opened the secure freezing area and retrieved a small quantity of the LG cell line. As the courier walked out with it, Luc already was having second thoughts about his decision.

The sun beat down in Culiacán, and all Tuesday morning the team worked hard. Some helped to build a cinderblock mission church; others paired with nationals to go into the communities. After they came together at noon for enchiladas prepared by the church members, the team retired to the sanctuary—the only air-conditioned room in the building—for an hour-long siesta spent writing in journals or sitting around singing.

Marnie had stretched out on one of the wooden pews and had almost drifted off when she felt someone near. She opened her eyes to see that Ben had slid into the pew and sat next to her head.

"Go back to sleep," he told her. "You look so sweet that way."

"How long have you been there?" she whispered up at him.

"About five minutes. They had me teaching at the university all morning." He reached down and stroked her hair gently. "Want to put your head in my lap?"

"Great idea." Marnie breathed in the familiar scent that was the combination of Ben's laundry soap and after-shave.

"Better?"

"Mmmm. Much."

"Hey, I have an idea," Ben said.

"What's that?"

"We have tomorrow night off. My translator gave me directions to this place with a great view. Can I take you to dinner?"

Marnie emerged for her dinner out in a flattering sleeveless dress. "Should I be more conservative?" she asked. "It's so hot here. . . ."

"Yes, it's hot, and so are you." Ben smiled. "You look great."

Marnie shook her head with amusement. "I didn't ask how we're going to get there with no car," she said. "Taking the bus?"

"Nope. I borrowed the pastor's pickup. He calls it his air-conditioned suburban." Ben made a grand gesture toward a dilapidated two-tone pickup. "What he means is that rolling down the windows conditions the air, and it works as well in the suburbs as in the city. I knew you wouldn't care. That's part of your charm. For us it's a chariot."

"You're right." Marnie was clearly amused. "A chariot, indeed. Good thing I'm not vain about my hair, since it's obviously going to be whipped around!"

"But on you . . . it looks great." Ben opened the door to let her in. *And it's going to take some willpower to keep this from being a romantic evening. I should be shot for doing this . . . to both of us.*

After dinner, Ben took Marnie's hand and led her outside down fifty steps and out to the balcony below the restaurant. Standing side-by-side, they looked out over the twinkling city lights. A gentle breeze made Marnie shudder from the unexpected cold, and Ben drew her close to shield her. The smell of her fragrance and the touch of her bare arm sent a rush of both pleasure and pain through him. He felt the awkwardness of years without a romantic interest. And he wanted to be a gentleman, hesitating lest he appear too eager. Mostly he felt the fear of his HIV exposure. *This would be the perfect moment to express my affection. Still, I've got to keep this from progressing . . . for her sake, . . . but . . .*

Caught in his whirling emotions, Ben looked into Marnie's face. He felt her warm breath and almost effortlessly turned her toward him for a face-to-face embrace. Marnie reached up and touched her lips to his in the most delicate, fragile of kisses.

Ooooh! he thought as she rested her cheek against his chest. *That wasn't nearly long enough. She didn't even give me a chance to respond. Is that my heart pounding or hers? Or both?*

He held her for a long moment. Then cradling her face in his hands, he whispered, "I love you," and gently pressed his lips against hers.

Back in her room, Marnie lay in the dark, watching the curtains sway in the breeze as she relived Ben's kiss. She didn't want to forget his scent, his touch, the look in his eyes, the sound of his voice as he'd said the words she'd longed to hear. Finally, she drifted into a deep and restful sleep.

Down the hall, Ben couldn't get comfortable. He felt deeply troubled by what he had let happen. *I love her too much to saddle her with a life of despair if I'm HIV positive. Why did I let it get that far? Why did I kiss her the way I did? Why did it feel so right?*

When the team met for breakfast, Ben sat with someone else instead of taking his place next to Marnie, as he had the previous two mornings. During the siesta, he napped instead of spending the hour with her. He was cordial, but something had clearly changed.

Chapter Ten

JANELLE PULLED HER CAR INTO THE country club parking lot. She checked her make-up in the mirror, straightened an earring that had turned sideways, and smoothed a blonde hair that wanted to do its own thing. Instead of buying a maternity dress that afternoon, she had bought something that flattered her figure. She wouldn't fit into it for long, but she didn't care. *Sometimes logic is overrated.*

When Luc met her at the door, he looked at her and made a great show of licking his lips. They both laughed. "So, what's all this mystery about? I demand an answer!" he insisted.

"Ooh, you must be patient, *monsieur*," Janelle spoke in a terrible French accent.

Sighing deeply, Luc held the door open and motioned for her to enter. They gave their names to the hostess, and soon their favorite waiter came to seat them.

"Hello, KJ," Janelle winked at him.

"Good evening, Mrs. Morgan, Dr. Morgan," he nodded at each of them as he spoke their names. "Right this way." He guided them to the table with the best view and seated them in front of the window.

Thirty minutes later, Luc picked at the house specialty—Pacific salmon—too distracted to eat. Every five minutes he asked Janelle what she wanted to talk about. But she just steered the conversation to other subjects as she savored her grilled chicken salad. After KJ had cleared their plates, Luc inquired, "Is your mother coming to live with us? Is that it?"

Janelle rolled her eyes.

"Just wondering. Gotta make sure you're not trying to butter me up for the big blow."

"No. Nothing like that, dear. You'll just have to be patient."

"You've finally realized just how desirable I am, and you needed a chance to get me off by ourselves to have your way with me?"

Janelle smiled broadly. She leaned forward on her elbows. "You do amuse yourself."

"That wasn't supposed to be funny." After another minute, he blurted out, "No—wait! You're going to law school?"

Janelle shook her head.

"You're joining the bomb squad to make sure nobody ever hurts me again?"

Janelle tried to keep a straight face, but she couldn't help but laugh. "Oh dang, you guessed it."

Finally, the waiter brought a dessert menu and handed it to Janelle.

"I don't get a menu, KJ?" Luc good-naturedly tried to alert the waiter, thinking he'd messed up.

"No, sir. Your wife already ordered your dessert for you."

Luc gave her a surprised look.

"Mystery solved," she told Luc. "It's a special dessert."

Luc leaned his head to one side. "All this mystique is about a *dessert?*"

"Oh, it's not just *any* dessert, dear. It's a very special dessert." Janelle turned to KJ and gestured toward Luc. "I'll have the same thing he's having."

"Very good, ma'am. I'll bring it right out."

Not more than two minutes later, their server reappeared

with two bowls covered by fancy silver lids. He placed them in front of the doctor and his wife and then looked at Janelle.

"Ready?" he asked.

She nodded. "I'll do the honors myself, thank you."

"Very good ma'am," he said, nodding deeply, a knowing smile on his face. Then he disappeared.

Janelle leaned forward and in a low, seductive voice said, "You may open it now."

Luc, with great dramatic flair lifted the lid. His look of expectancy turned to bewilderment. "Ice cream—with pickles? *That's* the surprise?"

Janelle positively glowed.

"I don't get it."

Janelle lifted the lid off her bowl to reveal the same thing. "Funny," she said. "I thought that's what you'd want. It's certainly *what I've been craving!*"

At that, a look of realization flashed across Luc's face. "Janelle, . . . you're not . . . we're not . . ."

Janelle, now both weeping and laughing, continued to smile. "What are you doing around New Year's Eve?"

He lifted his shoulders.

Then she reached into her purse and handed him a cigar. "Well, I'll tell you. Congratulations, Daddy!"

"You're sure?"

Janelle nodded. "I took the test—twice."

Luc dropped his napkin on the table, scooted the chair out, and took two steps toward his wife. "How could this happen?"

"You're an OB/Gyn. You're supposed to know stuff like that." Janelle wrapped her arms around him.

On Friday morning the team gathered in the lobby to head to breakfast at the adjoining restaurant when Ben emerged in his medical garb.

As everyone made their way through the lobby, Ben pulled Marnie aside and walked slowly behind everyone else. "I need to ask you a question."

"What's that?"

"Carlos Rivera called last night and said he wants to give me the grand tour of their hospital today. But, well . . ."

"What is it?" Marnie stopped and stared.

"He asked if you'd like to come along, too."

"Oh! How kind. But really, I couldn't. I'm giving my testimony at the park, and I promised a young widow I'd meet with her afterwards to try to answer some of her spiritual questions." She thought for another moment and her mood seemed to change. "Besides, the realities of my late husband's experiments are a bit close to home here."

"That's certainly understandable. My concern is that he seems to know so much about us. Why did he single you out the day we got here . . . and again now? He must know something."

"Hmmm. I see your point, although there's not exactly much to know about 'us'—right?"

Ben said nothing but gave her a slight nod and began walking again. "All right. Maybe I'm just paranoid." *But the man has good reason to hate Tim—and you by association.*

Carlos Rivera's limo pulled up to the large building. It boasted a new wing that bore the mayor's name. Carlos guided Ben inside, and they were met by the chief of staff.

Together, the three men toured the hospital floor-by-floor, and Ben was generous with his compliments. They stopped at last in the OB wing, which was colorful and fairly modern, though not state-of-the-art. Ben mentally noted the absence of baby warmers and monitors. Finally, they led him to the *in vitro* lab. The single operating room had an ultrasound machine in the hallway. *Can't do a transvaginal egg retrieval or Doppler flow studies with this model,* Ben thought. The egg lab was quite new, with much of it still in boxes. *Glad to see they have a good operating microscope.*

"You are so quiet, my friend," Carlos said, putting Ben on the spot.

Ben hedged and said, "You have the makings of a very fine clinic here, and it won't be long before you're equipped to do everything."

When Carlos pressed for details, Ben smiled. Looking closely at the equipment, he continued. "It would be my pleasure to talk with you about the future of your fine clinic."

"Future? I see. Well, you like *tamales,* yes?"

Ben nodded.

"Time to head for the restaurant, then. *Vámonos!*"

Once in the backseat of the limo, Carlos began again. "You like our clinic, doctor?"

"Oh yes. It's remarkable. The new wing, the new facilities and equipment . . ."

"Yet tell me frankly. You still think it would be unwise to bring our embryos here for transfer?"

Ben chose his words carefully. "Yes, Mr. Mayor. One of the keys to success is experience. And while you have certainly begun to assemble very good equipment, I wonder if your team is ready for such delicate procedures. I have no doubt that, in time, this will be the finest clinic around. But I wouldn't recommend transferring your embryos to the clinic yet. And let me repeat, I would consider it a great privilege, in return for your generosity in inviting our team here, if I could bring you and your wife to our clinic and perform the transfers whenever you're ready."

"Is there risk in sending the frozen embryos to my clinic?"

Ben shook his head. "Not a very high risk. They can be transferred frozen quite well. But the thawing, the timing, the

precise transfer to the correct depth—these require considerable skill and experience."

"Could you not come down and do the transfers here?"

"Yes, perhaps. But your equipment, sonography, and the
entire operating team would be unfamiliar. I just don't believe
we'd be giving your babies the best chance. And when dealing
with embryos, we want to give each tiny life the absolute best
chance for survival."

"Yes, of course. I see." Carlos sat quietly, thinking. "And
you are *certain* there have been no more 'mistakes'—that these
embryos are *my* children, not like the clones?"

"Absolutely sure."

Victor, Carlos Rivera's second assistant, extinguished his cigarette and entered the Hotel Real with Ramon. As they approached the front desk, the desk clerk recognized Ramon as
the mayor's right-hand man. Smiling, he asked, "Is there something I can do to assist you?"

Ramon smiled. "Yes. Could you pull up the fees for the
American team?"

The clerk looked puzzled and met Ramon's question with a
stare.

"The mayor is planning to cover all their expenses, you see."

"Ah, of course! Very good, sir!" He pulled up the information
on the new computer and printed it out. As he handed over
the papers, Ramon asked, "May I also see their documentation?"

The clerk, now enthusiastic about helping, removed all the
passports and birth certificates from the safe.

Ramon thumbed through the documents and jotted down
names. He looked up to meet the clerk's inquisitive eyes. "The
mayor is planning a dinner party and he needs the names of
each of our guests."

"I see. Is there anything else I can do to help you, sir?" Just then the phone rang, and the clerk stepped away to answer it. Ramon quickly jotted down passport numbers for Ben and Marnie. He also checked to be sure Ben had used his credit card to secure the rooms, noting that number as well. Finally, he located the room numbers next to each name and flashed a number to Victor, who quietly excused himself and headed for the stairs.

For the next ten minutes, Ramon occupied the desk clerk with conversation about the mayor, the weather, and the music playing in the lobby. He was lavish in his praise for the new hotel. When Victor returned, he nodded to Ramon, and after another minute of small talk, the two men departed.

On Saturday, the mission team had the day off, so the pastor arranged to take the group to the beach. Once they arrived at the coast, the group played games or sunbathed. Marnie tried to hide her unhappiness by playing volleyball, but it took concentration. At one point someone in the group teased about her romance, and it made for an awkward silence.

Back at the hotel, hours later, Marnie stepped out into the hall to fill her water bottle from the cooler. Ben had just slipped his key into the lock when he spotted her.

"Marnie!"

She looked up at him with sadness in her eyes.

"Have a good day?" he said cheerfully.

She shrugged.

"What's wrong? C'mon, where's that smile I love?"

"Are we okay?" she asked quietly.

"Why wouldn't we be okay?"

"Never mind." She started to turn back toward her door, but he followed her.

"Wait! Don't leave!" He put his hand on her shoulder as she reached for the knob. "Marnie, please don't be mad at me."

She spun around and looked at him with eyes that sliced right through him.

"Are you up for talking?" he asked.

"I've been 'up' for talking all week. The question is whether *you're* in the mood for it." She turned back and slid the key into the latch.

"I am. Will you meet me in the lobby in about fifteen minutes?"

"Sure," she said. She opened the door and shut it behind her.

Chapter Eleven

As Ben sat in the hotel lobby waiting for Marnie, he realized he hadn't felt this depressed since Tim had "resurfaced." *What will I tell her? It's all my fault. The last thing I meant to do was hurt her! I can't seem to be around her without making this harder on both of us. But if I tell her I might have AIDS, she'll stick by me, helplessly watching me die. I don't want to put her through that. I'm gonna have to back off—can't put her through that—not again.*

He looked at his watch every two or three minutes. *She's certainly in no hurry.*

At last, Marnie got off the elevator, sauntered over to the couch, and sat down next to him.

Out of the corner of his eye, Ben saw another team member approaching. "Let's take a walk, shall we?"

"Sure." Marnie's eyes stayed glued to the ground as they walked through the lobby. They passed through the doors and strolled down the street in silence. At the end of the block they stumbled onto a park, so they found a bench and sat down.

"What's on your mind?" Ben asked.

"I'd like to ask you the same question."

"Hey, it's been a great trip. . . . Got lots of good work done, and I think we've patched up relations with the Riveras."

"You know that's not what I mean, Ben." Marnie looked him square in the face. "Just answer one question for me. When you told me the other night that you loved me, what exactly did you mean?"

Ben sighed. "Do we have to analyze a beautiful moment? It loses some of its mystique when you dissect it."

"I see."

"But if you're wondering if I meant it or whether I was just carried away by the moment—the answer is yes to both."

Marnie stared at the ground, processing this information.

"I'm sorry I'm making this hard for you. I should be making it easier," he added.

"Making *what* easier?"

"I don't know. Everything. I've been selfish and you deserve better. I'm sorry."

"What do you mean? I'm ready to accept your apology once I figure out what you mean."

"I guess it's something I just can't explain. Maybe there's a private graveyard in my heart that I can't open for visitors just yet."

"Does it have to do with losing your wife?"

"Losing someone you deeply love leaves scars in the deep, secret places of the heart."

"I don't claim to understand, Ben, but I know it's hard. It was bad enough losing Tim, and he and I had nothing like the relationship you and Juli had. So is that it? This is about Juli? Do you think I'm trying to take her place, because—"

"No, no, it's not that . . . not at all. I just wouldn't want anyone to have to go through that again."

"So you would rather spend the rest of your life alone, refusing to take emotional risks?"

Ben smirked. "Sorry. There's just some painful stuff inside I need to work through. I need more time."

"You need to work through it by yourself?"

Ben nodded. "I think so."

"You don't want to share it with me?"

"Can't Marnie. I just can't." Ben shook his head. "You're gonna have to just trust me on this one."

"You're pulling away, and I'm supposed to just trust you?"

"I don't want you to get hurt."

"Too late for that. Ben, tell me honestly—are you having second thoughts about us—about me?"

"Not a chance."

"Well then, Ben McKay, if you're in pain, why won't you let me in? I didn't just open my heart to you—I threw open the windows. You've walked through the hardest days of my life with me. Why won't you let me walk in hard places with you?"

Ben shrugged. "It's something I have to deal with alone. It's just the way I've got to do this. It's for the best. It would be too hard—"

"I can't imagine that it would be harder than *this*—this horrible wall, this distance."

"I can." *I know you'd never leave. . . . You'd stay . . . and I'd know I'd done that to you.*

"So are you trying to spare me, or trying to spare *you*—you—always the caregiver? You, the one who's happy to give but not to receive?"

"Not fair."

"Think about it. I think you'll find I'm right, Ben. Your 'protection' feels like control."

Ben sat quietly for a long time. When he finally spoke, all he said was, "I just can't right now. Too much going on. Just give me a little time—a few months may be all I need."

Marnie wiped a tear from her face. "You say you need time? Don't you really mean you need *space?*"

Ben shook his head in frustration.

"Well, I am *so* here for you, Ben. But I'm not going to try to pry you open, as though you were some oversized oyster with a pearl inside. If I get any pearls, it will be because you give them to me. Giving your heart to someone else is a gift, a treasure. There's no pleasure in demanding it. So I'm going to quit trying. When you get tired of shutting me out, you know where you can find me."

Marnie sat for a long time waiting for Ben to respond, but he had nothing to say. Finally she told him, "Maybe you'd rather be alone to think." He shrugged and continued staring at the ground. So she left him sitting on the bench and walked back to the hotel. When she entered the lobby, the live band was playing "Save the Last Dance for Me."

She got to her room as fast as she could and threw herself across the bed.

Janelle entered her OB/Gyn's reception area and looked around. *All the other pregnant ladies here look so young—and beautiful; glad I'm not showing yet.* Though thrilled, Janelle needed some transition time to adjust to her new identity.

After thumbing through magazines for about fifteen minutes, Janelle heard the nurse call her name.

"Hi, I'm Ginny, Dr. Geman's new nurse."

Janelle nodded and wondered what had happened to Sharon. *This one must be fresh out of nursing school.* She followed Ginny back to a room where she recorded weight, took blood pressure, and handed Janelle a cup.

"Urine specimen?" Janelle asked.

Ginny nodded.

"I know the way," Janelle said, heading for the bathroom. A few minutes later, she returned to the exam room.

Ginny opened the chart, "Date of your last period?"

Janelle looked at her purse calendar and answered.

"Any cramping or bleeding?" Ginny looked up. Janelle shook her head.

When the nurse finished with her questions, she led Janelle back to Dr. Geman's office. Motioning to a chair she said, "Have a seat. He'll be right in."

Janelle waited only a minute or two before the doctor entered wearing scrubs and carrying her chart. "Hello, Janelle," he said taking her hand. "What have we here?"

"I'm pregnant." She returned his smile.

"So I see. And you seem pretty pleased."

"Oh, yes! A little scared, but very excited."

He glanced through her records. "You've been on the diaphragm for years. I take it that didn't work?"

"I don't think we can blame contraceptive failure. My husband's leg fracture kept him out of action for a while, but there was a time or two that he surprised me." She grinned sheepishly.

"Indeed, I've always said the diaphragm doesn't do much good on the dresser! And how is Luc taking the news?"

"Great."

Dr. Geman nodded and maintained a pleasant smile, but his voice grew a bit more sober. He sat on the rolling stool and scooted it toward her. "Janelle, there are a few things we need to talk about—not because I suspect anything's wrong but just to give you the best possible medical care."

"Oh no. Is this the pregnant 'old lady' speech?"

"We prefer to say 'more mature maternity patients,'" the doctor said with kindness in his eyes.

"Smooth. You polish the phrase nicely." Janelle laughed.

"As you know from the last three we've been through together, pregnancy causes a huge stress on the body. It changes every organ you've got. So we have to watch a bit more closely this time. Some of the risks increase with age."

"I understand."

"We'll need to keep an eye on weight and blood pressure and watch for certain birth defects. Genetic abnormalities increase with aging. We can offer some tests and even encourage a few, but I don't require them to follow your pregnancy. We can run some at this early stage . . . one called a chorionic villus sampling can be done very soon, and it can tell us if the baby has normal chromosomes."

"Will the test benefit the baby?"

"Not directly. But occasionally we find things that can be helpful at the time of delivery. They allow us to prepare so we can have the right people assembled."

"Is there any risk to this test?"

"We see a small risk of miscarriage with this type of procedure, but with placental localization with the sonogram, it's pretty straightforward in competent hands."

"Do you recommend it for me? You know we wouldn't abort the pregnancy no matter what."

"Right. Janelle, I have to offer the test. There's a huge liability risk if I don't explain and offer prenatal testing to patients over age thirty-five. But I don't require it and, frankly, if I had to make the choice, I probably wouldn't go that route. Still, some patients feel better knowing one way or the other."

"I suppose so. But I wouldn't feel good about putting the baby at risk for the 'knowledge.'"

"No problem. There are some other tests we can discuss later—some blood tests. And an amniocentesis. We can also use sonogram guidance that could give us some important information, if you wish."

"Thanks, doc, we'll cross the bridges one at a time, all right?"

"Sure." He nodded.

"Let me talk with Luc about testing, too."

Ben distributed tickets to the team members for their flight home. Marnie didn't expect that Ben would arrange to have her seat next to his. She just hoped she wasn't wedged between two large men.

After boarding the plane and finding her seat, she looked up to see Ben. He stood in the aisle next to her, holding his carryon. "Mind if I join you?" he asked.

"Not at all." She stood so he could scoot through and take the window seat. No one came to claim the aisle.

They settled in and made small talk, and soon Marnie forgot her frustration with him as they became engrossed in talking about the hospital, consulting with the mayor and with the doctors, and how they could set up an IVF clinic.

"I met the Rivera twins," Ben told her. "They're so little and sweet. Just adorable. Breaks my heart."

"How are they?"

Ben shook his head. "A tough life. I had to gown and glove to be around them."

Ben sat next to her again on the flight back to Washington, D.C. To her disappointment, however, he slept for most of the flight. While she listened to his breathing, Marnie closed her eyes, conscious of her arm touching his, occasionally wiping a tear.

Ben and Marnie emerged from customs at Reagan National to find Luc and the boys, Bill, and a crowd of others there to meet them.

"What a surprise!" Ben said, looking at Luc. "Good to see you, buddy." He shook his friend's hand, and Marnie greeted him as well.

"We couldn't stand to wait. We've got some big news," Luc said. "Jan will be here in a minute. She went to find a restroom."

"News? What sort of news? You can't tell us *now?*" Ben asked.

"Nope. Jan has to be here."

"If that's the way you want to play it," Ben pretended to sulk.

"Here I am!" they heard Janelle and turned to see her. After exchanging hugs, Ben said, "I'm sure surprised to see you here."

Janelle grabbed Luc and kissed him gleefully. Then she winked at Marnie. "We just couldn't wait to tell you!"

"Tell us what?" they said in unison.

Janelle gave Marnie a knowing look. "We're going to have another baby!"

"Oh, Janelle! That's wonderful! I'm so happy for you!" Marnie embraced her.

Ben smiled while the news sank in through his fatigue. "So that's what happens when you're off work on disability," he said to Luc. "And you tried to convince me you were reading medical journals the whole time. I'm up all night delivering the entire population of the world, and *you're* at home trying to increase it!"

As they all walked down the corridor together, Janelle took Marnie's arm and hung back from the others. "How did your trip go?" She glanced at Ben and then back to Marnie.

Marnie just shook her head. "We'll have to talk later."

"We'll do that." Janelle fell quiet.

Bill handed the keys to the Explorer to Ben and thanked him for the loan of the car. Marnie's heart sank. They'd have Bill in the car with them on the way home. She had hoped for some parting words of encouragement from Ben.

But Ben dropped off Bill first, even though it meant going a little out of the way. Then for the first few minutes the couple rode together in silence. Finally, Ben spoke. "I'm pretty tired. I'll e-mail you later tonight, okay?"

"Sure."

"But I need to see you again soon. How about dinner and a show on Friday night?"

Marnie wrinkled her brow and shrugged. "All right."

Chapter Twelve

ON HIS FIRST AFTERNOON BACK AT WORK, Ben walked with Luc to the doctors' café. As they ate ham and cheese sandwiches, Luc said, "I haven't had a chance to tell you, but while you were gone Tim's former research supervisor called."

"Really? What did he want?"

"He asked for all of Tim's notes and a sample of the special cell line he developed. And then this morning he phoned to say that the notes from Tim's last week of research weren't with the notes we sent."

Ben's eyebrows shot up. "Wait! He wanted a sample?"

Luc nodded.

"What did you tell him?"

"I went ahead and released one—a small one."

Ben leaned forward. "What? You did *what?*"

Luc just looked at him, not wanting to repeat what he'd just said.

"The LG cells?" Ben insisted.

"I didn't see any harm in it. All they're doing is sitting in the freezer. But I sent him only a small sample—not a lot."

"If it replicates itself, that's all he needs." Ben spoke gently. "Luc, I'm not sure I know all the ramifications, but those cells . . . remember, it was the mixed-up embryo transfer you did with *those* cells that led to the delivery of the Rivera twins. We have several hundred thousand identical cells, *each* of which potentially represents another 'twin' of those kids."

Luc rubbed his chin and chose his words carefully. "Sorry, Ben. I hadn't given it that kind of thought. The way I saw it, we've got a tissue culture of cells, and Harrison wants to understand the cell mechanic so he can develop tissue for transplantation."

"Sure, Luc, but we treat each fertilized egg and donated embryo with all the respect due a person. And these cells some-how produced the Rivera twins. So in my book the LG cells are due the same regard as any other embryo."

"I'm really sorry, Ben. I've never thought it through like that. So what *do* we do with the cells?"

"Buddy, I really don't know. We've got thousands of them. *If* we could figure out how to implant them, we *still* have the outcome of the Rivera twins' leukemia. So I think we sit tight, preserve them, and pray for deeper insight."

Luc shook his head in frustration.

Ben continued. "I guess it proves the adage, 'Just because you can do something, doesn't mean that you should.' Tim got out way past our ethical understanding, not to mention the biology."

"Okay, partner. I think you're right. This is so complex. How did you work it all through?"

"Ha! Like I've got it all worked out! Just trying to be con-sistent and err on the side of life."

Dr. Lowell, a short, thin, intense man, wore thick glasses and an expression of perpetual curiosity. He was the brightest assistant in Dr. Harrison's Dallas laboratory. Poking his head in at Harrison's open doorway, Dr. Lowell said, "Sir, I have an update for you."

Dr. Harrison looked up from his paperwork. "What can you tell me?"

"I've got good news and bad news. Can you come down to the lab for a few minutes?"

The doctor nodded, finished writing something, and stood to follow. As they walked, Lowell told him, "The results are remarkable. Though the LG cell line has been frozen for some time, when placed in culture with the fetal cells we obtained from abortion specimens, the cells 'switch on' with whatever cells we place them with. We're beginning to generate human skin tissue, blood cell lines, some nerve cells, heart cells—it's astonishing."

Dr. Harrison nodded. "That's incredibly good news. So what's the bad news?"

"Well, they'll make mature *tissue* cells, but they won't replicate themselves. And since the culture is not self-sustaining, we have none left."

Dr. Harrison swallowed hard. During the past week, he'd suggested to his superiors that he'd discovered the pathway to tissue for future transplantation and repair of damaged organs. He'd convinced them that Genevex would be the number one, knock-your-socks-off biotech firm. He'd even envisioned a Nobel prize for medicine. But now, as dramatic as these results were, they meant nothing until researchers could figure out the combination that would make the culture self-sustaining.

"We need more of the cell line, doctor."

Dr. Harrison stormed out of the lab and back to the office. But within minutes, he had calmed down and was already planning yet another call to Luc Morgan. *I'll have to think of a way to get some more cells. If we can just get more, I'm sure we can unlock the secret.*

On Thursday evening the phone rang. Marnie glanced at her caller ID and saw Ben's name. He had e-mailed regularly, but she had not spoken with him since their return earlier in the week. She had tried reminding herself that he was probably swamped at the clinic, but she also sensed him pulling back even more. His messages had arrived daily, but their contents were merely newsy, without much warmth.

"Ben, you sound terrible," she said when she heard his croaking voice.

"I *feel* terrible. And I hate to do this, but I need to break our date for tomorrow night. Can we reschedule?"

"What's the matter?"

"Probably just some bug."

"You're never sick. You're a doc."

"I know. That's why I went to med school. I thought it would make me immune!" He chuckled until a cough stopped him.

"Sorry to hear it. And, unfortunately, chicken soup is not my specialty."

"No problem. I don't need mothering."

"What *do* you need?"

"I need you not to be upset with me for breaking our date."

"Not to worry. I don't want to catch anything right now. But I *do* regret that I won't see you. What do you think you've got?" She didn't want the conversation to end.

"Probably some nasty crud I picked up in Mexico. Feels like the flu. I'm achy, got a fever, no energy—generally exhausted and miserable."

"When did you start feeling lousy?"

Suddenly, Ben grew defensive. "Hey, I'll be *fine*. Why don't you let *me* handle the medical end of things?"

〜❧〜

The following Wednesday Ben felt well enough to return to work, and he hit the ground running. When he got to the office, Lisa mentioned that a Dr. Harrison had been trying to reach Luc. Ben said he'd handle it. But Lisa, assuming Ben had the number, didn't leave messages in his box. And Ben, assuming Lisa would leave the message in his box, promptly forgot. Conscious that Luc and Janelle needed more time together, he put in long hours and came in on his day off to give Luc more of a break.

Marnie saw Ben at church and received daily e-mails, but other than that she had no contact with him for nearly three weeks. He diligently kept her informed about the events in his life, but he purposely kept her from knowing anything under the surface. He never dropped so much as a hint of the truth—that he was pining for her at a level approaching abject misery.

Then he felt ill again, missing three more days of work.

In mid-August, Ben couldn't suppress his anxiety as he filled out the lab paperwork for his five-month AIDS test and sent it with his blood sample. *What if I've made it this far only to find out that this flu thing is really HIV?*

He had a short fuse with the staff for the next few days, enduring the wait with mounting tension. But, finally, Dr. McLaughlin called to tell him the test was clear: "You've made it to five months—that's a good sign. Pass next month and you're out of the woods. Hope you have a great weekend."

"It's sure off to a good start! Thanks, Mark."

The minute Ben hung up the phone, he picked it back up and dialed Marnie's number. He got her machine, so he tried her on the cell phone.

"Hey, Ben, what's up?"

"What's with the heavy breathing?" he wanted to know. "Happy to hear from me?"

Marnie laughed. "You caught me at the club with Janelle. We're biking. And you sound like you're in a great mood."

"Aye, 'tis true." He almost sang in a thick Irish accent. "And I was wondering what you're doing tonight."

"Nothing that I can't change. What's up?"

"I need to see you."

"Is everything all right?"

"Everything is just great," Ben told her.

"What's the plan?" Marnie sounded tentative.

"Why don't you come to my place? We'll order out, and we can take a swim and talk."

In the eighteen months that Ben had known Marnie, this was the first time he had invited her to the home he'd shared with Juliet.

After dinner, Ben and Marnie took a swim. When they emerged from the water, Marnie modestly wrapped a sarong around her hips. She and Ben stretched out side by side to dry on the matching wood chaise lounges.

"Great place you've got here," Marnie said, looking up at the grapevine that covered the slatted patio. In the hot summer air, the lights from the pool danced in reflection off the side of the house, casting the evening in a dreamlike glow.

"Glad you like it, because I hope you'll be spending more time here in the near future." Ben scooted off his lounge, stood facing her, and then leaned down to kiss her.

When he had finished, Marnie gave him a questioning look.

"I know. I'm a total mystery to you."

"Well, now that you mention it." She smiled.

"Marnie, I have a story to tell you—a true story. And I think once you've heard it, my behavior in the past few months will make a lot more sense."

"Great. I'm listening."

He sat on the edge of his chaise and told her everything, from the prostitute to that afternoon's test results.

She sat silently for a long time. Ben couldn't read her expression. "What are you thinking?" he finally asked when he could no longer stand the suspense.

She crossed her arms and set her jaw. "I'm thinking that I'm sorry for all you've been through—the fear, the trauma . . ."

"But? . . ."

"But I'm also royally chapped." She spoke with a studied calm.

Ben sat up straight. "Why?"

"Because you assumed I would walk out of your life if you tested positive to HIV."

"No Marnie, that's just it. I knew you'd *stay,* and I couldn't do that to you."

Marnie sat stunned for a moment. "So what were you going to do if you tested positive? Go crawl in a hole somewhere and suffer alone? One way or the other I'd have found out, and I'd still be in your life in *some* way. You could have chosen to share it or not share it, and you chose not to."

"But you'd been through enough."

"And your pulling back from me emotionally was supposed to ease my pain?"

Ben shrugged. "Yeah, I guess."

Marnie stood and grabbed her things. "You don't get it, do you, Ben? You made all my choices for me in this; I had no say in it. You shut me out of your life instead of letting me walk with you in it." Her eyes clouded over. "Ben, I suppose your heart was in the right place, and from your point of view you were loving me. But you need to know that from where I sit you were cruel. And controlling. I just don't know about us anymore."

Ben sat speechless as Marnie walked back into the house, picked up her street clothes, and headed for her car.

On Saturday, Marnie did not return Ben's e-mails or pick up the phone when he called. She greeted him politely in church on Sunday. She even agreed when he asked to sit with her. But she didn't hang around to visit afterward. She went straight to get Emily from her class and took her out to lunch alone. But by Sunday afternoon she was reconsidering. That evening she got a short e-mail from Ben that said, "Grand Marnier, I was wrong. I can't say I totally understand, but I know I can't stand for things not to be right between us. Please? Forgive me?"

I need to give him another chance.

She wrote back, "I can't stand it, either. Let's try to talk it out. Truce."

Chapter Thirteen

LATE SUNDAY NIGHT, MARNIE'S PHONE RANG, and she jumped up to see the caller ID. When she saw Ben's name, she picked it up.

"*Bonjour,* Marnier. Miss me much?"

"Hey, how are ya?" She avoided answering the question.

"Well, obviously we have some stuff to talk about. But right now I'm calling because Janelle just called me. And I'd like to ask for the incredible pleasure of your company for a foursome—an evening of Shakespeare."

"What's playing?"

"*Antony and Cleopatra.* At Folger's Theatre."

"Luc and Janelle are Shakespeare fans, too?"

"You mean I've never told you?"

"Told me what?"

"The story behind Shakespeare."

"So tell me."

"It goes way back to med school when I introduced Luc and Janelle to each other. They've never forgiven me," he laughed. "See, I knew Janelle from the campus fellowship. She was a drama major, and I deluded myself into thinking I could act. So we did a lot of skits together. The local community held a Shakespeare festival during our senior year, and they wanted to perform *Antony and Cleopatra*. So they borrowed her from our school's drama department to play the leading lady."

"No kidding—a blonde Cleopatra?"

"Amazing what they can do with wigs and makeup. She was incredible."

"How fun!"

"After I saw her on opening night, I dragged my roomie to the next performance. He put up a nasty fight, but I won. Luc never was a big Shakespeare fan . . . until that night. He fell in love with the woman playing Cleopatra."

"He quickly decided to learn the Bard's English, eh?"

"Verily. Luc insisted that I introduce them. Of course, I tortured him for a while."

"You didn't want to date her yourself?" Marnie tried to suppress a twinge of jealousy.

"Honestly? Naw. Janelle's always been just a really great friend. Anyway, now they have three kids—with another on the way—two cars, Peaches the cat, and Napoleon the bearded dragon lizard."

"Amazing."

"Which brings us back to *Antony and Cleopatra*. It's the perfect drama for all of us to see together—just like old times."

"I'm there. When and what time?"

The usher led the two couples to their seats. Luc motioned for Marnie to go first, so they sat—Ben with Marnie to his left and Janelle to his right, and Luc on the aisle to Janelle's right.

After the first act, Janelle leaned forward to see that Marnie was occupied studying her program. Then she leaned close to Ben and asked, "You were AOA and Phi Beta Kappa, right?"

Puzzled, Ben nodded.

"That's what I thought."

"And what, pray tell," said Ben, "does a med school honor society have to do with Shakespeare?"

"It means you're supposed to be smart."

"Oh, uh-huh." Ben looked confused.

. Janelle looked over at Marnie, then smiled at Ben. After that she looked down at her own left hand and Ben's eyes followed hers. She twirled her wedding ring and said, "Men! Sometimes you really don't get it, do you? This is a hint."

Ben glanced at Marnie to make sure she was not paying attention. Then he smiled at Janelle. "Gee, wish I'd thought of that. Why don't you stick to watching the play?"

On the way home, Ben and Marnie stopped for dessert. Over sherbet ice cream and chocolate death cake, they fumbled for words.

"I'm sorry," Ben said. "I—"

"No. I need to apologize, too. I should have stayed and talked it out. Nobody ever resolves anything by walking away."

"Marnie, I have to confess. . . . I'm still having a hard time understanding why you got so upset. I can see how you thought I was being controlling. But there's a lot I still don't get, and I'd really like to understand."

She looked at his eyes, which pleaded with her for an answer. "Ben, sometimes I feel as if you treat me like a china doll. You're the strong one, and I'm the one you take care of."

"What's wrong with that?"

"It may *seem* the manly thing to do, but it doesn't work. There's a huge difference between a doll and a partner. Partners take care of each other. We've been learning about unity and oneness at church, and that's what I want in my relationships. And if you don't let others help bear your burdens, there can never be unity. It may feel noble to you, but it feels like distance from this end."

At this, Ben grew agitated. "So, what if I'd told you everything? And what if we got together? And what if I got AIDS? You've already lost one husband—twice."

"I recognize your selflessness in that," her voice remained calm. "And in one sense it's very sweet. But consider this. How do you think I'd feel, going through my entire life having never heard three special words from you?"

"I told you in Culiacán that I love you."

"Not those three. I meant, 'I need you.'"

A little over a week later, on Monday morning, Ben thumbed through his phone messages from Friday afternoon. When he tried to return the call from Dr. Harrison, he found that Lisa had apparently written down the wrong number. Having finished with calls, he glanced through the list of the day's patients. His mouth made a crooked grin when he saw Kim Murphy listed. *Lord,* he heaved a nervous sigh. *Are you trying to tell me something?*

At ten o'clock, after he'd completed her six-week postpartum checkup, he asked the nurse to have her meet him in his office.

"Is there a problem, doctor?" The red-head entered and sat uneasily on the edge of the chair. "You seem upset."

"No, no. Sorry! No problem at all." Ben felt himself stammering. "Um, remember the night you and your hubby offered me your box seats for a Redskins game?"

"Are you kidding? I had a baby that night. How could I forget?"

Ben got up and shut the door.

Ben picked up Marnie for the Cowboys-Redskins Monday night season opener, but he stopped short after pulling into her driveway. Before going to her door, he lay his head on the steering wheel and breathed a prayer. Then he took a deep breath, got out of his Explorer, and strolled up the walk.

Marnie answered the door and immediately noticed the logo on his cap. "You're looking pretty *brave*. A Cowboys hat in Redskins territory?"

An hour later, they found their seats at the fifty-yard line.

"These are great seats, Ben," Marnie said, "But I thought you said you could get *box* seats for this game."

"Did I say that?"

"Yeah, you did."

"Hmmm."

Ben appeared to lose himself in the game.

When the two-minute warning signaled before halftime, a red-headed usher stopped at their aisle. She motioned to Marnie and said, "I need to speak with you."

Marnie looked around, then pointed to herself. "Me?"

The usher nodded. "Former President Sullivan has requested that your party join him in his box."

"Oh my! Really?"

"Yes, ma'am."

The woman sitting next to Marnie exclaimed, "Did she say the president? Wow, are you a movie star or something?"

Ben leaned forward to answer her. "Yes. She is."

Marnie shoved Ben gently with her elbow. As she rose from her seat, she explained to the woman, "No, I'm not. President Sullivan is a distant relative."

"Oh." The woman stared.

Marnie slid her hand in Ben's, and they followed the usher up the stairs to the exit. There, a man in a dark suit, wearing an ear communications device, met them and took them to the elevators.

"I wonder how he knew I was here?" Marnie thought aloud. "I told Tim's mom we were coming to the season opener. She must have told him."

When the elevator door opened, the guide directed them to one of the boxes and opened the door. "Please wait inside," he said. "It will take a few minutes."

As Marnie entered the room above the fifty-five yard line, they heard the buzzer going off, signaling half-time. Ben thanked the usher and shut the door, leaving them alone inside.

"Why's it empty in here? Where do you suppose he is?"

"I don't think he's coming." Ben walked over to the window and waved.

"What?" She looked confused.

"I need to show you something, Marnie." He gestured for her to join him at the window. Then he held up his arms and motioned that he wanted to dance. "Come here. I have a question for you."

Marnie, now vaguely suspicious, complied with his wishes.

"But there's no music."

"Marnie, when you're with the right person, all the music is Rachmaninoff."

She relaxed in his arms. "What a lovely thing to say." She smiled up at him, inches from his face, remembering the first time he had ever held her—Rachmaninoff had been playing in the background.

Suddenly they heard the announcer. "Ladies and gentlemen, if you will turn your attention to the scoreboard, we have a matter of importance. . . ."

"I want you to see something," Ben told her.

"What's that?"

"You ready?"

"Uh-huh."

He gently lay a hand on each shoulder and turned her around so she could see the scoreboard. It said, "Marnie, may I have this dance."

"Ben McKay!" she whispered, his name catching in her throat.

Then the lights on the scoreboard went out for an instant, and a second sign flashed up: ". . . for the rest of my life?"

Ben removed his cap and slid down on one knee. Then he took her left hand in his and looked up at her. "Marnie, I love you. I need you. Will you marry me?"

Marnie's right hand flew up to cover her mouth. Tears spilled down her cheeks as she looked down at his face in disbelief.

Again the announcer spoke. "Ladies and gentlemen, if you will now look to Skybox number one, just above the Redskins Banner at the fifty-yard line, Dr. Ben McKay is proposing marriage to Marnie. Let's give them a little encouragement!"

The camera from across the stadium focused through the window and projected on the scoreboard the scene in the box—Ben kneeling, Marnie standing.

The crowd erupted—"Mar-nie, say-yes! Mar-nie, say-yes!"

She giggled, then tugged gently on Ben's hand, urging him to stand. She pulled him close until her face was an inch from his. Looking up, gazing boldly into his eyes, she whispered, "Yes! For always—yes." They kissed and the crowd roared. When they turned to wave to everyone, the scoreboard read, "Yes! Yes! Yes!"

After the game, Marnie and Ben exited the stadium, surrounded by myriad well-wishers who were calling out their congratulations: "Good luck!" "Best wishes!" A few who noticed Ben's cap threw in, "He's a Cowboys fan. It'll never work!"

When they got to the door back at Marnie's house, she reached to open it, but her father beat her to it. He and Emily greeted the couple with a big smile. "Hey, the Redskins may have lost, but I'll bet it was one fine halftime show!" Marnie's dad said.

That night, when Emily changed into pajamas and delivered goodnight hugs and kisses all around, Ben asked her, "Can I read you a story before you go to sleep?"

Emily jumped up and tugged on Ben's hand. "Let's go!"

Ben picked up a bag he had brought and excused himself to Marnie and Will. In Emily's room he leaned back into the rocking chair, and she grabbed her blanket and nestled into his lap. He let Emily reach inside the sack, and she pulled out a copy of *The Velveteen Rabbit.*

"Do you know this story?"

Emily nodded with a smile. Then she whispered, "Can I tell you a secret?"

Ben nodded.

"My Molly doll is real, just like the rabbit in the story."

Ben's eyes grew wide. "No!"

Emily grinned a toothless smile and nodded vigorously.

"What a great secret!" Ben said. "Thanks for telling me. And your secret is safe with me. Are you ready for me to read it?"

Again she nodded. So he began.

When he was nearly finished, Marnie peered in at the door. "You ready for me now?"

Ben motioned for her to join them, and she came over and sat on the ottoman. She waited as Ben completed the last line, then she took a deep breath. "Emily, can we ask you something?"

The child nodded. But before her mother could speak, she asked, "Is Ben going to be my daddy now?"

Marnie looked over at Ben in surprise, then back at her daughter. "Well, yes."

Emily threw her arms around Ben, and for a moment he felt as though the child he'd lost had been returned to him.

"How did you know, Em?" her mother asked.

Emily stretched up and whispered into Ben's ear. "Molly told me."

Chapter Fourteen

ON WEDNESDAY NIGHT BEN AND MARNIE sat down by his pool to make plans while Emily swam.

They stretched out on the lounge chairs and sipped on fruit drinks. "You know, it would be easier if we just eloped," Marnie told Ben, glancing over at him with a smile.

"Fine by me," Ben said. "How does tonight sound?"

Marnie laughed and motioned to Emily. "Sort of short notice on the childcare."

"Oh, details!"

"Seriously, Ben, when did you have in mind?"

"Whatever works best for you, babe."

"I'd say the sooner the better. We don't have to have an elaborate deal. It's the second time for both of us."

"You'll get no complaint here," Ben said holding up his palms, "but . . ."

"But what?"

"Well, there *is* the little matter about my needing a final HIV test next week."

"What difference does *that* make?"

"None, as you've made so abundantly clear. Besides, the odds of HIV infection now are really slim."

She smiled. "But no matter what, I'm here to stay. So let's get on with the ceremony, while the weather's still good."

"Great with me!" Ben laughed. "But the best time in terms of the clinic schedule is in a little less than three weeks. That's kind of short notice for your work schedule, isn't it?"

"It's fine. In fact, it'll seem like forever."

The following week Ben sent in his blood work and waited for a response. When Dr. McLaughlin's office didn't call, Ben tried to be patient and gave them an extra day. But finally, he got on the phone and asked for his results. The nurse couldn't find a record of them. Perhaps the doctor had them.

But Mark didn't return Ben's call that day. Instead, the nurse called the following afternoon with bad news. "Dr. McKay, the lab seems to have misplaced your sample. I'm terribly sorry, but could you send over your blood work again?"

Ben was incensed. "I've already waited three extra days, and now you're telling me we have to rerun the tests?"

"I can't tell you how sorry I am, but yes, doctor, that's correct. They'll do it for you at no charge. I'm so sorry. They've been really swamped."

I'll bet they'd be swamped in a birdbath, Ben thought. He almost said so. Instead, he swallowed his anger, complied with instructions, and began the long wait again.

Two days later, Dr. Geman knocked quietly on the door of the exam room.

"Come in," Janelle called out.

He entered, followed by Ginny, his nurse. Janelle lay on the table with her tummy exposed.

Ginny had taken Janelle's vitals only moments earlier. Dr. Geman seated himself on his stool and glanced through the chart. "Let's see . . . you came in two months ago and then again last month. So you're at . . . um . . ." He began to mentally calculate.

"Sixteen, seventeen weeks," Janelle told him.

He nodded and kept reading. "Weight, blood pressure fine. Urinalysis negative. Good." He set down the chart and gave her his full attention. "So, how are you doing? Any problems?"

"No. I'm great. I didn't have much morning sickness, and my energy has returned."

"Let's just see here." He pulled a tape measure from his pocket, stretched it from the pubic bone to the top of the uterine fundus, and read it. *Should be over halfway up to the navel, but it seems just a bit small.* He put the tape back in his pocket and palpated on the uterus with his warm hands. After that, he picked up the Doppler from the counter, smeared it with acoustic gel, and placed it on Janelle's abdomen. He searched briefly and then heard the rapid "whoosh" of the baby's heart. "Loud and clear. That's good."

He smiled down at her. "All right, since we've decided not to do any of the chromosome tests, let's take a look with the sono. I'd like to have a peek at the baby—just a general scan—and then maybe do some blood work."

"I get to see the baby?" she said, her voice elevating. "Can we tell if it's a boy or a girl?"

"Unlikely. I'd have to get a 'perfect view.' But we can get a general assessment—see how the baby's growing."

Janelle nodded and Dr. Geman and Ginny exited to get the machine.

A minute later, Ginny and another nurse wheeled in the portable unit. Shortly after that, Dr. Geman returned and began smearing her abdomen with copious amounts of warm gel. He scanned silently for a few seconds and then began the "travelogue."

"All right . . . here's the baby's head. He's lying transverse, kinda sideways, which is normal for this stage of pregnancy. . . . Let me freeze this for a picture and a measurement."

Janelle stared at the screen, wearing a beatific smile.

"Now, let's measure the legs." He adjusted some of the dials. "And another measurement . . . looks good. I can do a measurement of an abdominal circumference—the waist size. That can also help demonstrate the growth. . . . Now, if I punch in this button, the computer'll chart the measurements and project a due date. How 'bout that?"

"Great, because as you'll recall it could be one of two," Janelle said, a sly smile on her face.

"Voilà!" He read the date and saw that it was a bit later than they had previously estimated. He noted that the head measurement was the one throwing off the projection. "Hmmm, let me remeasure the head—though there is some 'fudge factor' in sono measurements." He remained quiet for a moment as he remeasured. "Let me just take another look here."

Ginny leaned closer to see what Dr. Geman was reading on the screen.

He studied it closely. *Both the diameter and the circumference of the skull are lagging slightly behind the other measurements, but the baby's tone and movement look good.*

"What do you think, doc?" asked Janelle, the faintest hint of fear in her voice.

Dr. Geman took Janelle's hand in his. "Everything should be okay, but with the discrepancy in estimated due date and your age risk, wisdom would suggest that I set you up to see the materno-fetal guys for a high-level sonogram—just to be sure. I haven't detected anything specifically, but we want to play it safe."

"I understand," Janelle spoke faintly. "Will you call Luc and explain it to him?"

"Sure. It's just a precautionary measure. We'll draw a little blood. That will give us some clues about how different parts of the baby are developing. It'll even let us check about certain genetic abnormalities."

Even as he spoke, Dr. Geman could see that Janelle had zoned out, mentally drifting to scary places. When his voice fell silent, Janelle looked up at him. "Thank you, doctor. I guess I'll get dressed now."

Ben's workload picked up significantly for the rest of the day after Luc was called out by Dr. Geman. No one knew what had happened, but the doctors customarily handled lots of emergencies, so no one thought much of it when Luc left. Ben was focused on waiting for his own results from Dr. McLaughlin's office, having instructed Lisa to track him down when the call came. When it finally did, Lisa found him in the hall, looking at a chart for one of the three patients who waited in various rooms. She told him, "Dr. McLaughlin on line four."

Ben hurried to his office and picked up the line. "Mark!"

"Hey, I hear you're getting married! That's great! But I thought you wanted to 'retreat to the cave' and do manly things. Eat raw meat, snore . . ."

"So . . ." Ben hesitated. "I take it the results are good?"

"Of course! I told you the chances of flipping this late are slim. Nice to give good news. After all you went through for going above and beyond, you didn't deserve the 'black bean.'"

"It's negative?" Ben repeated himself.

"Yeah, man. Forget about it. Go enjoy your new bride. I hear she's a real honey. Congratulations! You can worry about something else now!"

As Janelle drove home, she realized she didn't even remember putting on her clothes. She fought tears, resolving not to let them obstruct her view of the road. *I hope Dr. Geman called Luc immediately. Maybe he'll be there to meet me when I get home . . . naw . . . wishful thinking.* When she pulled into the driveway, the automatic door opened to reveal an empty garage.

She parked the car and pressed the remote to shut the garage door. But instead of getting out, she rested her head on the steering wheel and sobbed. *Lord, I don't want to be alone with this.*

After she let it all out, Janelle fumbled in her purse for a tissue. She stared straight ahead for a few minutes. Then she turned on the CD player, tilted the seat back, and listened to the music. A few minutes later her cell phone rang. Luc's mobile number lit up on the display. She turned down the music and answered. "Luc!"

"Honey, how are you? Where are you?"

"In the car . . . just pulled into the garage."

"Good! I tried the house phone, and you weren't there yet."

"Where are *you?*"

"Not far." Just then the garage door opened and Luc's Jaguar appeared in her rearview mirror. When he pulled alongside, she could see his solemn look.

He jumped out of his car, and Janelle opened her door just as he got to it, banging Luc in the knees. Ignoring the pain, he wrapped her in loving arms. They held each other for several minutes before Luc guided Janelle toward the house. Once inside, they went to their bedroom and sat together on the bed.

Without prompting, Janelle told Luc every detail of her visit to Dr. Gemen. He listened patiently, squeezing her hand as she talked. She knew Luc had talked with Dr. Geman, but she needed to go over everything he'd said. Then she asked, "Did he give you any more details?"

"Nothing you don't already know. Yeah, it's scary, honey, but really the high-level sono is the right thing to do medically. It doesn't mean anything's wrong."

Janelle searched his eyes for a hint of his real feelings. "So you're not scared?"

"Sure, I'm scared. And I knew you would be, too. I didn't want you to be here alone."

Janelle snuggled under his arm and breathed, "Thank you, honey."

Luc held her for a few minutes before she looked up at him and asked, "What will we do?"

"Janelle, no matter what happens . . ." He paused to gain composure. "No matter what, we'll get through this together."

She nestled next to him again, and he kissed her forehead. She began to weep.

Luc continued, stroking the top of her head as he spoke. "I'm committed to this child, even if it's not perfect from a human perspective. Isn't that what we believe, that all life is precious? We have to trust God to give us the grace to handle anything—no matter what happens." He squeezed her tight again.

"How will I ever wait two weeks to know more? It'll seem like an eternity."

"Not to worry. I've already pulled a few strings—got you an appointment in three days."

Chapter Fifteen

ON THE DAY BEFORE BEN AND MARNIE'S wedding, Janelle entered the reception room of the materno-fetal doctor. Even though she'd waited only three days for her appointment it had seemed like decades.

She signed in, and in a few moments the receptionist ushered her back to a room.

After a short wait, the doctor entered. "Well, Mrs. Morgan, so nice to finally meet you. I'm Dr. Lucinda VanVleet," she said, extending her hand.

"Nice to meet you."

"I've worked with your husband for years, but I don't believe you and I have ever met. Now, don't worry. We do lots of these, and we should be able to get a good look."

Janelle settled back on the exam table and, once again, felt the warm gel on her belly. Soon Dr. VanVleet began the systematic study.

She spoke in a gentle voice. "Now, just so you know, I'll be looking carefully organ by organ and taking lots of pictures. I'll tell you what I find once I've looked at everything."

Janelle nodded and settled into the silence of the darkened room.

Dr. VanVleet slowly moved the slick transducer across Janelle's abdomen. Pictures appeared on the screen; the doctor clicked the photographs; then more pictures. She took numerous measurements and then punched the keyboard and called up a variety of graphs and other numbers. It was totally unintelligible to Janelle, though she could see the screen. She just watched her baby's heart beating.

Not until she had finished did Dr. VanVleet break the silence. "That's all, Mrs. Morgan. I'll let the nurse get you dried off, and you can dress and meet me in the office." She stood to leave.

"What did you find, doctor? Is everything all right?" she pleaded.

"Let's go ahead and get dressed first. We'll meet in my office. Give me a few minutes to study all these measurements. And is there somewhere we can contact your husband? I'd love to talk with him, too."

Janelle's heart sank. "He was planning to come with me, but he got delayed by an emergency. He should be here any minute." Janelle spoke softly, not making eye contact. As a doctor's wife, she knew all too well that the invitation to "talk to you in the office" meant that the news was bad, perhaps very bad. When Dr. VanVleet flipped on the light as she headed out, Janelle thought she saw tears in the doctor's eyes.

Janelle dressed and was escorted to the consultation room. She looked around at the beautifully appointed, massive wooden desk and shelves filled with books and pictures of golfers and golf memorabilia.

After a long ten minutes, Dr. VanVleet returned and took her seat in the big leather chair behind the desk.

"I see you like to play golf. That's a lovely photo of Pebble Beach," Janelle said.

"Thank you." Dr. VanVleet smiled kindly. "My university team placed second in the Women's Collegiate Open." She put the chart down on the desk and shuffled through the sonogram pictures. Then she looked up at Janelle and spoke gently. "We have a problem, Mrs. Morgan. I'm sorry."

Janelle swallowed hard and looked away.

"I've scanned the baby from many different angles and obtained some good measurements, but I'm afraid I see serious growth problems."

"Will our baby be all right?"

Dr. VanVleet paused and sighed deeply. "We'll do another sonogram to follow the growth and confirm the findings, but I'm afraid your baby has a genetic problem. It may be a chromosomal difficulty that will, in all likelihood, lead to severe developmental problems."

"Down's syndrome?" Tears rolled down Janelle's face.

"No—probably not Down's. It's a problem that may make it impossible for the baby to survive for very long."

Before she could finish, Janelle burst into tears. She saw Dr. VanVleet nod toward the doorway and turned to see Luc. He knelt beside Janelles's chair and wrapped her in his arms, holding her while she cried. He looked back at Dr. VanVleet, who shook her head and glanced down at the pictures.

After a few minutes, Janelle choked out, "There's something wrong with our baby." Taking a shallow triple breath, she added, "He's not normal. He may not even live." She buried her head in Luc's shoulder.

Still holding Janelle, Luc looked back at Dr. VanVleet and said softly, "What exactly did you find?"

"Dr. Geman was right. BPD and head circumference are lagging far behind. Plus, I noted some changes in the spine, feet, and cardiac exam. I'm pretty sure he has Trisomy 18. It fits the lower alpha fetoprotein, hCG, and serum estriol that Dr. Geman had ordered. Not all the babies with this problem have sono findings."

"And the brain stem?" Luc asked.

The doctor subtly shook her head. "Possibly Dandy Walker

syndrome. Significant cysts in the posterior fossa. I'm sorry, Luc."

"Thanks, Lucinda," Luc said, his eyes glistening now.

Dr. VanVleet quietly got up and left them alone in the office, closing the door behind her.

Later that evening, Janelle sat down on the bed next to Luc. "How did you ever make it through the rehearsal tonight without telling Ben and Marnie what's going on with us?"

"Must be that male ability to compartmentalize. It's their moment. Not the time."

"What did they say when you told them I didn't feel well?"

"I just told them that pregnant women are a sensitive lot. They laughed, sent their best, and went on with the show. Good thing they didn't press the issue. I was on the verge . . ." Luc swallowed hard.

"Good. I didn't want to hurt their feelings by not coming, but I just couldn't go." Janelle began to cry again.

Luc held her tightly. "Of course not, Jan. Of course not. We got quite a shock today. I felt like I was in a daze at the rehearsal. But still, God knows they've had enough heartache—both of them. I don't want to take anything away from their happiness right now."

"I know. I just hate that our dear friends are getting married tomorrow, and all I want to do is cry."

Saturday morning, Marnie rose before dawn feeling a little jittery. The day was overcast, but it didn't matter. *Even if we had a Virginia downpour, I wouldn't care. Tonight I'll be Mrs. Marnie McKay.*

She smiled at the thought. Sipping French vanilla coffee, Marnie checked her e-mail and was delighted to find a message from Ben sent before five that morning: "To my Grand Marnier—I couldn't sleep. Today you'll become my bride and make my life complete. As Robert Southwell said, 'Not where I breathe, but where I love, I live.' All my love, Ben."

How very sweet. Marnie printed the note and stuck it in her journal. A glance at the clock told her he'd already left the house to go jogging, and he'd probably not check his personal e-mail again until after the honeymoon. So she wrote, "You are the sweetest. By the time you read this, I'll be your wife. And, although it's hard to imagine, I'll love you even more then than I do at this moment."

She pulled down the carry-on cosmetic bag from her closet shelf and finished packing. Ben had told her to pack for both cool and tropical locations.

At ten, the florist brought her a dozen red roses with a note that said, "Only a few hours until always. I love you, Ben."

In the gazebo of the Bishop's Garden at the Washington Cathedral, Emily, Will, Carolyn—Ben's sister from Dallas—Luc, Janelle, and other friends and family gathered. It was one o'clock. Marnie had found the perfect tea-length ivory lace dress, and she wore her dark hair pulled up in a twist. After a short reception in the garden, Marnie and Ben pressed close to each other in the back of a black limousine and were whisked away to Dulles International Airport. They talked gently about their day and all the sensations they'd just experienced. Ben took Marnie's hand and touched her fingertips to his. "Do you remember the first time our fingers touched like this?"

"Of course."

"Where were we?"

"Kiev. The boat was cruising under the bridge."

"Wow, you *do* remember. And have I mentioned that you look ravishing?" As Ben spoke, his face was only an inch from hers.

"Mmmm, I'm not sure we've had much of a chance to talk today," Marnie giggled.

"No. And yet we certainly did a lot of communicating." Ben grinned.

"That we did," she smiled back.

Ben kissed her fingertips, and then he leaned down and kissed her. She moved in even closer to her groom. "Tell me I'm not dreaming."

"If you are, I won't wake you. Sweetheart, today you pledged to be my wife. I hope it's not a dream, because I sure got the better end of the deal. I've always said a man should marry above himself. Well, I definitely did that today."

"*Au contraire*. It is *I* who got the better end of the deal," Marnie insisted. "But I'll allow you your illusions."

Later, when they had taken their seats in first class, Marnie looked over at Ben. "So this flight is going to San Francisco? I thought you said we were doing 'tropical.'" Marnie feigned alarm. "Where are you taking me, *monsieur*?"

"Tonight, San Francisco. Tomorrow, who knows? That is, if we're still alive after the earth moves under our feet tonight—and I'm not referring to a San Francisco earthquake."

Marnie laughed.

The flight attendant interrupted their flirtations by handing out menus. "We'll be serving dinner once we reach a cruising altitude. You have your choice of shrimp scampi or beef Stroganoff. You can make your cocktail selections from this." She handed them a small menu.

After she left, Ben turned to Marnie and spoke out of the side of his mouth. "Only four hundred hours until we're finally alone."

"It feels like that, doesn't it?" Marnie commiserated.

"So—time for a subject change before I hyperventilate?"

"Good idea." Marnie smiled.

"I hope you'll like it in Des Moines tomorrow."

"What?"

"Just kidding. We're not going to Des Moines, although I'm sure it's a great honeymoon location—for somebody else."

Marnie rolled her eyes and shook her head.

Then Ben got serious. "Actually, I really *do* hope you'll like where we're going."

Marnie squeezed his arm. "Ben, surely you know that it doesn't matter to me where I am for the next week—just who I'm with."

After they had finished dinner, Ben napped, but Marnie wanted to write in her journal first. She described the day and ended her entry with, "Emily, a perfect little lady, stood up with me. Ben wore a black silk suit, and I couldn't help asking myself over and over, 'Do I really get to spend the rest of my life with this sculptured hunk of manhood?' I had never known a touch and look so tender as when he took my hand from Dad's. Bob King married us, but I'm not sure we once looked at him. We were so immersed in our own delight. After so much heartache—today, absolute pure joy. We had a little reception there in the garden—short, but lovely—and how wonderful to drink in the moment with intimate friends and family. God is so good."

She shut the book, tucked it in her carry-on bag, and rested her head on his shoulder in sweet sleep.

A white limousine awaited them in San Francisco. It slipped through the cool, clear night, taking them to their hotel on Nob Hill.

Marnie gasped as they pulled up. "It's magnificent," she whispered. She looked over at Ben. "Just like you."

Chapter Sixteen

BEN GUIDED MARNIE THROUGH THE HOTEL LOBBY. Their steps echoed across the marble floors. At the front desk, Ben smugly announced, "Dr. and Mrs. Ben McKay."

"Oooooh, I like the sound of that!" Marnie told Ben quietly.

He winked at her. "Me, too."

The clerk handed them electronic room keys and escorted them to a private elevator that took them to their floor. Marnie's ears popped as the elevator carried them higher and higher.

The door to their suite opened onto beautiful furnishings and elegant window treatments. An atrium dining room led to a balcony that overlooked the city and, beyond that, San Francisco Bay.

Holding hands like excited school children, they explored their accommodations. Peeking into the bathroom, they found a marble bath with jacuzzi jets. Matching plush terry robes hung on a rack near the steps up to the raised tub.

Ben led her through the atrium out to the balcony, high above the city. He slipped his arms around her waist from behind, and they both stood drinking in the view and the moment. "I love you," he whispered in her ear and then kissed her neck tenderly. The bellboy knocked on the door and brought in their luggage.

After sending him on his way with a tip, Ben turned on the stereo system. "Amazing," he called out to her. "Marnie, can you imagine? They've got a CD loaded into the system already, and it's the one that was playing when I held you for the first time."

"Rachmaninoff?"

"That's the one."

"That *is* amazing." Marnie suddenly caught on. "No, *you're* the one who's amazing!"

Ben turned the volume to play softly and motioned for her to join him. They danced and snuggled and exchanged gentle words and expressions of affection. Then Marnie whispered, "I'm a little tired. I think I'll get ready for bed—maybe take a bubble bath first. Why don't you come join me after a while? I'll leave you a bathrobe on the bed, if you like."

"Mmmm, sounds great," Ben agreed.

Marnie found her way to the bathroom and shut the door. She lit three votive candles, turned off the lights, and opened the door. Then she drew the water, pouring in generous amounts of bubble bath. She slipped into the warmth, feeling blissfully happy and full of anticipation. But she also had a bit of the same jitters she'd had that morning. In the other room she could hear Ben making a call or two to arrange more details and to check on flights.

A few minutes later, inspired by the ambiance, Ben turned out the rest of the lights in their suite and carried the dinner candles into the bedroom. Finally, he knocked gently as he entered.

Marnie felt her heart begin to pound.

"Mind if I turn on the jets?" he asked. His hand was on the dial as he stood before her in the terry robe.

"You've never taken a bubble bath, have you?" Marnie said.

"Uh, no, can't say I have!"

"Sure. Turn them on. Let's see what happens!" Marnie was amused, knowing Ben had no clue.

Ben pressed the button, and the water began to rumble. Then he took off his robe and slipped into the bathtub next to her.

Ben was still adjusting to the hot water when the gurgling action of the jets began to take effect. Within seconds, they were engulfed in bubbles, which rose to one and then two feet above the edge of the tub. Soon bubbles surrounded everything except their faces.

Marnied pointed to the dial. "Ben, you've got to turn it off or we'll drown in bubbles before we can consummate our marriage!" She was having trouble controlling her laughter.

"I can't. Why would they put that dial so far out of reach? I don't want you to catch sight of me in the buff, covered with bubbles from stem to stern!"

"I'll close my eyes. I promise!"

"No peeking!" Ben got out and turned off the jets.

"Can I open them now?"

"No! Don't you dare!" Ben scooped excess bubbles out of the tub onto the marble bathroom floor. Then he slid back into the water and pulled Marnie close. "You can open your eyes now," he said. "You should have warned me, you rascal!"

"What? And miss the first sighting of Bubble Man?"

As the giggling subsided, Marnie snuggled close and tilted her head up. And as the mirrors reflected the flames dancing around them, they began to kiss. "You definitely were worth waiting for," Ben whispered.

Luc logged off the Internet and headed into the bathroom.

"What did you find?" Janelle asked quietly.

"More of the same. " He looked up and saw her reflection as he spoke.

"Tell it straight. You know me; I don't want it sugarcoated." Janelle leaned against the sink cabinet.

He turned to face her, then hung his head. "Pretty bleak. Severe mental retardation. There's no therapy available, and usually the baby doesn't . . ."

"Go on."

"Do I need to?"

"I guess you don't. The baby doesn't usually make it through delivery?"

"Something like that." He stared at the plush carpet.

"At the moment, I have an even scarier thought."

"What could be scarier than that?"

"I noticed a little spotting."

Luc raised his eyebrows. "Any cramping?"

"Just a little."

He glanced at his watch. "Ten P.M. Why don't we go over to the office and take a look?"

Janelle sighed deeply. "Let me call Sheila and see if she'll come watch the kids for an hour."

"Good idea."

Luc and Janelle drove along Route 50 in silence until they passed a Methodist church with a lighted cross on the front. "Sure is pretty at night," Janelle said, pointing to it.

Luc nodded, then reached over and squeezed her hand.

Once they arrived at the clinic, Luc unlocked the doctors' entrance and punched in the code to disable the complex alarm system. He flipped on a light and escorted Janelle down to the sono room.

Janelle stretched out on the table. "Strange. I've never been sono'd here."

"Yeah, I guess that's right," Luc agreed. "Everything here is so new. This machine is better than the one that got torched." He greased Janelle's abdomen with gel, flipped on the sono, clicked off the lights, and sat on the wheeled stool. Then he slid over to the bedside and picked up the transducer to find his child's heartbeat.

Moving across the abdomen, he found the baby's head. Then he moved down into the chest.

Both he and Janelle stared at the screen, searching for motion.

Luc got a good cross section view through the heart and watched. *The easiest thing to find is a moving, beating heart. . . . Where is it?* He held his position and watched . . . and watched. *C'mon! Where are you?*

Chapter Seventeen

THE NEXT MORNING, MARNIE AND BEN threw their luggage into the trunk of a cab. Ben still hadn't told her where they were going, so when she saw the air traffic tower of the San Francisco airport she said, "So, we're flying again?"

"Much easier that way," Ben said with a smile.

"Good. Any tropics within driving distance of San Francisco would mean a very high cab fare!"

The driver dropped them off at the curb, and Ben pulled out the itinerary. When they reached the front of the line, the ticketing agent took it from him. After asking the usual identity and security questions, the agent printed out the tickets, wrote the gate information, and told them, "Enjoy your time in Maui."

Marnie remained calm until they'd walked far enough away not be overheard. Then she stopped and turned to Ben. "Maui!?"

Ben smiled. "Kaanapali Beach."

"Oh, Ben. No kidding? I've always wanted to go to Kaanapali! Ever since I was a little kid living on the West Coast."

"I know. I asked Janelle to find out your dream vacation. She told me you and Tim went to Maui a couple of years ago, but that you and Emily had mostly island hopped while he was out deep-sea fishing—and that you'd always *really* wanted to stay at the Hyatt in Kaanapali."

"We're staying at the *Hyatt?*" Marnie's eyes lit up.

Ben nodded. "In the presidential suite."

She was so thrilled that her eyes clouded over. "I didn't think I'd ever get back there . . . though I've dreamed of it! I figured *we'd* never get to go there."

Ben cocked his head and smiled tenderly as he enjoyed her response.

"One more thing," he added.

"What's that?"

"We'll be driving a 1968 navy-blue Mustang convertible. I'm told it's your favorite car, and we certainly don't want to look like other tourists."

She took a tissue out of her purse. "Oh Ben, it just keeps getting better and better with you." She hugged his arm, and then they walked toward the gate.

After an afternoon of strolling on the beach, Ben and Marnie checked their e-mail for the first time since they'd left D.C.

"Dad says Emily's doing great," Marnie said, the motherly relief showing in her voice. "But I'm going to call first thing in the morning. I need to hear her voice."

Luc tried to call Dr. Geman on Sunday, but his partner was taking calls, so Luc waited until Monday to talk to Geman himself. After the two physicians spoke for a few minutes, Dr. Geman asked to talk with Janelle.

Luc handed her the cordless phone. "Your turn," he said.

When Janelle came on the line, her doctor asked, "Are you okay?"

"Yes, I guess so," she said, speaking barely above a whisper.

"You have a couple of options, which your husband and I

just discussed. We can wait for spontaneous labor, which could be days or weeks."

Janelle shuddered. "I feel like a walking tomb already. It's eerie."

"I understand," Dr. Geman said. "Another option is to do a D&E, which is an abortion-like procedure. But it isn't very pleasant for anyone, and the infant's remains—"

"No, doctor. That option is too much like shredding a child. I want to hold my baby." A sob caught her again.

"Yes, I understand. I'm not recommending that—just offering the options. The other possibility is prostaglandin induction. In that case, we commence a labor and vaginal delivery similar to regular labor, though perhaps harder and faster."

"Can Luc and I discuss it and call you back?"

"Certainly. Take all the time you need."

Janelle thanked him, hung up the phone, and turned to her husband. "What do you think I should do?"

Luc paused before answering, looking at his wife with compassion. "If we wait, there is some risk. The occasional problem with maternal blood clotting can be dangerous if labor doesn't begin for four weeks."

"I don't think I could stand waiting another four weeks."

"Right. I'm pretty sure we don't want to go that route. But we need a little time to get used to the idea. If we opt for the prostaglandin induction, it would allow the baby to deliver vaginally, intact. I'd lean toward that option if nothing happens soon."

Janelle nodded. "I'd like to have a memorial service."

Luc agreed. "Shall we ask Ben?"

Janelle nodded once more, and her tears began to flow again.

After a breathtaking sunrise at the top of Haleakala Crater, Ben and Marnie took a helicopter to see Hana and the Seven

Pools from the air. They spent the afternoon working out in the hotel's fitness center and lounging by the pool. In the early evening, they took a drive up the west coast to watch surfers. Along the way, they spotted a rustic chapel on the edge of a cliff. They drove up to it and found the place empty but unlocked. Ben took Marnie's hand and they entered.

They sat down in one of the wooden pews that faced the picture window overlooking the coast. After sitting together in a lengthy silence, Ben looked down at Marnie and saw her wipe a tear. He gave her a puzzled look, and she smiled. "It's just joy, Ben."

Squeezing her shoulder, he nodded solemnly with a gentle smile. Then he put his arm around her and bowed his head. "The two shall become one flesh. . . . Thank you, heavenly Father. For the beauty of your creation. For the beauty of marriage. Make us one, O Lord, as you have already begun to do."

After a few minutes, they returned to the car, hand in hand, neither of them speaking.

That night Marnie checked e-mail before calling D.C.

"Anything from Luc?" Ben asked.

"No."

"Hmmm. That's strange. He said he'd let me know how the weekend call went."

Chapter Eighteen

THE NEXT MORNING, LUC MORGAN'S PHONE RANG a few minutes before the office opened. He picked it up, expecting to hear from one of the family or friends who had access to his private back line. But the voice he heard sounded only vaguely familiar.

"Doctor Morgan?"

"Yes?"

"This is Dr. Steven Harrison."

Wonder how he got this number. Luc felt his anxiety level rise. "Ah, yes, Dr. Harrison. How are things going with your work?"

"Splendidly," the confident doctor said. "But I've been trying to reach you for weeks. Don't you ever return calls?"

"What? I thought Dr. McKay was handling it. Didn't he call you?"

"No. I've heard nothing from either of you."

"Hmm. Sorry. Well, what can I do for you?"

"We're learning things from the cells and the genetic machinery that are very exciting—very encouraging. In fact, I believe that in my lifetime, the things we learn from the mouse research will lead us safely down the path of human research."

"I'm glad to hear that," Luc said flatly. "And thank you for the update. I was hoping the report would be good."

"Indeed, doctor. But I'm calling not only to give you the positive report. I also need to ask another favor."

"What do you need?"

"As you know, Dr. Sullivan's work was cutting edge, and his research and the biological material have been invaluable in the rapid advances we're making. We owe so much to your late colleague. In the spirit of his memory I need to pick up more of the tissue culture. I can't tell you how important this work is. . . ."

"I do appreciate your call," Luc interrupted, "and your diligent work. But my partner, Ben McKay, and I are of one mind that the cell culture will not be subjected to any further research until some key ethical issues are addressed. Meanwhile, we will keep the material cryopreserved."

"What ethical issues?" Dr. Harrison became animated. "We're talking cells, a culture dish of cells, and state-of-the-art research that could save millions of lives. What could be more 'ethical' than that? If my research can produce skin cultures to graft burn victims, cardiac cells to help heart attack victims, nerve cells—don't you understand, doctor? Can't you see the good that can come of it?"

Sensing the anger rising in Harrison's voice, Luc spoke slowly and calmly. "Yes, Dr. Harrison. I do understand. But the question of personhood at its earliest stages in these cells gives us pause. Although much good can come of the research, we must consider the lives of these humans in embryonic form. Believe me, I'm still struggling to fully understand the implications of what Dr. Sullivan's research uncovered."

"But isn't your commitment to healing people? To doing good?"

"Of course. But at the same time, I must try to 'do no harm.' And if these cells represent persons, . . ."

"Good day, doctor," Harrison said, slamming down the phone.

Luc looked at the receiver in disbelief.

Wednesday evening around six-thirty, Brock poked in his head at Courtney's office. "Want to order out?" he asked. "I'm in the mood for pizza, and it looks as though I'm going to be here for a while."

"Pizza—the all-American food. I've developed a taste for it."

"How do you like yours?"

"Everything but anchovies."

"Okay if we hold the sausage, too?"

"Make the call. Brock, why are you working late again? I thought you were going to try to unpack some boxes at home tonight."

Brock stepped in and pulled up a chair. "I talked Luc into leaving early. He just couldn't seem to focus. With Ben gone, he's doing the work for two, and he needs to be with his wife. I wrecked my own marriage by not being there for a hurting woman. The least I can do is help somebody else avoid my mistakes."

Courtney put down the specimen she was examining and looked at him. "If I may ask, what happened?"

"Not much to tell, really. It was the typical neglected medical marriage. She worked; I went to school, and then I was busy building a practice and getting my strokes from appreciative patients. She wanted me around, but I was never there. When she lost her parents in a car accident, I went to the funeral and flew back the next day. She stayed to pick up the pieces of everything except herself. She grew distant from all the hurt. By the time I wanted her around, she had her own life. I tried to change, to get us some counseling, but it messed with the predictable world she'd built. So she took our two girls, half the money, and split."

Courtney winced.

"She found herself a new guy in New Orleans. So I had to

get out of there. I couldn't stand running into them or hearing from friends who'd seen them."

"It sounds so difficult—for both of you. I'm sorry. In Taiwan, marriage and ancestors and children are everything, but so is the work to provide a better life for them. As far as I can see, marriage stinks."

"Oh, I'm all for the institution," Brock insisted. "That's what was so painful. I had my priorities all out of whack and I pursued the wrong thing. In the end I got what I asked for—all the work I want with no one to complain to about my long hours." Brock sat thoughtfully for a moment. "How about you, Courtney? Ever married?"

She shook her head.

"Any romantic attachments?"

She shook her head again and looked at her shoes. "I'm married to my lab, I guess."

"So you don't want to date?"

"I have had little time for anything except study. Success is important to me, as it is to my family. Where I'm from, academics is key, and I spent my time working to be accepted in the U.S. program. Once I was accepted, the highest priority was to send home grades my father would consider worthy. Also, I have not yet found many men who are interested in a woman scientist."

She smiled hesitantly. "Actually, your American dating customs feel a little awkward to me. Some of my colleagues at the Smith clinic even told me I needed some life experience to go with all my book knowledge."

"Interesting."

"But how? We worked such long hours there."

Brock smiled. He had noticed that Courtney often didn't understand the office humor. She seemed smart and kind but perhaps a little too trusting. With a little make-up and her hair down, she would be attractive, but he had never seen her in anything but the white official uniform of a doctor. "So no prospects, huh?"

"No. And as you know, the hours here are not conducive to a social life."

Brock nodded, considering her last comment. "Well, let me go order the pizza, and we'll see if we can make it out of here before eight, okay?"

Dr. Harrison dialed Carlos Rivera's number. On another line was a translator he'd secured for this call. Ramon answered the phone, and the translator identified Harrison as the U.S. surgeon general's appointee for special research. He informed Ramon that they were calling with news that might be of importance to the health of the Rivera twins.

Ramon assured the translator that Carlos would want to be interrupted to take a call from the doctor, and that he probably would not need translation. When Ramon put the call on hold to get the mayor, the translator relayed the information to Harrison.

"Thanks. I'll take it from here," he said.

After an elaborate introduction, Dr. Harrison told Carlos, "I'm aware of some of the research by the horrible doctor who took liberties with your wife's eggs, producing her, uh, the twins. I know of the lawsuit and your heartache." Harrison still didn't know exactly what the embryos were, but he knew enough to sound as if he did. "I know your embryos are now at the Novacef clinic, being stored with the special cell line."

"I am not sure I understand. What is a cell line, doctor?"

Harrison fell silent, then stammered. "Uh, well, perhaps you didn't know. See, there is a group of cells being stored at the clinic—cells that could be of enormous help. They may well hold the cure for your children."

"What?"

"Yes, the special cells that contain the fusion of your wife's eggs, the cells that led to the birth of your daughters. Perhaps we could use them to find a cure for them."

"How do you know this, doctor?"

"In my work for the U.S. government it's my job to know when people are doing illegal research. I also consult with a biotech firm that's in the business of diagnosing and treating genetic problems such as the ones you are facing. Only you and I and the doctors at the clinic know these cells exist."

"And how do you think they could help my children?"

"They are the cells from which your children were created. Perhaps we could grow organs that might perfectly match their genetic structure. All we need is a sample of them. But at the moment, the doctors at the clinic have refused to help."

"That is no surprise."

"I imagine the cells are legally yours, or at least your wife's. Maybe all that is necessary is for you to request them, perhaps through your attorney."

"No," Carlos insisted. "If these doctors have not told me about these cells, I doubt they will *give* them to me. And the legal process is too slow. The twins are very sick now. We do not have time to waste if they can be helped. And the doctors at the clinic will certainly ask how I know about the cells. There may be a better way to get them."

"What's that, sir?"

"Let me think about it. Thank you for calling, doctor. Most interesting."

"I thought you'd think so. Let me leave my number."

"Ramon, it is Carlos."

It was after two in the morning, and Ramon struggled to focus, having been jarred from sleep.

"Señor?"

"Concerning our conversation this afternoon, after the call from this Dr. Harrison. I have some instructions for you."

"Sí?" Ramon fluffed a pillow and sat up.

"I have spoken with my attorney, and the legality of the cell cultures is uncertain. But Dr. Harrison believes they will help our babies, and there is much money to be made from them. Apparently, the selfish doctors want to hoard it all for themselves. So we must take them. Dr. McKay is out of town this week; perhaps this is a good time for our good friend Victor to see what he can find out. He will have to work quickly."

In the early hours of the morning, Brock threaded a long needle down the guide of the transvaginal ultrasound probe. Traversing the patient's vagina, the probe entered the abdominal cavity through the posterior wall into the ovary. The thirty-six-year-old woman on the table had been a clinic patient for years. She had been scheduled for an IVF cycle the week after the clinic bombing, so she'd gone to a doctor in Fairfax, but with no success. Now she was back. Brock was particularly eager to see this procedure result in a successful pregnancy. She'd been through six years of treatment already.

He aspirated her eggs with minimal sedation. "We've got fifteen mature follicles here. It'll be interesting to see what we end up with," he told the nurse assisting him. Brock applied gentle suction and an easy flushing of the cyst wall within the ovary to obtain the eggs—one at a time, each cyst yielding one ovum.

"It feels great to be in a cutting-edge clinic again," Brock said to the patient, who was groggy but still semi-conscious. "They've done a lot with IVF procedures, even in the past few months. We can do so much more for patients." Brock's voice helped the patient remain relaxed. She wouldn't remember much of what he said, but patients were more calm when he soothed them with his "vocal anesthesia."

As he worked, he asked the nurse for various instruments, which he usually referred to as "toys." After retrieving each egg, Brock carefully passed the specimens through a special window into the lab, where Courtney immediately labeled them for identification.

By the time he'd finished harvesting all the accessible eggs, Courtney had graded fifteen for quality. With medications to stimulate patients' ovaries into producing multiple eggs in a single cycle, harvesting ten to thirty eggs from each patient had become routine at this clinic. While it had been difficult to successfully thaw eggs in the past, the technology had advanced enough to make egg storage almost as reliable as it was for sperm. Courtney was still working to perfect the process, but they'd come a long way. Now she selected the four most promising eggs and froze the rest for later use. One at a time, she immobilized each egg with light suction and a specially-made pipette. With the egg stabilized, she could "scratch" its edge to help it "hatch." Or she could draw up a single sperm for injection into the egg, depending on whether the couple's fertility problem related to a low sperm count.

When Brock finished with the patient, he came into the lab with Courtney to find out how it was going. "I love to coax the best sperm to swim into my needle," she said with a smile— one of the few he had seen.

"You like to see them surrender to your expert care, don't you?" hoping her cordial mood would continue.

She nodded.

"How many have we got?"

"We started with fifteen. I froze eleven and used four, but two didn't make it through the ICSI procedure. So that leaves two. We've got a grade A cell and a grade B."

"Not fabulous, but, wow, an A—that's rare." Only about five percent were graded as A's.

"Right. Even though she only has two, I'm hopeful. At her age, I'd prefer to transfer a minimum of three. But with the high quality, their chances are still good."

"Great work," Brock told her.

"Thanks," she said in her usual professional tone.

Brock and Courtney worked long hours all week. With Ben on his honeymoon and Luc distracted by the loss of an infant, they pulled the extra load without complaint.

Chapter Nineteen

By FIVE-THIRTY FRIDAY EVENING Courtney and Brock were the only two employees left in the office.

"May I ask a favor?" Courtney said.

"What's that?"

"My car's in the shop. Could you give me a lift home? I know it is out of your way, but . . ."

"Sure, Courtney. I'd be glad to." Courtney was so fiercely independent that Brock knew even this simple request had been difficult for her. She had accepted him as her friend.

It was late enough that the last rays of the sun were dwindling when Courtney punched in the security code. She and Brock left the office and walked to his car, unaware of the figure who watched from the shadows near the rear of the building. The silent figure flicked away his cigarette, pulled on surgical gloves, and quietly walked toward the physicians' entrance. With the confidence that comes from practiced skill, the man manipulated the lock and slid back the door. He silenced the beeping alarm system by attaching an electronic device to the touch pad. *Not quite as simple as at the other clinic,* he mused. Nevertheless, he had bypassed the code in under thirty seconds.

He moved quietly down the hall and found the door to the lab.

Five minutes after Brock turned onto Route 50, Courtney rummaged through her purse and cursed.

Brock glanced over in puzzlement. "Don't like my driving?"

"No, it's not that," Courtney said, in disgust. "I left my cell phone in the lab."

"And I'll bet you need it tonight."

"Yes."

"No problem—really. I was just thinking I should have brought home the new Red Journal I was reading. I'll get it from my office while you get your phone."

"Thank you. You are probably lying, but I appreciate it."

The remark caught Brock by surprise, and he laughed. Courtney looked quizzically at him.

"I've been accused of lying to cover my back end before, but never of lying to be nice! Not my style. But I appreciate the compliment."

Back at the clinic, Brock opened the doctors' entrance door. He reached to turn off the alarm, but then saw that it was not activated. "Didn't we arm this when we left?"

"I thought so," Courtney said.

"Hmm. Maybe it didn't activate." Brock looked back out the door and around the parking lot. "No other cars. I guess Luc hasn't been here. Well, you find your phone, and I'll zip back to the office and grab the journal. Meet you back here in a flash. If the alarm system doesn't activate when we reset it, I'll have it checked out."

They went in opposite directions. As Courtney started to punch in the combination for the lab, she saw that the alarm was deactivated there, too. "Brock!" she whispered.

But Brock didn't hear her.

Inside the lab, Victor had not heard the car pull into the lot, nor had he heard the clinic door open. The sound of voices inside the office was his first warning. He turned off his flashlight, pulled his gun, and crouched by the door, hoping no one would come into the lab but ready to spring if someone did.

The sliver of light from the hallway widened as the door was slowly opened and a woman cautiously leaned in. He grabbed her, pulled her on into the darkness, and clamped his hand over her mouth in one motion. Next, he made certain she felt the gun he now shoved into her back. Putting his lips to her ear, he whispered forcefully in heavily accented English.

"Open that." By the hall light reflected into the dark room, she saw that he was gesturing with his gun toward the refrigeration unit.

She tried to shake her head and say, "No money, no drugs," but his hand muffled her words.

"Open it!" he insisted, tightening his already vicelike grip.

"But . . ."

Victor put the gun to her head.

Together they shuffled to the door. She punched in the code, and a buzz indicated that the lock had released. Victor took his hand from her face to open the door, and Courtney took her chance.

"Brock! Help me!"

Victor knocked her hard on the head with the butt of his gun, and she fell to the floor. He stepped over her to the refrigeration unit, but already he heard running steps in the hall. A large silhouette paused in the light of the doorway. Without hesitation he pointed his gun and pulled the trigger. There was a flash of light and a cracking sound. The man fell backward from the force, blocking the doorway as he hit the ground. Victor waited a moment and listened for others. Hearing nothing, he jumped over the man who lay gasping for air and clutching his chest. Then Victor slipped out the back door.

Courtney groaned as she regained consciousness. Her hand touched the painful bump on her head. Becoming more fully conscious, she recalled being grabbed in the darkness. In the stillness of the lab, she peered toward the light of the open doorway and, to her horror, saw the body lying against the threshold in a pool of blood. Crawling over to Brock, she tried to assess the situation by the light from the hallway. She could see his ashen face, the blood on his shirt, and the dark stain widening between them.

She cradled his head in her hands and pressed her fingers against the side of his neck to check his pulse. Gazing at the entry wound in the center of his chest, she knew. . . .

She reached up to the desktop, grabbed her cell phone, and dialed 911.

Brock struggled to remain conscious. As he strained to speak, she heard the sound of gurgling blood in his lungs. The entry wound was just to the left of the sternum. She pulled her lab coat off the chair at the desk and applied pressure. She knew by the copious blood flow and the sound of his breathing that the bullet had hit both heart and lung.

When the operator answered, Courtney tried to speak calmly. "Dr. Gaylen has been shot. Send an ambulance." She gave the clinic address.

"A shooting?"

"Yes."

"Is the gunman still there?"

"I don't think so."

"All right, we'll send the police as well."

"Yes." Courtney hung up.

Brock was struggling to speak. She put her ear close to his mouth in an effort to decipher his whispers. "Daughters . . . love them . . . Wife, tell her, sorry . . . sorry . . ."

Gurgling sounds continued. Blood had soaked through the wadded lab coat, unstaunched by the pressure she applied. Brock fell silent, and Courtney felt his pulse cease. She held him and wept until police arrived five minutes later.

Officers quickly secured the building, and she was led to a chair and bombarded with initial questions that might indicate what had happened and who they were looking for. Through an emotional fog, Courtney heard herself tell them the gunman had an unrecognizable accent. No, she didn't see his face, but he was tall. It seemed to be a robbery. Somehow, he had turned off two alarm systems. He wanted in the refrigerator. "Must have thought it was a safe, but there was no money, no drugs. Just tissue and lab preps."

The paramedics had now arrived. Quickly they ran through the mandated trauma procedures, but without enthusiasm. Then an ER physician, somewhere at the other end of a radio monitor, officially pronounced Brock dead at the scene. Courtney just stared. She had already known that he was gone, but the disembodied pronouncement over the radio receiver made it seem so irrevocable. *This isn't happening.*

As paramedics assessed her head injury, she watched the crime scene investigator move in with his camera bag slung over his shoulder and a carrying case in either hand. Paramedics led her to a waiting ambulance. Soon, Brock's body would follow.

He was so alive. Was it only thirty minutes ago?

She had a possible concussion, but it didn't look like the

hospital would need to keep her overnight. A detective would want to talk to her again in the morning at the clinic, along with everyone else. No one could use the lab until they released it.

She nodded obediently but numbly at each bit of information she received, and wondered how she would get home.

Ben and Marnie had checked out of their rooms on Maui less than an hour before the phone in the presidential suite rang. Finally, a hotel operator cut in. At the other end, Luc Morgan told himself there was nothing Ben could do anyway.

Chapter Twenty

On Sunday night, when Ben and Marnie returned, Will and Emily met them with hugs at the airport. Ben noticed that Will seemed reserved as they described their trip.

Will handed his car keys to Ben, who drove them all to Marnie's place. Ben would live there for a while, so Emily's schedule could remain consistent, and Marnie had enough room for everyone. Ben would rent out his house.

"How was *your* week?" Ben asked Will.

Will shook his head.

"What's wrong?"

"Janelle. They have to induce on Wednesday."

"But she's only . . ." Ben glanced at Emily and stopped himself.

"Right," Will said. "And that ain't all." He handed Ben the Saturday newspaper. "I hate to be the bearer of bad news, but it's been a tough one."

Ben and Marnie gasped involuntarily as they read the headline: "One Dead, One Injured in Clinic Robbery."

On Monday morning Ramon Gomez checked the weekend's phone messages. One urged that Carlos Rivera contact Dr. Harrison at once.

There were no polite formalities when Harrison came on the line. "What happened?" he demanded.

"What do you mean?" Carlos asked.

"I'm talking about the clinic break-in. Murder? You had no reason to use force."

Who did this *gringo* think he was, to use such an accusing tone. And what if someone else was listening?

"Do not speak to me as to a child," he said with a whisper that knifed through the telephone receiver. The intensity of his words was lost on the man to whom they were directed.

"Making a move on the clinic was completely unnecessary."

"And you are suggesting that I am in some way responsible?" Carlos asked in a tone of caution edged in warning.

"Of course. Who else would've wanted in that refrigeration unit?"

"You, doctor, could answer that question better than I. I doubt you have had a better idea for getting the cells quickly?"

"Yes, in fact, I do. You just keep up relations with the doctors at the clinic. I have other means at my disposal for obtaining the cell sample. I'll be back in touch."

After Carlos hung up, he sat thinking for a long time. *That man could be dangerous.*

The next evening, Marnie and Emily stood at the airline gate, awaiting Ben's flight from New Orleans.

Ben greeted his new family. "It's good to see you two, but you really didn't have to drop me off and pick me up. I could've left the car here. Hate for you to be out this late." He gave Marnie a tender look.

"Tell me about the funeral," she said. Emily grabbed her Mom's hand, and they all headed for short-term parking. "Did you have to do anything?"

"No. Just watched. It was about eighty miles outside of New Orleans. He was from a place called Kentwood. Not a bad drive—good highway. A simple service at the Baptist church and burial in the church cemetery on the grounds. The family pastor did a nice job—mixed the gospel hope of resurrection and some terrific stories of Brock's childhood. Kentwood's got two stoplights, a railroad track, and a chicken place. Afterwards, the community fed us, and I ate stuff I didn't even recognize. All the guests went back to the family place, maybe two miles or so from the church."

"Lots of people?" Marnie asked. They exited the terminal and walked to the parking area through the late September chill.

"Oh yeah! They have big families there—and his wife and daughters came."

"Really? His ex? What was that like?"

"The family just swallowed them up—loved 'em like nothing had ever happened. She had enough class not to bring her boyfriend. Brock's family was huge. And I suspect most of them knew he'd stayed too busy to be much of a husband and dad. Pretty sad."

They had exited the parking lot and made it to the highway, before Ben continued. "I met one of his former partners. He gave me a lead on a reproductive endocrinologist in New York who may be interested in moving to D.C."

"Wow, it would be great if you could fill the job quickly."

"Yeah, it would. I called him from the airport on the way back, and he called back on the cell phone before I boarded. It sounds promising."

Janelle lay in an L&D room at the end of the hall, away from the traffic and all the normal laboring women. She wore a flowered gown that opened in the back and a hospital ID band on her wrist. An IV dripped medications. Luc sat on the reclining chair next to the window, silently holding her unencumbered hand. The sound of piped-in music camouflaged other noises in the room.

A nurse came in and said, "I brought you some Phenergan for nausea. You'll probably feel queasy after the doctor inserts the prostaglandin. It's tough trying to encourage a uterus to labor before it's ready."

When the nurse exited, Janelle noticed that the door bore a card marked with a lily sticker. "What's that for?" she asked Luc.

He spoke gently. "It's to alert personnel of the fetal demise. They don't want anyone walking in here and saying, 'So, you're gonna have a baby!' or 'Is it a boy or a girl?'"

Janelle gave him a sad smile.

"Before we instituted the lily on the door, some very nice people said some very hurtful things. And I'd really hate to have to deck somebody today."

Dr. Geman knocked and entered. After inserting a vaginal prostin suppository, he warned Janelle, "These dissolve fairly rapidly. But I have to warn you—they cause fever, nausea, diarrhea, and a generally miserable feeling."

"Thanks for the warning, doc," Janelle said, far more cheerfully than she felt.

For the next two hours, they sat waiting for something to happen. Then they heard a knock on the door, and Ben looked in.

"Hi. Glad you're here." Luc said. He started to stand, but Ben motioned for his friend to stay seated. He approached Janelle and softly said, "Hello." Then he leaned down to kiss her on the forehead. He noticed her fragrance. *She's perspiring.*

He looked in her eyes. "I'm so sorry." Then he walked over to Luc, put his arm around his friend's shoulder and said again, "I'm *so* sorry." He turned back to Janelle. "Marnie sends her love." He glanced around to assess the medical situation. "Nothing much happening yet?"

Janelle reached out for his hand, "Not much yet, though I'm running a fever."

"And she's had some bouts of nausea," Luc added.

Ben turned his attention to Luc. "How are *you* doing, partner?"

Luc nodded. "Hanging in there." He motioned to his wife, "Wish she didn't have to go through this. No one should have to go through this."

Ben agreed and pulled an empty chair nearer to his friends. For the next fifteen minutes no one said much, content with the silent company. But when Dr. Geman returned to give Janelle a second suppository, Ben stood to excuse himself. "May I pray with you before I leave?" he asked.

Everyone, including Dr. Geman, agreed. So the three men surrounded the bed, and Ben took Janelle's hand. He asked God to give comfort and grace. And he gave thanks for the brief life that had been entrusted to their care—a life of eternal significance, though so very short here. Luc and Janelle both wiped their eyes as he departed.

The second dose brought some mild cramping in the two hours that followed. At hour four, another dose brought labor with a vengeance. Luc held Janelle's hand, rubbed her back, stopped touching her—whatever she asked for.

Janelle gasped, having gone from mild discomfort to hard, almost unrelenting contractions in the brief quarter hour since the last dose. Sweating profusely, she began to vomit. Luc sat helplessly, doing what little he could to assist. The nurse brought some Nubain to ease Janelle's pain, and before long she blurted out between gasps, "It's coming!"

"Okay." Luc punched the nurse call button

The ward clerk answered. "Yes?"

He spoke calmly. "Please send a nurse, and page Dr. Geman."

Janelle shouted, "It's coming! I feel it—it's coming!"

Luc pulled back the sheet to see that the baby was, in fact, delivering.

When the nurse entered, Luc looked up and said, "Breech," noting that the baby was coming bottom first. With the bag of waters still intact, a gray balloon with a tiny human inside emerged. Luc gently parted Janelle's legs and assisted with the delivery. When the sac burst, a brown-tinged fluid gushed across the bed. With no time to break down the bed and put up the stirrups, he did the delivery with the bed flat.

Janelle let out a groan. With one push, she delivered a still-born baby boy.

The nurse opened a cabinet and quickly pulled out a delivery pack. Luc cut and clamped the miniature cord. Then, with his hands still wet from the fluid, he carefully wrapped his son in the blue receiving blanket, held the baby to his chest, and sat down on the side of the bed.

Janelle's medication had taken control and she relaxed back into the pillow once the hard pains ceased. With anxiety in her voice, she asked, "Does he look okay?"

Luc recognized the terror common to all moms of stillborns. He knew she feared the worst—that she'd delivered a monster. With tears running down his cheeks, Luc looked down at their son, Samuel. "He's beautiful, honey. Just beautiful."

Janelle tentatively held out her arms, and Luc handed her the baby. Neither of them spoke for a few minutes; they just kept peering into their baby's tiny face. Then Janelle cooed, unwrapped him, and touched his hands and feet, finding many points of beauty.

They heard a knock. Dr. Geman came in to handle the delivery of the placenta and cleanup. Seeing Janelle loving her child, he stopped to acknowledge their loss. "We're on holy ground," he whispered to Luc. "He's beautiful."

That evening, Ben and Luc met in the doctors' cafeteria. Over coffee, they commiserated over the events of the past few days.

In the middle of discussing the hiring of a new endocrinologist, Luc stopped. "Ben. About the clinic break in—I wonder if the robber was really after drugs."

"That thought had crossed my mind, too," Ben said. His voice and face conveyed an ominous expression.

Chapter Twenty-One

DR. HARRISON NOSED AROUND AND CONTACTED a high-ranking friend who was on staff at the same hospital where Drs. Morgan and McKay had privileges. From this doctor he learned about Travis Sudderth. Harrison checked further and found that Dr. Sudderth had past narcotics problems in the military residency where he had served. The records were sealed, but Harrison had enough clout to get access. He found, too, a record of enormous debt—big house, big car, an antique bottle collection. Sudderth's financial dilemma, combined with his current drug problem, could cost the self-important physician his license for good.

Harrison had all the ammunition he needed. *He's not getting the income he needs while he's in detox. And since McKay blew the whistle on him, he may be happy to get even.*

Dr. Harrison made a phone call to the unit in Atlanta where Dr. Sudderth was in therapy. He offered him an early-out in exchange for some cooperation. Sudderth asked what would be required, though he was desperate enough to go for anything.

"I need some information—of possible national interest—from Novacef. Some cell samples. If you agree to get them for me, I'll get you early release. All you'll have to do is check in weekly with Dr. McKay and have weekly drug tests and random testing."

"Ophelia?" Leigh Rivera called out.

The nurse ran down the hall to the expensively furnished nursery. "You called?"

Leigh had been cooing as she rocked eighteen-month-old Gabrielle. Now she looked up at Ophelia and motioned to a crib with her head. "Liliana's fussy. Will you rock her? My hands are full."

"Certainly," Ophelia said as she scooped the twin out of her crib. "I was just doing a load of visitors' gowns."

Leigh nodded. She, Ophelia, and the night nurse didn't need to gown and glove because they had such regular contact with the girls. But they were meticulous in their hand washing. Everyone else had to suit up to touch the twins.

The two women sat humming and patting. After a few minutes, Leigh shook her head and said, "I'm afraid Gabrielle has developed a fever. She feels hot. Is Liliana okay?"

Ophelia nodded slowly. "She feels fine . . ."

"But?"

"Well, it seems like maybe her appetite has been a bit off in the past few days."

Leigh looked distressed. "I hadn't noticed, but then you've fed her more than I have." She sighed. "When they had their check-ups last week, they were lagging behind on the growth chart, but still they seemed to be doing better."

"Perhaps I am too fearful, *señora*."

"No, Ophelia, you're usually right about these things. Please get me the thermometer."

Balancing Liliana on her left shoulder, Ophelia reached for the ear thermometer. She pressed the button on it and gently rested it in the sleeping Gabrielle's ear as Leigh held her.

"What? What is it?" Leigh asked, seeing Ophelia's alarm.

"It is one-hundred-and-one degrees. I'll call the doctor, *señora.*"

Leigh tried not to panic as she listened to Ophelia speaking in rapid Spanish. According to her answers, Leigh determined that the pediatric oncologist wanted to know the twins' fluid intake, their daily weights, the number of diapers, how wet . . . As Leigh heard Ophelia tell the doctor that they were on their way, a wave of nausea rushed over her. *Not again!*

As calmly as she could, Ophelia explained that the doctor was being conservative, wanting to rule out a relapse of the twins' leukemia.

"Okay, you get the girls ready and I'll call my husband to let him know."

"Sí, señora."

When Carlos came on the line, he expressed his indignation over being called out of a meeting. "I am very busy. What is it?"

Leigh explained.

"The girls were fine last week. Did the doctors miss something?"

"I don't know. . . ."

Carlos had only recently informed his wife that he'd instituted a lawsuit against Luc Morgan. He'd convinced her, however, that the suit was only to help pay for the children's medical expenses.

"I am in a meeting," Carols said, his voice agitated, "but I will meet you at the hospital as soon as I can satisfactorily conclude matters."

Janelle had spent the previous week trying to catch up on her rest, but she had been sleeping fitfully. She awoke late one morning to the alarm. Luc hadn't even kissed her on his way out, but when she realized that he'd reset the alarm, she gave him the benefit of a doubt. *He just wanted to let me sleep.* She still had plenty of time to get the boys to school, so she slowly shook herself fully awake. Feeling moisture all over herself, she realized her milk had refused to dry up despite the Parlodel she had been taking.

As if losing a child isn't bad enough. Now I get to enjoy ice and breast binders. . . . I feel like I'm going to burst in more ways than one. She changed into street clothes and thirty minutes later stood red-faced in the garage. "Just get in the car!" she yelled at her sons.

They stared, wide-eyed, at their mother. They rarely saw her looking like this—with hair uncombed, wearing a baggy T-shirt and old sweat pants.

"Get in now!" She held her temples as if she had a raging headache. The boys scrambled over each other and quickly clicked on their seat belts.

The four of them rode to school in silence. When Janelle pulled into the loop in front of the school, they piled out. The oldest, who got out last, turned to her and said, "Sorry, Mom. It's my fault we took so long. I couldn't find my backpack."

Janelle nodded and waved him off, mumbling, "It's okay." She watched him walk away with his head down. *So grown up. They hardly need me any more. And certainly not if I'm going to rage at them for no good reason. I'm a terrible mother. The breast leaking will probably last for months. Nobody cares about my pain. Nobody even remembers my baby.*

Two days after the emergency admission, Leigh and Carlos sat in the intensive-care waiting room. The doctor was to join them soon. He had sent them straight from his office to the

ICU isolation unit, and Leigh had spent the last two nights sleeping at the hospital.

The short, dark physician showed graying strands of hair. Wearing a grim expression, he entered the room and sat across from the couple. "I will be frank," he told them. "I am sorry to tell you that things do not look good. The remission did not last nearly as long as we had hoped. And in addition to this relapse of their atypical leukemia, they have some unusual antibodies. I am not sure why. We are continuing to search for marrow matches using the computer registry of donor types, but so far, we have found nothing very close. It is unfortunate that they have no other siblings, though that would still not guarantee a match."

He waited a moment for the force of his words to sink in, then continued. "They need chemotherapy and, possibly, another bone marrow transplant."

"What you said about siblings, doctor. What did you mean?" Carlos asked.

"Just thinking out loud—potential donors. Other family members would be good."

"I see," said Carlos, who had kicked his thinking into high gear for a possible solution.

The three sat in silence for several minutes. Finally, the doctor rose and said, "I will let you know if anything develops in the search for a bone marrow donor. But we will need to proceed quickly. I will begin to make arrangements and call other consultants, but I would like your permission to move ahead."

The Riveras stood, shook his hand, and thanked him. After the doctor turned and disappeared through the double doors, Leigh wailed in her husband's arms.

He patted her back as she cried. When she had settled down enough to hear him speak, he said gently, "I have an idea."

"What?" Leigh stopped short and looked at his face.

Carlos looked at her for an uncomfortably long time. Then

he said, "I think I know a way this could work. We have seven embryos frozen. We could have another baby. A sibling."

Leigh was dazed by the suggestion. She remained silent for a moment, then thought aloud, "But is there time?"

"We need to ask, to find out if there is a way to give ourselves more time."

"Oh, Carlos, we can't lose our girls." Having said this, she sobbed into his chest.

"We will find a way."

"Dr. Harrison, this is Carlos Rivera in Mexico." The mayor motioned to Ramon to sit down while he made the call.

"Yes, hello!"

"Doctor, I must know something."

"How can I help you?"

"You said the Novacef clinic has some special cells that you believe could help our twins?"

"That's right. In fact, I'm sure they could."

"Our girls are very sick again." Carlos thought for a minute, then spoke again. "And you requested these cells from the doctors, but they refused to send them?"

"Correct."

Carlos was silent again, so this time Dr. Harrison filled the void. "The doctors don't know what to do with these cells. They're not research specialists, so they're just keeping them. And they say it is wrong for us to use them in research—that it would be experimenting on people."

"I see. So you do not think their interest is purely economic?" Carlos sounded suspicious.

"It's hard to say. Anyway, I've made some arrangements. I think we'll be able to get the cells before long. And when we do, I'll do all I can to help your children."

"How do you plan to procure the cells?"

"It would be better if I didn't say. . . . But your mistake may make it more difficult."

Carlos's temper flared. "What makes you so sure it was *my* mistake? You read the reports. The woman said the robbery attempt was drug related."

"Easy there. Don't worry. Your secret is safe with me. I'll let you know when there are further developments."

Carlos hung up the phone and stared at his desktop for a moment. Then he looked up at Ramon. "Once we have finished our business with Dr. Harrison, we may need to pay him a personal visit."

Ben guided Marnie down the ramp, and they found their seats on the New York shuttle. Marnie had decided to accompany him on the trip to interview the new doctor.

Once they'd fastened their seat belts, Ben told her, "I had an interesting call from Carlos Rivera this morning."

"Yeah?"

"Guess I made a good impression on him during the Culiacán trip. I think he trusts me more than he does Luc, which is understandable—at least until we resolve the suit."

"What did he want?"

"He asked if I was serious about doing the embryo transfer. Remember the seven Rivera embryos Tim left me?" He looked over at her.

Marnie nodded.

"Well, they want to try a thaw/transfer cycle. I'm hoping we can help 'international relations,' so I agreed to handle it."

"I'm surprised they'd want another baby right now."

"In fact, the girls have had a relapse."

"Are they okay?"

"It doesn't look good."

"That's so sad."

"That's part of what has motivated this."

"Hoping to ease the pain?"

"Not so much that. Hoping for a sibling bone marrow donor."

Marnie looked aghast. "And you agreed?"

"Sure."

"A baby to be *used* as a tissue donor? Isn't that immoral—to have a baby for the purpose of treating another baby?"

"Ahhh, good question, babe. Here's the deal. The tissue donation is *a* reason for them to conceive, but not the only reason. The harvest procedure doesn't harm the baby—it's not like we're sacrificing a life. So, we have a baby that the Riveras desire anyway, plus a real chance that the ailing twins could be helped. It's a win-win, good-deal possibility. They may get a new baby, a tissue donor, and it gives the frozen embryos a chance."

"You don't still freeze embryos at the clinic, do you?"

"We freeze gametes—eggs and sperm—but not embryos. I'm not crazy about cryopreserving embryos unless the parents involved have a definite plan for using every fertilized egg. I had a patient once who had seven embryos—three were transferred to her uterus and the remaining four were frozen. She got pregnant on the first try, but when she delivered we had to remove her uterus. That left her with a bunch of frozen embryos and no uterus to deliver them."

"What did she do?"

"Paid fifty grand for a surrogate."

"Wow."

"She figured it was better than letting embryos thaw and die—and I agreed with her. Sometimes we don't have the perfect solution, but we can at least choose the best solution among the options. Anyway, the clinic originally decided to do freezing back during my leave of absence after Juli's death. Luc and I hadn't clarified and codified the clinic's position on cryo-preservation. It seems so strange to leave tiny humans in a 'suspended state.' Today, we no longer do it. But we're still left with the Riveras' frozen 'unchosen' from earlier days.

"I don't know exactly what that means to the soul and eternal significance of the embryos, but I'm certainly in favor of transferring and giving them a chance to grow and live. The seven Rivera embryos were the only ones not destroyed in the blast, because Tim took them—and all the LG cells—when he disappeared. This is a chance to give *them* a chance."

That evening, Ben and Marnie had dinner with Ken Edwards and his wife, Myra, in New York City.

"I have a really good feeling about them," Marnie told Ben afterward.

"Me, too," Ben said. The informal interview with the endocrinologist had gone well, and Ben had arranged to meet Dr. Edwards at his own office the next morning for a more technical discussion.

"He's a general endocrinologist—not a reproductive endo guy. I'd prefer an RE," Ben told her. "But he does mostly infertility in his practice, so I think it could work. And we need somebody fast. The part-time doc we've got coming over from the med school is doing us a big favor. But she'd rather be home more with her kids, and I sure want to honor that."

Chapter Twenty-Two

Awake again.

Janelle stared at the red LED digits on the clock. *Three-fifteen.* Luc lay beside her, sound asleep. She listened to his rhythmic breathing and watched the covers on his chest gently rise and fall. *How can he sleep so well when I can't sleep at all?*

Ten days had passed since the funeral. She could still see the baby lying in the casket with too much makeup on his tiny face—someone's failed attempt to give color to his gray-blue skin tone. The smell of cut flowers had always reminded her of romantic garden walks. Now, the scent would forever be associated with death. The tissues. The tears. The hugs. The platitudes:

"The baby had something wrong, anyway."

"Its death was God's will."

"God has his way of taking care of these things."

Publicly, Janelle had responded with kindness, but when she was alone, she threw pillows at the floor. Her sister had flown across country from Washington state to handle the boys. She'd been glad to have her there during the visitation, when so many well-meaning people had made so many callous statements. *Where do people in this country learn such messed-up ways of dealing with others' grief? Soap operas?* When her sister had returned to Washington, Janelle felt as if a huge part of her own heart had gotten on the plane and left with her.

Janelle turned over, then turned again. Restless. Sleep wouldn't come, nor had it since their baby's diagnosis. She'd slept some around the time of delivery, but that had been the artificial drug-induced kind, not the restful sleep she craved.

She'd lain awake most of the night after the graveside memorial service. She couldn't remember any of what Ben had said, but his presence had its usual calming effect. *So many times he has shut us out of his anguish over Juliet, but he always enters our pain with such abandon.*

But then there was Luc. He seemed so unmoved. So together. So little comfort. *I've never seen him like this—"business as usual" while I'm dying inside. He just doesn't understand. But then, I don't understand. Can't think straight, can't move ahead.*

All the sights and sounds and longings for her baby swirled around in her head. *I want out, and there's no way out. I don't want to keep feeling this way. But I don't want to take more sleeping pills—they only get me off to sleep so I can wake up two hours later.*

"Dr. McKay?"

"Yes?" Ben knew immediately from the accent that he was speaking to either Carlos or Ramon.

"This is Ramon Gomez. Please hold the line for Mayor Rivera."

In a moment Carlos spoke. "Dr. McKay! I have good news."

"What's that?"

"Our girls responded quickly to the latest therapy."

"That's wonderful!" Ben wondered why Carlos was telling him. "So the marrow transplant worked?"

"No, we used chemotherapy this time—apparently a specific one designed for leukemia. The elevated counts came down dramatically and quickly. Now our girls have got some normal cells growing. We are still keeping the twins in isolation, but they are in remission."

"Great!"

"And the reason for my call . . ."

"Yes?"

"My wife and I are ready to come to your clinic. We would like to do the transfer as soon as possible—quickly. This month instead of next, if we can."

"That's fine. It will have to be during your wife's fertile time. We'll do a natural cycle. Any idea how long it's been since her last period?"

"Yes, she said to tell you she is on day seven now."

"Then we'll need to get you up here in the next few days. And as I told you before, the clinic will cover your expenses."

Three days later, the nurse knocked at the door of Ben's office and leaned in. "I just had a call from a very weepy Leigh Rivera. She phoned from the Marriott—the kit says she hit her LH surge this morning. Can't believe it happened so early—day ten."

"No problem. Just tell her to get down here."

Of the four embryos Courtney thawed, one failed to survive. So she and Ben transferred three. With the lawsuit still pending, Luc stayed clear. Leigh was as sweet and naïve as before, but Carlos had exploded when Ben told him he could go in only for the transfer, that clinic policy disallowed access to the lab for nonstaff members.

Later, Ben found Luc to give him a report.

"Ever wonder if this guy could be dangerous?" Luc asked.

"So smooth and slick on the outside, but like a stick of dynamite waiting to explode. I've just got this feeling."

Ben nodded. "After seeing his temper today, yes."

When they finished talking, Ben stood to leave. Then he turned back. "By the way—I got a call this morning from administration. Sudds is back. I've been set up as his advisor, so he'll be hanging out here from time to time."

"Oh joy. How did he get out so fast?"

"Connections, apparently. And he wants me to be his 'recovery supervisor.'"

Chuckling, Luc replied, "See? No good deed goes unpunished!"

"Yeah. That's what I said."

For the next few days, Leigh came alone so the doctors could monitor her progesterone levels. Everyone breathed a sigh of relief that Carlos was staying away.

A few days later, Travis Sudderth timed his visit to the Novacef clinic for an hour when he was pretty sure Ben would be over at the hospital.

"Good morning!" he flashed a big smile at the receptionist. "And you are? . . ."

"Lisa."

"Aaah, Lisa. Lovely name. I'm Dr. Sudderth—colleague and friend of Dr. McKay's."

"I'm sorry. He's not here right now."

"No problem." He continued smiling. "I'll wait around."

He then helped himself to the door that led back to the offices and the lab, pretending not to notice Lisa's reaction to such bravado. As he scoped out the office setup, he passed Courtney's office. She was leaning over the cabinet, filing charts, and he stopped to appreciate the view. "Well, hellllllloooooo there," he said.

Startled, Courtney turned.

"I'm one of Dr. McKay's friends from the hospital. Can't believe he's never mentioned *you*."

Courtney tentatively reached out her hand, obviously flustered. "Uh, I'm Dr. Pak. Courtney Pak."

Sudderth took her hand and held it warmly. "So, how long have you been working here? Can't be long—I'm sure I'd remember if I'd met you." He poured on the charm, and she seemed receptive.

"I've been here since the new clinic opened."

Sudderth sat down, so Courtney went behind her desk and sat, too. He eyed the diplomas on the wall. "Wow. Impressive. So you trained at Smith?"

She nodded.

"Great place. I've referred there often."

"Yes, very good clinic."

"So, you must do the embryo work."

She nodded.

"I concentrate mostly on gyn surgery, but I have quite an interest in what you do. I'm also involved on the research end—culturing kidney, heart, and liver cells for future potential use in transplantation. I'll bet your work in embryology is fascinating, though I prefer working with grownups," he said, chuckling. He could tell his humor was lost on Courtney but hoped his charm was hitting the mark.

Courtney blushed and looked at the floor.

"Hey, if you aren't too busy, I'd love to see your setup."

Their eyes locked.

He continued. "How about a quick tour of your lab?" He gestured in the general direction of the front desk. "They told me McKay's over at the hospital."

"We don't have any transfers today, but I can show you the lab. Sure."

Sudderth watched as she punched in the code, slid her card, and then pushed the door open.

"Wow, tight security in this place!" he said.

"Yeah, the last clinic got bombed, and you probably heard about the recent robbery attempt."

"*Really?* Druggies, probably. No, hadn't heard. I've been out of town for a while."

"Well, we take more precautions now." She gestured around the lab. "This is where I work. There's the pass-through window to the operating suite where we harvest the eggs." She pointed. "This is where I do the procedures."

"Wow!" he said, too enthusiastically. "Looks like an incubator with a huge microscope."

"Actually, it's very much like that," Courtney half-smiled. She pointed again. "And that's the cryo area. We've got freezer storage for the sperm and the new egg work I've been doing—trying to perfect the freeze-thaw of eggs without losing viability."

"Freezing and thawing eggs—I didn't think that was doable! And where do you store the eggs and embryos?" Sudderth asked innocently.

Courtney pointed to the special freezer. "But we don't freeze any embryos. The doctors here have some ethical concerns about that. These have been shipped here for adoption rather than destruction."

"Adoption of embryos? Amazing. What will you come up with next?"

"I'll be late again tonight," Luc told his wife over the phone, just as she had put the finishing touches on dinner. Making a meal was about the only thing she had accomplished all day. Once she had gotten the boys off to school, she had gone back to bed and stayed there for hours with the covers pulled over her head.

"Thanks for telling me," Janelle said, emotionless.

"You mad?"

"No, I'm fine."

"Fine—as in frustrated, insecure, neglected and emotional? Or fine, fine?"

"Very funny."

"I'm serious. You say you're fine, but you sound mad."

"Dogs go mad; people get angry."

Luc's voice revealed his growing annoyance. "Are you angry?"

"I said I wasn't."

"Something's bothering you. What is it?"

"I said I'm fine."

"Fine. That's just *fine*. I'll be home around nine. See you then."

Janelle hung up but kept her hand on the phone for another minute. *You get up, get dressed, work all day—even stay late, come home and eat, read the paper, watch TV, go to bed. How can you live as though nothing has happened? Our son is dead!*

⁓❧⁓

Ten forty-five in the morning.

Janelle moved the covers, rolled over, and propped herself on her right elbow so she could answer the ringing phone. "Hello?"

"Hey, girl, it's Marnie."

"Oh, hi."

"How are ya?"

"Okay."

"Want to do the workout thing this afternoon? Maybe go eat somewhere afterward?"

"No thanks, Marnie."

"You okay? You sound tired."

"Just haven't been sleeping really well."

"I'm sorry."

"Yeah, well . . . thanks. I guess with leaky breasts, being a witch of a mother, a husband who's acting like a jerk . . . No, I don't really feel up for a workout."

"I'm sorry."

"I know, I know," Janelle cut her off.

"It's been a while since I've seen you. I miss you."

"Thanks, Marno. I'm just not up for it yet, okay?"

"Sure. Some other time."

Ben slid between the covers, having just returned from doing a late-night delivery. When Marnie stirred and mumbled, "What time is it?" he reached over, pulled her to him, and held her tight.

"It's too late for you to be awake."

"How'd it go?"

"Happy mother, happy father, beautiful baby, and—if I may say so—a mighty slick delivery."

"Good to hear. Missed you," she said sleepily.

"It's way better coming home to you than to an empty house, but still—I was gone only three hours!"

Marnie struggled to wake up. "I may be an old thirty-something lady, but we still get a full twelve months to be newlyweds, right?"

"No argument here." Ben pushed her hair back out of her face and kissed her deeply. "Besides, you're not old. In my professional medical opinion you are quite a babe—a fox among foxes. So don't gimme that 'old lady' stuff."

"Good of you to notice," she said, stretching until she managed to rouse herself enough to talk about what was on her mind. "Honey, I'm a little worried about Janelle."

"Mmm. Janelle? Why?"

"I mean, more than the usual concern for someone who's going through what she is."

"What's up?"

"I called her today. She's so distant. Not herself. She just cut me off. I know she's hurting, but I wonder who else she's got if she's not talking to me."

"So you're worried about your friendship?"

"More than that. Something deeper."

"What do you mean, then?"

"I'm not sure. Something doesn't feel right."

"Want me to talk to Luc?"

"I don't know. Maybe if the opportunity presents itself. I'm not saying I want you to do anything. I'm just concerned."

On Saturday evening, Janelle finished putting ravioli, French bread, and green salad on the table. Then she called her family, and they gathered to eat. During the meal, the boys engaged in lively conversation with each other and with their father, but Janelle just observed. *They hardly need me any more. I'm starting to be more of a burden than a help. I'm always so depressed. No one understands how I feel.*

When they were nearly finished, Luc looked at her plate, then at her. "Aren't you eating anything tonight, hon?"

"Not real hungry, I guess. Maybe I had too much for lunch."

"No way, Mom! You only had half a slice of pizza for lunch, remember? You ate the part I didn't. . . ."

"Why is everyone suddenly so concerned about my eating habits?" Janelle snapped angrily at her child.

They all grew quiet and stared at her.

Suddenly, she burst into tears, covered her face, and ran back to the master bedroom. She closed the door, flung herself across the bed, and sobbed. *Why God? Why all the pain? Why all the sadness? Why does life have to be so painful? I just can't take it any more!*

After a minute or two, Luc came in. He put his arm around her. "It'll be all right, Janelle. It'll all work out. We can make it through this together."

"Together?" She flipped over to glare at him. "How can we make it together when you're never here? And on those rare occasions when you *are* home, you sit glued to the TV. You don't even talk to me! And you *certainly* don't ever talk about our baby."

Luc sat back, dumbstruck. "Honey, calm down. You're just upset because, . . ."

"How *dare* you patronize me!"

Janelle got up and left the room while Luc stayed put. After the boys had gone to bed, Luc told her he had to go back to the office for a few hours.

Once again, she was alone.

Chapter Twenty-Three

ON MONDAY MORNING, BEN AND LUC MET early at the club for a game of racquetball. As they sat on the bench changing their clothes after the match, Ben looked over at Luc. "Hey, buddy, can I ask you a personal question?"

"Sure. Fire away."

"How are you and Janelle doing?"

"Why do you ask?"

"Nothing in particular prompted me. But I've noticed you're working really long hours. And it's been a while since Janelle and Marnie worked out. Just wondering."

"To be honest, I'm doing all right, but Janelle is just crushed."

"Pretty depressed?"

"Sure. Very sad."

"Some postpartum depression?"

"Don't think so. She's not clinically depressed, if that's what you mean."

"You think hormonally she's back to normal?"

"Uh-huh. That's not to say she's done grieving. But she's up and dressed. We had breakfast together this morning. She has dinner on the table. You know, she's functioning pretty well, considering all we've been through. I think she'd bonded with the baby a lot more than I had. But she hasn't said a lot about it."

Janelle opened her eyes and glanced at the red digits glowing in the dark. *One-fifteen. Awake again.* She lay staring at the ceiling fan. After thirty minutes of trying to fall back to sleep, she got up and used the bathroom. Then for the third time that week, she sat on the vanity stool and stared into the huge mirror. As she looked at her reflection, tears streamed down her face. *I want my baby . . . and I don't* want *to forget. If I don't remember him, no one will.*

One of the women from their church had dropped by the previous afternoon. But when Janelle hinted that she had ongoing anguish, her feelings had been met with, "All things work together for good," and "Just trust God." *I believe those truths. So why did they make me so angry when she said them?*

She wept for her loss; then for what she saw happening in herself; then for how far away Luc felt. She went to the medicine cabinet, took another sleeper, and then one more in the hope of some relief, some escape, some end to the pain. *What's the point in going on?*

When Ben awoke the next morning, he told Marnie, "I'm not feeling too great."

She rolled over and felt his forehead. "You do feel a little warm."

"Kind of achy, too. And the barbecue we had for dinner last night isn't agreeing with me."

Marnie got up and brought the thermometer from Emily's bathroom. In a few seconds it beeped.

Ben took it out of his ear and read it. "A hundred point eight. Just what I don't need."

~✦~

"Thanks for seeing me, Mark," Ben said. "I'm feeling kinda whipped, I must confess."

"I'm not surprised!" Mark quipped, trying to lighten the mood. "Marry a young woman—you forget your age." He extended his hand to Marnie.

Ben, still smiling at the remark, said, "I agree heartily. Mark, meet my bride, Marnie. Hon, this is Dr. Mark McLaughlin."

She shook his hand. "Thanks for all your help, doctor."

"Call me Mark," he insisted. "Ben and I go way back." He motioned for them to sit down.

It had taken him only seconds to note that Ben's eyes looked a little jaundiced—probably not enough for anyone but a trained physician to notice. "Tell me what you've been feeling and when it started. You know the drill."

"I just feel so tired," Ben said weakly. "I've been taking it easy off and on since I got that flu in Mexico, but I can't seem to bounce back. I mean, I could sleep twenty hours a day. And my taste buds are shot. Nothing tastes good, and I really like food!"

Mark leaned forward across the desk, looking more closely at his eyes. "Look down."

Ben complied.

"Yep. You look a little jaundiced. Tell me about that 'Mexican flu.'"

"I was down there for about a week. Didn't take any chances, but came back and got sick. Nausea, vomiting, the whole nine yards. Ever since then, this thing keeps coming back periodically."

"That was when?" Mark asked, now taking notes.

"About four months ago."

"Okay, but what you're feeling now may be something else. It's pretty unusual to get jaundice with 'el tourista.'"

"After the first time, I got sick again—I guess about six weeks later. But it went away pretty quickly. I had mostly the same kind of symptoms. I figured it was a G.I. bug."

"Anybody else in the family get it?"

"No, but I wasn't married at the time."

After doing an examination and taking Ben's full history, Mark met Ben and Marnie back in his office.

"Well, did you find anything—or am I just getting old?" Ben asked.

"No, buddy. You are slightly jaundiced, with mild hepatosplenomegaly."

Ben looked alarmed.

Marnie saw his face and asked gently, "What's that?"

"That's an enlarged liver and spleen," Mark told her. Then he looked back at Ben. "Your urine tested positive for protein and urobilinogen; looks like hepatitis."

"From Mexico?" Marnie asked. "He got hepatitis from eating or drinking something in *Mexico?* We ate most of the same stuff."

"I doubt it. But I need to run some tests and see what it is. Ben, you've had the Hep B vaccine right?"

"Yep."

"And we covered you with gamma globulin after the 'Chevy incident.'"

"Right. You don't think it has anything to do with that, do you?" Ben pleaded. "I thought that was behind me. You covered me with gamma globulin for Type A, and I got vaccinated for B. Don't tell me this is a non-A non-B, and the gamma globulin didn't cover it for me."

"I don't really know. Just trying to think it through. I did keep the blood samples from all your HIV tests for a study I'm doing, so I can retest for a few other things. I'm sure we can sort this out. Given a little time, a little rest—we'll have you good as new. I'm gonna admit you directly to the medicine ward and start the work up. It's a bit puzzling, so I'll put you on isolation until we know more precisely." Mark reached for the phone, called his nurse, and made arrangements.

While he did this, Marnie turned to Ben and said, "So am I at risk?"

"For now you're gonna have to stop kissin' on me, and we'll have to be careful."

She breathed a little sigh. "That stinks. And I guess you're out of work for a while, too."

Ben nodded.

Marnie added, "Good thing Ken Edwards is starting at the clinic soon."

Ben nodded again, a look of frustration on his face.

Mark jotted down the admission orders and gave them to Marnie. "We'll have things ready for him when he arrives. Just take him over to admitting, and I'll be there after I finish up here at the office."

"Thanks," Marnie said with gratitude, obviously trying to mask her anxiety.

"Thanks, Mark," Ben said softly. "Chevys. I've never liked Chevys."

Following the transfer of the three embryos, Leigh Rivera had been coming back to the clinic for blood work. About two weeks after the transfer, Courtney called her at the Marriott.

"Dr. McKay is sick, Mrs. Rivera, otherwise he would be making this call himself. But he asked me to call and tell you that your beta hCG level is close to three hundred today. And I'm sure you realize that anything above a five means we are tentatively optimistic."

"You bet I know what it means—I'm pregnant!"

"Yes. And we need you to come back tomorrow for a follow-up test to make sure the level is rising."

"Yeah, I know the routine. Just like last time. Of course my hCG was initially higher, but then I ended up with twins, too!"

"Any bleeding or cramping?"

"No, no problems at all. And right now I feel just great! Thank you so much, doctor!"

As Ben and Marnie walked through the lobby on the way out of the doctor's building, Marnie tried to hide the fear in her eyes. She knew she'd failed when Ben asked. "You okay, babe?"

"I should be asking *you* that," Marnie said, her voice quivering.

Ben reached over and touched her cheek.

"I'll go get the car and pick you up at the door," she insisted. "Save your energy."

Ben didn't argue.

Within fifteen minutes, they were sitting at the hospital admissions desk.

"Dr. McKay!"

"Hello, Louise," Ben said. "Nice to see you."

The admitting nurse smiled at him, "Yes, doctor." She looked over at Marnie and nodded, then turned her focus back to Ben. "So you'll be joining us here at the Great Memorial Hotel?" she chuckled.

"Indeed," Ben said, "I hear you have outstanding food and the staff—beyond words. " He forced a smile.

"Oh, sure—right." Louise rolled her eyes. "So let me have those orders, and I'll finish getting you into the computer. It won't take a minute. Dr. McLaughlin already has you started."

She typed away on her keyboard. "Yes. Here it is." She thought a minute and then spoke again. "All right, now I know you know all this, but I have to ask—do you have a living will? It's required that we ask all admitted patients."

"I know, Louise," he said, looking tired. "Yes, I've got it covered." He looked over at Marnie. "Guess at some point we ought to discuss this stuff."

She nodded sadly.

"Here are your wristbands," Louise said. "Please check and be sure I've spelled your name correctly. I'll call Leighton in transport, and we'll get you right upstairs."

"I can walk, Louise."

"I'm sure you can. But you're on my turf now, so you get the 'red carpet.'"

About ten minutes later, the transporter appeared with a wheelchair.

"Hey, Dr. McKay. Ready to take a ride?"

"If I must."

He pointed to the seat. "I have my orders."

Marnie walked next to Ben. Feeling insecure, she kept her hand on his arm or shoulder the entire time he was being transported. She had, in fact, hardly stopped touching him in some way since they got in the car to leave Dr. McLaughlin's office.

When they arrived on the med floor, a nurse handed him a gown, a urine cup, and an assortment of forms. Ben held up his palms. "I'll stay in scrubs, if that's okay. A doc has his dignity."

She shrugged. "Whatever."

She ran through her questions about current medications and allergies. She requested the order sheet from Dr. McLaughlin and told them, "I'll get the lab started."

Before long the phlebotomist showed up. "I'm here to feed some thirsty vampires. Need to draw some blood—by the gallon."

When Marnie realized that Ben was in isolation and every-one around him was gowning and gloving, she grew a little panicky. "Should I be wearing a mask?" she asked Ben.

"No. Nobody's wearing a mask—it's not airborne," he told her. "Really, hon. Don't worry so much. I'm gonna be fine."

Before she could respond, the dietician walked in. She spent fifteen minutes discussing food preferences before telling Ben about his special diet.

Marnie went home to get some of Ben's things and to pick up Emily from school. When she returned, she found Ben look-ing alert but sad.

She kissed his forehead, then sat down quietly next to him. "You hate this, don't you."

Ben nodded and remained silent for a long time. Then he looked over at her, reached for her hand, and stroked it. "Mark McLaughlin was just here . . ."

"And?"

"There's little doubt about it being hepatitis. We'll have to wait and see if it's A, B, or some strange deal."

Marnie shook her head slowly.

Ben continued, "So we're basically waiting to see how my liver will respond and how much liver function I'll lose."

She put her head down on the bed and ran her hand gently up and down his forearm. "You're a strong man. I'm optimis-tic." The way she said "optimistic" sounded anything but, and as soon as she was sure Ben wasn't looking, she wiped away her tears.

"Sudds! What are you doing here?" The plastic surgeon greeted Travis Sudderth at the sign-in table for the quarterly staff meeting. The hospital required all attending physicians to be there, and their attitudes about it showed.

"You know I wouldn't miss one of these," Travis Sudderth said with a smirk. Then he added sarcastically, "I *live* for these meetings!"

"Yeah, don't we all. Hey, I just heard you had a 'required leave of absence.'"

"Ah. Rumors. Greatly exaggerated. Actually, it was just a big misunderstanding, but it's all worked out now."

The two men ambled over to the coffee and donuts. Dr. Sudderth lingered, sipping his coffee, shaking a few hands, making small talk—all the while his eyes scanning the crowd. Just as the meeting was starting and most of the doctors had found seats inside the spacious auditorium, the slender white-coated figure of Courtney Pak appeared. She made her way through the glass doors into the atrium and to the registration table.

With impeccable timing, Dr. Sudderth walked over and came up behind her so that as she turned she "accidentally" bumped into him. He exaggerated the move with his coffee cup. "Whoa! Almost got me!" He flashed her a big grin.

"Oh! I'm so sorry!" Courtney insisted.

"Hey, no problem, Courtney. . . . It *is* Courtney, isn't it?" She nodded.

"I never forget a beautiful face. How are you?"

Courtney blushed and stuttered. "I-I'm, uh, I'm fine, thank you."

The doctor pointed to himself. "Sudderth . . . Dr. Sudderth. You remember? From the office? But you can certainly call me Travis—and call me often!" He had practiced his smooth spiel to perfection. Courtney didn't quite seem to catch the nuance of flirtation, but she smiled back.

"Can I get you some coffee? Or a donut?" he asked.

"No, thank you." Courtney spoke awkwardly.

"Well then, let's go in." Sudderth pointed the way, taking command of the situation and walking closely beside her. They entered the auditorium. He gently guided her around the back of the aisle and sat next to her, trying to entertain her during the interminable meeting.

She seemed to enjoy all the personal attention, and being "accepted" in the staff meeting. The group voted in favor of everything, as they always did. Sudderth kept his chatter running the entire time, leaning close to whisper in her ear whenever he wished to amuse her with a comment.

As the meeting ended and they stood to leave, Sudderth said with surgical precision, "Do you like French food?"

She thought a moment. "Yes. I do. Some things."

Sudderth realized that she thought he was merely asking her opinion.

"You on call tonight?"

"No, I'm off this weekend."

"Great, what time do you get off?"

"Around five-thirty."

"Then I'll come by the office and get you. I've heard of this new French restaurant that I've wanted to try, but I hate to go alone. Will you do me a favor and join me?"

Courtney looked at the ground. "Uh, okay. But, what should I wear?"

"You look terrific as you are. But if you like, I'll drive you home, and you can change."

Chapter Twenty-Four

THAT EVENING, DR. SUDDERTH, IN HIS RED Porsche, followed Courtney from the clinic to her fashionable townhouse. As she changed for dinner and applied some makeup, he studied the décor in her black and white, modern living room, trying to learn more about this woman.

Twenty minutes later, she emerged in a clingy black number with slits up the side.

Elegant and provocative. She looks pretty good. Maybe this won't be so bad after all, Sudderth thought. After complimenting her generously, he escorted Courtney to his car and opened her door. He eyed her legs as she slipped in, but she remained oblivious. "This is amazing," she said, running her hand along the leather seat. "I've never been in a Porsche."

At this, Sudderth smiled confidently, feeling like a cat that had snagged the canary.

On the way to dinner, after some brief chatting, Sudderth asked Courtney about her job. Once she had launched into a discussion of her work, he asked carefully, "How do you feel about the limitations in your lab?"

"What do you mean?"

"Well, for example, you told me your frozen embryos are all

transferred in. Your docs don't go for cryopreserving anything in their own clinic."

"Yes, they are certainly more rigid than the people at Smith, but we freeze sperm and eggs—just no embryos."

"And that doesn't bother you?"

Courtney shrugged.

"I'd think someone as brilliant as you might find that limiting."

"I keep my focus on embryology. I want to be the most skilled technician I can be, and I honestly don't spend a lot of time wondering about their ethical concerns or limits."

"So you don't share their convictions?"

"Not really. But in any lab you live with policies you yourself might not make. That's life. I always try to work within whatever limits I am given. I think it makes people more creative—to have to find ways to work within boundaries."

"That's interesting. So they didn't require that you share their views as a condition of employment?"

Courtney shook her head. "No, they're not like that. They're really very nice."

"Since you're an embryologist, what's your take on what you're working with?"

"What do you mean?"

"I mean, is it tissue to you? Or do you think embryos are people?"

Courtney thought for a moment. "I hope this won't offend you, but in my mind, nobody is human until birth. They are gametes, fertilized eggs, pre-embryos. That's the language we used at the Smith Clinic, and it makes sense to me."

"Why would that offend me?"

"If you believe an embryo is a person at fertilization, then . . ."

"No, don't worry," Dr. Sudderth insisted. "That's not why I'm asking. I don't mean to be taking issue with you at all! Not at all! I perform elective abortions, so you won't get any argument from me."

Courtney smiled shyly. "I wasn't sure." She paused and thought a moment, then continued. "I love to help people with fertility problems, and I'm always amazed by the process— watching the sperm that I choose penetrate the egg. I love observing cell division and watching the pre-embryo begin to develop."

Sudderth nodded. "You must be very, very good at what you do."

"I confess," she said, looking at him, "I take great pride in my ability. But I guess I'm a little touchy. When people say I must think I'm God or I'm playing God, it does bother me. I don't think I'm playing God. And I know I'm not God. I don't think much about God at all, really."

"Yeah?" Sudderth liked her answers. He saw that he could get what he needed from her with a minimum of moral self-searching.

"My parents are Buddhists, but I've not practiced since I was a child."

"Interesting. Then it'll be easier for me to tell you about the research I'm involved with."

"What do you mean?"

"I mean, I didn't want to offend you, if you had a problem with it. But it's really very exciting."

"What *are* you doing?"

Sudderth thought quickly. "I'm working in association with a research center that's doing genetic engineering and stem cell research. We want to see some major diseases cured in our lifetimes, and that's looking more and more like a realistic goal."

"Really? And what's your involvement?"

"I'm involved on many levels, but one of my key responsibilities is to procure tissue specimens for the research center."

Several hours later, after dining on fine French food and wine, Courtney shut her front door, leaned back against it, and smiled. *Good looking. Smart. Wants to help hurting people.*

As she headed for the bedroom to change, she considered his thoughtful manners, the way he had leaned forward to listen to her every word—even scooted his chair closer. And what a great ending. He had left her at the door with a tender kiss on the hand. And that had left her wanting more.

"Hello, darling. I miss you! How do you feel this morning?" Marnie asked Ben when he called.

"Great, babe. I'm calling with good news."

"I could use some! What's up?"

"I get to come home today."

"Yay!"

"I agree. Mark says the week here has helped a lot. I've responded well to the diet and rest. My labs have nearly returned to normal, my energy's returning . . . and it looks like there's minimal liver damage."

"That *is* good news!"

"Yeah. I'm moderately jaundiced, but all in all, Mark said I should be back on my feet in no time, though he gave me strict orders to take it easy for a month. Now you want to hear the real bummer?"

"What?"

"Mark did manage to pinpoint the infection. It first turned up in the blood specimen one month after the Chevy delivery, so apparently that's where I got it."

"And after all that testing, after being so careful—what a rip!"

"Can you believe it? All from just trying to help out in an emergency. Reminds me of a saying we have."

"What's that?"

"There's no such thing as 'It's too far to walk to get gloves.' See if I ever bare-hand it in the back of a Chevy again!"

"Then let me come get you—in a Ford!"

Courtney handled the call for Ben from Culiacán.

"Dr. Pak, this is Dr. Zazueta. You assisted Dr. McKay in the treatment of Mrs. Rivera, yes?"

"Yes, I'm the embryologist."

"Then I am pleased to report—Mrs. Rivera made me promise to call—we have a pregnancy at six weeks. All labs have come back normal. We visualized the heartbeat—one baby this time. Everything looks wonderful. You understand? My English is not so good."

"I understand perfectly. Thank you so much, doctor."

"You will be sure and tell Dr. McKay?"

"Yes. He's out of the office today, but I will tell him as soon as I can. Thank you so much for letting us know."

A week later, Ben woke early. He lay next to Marnie in their bed, watching her sleep. She stirred slightly, then opened her eyes. Noting her puzzled look, he reached over and pulled her close. "Just thinking how grateful I am that you're here and I'm better," he said.

"It's been good to have you back this week. I hated sleeping alone."

"Me, too," he said. "It's good to be back in our own bed. Whose idea is it to wake up patients to take their blood pressure all the time? I'm convinced it's a ploy by insurance companies. Patients beg to go home so they can get some uninterrupted sleep."

After a moment Ben continued, "I think I'm going to start back at the office today."

Marnie sat up. "What?"

"Don't worry. I'll take it easy. It'll just be during daytime hours. Charts, dictations, simple office visits."

"Oh, Ben. I thought you planned to take it easy."

"I have been! And I'm fine."

"What did Mark say?"

"Don't worry. I'll just spend a few hours at the office. I'll let him know if I have any problems. I promise."

"You're the doctor." Marnie chose not to argue, and she lay back down for a few more minutes, appreciating the security of Ben's arms. Finally, she worked up the nerve to ask what had been concerning her most. "Ben?"

"Hmmm?"

"I'm sort of scared about something. I've been feeling a little sick to my stomach with no energy. Any chance I have hepatitis?"

Ben flipped on the light and put his index finger under her chin and lifted her face so he could look into her eyes. She couldn't tell if his expression was love or professional concern as he checked for jaundice. "It's unlikely that you would contract it now. But just to be safe, I'll call Mark and see if you need to drop by for a blood test."

Ben had been back at work for a few days, but he felt worse instead of better. Even watching games on ESPN held no appeal for him. So he called Mark.

"It's probably just going to take time," Mark said. "You're not trying to work full-time are you?"

"No, part-time."

"No night or ER call, either, right?"

"Right. Just like you said. Though now I've got an exhausted partner who needs some rest himself."

"Can he trade call with some other OB's?"

"Yeah, he's done that. I guess I'm just champing at the bit to get back to full-time practice and pull my weight."

"Sorry, man. Your body has taken a beating. I want to you to keep taking it easy for a while."

On Sunday morning, the early November air was unseasonably warm. With the sky a blue backdrop for the golds and scarlets of autumn, the drive home from church lifted everyone's spirits.

Marnie and Ben dropped off Emily to play with a friend, and Marnie asked, "How would you like to take a drive later?"

"Did you have somewhere special in mind?" Ben asked.

"Actually, yes. My surprise. Hungry?"

"Sure. Though I'm also a bit tired."

"It's a short drive, and you can stretch out and rest all you want. I've got the makings for a picnic in the fridge. Fried chicken, chocolate chip cookies, and a snack to tide you over."

"You planned ahead, huh?"

Marnie cocked her head to the side. "Uh-huh," she said with a ghost of a smile. "I've had something sort of special in mind for the past few days. Just waiting for the right time."

Ben reached over and squeezed her hand.

When they got home, Marnie packed the car. In the trunk she hid an ice bucket, glasses, and sparkling grape juice. She had not yet decided whether she would bring it out. That would depend on Ben's reaction to her news. She caught herself biting a fingernail.

"I'll drive," she said after he came out to the garage to join her.

"You sure? My, my, you're a mysterious one, aren't you?" Ben studied her face for clues.

Marnie reached up and pecked him on the lips. "Hope so. Get in the car."

"Yes, ma'am," he said playfully.

Within a few minutes, they were headed into Washington, D.C.

"You take me to the city for a picnic?"

"Just wait," she told him.

"All right. But I think I'll wait in comfort." Ben adjusted the seat so he could recline and stretch out. After a minute he reached over and turned on the CD player and started humming along to an old John Denver tune.

Marnie tapped the steering wheel with her index finder as she drove. *I wonder what he'll say. . . . I'd better not expect too much—give him time. He lost Juli during her pregnancy, so this could get complex. . . .*

"Marnie?"

"What?"

"You didn't answer me."

"Huh? Oh, sorry. Guess I didn't hear you."

"You okay, babe?"

"Sure."

Ben reached over, took her hand, and began to stroke it gently. "I just asked if you brought any other CDs along."

An hour later, Ben rested his head in Marnie's lap as they stretched out on a blanket. They'd found a secluded spot on Roosevelt Island, overlooking the Potomac, and after lunch they reclined, enjoying each other's warmth and the rustling autumn leaves.

Occasionally, Marnie leaned down and touched her lips to Ben's face in the most tender of kisses. After a long period of quiet, she spoke. "Ben?"

"Hmmm?" He lay with his eyes closed.

"I love you."

He looked up to see tears in her eyes.

She held him in a long gaze. "And I'm going to have your baby."

Ben blinked, sat up, and stared at her.

She wiped her eyes, but that didn't stop the tears.

Ben drew her to him and held her close. He buried his face in her hair.

Marnie rubbed her right hand up and down his arm while he held her, waiting patiently for a response. After what happened to Juli, she knew it might take time for him to adjust to the idea.

After a moment or two, Ben wiped a tear. "I'm sorry, hon. Tears are probably not the initial response you'd hoped for."

"No need to apologize, sweetheart." Marnie leaned against his chest as she spoke. "Sorrow . . . joy. All mixed up. I know."

At this, he squeezed her harder and kissed the top of her head.

He spent a moment silently composing himself. Then he said, "This really is great news."

"Ya think?" Marnie pulled back to look at him.

"Ohhh, yeah." Ben rubbed his eyes again. "I'm thrilled, really I am. For you. For us."

"I'm glad you're glad, sweetheart," Marnie drew close again.

"It's not like we're young things—I mean, I'm an old geezer, but then you're what? Twenty-four?"

Marnie giggled. "Thirty-five."

"A young thirty-five. That sure happened fast. You can't be very far along."

"I'm about a week late. Very early. Just wanted you to have as much time as possible to get used to it before we start telling people."

"How thoughtful. Thanks, honey." Ben shook his head.

"Here I've been thinking about getting over being sick, and apparently you've been thinking about colors for the nursery." Ben sighed and smiled into Marnie's face. "Just imagine the adventure we have ahead."

"I'm concerned about how to tell Janelle. It feels a little like survivor guilt," Marnie said.

A chill of understanding swept over Ben. "That'll be a tough one."

Marnie nodded and fell silent for a minute. Then she told him, "Mark ran a pregnancy test when I went in to get checked out for hepatitis."

"I can't believe you didn't tell me!"

"I told you I didn't have hepatitis," she said with a giggle. "And I don't! Plus, I wanted it to be special. But, believe me, it about drove me crazy waiting to tell you."

Ben stretched out on the blanket, and Marnie lay across his chest. He held her and closed his eyes. Then within his heart he looked deeply into her soul, to the place where words were unnecessary. And he nodded.

Thirty minutes later, Ben packed up the picnic basket and started for the car, while Marnie folded the blanket. He opened the car trunk, and Marnie came a moment too late to prevent him from seeing the wine glasses and the bottle she'd hidden.

"Did you forget? . . ." Then he saw her expression. "No, you didn't, did you."

Marnie shook her head. "Some other time. Not today."

"Oh, Marn." Ben reached out to touch her again.

"There'll be many other opportunities to celebrate before your child arrives."

"Our child," Ben corrected.

"There's something very special to me about saying '*your* baby,'" Marnie said sweetly.

Chapter Twenty-Five

I made it until four-thirty this time, Janelle told herself after looking at the clock, *probably because I didn't fall asleep until after one.* She dragged herself into the bathroom again and sat on the stool. *When you get down to it, nobody really cares. But it doesn't matter, anyway.*

She went to the cabinet, took out the new prescription for sleeping pills, and took one. She stared at the bottle for a full minute, and suddenly a wave of calm came over her. She made a decision. *See Jesus. See my baby. Put my family out of their misery. Should I leave a note? No. Really, there's nothing to say.* One by one, she took every pill in the bottle. Then she opened the Percocet, medicine for the cramps she'd been given after the delivery. She took the rest of those, too. Then she walked to each of the children's rooms. At each bed she watched her children sleep, touching each one softly. *It's for the best. I'm no good to you now. Nothing will ever change.* Then she shuffled back to bed and kissed Luc on the cheek. He stirred but didn't awaken. *It'll be better for you. . . . You can find someone who makes you happy.* Then she lay down to sleep forever.

Luc awakened to the alarm at six A.M. Janelle, with her back to him, didn't stir. He nudged her and said, "Honey, time to get up." She didn't move. He shook her gently and turned up his volume a bit. "Honey . . ." No response. He turned her toward him, and she felt cool to his touch.

Shouting to awaken the kids, Luc pulled open Janelle's eyelids. Seeing that her pupils were tightly constricted and unresponsive to the light, he put his hand under the angle of her jaw to check her carotid pulse. *Weak and thready.* At the same time, he anxiously watched for evidence of breathing. *Some shallow movement of the chest.*

He pulled the pillow from under her so that her head lay flat on the bed. Then he tilted her jaw up to keep her airway open.

Luc bent and put his ear to Janelle's mouth so he could listen for improved breathing, and at the same time, watch for increased movement in her chest. But, to his terror, he now detected no sign of respiration. Keeping Janelle's jaw tilted up, Luc covered her mouth with his own and delivered two breaths. *Gotta get some air in her.*

"Dad!"

Luc looked up to see eleven-year-old Ryan standing in the doorway, a look of horror on his face.

He took his mouth from Janelle's. "Call 911!"

"What happened, Dad?"

"Mom's sick. We need to get her an ambulance. Dial the phone and bring it to me!" Luc planted his lips back on his wife's and exhaled again. *She may have taken too many sleepers or something.*

When the ambulance arrived, the paramedics hovered around Janelle.

Luc told his sons, "Just stay back. We're taking care of Mom." They all took a step back and watched helplessly as the medical team worked.

One of the paramedics, seeing her pupils, turned to Luc, "Is she on any medications?"

"She must have taken a pain pill with the sleeper. She hasn't been eating well lately. Probably the combination of the two knocked her out."

Ryan touched his arm. "Is she gonna be okay, Dad?" Tears streamed down the boy's cheeks. He looked up and saw the moisture in his father's eyes.

Luc put his hand on Ryan's shoulder and spoke confidently. "You betcha, son. I wouldn't let anything happen to your mom."

They watched as the paramedics prepared Janelle for transport. With the oxygen mask on, she began to take on a more natural color, and Luc sighed with relief.

"Ryan?"

"Yeah?"

"I need you to call Sheila and see if she can stay with you. I gotta get dressed."

"Can't I come with you?"

He shook his head. "Sorry. But I'll call you soon and let you know about your mom. I promise."

Luc, having slept in scrub pants, went into the bathroom to pull on his scrub shirt. He stood aghast when he saw the two pill bottles lying empty next to the bathroom sink. *She did it intentionally! Oh, Janelle! Good night. . . . Please, God, let her be okay.* Luc watched the flickering reflection of the flashing lights off the bathroom window pane. *What will people think of me when they hear that my wife tried to commit suicide?*

Luc convinced the paramedics to let him ride with them in the ambulance. At the hospital, they rushed the patient into ER, where the medical team sprung into action.

"What's the status? Did she respond to the IV? Do we know exactly what substances were ingested?" asked the attending physician.

Luc gave him the empty prescription bottles. "Sleeping pills and analgesics—I don't know how much, but a large dose."

A nasogastric tube was quickly threaded through Janelle's nose into her stomach to pump its contents. Finding numerous capsule fragments in her aspirate, they forced "charcoal" into her stomach. The black substance would absorb residual medication. When an oxygen mask was in place, the transport mask was returned to the ambulance team. Next, they changed the IV bag and started her on Narcan—a narcotic reversal agent. They prepared to use the IV line as access for any medications they might need should she go into cardiac arrest.

The ER doctor noticed Janelle's leaky breasts and turned to Luc. "Do you have an infant? Is she breastfeeding?"

Luc shook his head. "Stillborn. She took the meds to stop lactation, but they didn't work."

Everyone looked up momentarily when they heard this. The physician said, "Oh."

Cindy, a hospital volunteer, recognized Luc from church. "Is there anything I can do for you, Dr. Morgan?" she asked. "Would you like for me to call Chaplain McKay for you? Isn't he your partner?"

"That would be great. Would you mind?"

"Not at all. Glad to help."

"Your wife's blood pressure is low but decent," the attending physician told Luc. Then he read the pulse oximeter they had hooked on her finger. "And with the mask oxygen, her blood gases have returned to adequate levels."

They spent the next hour drawing labs. Cindy leaned her head in the door and looked at Luc. "I'm still trying to locate Dr. McKay. Sorry it's taking so long."

Luc shrugged. "Thanks for trying."

When the lab results came, the doctor told Luc, "We can transfer her to ICU to sleep it off."

Having read the numbers, Luc knew for certain that Janelle had purposely overdosed. He stepped out into the hall and wiped the tears from his eyes. He felt an odd combination of fear and enormous relief that Janelle had survived. When he had sufficiently gathered his thoughts, he pulled out his cell phone and called his kids. Then he headed for a staff rest room. Once inside, he locked the door and sobbed into his hands. *It's all my fault. Didn't see it coming . . . should have seen it. What do I do now?*

When Luc returned, the ER doctor told him gently, "I'd like to order a psych consult for your wife when she awakens, okay?"

Luc nodded. "She's been pretty depressed since the delivery."

Luc stepped outside and leaned against the wall again. He heard the doctor say, "Looks like trouble for our fine Christian doctor."

"Hey, Man—don't be so critical," snapped one of the nurses. "Postpartum depression can be bad enough even when the baby lives."

━≈⊱⊰≈━

Ben signed in. "I'm here to visit Janelle Morgan," he told the psych nurse. Then he made his way down the hall in the locked wing. He'd walked down this corridor many times during his days as a chaplain, so he was no stranger to life on the psych ward. But it had been nearly a year since he'd heard his own steps echo here. Besides, this felt different. This was Janelle. He stopped outside her room and gently tapped. "Hello?" he said softly, cracking the door just a little.

"Come on in, Ben," Luc replied in a low tone. "Glad you're here."

Ben entered and quickly scoped out the situation. Luc sat perched near Janelle's bed, looking helpless. His whisker growth, even after only a day, accentuated his wrinkles. "How's it going, buddy?" he asked.

Luc shook his head. "Our neighbor still has the kids, and I don't know how I'll explain all this. Or what I'll tell the office."

"Don't worry, Luc," Ben interrupted. "We've got everything covered there. And Janelle's gonna be okay. That's what really matters."

"I know." Luc's tone reflected his gratitude. "I just don't understand. I thought we were getting through it. How could I miss this? I spent half an hour on the phone just yesterday with a patient, a seminary wife, who has postpartum depression. Her husband tells her to 'Just trust God and get over it.'"

As Luc spoke, Ben glanced over at the figure in the bed. Janelle looked nothing like herself. She lay in arm and leg restraints with white cloth wraps tied to the bed rail so she wouldn't try to climb out or remove the tubing taped to her nose.

Luc buried his head in his hands, and Ben put a hand on his shoulder. Then he moved closer to the bedside, near Janelle's head. He got there just in time to catch a flicker of her eyelid.

Ben turned back to Luc. "Has she been awake much yet?"

"Not really. A few moans. But she's been pretty zonked since this morning. After they got her stable, they decided to let her sleep it off and gave her some antidepressant that her doc thought would help. After hearing the story, he told me we had a pretty classic case of postpartum depression, magnified by the loss of our baby."

Ben nodded his acknowledgment.

"I see it all the time at work," Luc looked down at his hands, "but I missed it in my own wife."

"Don't beat yourself up, buddy. We all cope in different ways and at different paces. Your heart's been in the right place. Why don't you go home, clean up, and check on the kids? They really need you, and just seeing you will make a world of difference."

"I really ought to stay here. I don't know what to do or say, but I feel like I need to be here."

"Just take a few hours, Luc. I'll stay here and sit with 'Nelle. I can give you a ring if she wakes up. You can't be in both places at once, and the kids haven't seen you since the ambulance drove away. I've got it covered here."

Luc nodded. "I could use a shave and shower."

"That you could!" Ben said with a grin.

"I've got my beeper," Luc told him. "Just have the service page me if she wakes up. Otherwise, I'll be back in a couple hours . . . after dinner."

"Great. Take off. She'll be fine."

When Luc rose, Ben noticed he stood with slumped shoulders, as though he bore some huge weight. Luc picked up his jacket and headed out of the high-risk wing.

Ben returned to the chair and sat patiently. Moments later Janelle's eyes opened again.

"Hello, my friend," Ben said. "I know you're awake."

"I just couldn't face him," she muttered, her voice hoarse. "What can I say? I can't even do *this* right. And get this blasted thing out of my nose." Janelle coughed and tugged at the restraints. "Why did they have to tie me up like a criminal?"

Ben stood and moved closer. He unfastened the restraint on her left hand, gently lowered the side rail on the bed, and sat beside her. He took her hand and with kindness in his eyes, he looked into hers.

"Ben, I'm such a fool. I couldn't even do a decent job of killing myself."

"Actually, you did a fine job. But for the grace of God, you wouldn't be with us now."

"What?" Janelle blinked, still in a fog.

"Janelle, if you hadn't married a doctor—and one who could keep his cool under fire—you wouldn't be here. You took plenty enough to do the job. Luc kept you alive long enough to get you here and get reversed and—pumped. That's why you've got that nasty tube."

"Why would he even care? He hasn't been any help at all. He's been sitting there most of the day reading a medical journal!" Her tone began to escalate, but she gagged on the tube in the back of her throat.

"I'm sure that's how you feel, Janelle. But he's a good man, and he's hurting too." Ben walked over and picked up the journal. "Ah yes, the *Journal for Psychiatric Nurses*. A real page-turner, no doubt! Did he ever turn a page?"

"But our baby," she sobbed and choked. "Our baby boy is dead. And Luc doesn't even care."

"Ohhh, he cares. He just shows it differently than you do. I could tell at the office. His mood has been reserved, and when he does sonos on the women in early pregnancy, it still tears him up."

Janelle was clearly surprised at this revelation. "So why doesn't he tell *me*? Why doesn't he show *me* he cares?"

Ben smiled tenderly. "In his mind, he *is* showing you that he cares. He shows it by being strong, by taking care of business, by forcing himself to remain unemotional. He sees himself as your rock, afraid that if he shows weakness, everything will fall. Remember, Luc and I are a lot alike, and I've actually had a little experience with trying to shut out the world, trying to close the doors on all the pain."

Ben continued. "Let me ask you a question: Where's your baby's crib right now?"

"In the attic."

"Who put it there?"

"Luc."

"Did you see him put it up there?"

"No."

"Right. See? He's dealing with this privately, doing what he thinks will make it easier for you behind the scenes."

Janelle was silent, and Ben was comfortable with it. After many minutes she gave him a pleading look and reached up to him with her free arm. Ben unfastened her other wrist, and she wrapped her arms around his neck. Through gagging and sobs she cried out, "What have I done? What have I done to my family?"

"It's all right, Janelle. You got a bit overwhelmed by everything that's going on. Losing a child. Geez. There isn't much in life that's harder than that." The memory of Ben's own loss made his eyes watery.

Feeling the moisture against her cheek, Janelle pulled back far enough to see his genuine tears. "Ben," she croaked, "how did you ever make it through? When Juli and your baby died? How did you *do* it?"

Ben struggled to form the words. "Just grace, Janelle. I didn't have the strength to go on. Somehow time and life just went on, and I caught up with it later."

They sat eye to eye. Finally, Ben broke the tension by adding, "Plus, I didn't have the hormone storm you have!"

Janelle gave a weak smile. "So, do you think I'm crazy?"

"Of course I do!" Ben paused for effect. "But no crazier than the rest of us. If my experience is worth anything, it tells me you're one of those unlucky women who get swamped with the hormonal changes that happen at the abrupt end of a pregnancy. Couple that with enormous grief and loss—it kinda threw you over the edge."

"You mean I won't always feel this way? I just can't handle this."

"Trust me. Once we docs actually wake up and recognize what you have, we're actually pretty good at treating it. You'll feel better very soon. The joy will return."

"But if I don't remember him—the baby—who will?" Janelle began to tear up again. "I don't want to forget him."

"You won't, Janelle. You can't. Your baby and those memories—the value and significance of that one tiny life—they're eternal. God wasn't surprised at any of this. Though we don't understand, we have to try to trust that He has it all together."

"I'm not sure I can do that."

"Then, I'll trust Him enough for both of us right now. And you can owe me for later, when my life takes a turn."

Janelle looked alarmed, but then she saw his smile. "Don't even say that. With Marnie in your life . . ."

"Yeah, she *is* something special, but you have a lot of people in your life who love you, too—including Marnie and me."

"And you really think there are some medications that will help me?"

"You know I'm not one to throw medication at every problem. But in your case—absolutely."

"And I'm not a wimp for needing them?"

"If a piano falls on your head, are you a wimp for asking someone to remove it?"

"Uhhh. No? Is that the right answer?" She forced a smile.

"Correcto! What happened to you makes the piano look like a marshmallow."

"What makes you so smart?" Janelle blinked away a tear. "You always know the right thing to say."

"Well, if that's true, it comes from years and years of saying the *wrong* thing."

Janelle sighed. "What about this tube in my nose?"

"Oh you mean the 'blasted thing,' as you so fondly referred to it?"

"Verily, doctor, the selfsame one."

Ben smiled at the Shakespearean allusion, and he saw the hint of a sparkle in Janelle's eyes. The antidepressant shot had made some impact.

"Tell you what—I've already violated a bunch of rules by untying you. Let's go for the *trifecta*." With a huge grin on his face, Ben pushed the nurse call button.

"Yes? May I help you?" The nurse's voice came through the intercom.

"This is Dr. McKay. Could you bring me a pair of gloves—medium? And some four-by-fours. I'll D/C the NG tube on Mrs. Morgan."

"Yes, doctor," came the professional reply.

Ben turned back to Janelle. "Piece of cake."

"Nice to have 'the power,'" she managed, with a grin. "But what did all that gibberish mean?"

"D/C the NG tube?"

"Uh-huh."

"Discontinue the nasogastric tube."

"I knew that."

Ben changed the subject, "Hey, I promised to call your hubby when you woke up."

"Oh, man," Janelle groaned. "Now, *there's* a conversation I'm dreading."

Chapter Twenty-Six

COURTNEY AND LISA SAT IN THE EMPLOYEES' lounge, finishing up the Chinese food that a drug company rep had delivered, a public relations touch the company hoped would be remembered when it was time to order.

"Mmmm. Not quite like home, but that tasted great," Courtney said, savoring the last bite. "Almost as good as the linguine I had with Travis last weekend."

Lisa raised her eyebrows. "Travis, eh?"

Courtney nodded.

"I noticed that he's been taking you to lunch every week after his meetings with Dr. McKay."

"We've been to a few nearby restaurants. A couple of really nice ones—and a dinner show."

Lisa swallowed hard. "Just be cautious. I hear he's quite a lady's man—love 'em and leave 'em type. Ask Darlene. She'll tell you."

Courtney gave the receptionist a Mona Lisa smile. "He's never been that way with me. He's been a perfect gentleman. Charming. Not at all pushy. In fact, I almost wish he'd move a little faster."

"Then you must be really special to him."

"I like to think so."

Marnie and Ben sat up in bed, talking about their dinner out that night with Janelle and Luc.

"How did Janelle seem to you, compared to how it went in the psych ward?" Marnie asked.

"Actually, great. I think it helps that she and Luc did the outpatient psych appointment together."

"I know your own conversation with her helped a lot, too. She mentioned it more than once."

Ben smiled and shrugged. "Nice to think maybe I helped a bit. But the therapist they saw really knows her stuff. If nothing else, they both needed to see how differently they handle grief—and how isolating that was, especially for Janelle."

"I guess a lot of people never learn that. Janelle said she was surprised to learn how many couples split up after losing a child. She said it made her realize that maybe she was more normal than she thought."

"I'm sure that's true."

"She said Luc copes by being strong, and she copes by falling apart. Pretty polarizing stuff."

"I'm glad she sees it. That's how Luc's been since I met him—not unlike me."

"Yes, O cave dweller," Marnie said with a smile.

Ben chuckled. "Sad, but true."

"It's easy to feel it as rejection instead of love."

"So I'm told." He leaned over and pecked her forehead. "But I think it's really the way most of us men think. We try to shut the painful compartment off and stay strong. It feels noble, heroic even. But, I've been trying to learn your language, to talk about feelings and really try to understand. So, are we talking about Janelle and Luc or us here?" Ben asked.

Marnie looked him in the eye. "When you love someone,

you appreciate any insight you can get into knowing how they think. So I suppose we're talking about both."

Ben raised his eyebrows. "Good answer." He leaned over and kissed her cheek. "But in their case, I don't think it was *totally* about communication and understanding. The storm caused by hormonal changes is not to be underestimated. The women in my practice who have true postpartum depression—when they respond to medication, it's amazing. When we regulate hormones, within a couple of weeks it can be like night and day. That makes it all the more tragic when a patient actually kills herself."

Marnie slowly shook her head, her eyes widening. "Thank God Luc found her in time."

It was eleven at night when Travis Sudderth picked up his ringing phone at home.

"Dr. Sudderth? Harrison here."

"Oh, hello."

"Need a progress report. When can I expect the material we discussed?"

"Well, good evening to you, too! Ya know, you need to loosen up, learn to relax a little. We're not talking about stealing hubcaps here."

"Dr. Sudderth, we're running short of time. Need I remind you that your 'special status' from the rehab clinic can easily be revoked? Or should I remind you about your licensure status?"

"Doc, listen up. I'm in. I know my way around the clinic, know all the security systems. But the 'material,' as you like to call it, is not only locked up. It's frozen, as you know—kept in storage with a bunch of other material. Donated embryos and cryopreserved gametes. I assume you want the 'right' material?"

Harrison spoke sharply. "When can I expect it? This isn't a game."

"I have a plan—a beautiful plan. By next week the goods will be handed to me on a silver platter!"

"How are you going to do that?" Harrison pressed. "They already turned me down flat."

"You just gotta know how to work the system. I've still got the number of your contact for pickup and transport. Tell him to be ready."

"You better not be pullin' my chain," Harrison growled. "Or I'll jerk you outta there so fast, you'll never practice again!"

"Dr. Harrison, trust me. I've got it all under control."

"And you'd better stop ignoring my phone calls."

Sudderth started to speak, but he heard a click and then the dial tone.

Good-bye to you, too, jerk.

That Friday, Courtney heard the staff nurses ooohs and ahhhs of appreciation in the hall. "Dr. Pak's got an admirer!" Lisa announced. Courtney looked out to see the reason for all the commotion. "I have a special delivery for a special lady." She stood holding a mixed floral arrangement.

Embarrassed but flattered, Courtney thanked her, took the flowers, and shut the door. She hurriedly opened the card and read it: "Can't wait to see you. Pick you up at six, Travis."

A few minutes later, one of the nurses knocked on the door. "Come in."

Courtney's door opened slightly, and a face peeked in.

"Hi, Darlene. Did you need something?" Courtney asked.

"Can we have a moment for some 'girl talk'?"

Courtney motioned to the chair.

"I'm just concerned about something."

"What's that?"

"Can I ask a personal question?"

Courtney nodded.

"Are the flowers from Dr. Sudderth?"

"Why, yes. They are." Courtney again seemed pleased.

"Well, I don't know how to say this nicely, but . . ."

Courtney's tone changed. "You have a problem with that?"

"Well, uh, it's just that—he has a reputation, you know."

"People like to gossip, Darlene."

"But I know from personal experience, Dr. Pak. Rather intimate experience. And I found out afterward that I had joined a long string of conquests. The girlfriend after me dumped yellow paint on his car, after she slashed his waterbed."

Courtney's air grew superior. "While that may be the case, Darlene, he's been nothing like that with me. He's been a perfect gentleman, and I have no reason to question his intentions."

Darlene stood to leave. "Okay. All right. Just don't want you to get burned like I did."

Courtney softened. "It's good of you to care. And I sincerely appreciate your concern for me."

At 5:45 P.M., Travis stood in Courtney's open doorway and elaborately cleared his throat. She looked up from some charts.

"Nice flowers," he said with a grin. Courtney smiled broadly. She rose to greet him.

"Thank you, Travis. They are beautiful."

"Welcome." He walked into her office with a swagger, gave her a warm hug, and kissed her on the cheek. "Ready to go? Got everything covered?"

Courtney nodded. "The new R.E., Ken Edwards, has call this weekend."

"Great."

"Tell me about this place where you're taking me," she said.

Travis looked around at the artwork on her walls. "You said you like learning about American history, so you're going to love it." He held up his arm, exposing his expensive watch, and pointed to the painting on her wall. "Nice art. I don't recognize this piece."

"It was done by a friend, Liz Gonzalez."

"Mmm, very nice." Then, as if just remembering something, Travis said, "Hey Court, did I ever tell you about this watch?"

"Not that I recall." She moved closer to see it.

He slipped it off his wrist and handed it to her. "It was a gift. Presented to me for my involvement in a research project. I think I mentioned it to you. It's actually a big government project. Working with stem cells to reverse various disease processes."

"My predecessor—Dr. Tim Sullivan—was involved in some government research as well," Courtney told him.

"Tim and I were quite close. But it was pretty hush-hush, cutting-edge stuff. He did most of the lab work; I helped procure tissue and handled the practical medical end of things."

Courtney examined the watch briefly and handed it back to him. "It's lovely. Very nice." She started to ask more about his work, but he stopped her.

"Hey, it's the weekend! Let's get outta here. We can talk shop some other time."

Courtney turned her back to fetch her things out of a closet. Travis came up behind her and helped her on with her coat, then they headed out the back through the doctors' entrance.

"Do we need to drop by your place and pick up luggage?"

Courtney shook her head. "I stowed my suitcase in the trunk. The weather is supposed to turn tonight. If we're going to make a three-hour drive before the roads freeze over, we'd better be going as soon as possible."

Travis gave her the thumbs up. "Great thinking." He pointed the way to his Porsche, and they drove over to her car. After discreetly moving her suitcase, they left her vehicle in the secured clinic lot. Since physicians often spent the night at the neighboring hospital, it didn't matter if anyone saw Courtney's car there.

Later, as they sat in rush hour traffic on the Beltway, Courtney said quietly, "Travis? Can I ask you something?"

He looked over at her and winked. "Ask me anything."

"How well do you know Darlene Jones?"

Sudderth considered his response until the silence grew awkward. Finally, he told her, "We were lovers for a while. It ended badly."

Courtney had not expected such an honest answer. "She warned me about you."

"I admit, I didn't handle it very well. We made a bad match intellectually. I can see where she'd be very jealous of you."

Courtney nodded. "Hmmm. Interesting. I think she is."

Shortly after nine that evening, Travis and Courtney checked into the Kingsmill Resort in Williamsburg. Once they were inside their room, Courtney breathed, "It's fabulous."

Travis looked unhappy.

"What's wrong?" she asked.

"It's got a king-sized bed. I specifically asked for two queens. And after our conversation in the car on the way up here, this looks bad. I can sleep on the couch. C'mon, let's get unpacked. There's a candlelight dinner waiting."

The accommodations and Travis's response caught Courtney off guard for a moment. Then she shrugged and turned to unpack.

All evening, Travis was warm and romantic. When they returned to the room after dinner, they opened the curtains to a breathtaking view of the lake from their fifth-floor balcony.

Courtney picked up her coat and handed his to him, gesturing that she wanted to go out.

"Care if I smoke?" Travis joked, then breathed a puff of steam into the cold air. At first, Courtney didn't understand, but when she figured out his humor she laughed and squeezed his hand.

"You know, Travis, I've dated only a few Americans, but no one else has been so much fun." She reached out to him, and they stood holding each other in the freezing night air.

After a minute, Travis said, "Your teeth are chattering. Better go inside before you're an ice sculpture."

They stayed up late watching a television movie. But when bedtime came, Travis went into the bathroom and changed into a bathrobe, then made a bed on the couch. He walked over to Courtney, kissed her on the forehead, and said, "Good night, sweetie."

Courtney, who had hoped for more show of affection, turned off the lights and undressed in the dark, then slid into the empty bed. After a few minutes, she spoke into the dark. "Good night, Trav. I'm sorry about the rumors. You've been a perfect gentleman."

"That's okay," he assured her. "That's life at a hospital. If I'd done everything I've been accused of, . . . but I really care about you, and I don't want to rush things. I think you're gorgeous, though, and I'd be lying if I said I hadn't struggled to control my passion."

This was all Courtney needed to hear before falling into a deep and blissful sleep.

On Saturday morning, after Travis showered, he walked out into the room wearing only a towel. "Court, have you seen my watch?"

Jolted from her sleep, she sat up, frowned, and shook her head.

"Funny, the last time I remember having it, we were in your office. But you gave it back, right?"

"I'm sure I did."

"Hmmm. I really don't remember. I must've just set it down. I was so focused on you, I must have done it absentmindedly. Oh well, we have to go by your office anyway to pick up your car."

"Sure. We can check then," Courtney assured him.

He nodded and went back into the bathroom.

Chapter Twenty-Seven

TRAVIS AND COURTNEY TOOK A LEISURELY WALK through Williamsburg, shopping and talking with craftspeople, especially the glassblowers. Travis had acquired a good working knowledge of glass from his bottle-collecting hobby, and he impressed Courtney with his ability to pick up a bottle and tell her if it was made before or after 1750. In the early afternoon, they took a horse-drawn carriage through the colonial village, ending at Chowning's Pub. They warmed themselves by the fire outside the restaurant as they waited for a table, and Courtney loved watching Travis charm the hovering crowds. After a long, leisurely dinner, they lingered over drinks and talked of everything from politics to poetry.

They took another walk, this time around the resort in the cold night air. When they returned to the room, the clock read 10:15. Once inside, Travis shut the door and pulled Courtney close. "Thanks for an incredible day." He kissed her with escalating passion. Suddenly, he pulled himself away. "Sorry. I'd better stop. Good night," he whispered. Then he pulled her close again. After another minute, he felt her breathing change. She looked at him and whispered, "Travis, you really don't have to stop—or sleep on the couch tonight."

He raised his eyebrows and asked innocently, "I don't?"

She shook her head.

On Sunday afternoon, Travis and Courtney made the three-hour drive back to Northern Virginia. During the trip home, they kissed at every stoplight. Courtney felt loved and understood, and she imagined what it would be like to be in a long-term relationship.

When they arrived back at the clinic to look for Travis's watch, Courtney punched in the code. Once inside, Travis grabbed her, and they stood and kissed for several minutes more. Then he took her by the hand and led her back toward her office. When Travis spotted the lab down the hall, he gestured to it dramatically and said, "Courtney?"

"Yes?"

He waved it off. "Oh, never mind. Just a thought but nothing important for now. You're all that's important."

"Oh, come on. You can tell me."

He kept walking. "No, I don't want to break the mood of this incredible weekend." When he arrived at her office, he plopped down in the chair behind her desk.

"There it is—your watch! On the desk behind one of the photos!" When Courtney walked in front of him to get it, he reached out, grabbed her around the waist, and pulled her into his lap.

"Remember? I told you I got it as a gift?" Travis reminded her.

"Yes, for your work on the government research."

"Right. It's still ongoing, and I still have some connections there. That's what I wanted to ask you about."

"Really? Well, ask away. Anything I can do to help?"

"Well, I really don't know. I'm not sure . . . but Tim Sullivan and I were working with some very special cells. *Very* special—none like them in all the world. In fact, I believe we did with them what no one else has been able to accomplish."

"Yes, I know about the cloned egg cells. I imagine it was illegal when he did it, but it probably wouldn't be now. And it's so remarkable! We still have the cell line."

"You what? No way!"

"Yeah, I helped Dr. Morgan ship a sample to a government contact he had," Courtney told him.

"I thought it all got lost in the fire!"

"No, they're here," Courtney said confidently. "I have them in the lab, though Drs. McKay and Morgan are pretty protective of them. From what I understand, they're a unique cell line—chromosomes from one egg fused with another egg. I don't know how Dr. Sullivan got them to grow, but he used a fairly simple technique, from what I understand," she said with assurance.

"I can't believe you still have some of that tissue culture. The people I'm working with in the government could sure use it! And I was just going to ask if you could lend me some of Tim's old journals!"

Courtney moved from his lap and leaned back against her desk so she could look at him. "I could ask the doctors about giving some for the government research." She paused a moment. "Though I think they've already been asked for more and refused. I don't know all the details. Something about a lawsuit."

"No," Travis interrupted. "No, I'm sure you're right. I don't think that would work." He looked down and shook his head. "I can't believe the tissue culture just sits in there frozen, when we could be using it to develop a cure. Just unbelievable. We were so close. Tim and I really thought, . . . but then, the accident, his death, the fire."

Courtney stared at the wall thinking hard. "You really think you could make some headway with these cells?"

"Not me alone, but I could with the incredibly skilled people I work with. Like you, they're at the cutting edge of research."

Courtney leaned down and slowly brought her face in front of his. She kissed him tenderly. "I have an idea."

"What, Courtney?"

"Do you have a way to get the cells to your lab?"

"Well, yes. I still transfer biological material almost every day to the lab. But not usually cryopreserved tissue."

"Listen. We got a shipment of frozen embryos for our donation service on Friday morning. We still have them in the liquid nitrogen capsules in the lab. I could move them into the unit, take a few of the samples of the cell line, and put them into the capsule. We can send you off with them today, if your contacts work on Sunday. Oh, that could be a prob—"

"No, no!" Travis interrupted. "No problem at all! They're always available. But I'd hate for you to, you know—break protocol."

Courtney shrugged. "Nobody goes into the lab but me now. I'm certain I could give you half of the material, and no one would ever know. And maybe you could do something really positive with them."

"Courtney, I just don't know what to say. You're fantastic!"

She got up to make the transfer, with Travis watching over her shoulder.

"Do you want any of these embryos for your research? I haven't logged them in yet, so nobody . . ."

"No, no. Thanks, but you've done enough already."

She efficiently made the switch, taking the LG frozen vials out of their specially locked areas and placing them in the liquid nitrogen capsule.

As she worked, Courtney seemed to grow increasingly tense. Pointing to the capsule, Travis said, "I always thought these things looked like miniature space ships." He hoped the humor would cut the tension. When she had finished, Travis lifted the capsule. "Boy, hope this'll fit in the Porsche!"

She laughed. "You can put it in *my* seat—for now, anyway."

"Where is it?" Dr. Harrison burst through the doors of the lab at 8 A.M. Monday and barked at the first person he saw.

"Good morning, sir. What do you need?" one of the techs asked.

"The cryo transport from Washington, D.C. It should've been here an hour ago."

"Yes, sir. Look down at the main lab. Dr. Lowell signed for it, I think."

Harrison nodded and grunted his thanks. He turned and rushed off down the hall toward the elevator. Moments later, the tall doctor stood peering over the shoulder of Dr. Lowell, who was busy at work among petri dishes and microscopes. "How's everything look?" Harrison wanted to know.

"Just great, Dr. Harrison," the young doctor answered with enthusiasm. He turned to look up at his boss. "We've got a great sample—gotta be four times what we got last time! Appears to be just perfect. Want me to proceed same as last time, try to revert it all back to embryonic?"

Harrison shook his head, and the smile faded from his face. "Don't think so. We hit a dead end last time, so I want to develop the line first—perhaps take part of the sample to maturity. There's something about this cell line . . . these cells. No other lab has been able to duplicate the process. I wonder how they'll respond to the usual stimulation we use to move them to mature cell types. Then we can use the rest to try to 'back up' to totipotential. Once there, we can make all the cells we want. How's the primate work going?"

"Terrific, doctor. I can go from stem cells to mature lines, and I can take intermediate cells back to stem cells. I haven't quite got all the way from fully mature back to stem cells, but with this new delivery we really don't need to, I don't think."

"Okay, let's get crackin' on these. Genevex needs something fast. Let's run a fourth of the samples down the fast track. Make some kidney cells, blood—we should be able to get some good results in a month and get those people off my back. I've got a few ideas on how to turn those cells totally around. Then the sky's the limit."

Dr. Lowell folded his arms across his chest. "Well, good enough, doctor! I'll separate the samples and get on the cultures right away."

The week after the trip to Williamsburg, Courtney phoned her parents. She told them she was involved with a doctor in a relationship that had real possibilities. She felt more cheerful than ever, and she had even bought a new, classier wardrobe. But the week had passed without a word from Travis.

The following Monday, she called and left a message at Travis's office. While she was at a regularly scheduled staff meeting, he returned her call and left a warm voice-mail message apologizing. She listened to it three times. "Hi Court, Travis here. Sorry I haven't been around. I've had a whole slew of scheduled surgeries. But pencil me in for lunch next week, after my regular meeting with Ben, okay? We'll catch up then. Bye."

The next Monday, Courtney still had not heard from Travis. She was downhearted but not terribly concerned. She called his office, but he didn't take the call or return it.

Two days later, she found out from Ben that Travis had asked to meet with him for breakfast at the hospital instead of at the Novacef office. It seems he had "so many charts" to work on. Travis sent the message through Ben that he'd have to cancel their lunch date because he had a surgery scheduled. So during the noon hour, she went out and bought a playful card. Inside, she wrote, "I had a wonderful time with you in

Williamsburg, and I'm looking forward to checking out that Thai restaurant you said we should go to. Don't make yourself so scarce." She added a smiley face and signed her name.

On the Wednesday before Thanksgiving, Janelle slid an apple pie into the oven then ran outside to retrieve the mail. Tossing aside the grocery store ads, the electricity bill, and three catalogs, she paused at an envelope personally addressed to her from Marnie.

Seating herself at the kitchen table, Janelle opened the card and read: "Dear Janelle. I don't know how to tell you this. I keep writing a note and throwing it away, but the fact is—no matter how I say it—it's just plain hard. I want you to know that Ben and I are expecting a baby. I know the news is probably difficult for you to hear right now, and I also know you will be happy for us. Yet, I didn't want you to have to respond in person. Call me when you feel like it."

Janelle cried, took a walk, and then picked up the phone.

On Thursday morning before the rest of the staff arrived, Carlos summoned Ramon into his office.

"Yes, sir?" Ramon stood in front of his desk.

Carlos gestured for him to sit down. "I have a task for Victor."

"Victor? Really?"

"Yes. I know you think he botched the last job—and he did. But he also did what he had to do. It was messy, but he left it as clean as possible. He exercised level-headed thinking in a crisis. At least we have no witnesses to trace it back to this office. He will pay for his mistake later, but for now we need him."

Ramon nodded. "I see."

"Which is why I wanted to talk with you."

Ramon said nothing but raised an eyebrow.

"There is one person who still makes me nervous," Carlos continued.

Again Ramon said nothing.

"Dr. Steven Harrison in Dallas. Victor is familiar with his facility. He's a loose end, and eventually we'll also deal with that—but not just yet."

"Yes, *señor*."

"I don't want Victor to act yet. I just want him to gather the necessary information."

Ramon nodded.

"The twins have stabilized. But if they get in trouble again, we may need the doctor's help. So it is too soon to do anything, uh . . . permanent."

"I will make the call."

Knowing Courtney had no family in the area, Ben and Marnie invited her to spend Thanksgiving with them and a group of singles from their church. Courtney dreaded the thought of making small talk all day with people she'd just met. Ben convinced her to come anyway. The turkey, dressing, and peach pie tasted great; it was fun to watch the football on the large screen TV; and the McKays' friends kept her smiling—if not laughing—all afternoon. The close-knit group somehow managed to make her feel included. What interested her most was that, before dinner, when they circled the table and named the person or thing for which they were most thankful, most of them said something about Jesus Christ.

She hurried home to check her messages, hoping Travis had called. But there was nothing. She sat in her living room staring at the wall, thinking of Ben and Marnie's life, full of family and friends, and wanting the same for herself.

At half past five on Friday, the day after Thanksgiving, Luc and Ben remained at the office tying up loose ends for the weekend. Luc wandered back and plopped down in one of Ben's chairs.

"Hey, congratulations, Papa! I didn't know you had it in ya. You must be feeling better'n I thought."

Ben nodded. "Thanks, Luc, and I've been wanting to thank you for covering for me while I was sick. I know you wore yourself out."

Luc nodded. "No problem. And thank *you* for helping with Janelle."

"How *is* she?"

Luc spoke quietly. "Really well, actually. The combination of meds, therapy, and learning to communicate better—I have to say, things are probably better than they've been in a long time. Again, thanks for your help. You've been a good friend to both of us."

Ben looked down at his desk momentarily. "Glad I could help some. But these things take time. Don't be in a big rush."

"It's been sort of humiliating, I have to confess," Luc told him.

Ben looked at him, waiting for an explanation.

"All the ER people who saw her come in, all the neighbors who saw the ambulance . . . There's really no good answer when folks ask what happened. And all the employees in the psych ward. Not a great witness."

"I wouldn't concern myself too much with that," Ben said quietly. "One thing I've learned. We worry so much about what people think of us. But the truth is, they really don't think about us much at all. Your reputation has the strength of many years. We're all fragile at times."

"Yeah, I guess you're right. Well, enough about me," Luc insisted. "How about you? How are ya?"

"Better."

"I'm really happy for you, Ben."

"Thanks, Luc," Ben spoke gently. "Kind of you to say so."

"Marnie feeling pretty well?"

"Yes, she's just fine."

Luc treaded carefully on what he knew to be sensitive territory. "I imagine you're a little nervous after what happened to Juli. . . ."

Ben shrugged, nodded slightly, and remained silent. It was clear from his response that he was done talking.

Luc got up. "Well, I'm glad to see you're getting your energy back."

Ben picked up a chart. "Thanks."

"Have a good weekend."

"You, too."

As Luc disappeared down the hall, Ben put down the chart, folded his hands, and closed his eyes.

Chapter Twenty-Eight

THAT NIGHT TRAVIS SURPRISED COURTNEY by showing up at her door around ten-thirty with flowers. He apologized profusely for his absence. Having brought a video, he suggested they could watch it together. So Courtney ordered out for some pizza, and they stayed up late.

The next morning, Travis had nearly finished dressing when Courtney woke up. She looked at the clock. *Six-thirty?* "Leaving so soon?" she asked, clearly disappointed.

"Got a seven-thirty case."

"On Saturday?"

"Yeah, sorry. It's a long story."

"When will I see you again?"

Travis shrugged. "Hard to say. 'Gentle Ben' has me under a load of charts, so I'm pretty swamped at the moment. But I'll call when things slow down." He gave her a swift kiss and disappeared out the door.

When she hadn't heard from him by the following Thursday, Courtney told herself to be patient. She had warmed her lunch in the microwave and was almost to the employees' break room when she overheard Darlene saying, ". . . so typical of Travis." She stopped outside the door to listen.

She heard Lisa groan. "Oh, that is so low."

"Yeah," Darlene said. "They went out for drinks last Friday. I guess Cindy's too new to know the scoop on Sudderth. She didn't know what he was like when she said she'd go with him."

"So what happened?" Lisa asked.

"She left him sitting right there in the restaurant after he made some rather aggressive suggestions."

"So I guess the Travster had to spend the night alone on Friday."

"Oh, poor baby," Lisa said sarcastically. Then, with an air of victory, she added, "Serves him right. That ought to put a damper on his love life."

"Didn't stop him for long," Darlene continued.

Courtney gasped silently, afraid Darlene somehow knew where Travis had spent Friday night.

"There's more?" Lisa muttered with a sigh of exasperation.

"Of course. The guy's unstoppable. This coming weekend he's apparently invited Ginny, Geman's new nurse, to spend the weekend with him in Annapolis."

"Is she going?"

"She hasn't said yet. But they're supposed to meet for lunch tomorrow in the doctors' lounge."

"That guy is a *disease*," Lisa said with disdain.

Courtney walked back to her office, slammed the door behind her, and threw her lunch in the trash.

The next afternoon, Travis and Ginny sat in the doctors' cafeteria, leaning intimately toward one another across the table. They didn't notice Courtney approaching them from across the room.

"Hello, Travis," she said coolly. She looked at Ginny and then glared back at him. "I see the snake has come out from under the rocks again."

"What? What do you mean?" Travis stood. "Uh, Courtney, I was just having a business lunch here with Ginny, Dr. Geman's nurse. Ginny, this is Dr. Courtney Pak."

Courtney nodded at Ginny then looked back at Travis. In a voice loud enough to be heard by everyone within twenty feet but calculated not to make a scene, she said, "Don't worry . . . I'm not planning to stay. I just wanted to see how you were doing. Is the Zovirax working for you? I hope everything clears up before you start dating again. Take care of yourself." She turned around and left.

Travis's face was as red as Mars. He looked at Ginny. "I don't have a clue what she's talking about."

"I know what Zovirax is, Travis. Remember, I work in a Gyn office."

Travis spoke, almost in a whisper, as the rest of the doctors in the café returned to their conversations. "Listen, Ginny, I don't have herpes. Never have—never!"

"That's really a private matter, Travis." Ginny's tone had turned from warm to cold. "None of my business." She stood to leave. "I have other commitments that will prevent me from joining you for the weekend, though I do appreciate the invitation." She excused herself and departed.

Ben, who had been sitting two tables over, stared after Courtney as she disappeared through the door. He looked down at his tray and shook his head.

Dr. Harrison raised his head from the microscope and muttered, "How did he *do* it? I've got most of his records. We've done everything exactly as he did."

He went back to his office, fired up his laptop, and opened a file to add a new entry:

4 December

I'm guessing Sullivan encrypted or destroyed the actual process of stimulating the enucleated egg once he implanted the nucleus from the other egg cell. Can't seem to get the same results he did. We can get the cells to grow forward—to mature—but not to replenish. Still dependent on his samples; can't seem to make our own. Can't get them to reverse to embryonic. Something is missing from these records of his, or something happened by accident. Will review the data of the initial harvest and nuclear transfer. But *something* is missing.

He sat a moment, thinking. *If Genevex knew about this, I would be so cooked.*

After work that afternoon Ben wandered into Courtney's office and found her sitting at her desk, writing. "Got a minute?" he asked.

She nodded and gestured for him to sit down.

"How are you?"

"All right." She folded her hands and looked at him. "What's up?"

"Just wanted to make sure you're okay."

"Why would I not be?" She tilted her head slightly and awaited a response.

"I'm here as your friend. Can we talk?"

"What about?"

"I was in the doctors' cafeteria today."

She froze. As the ramifications of his words had time to sink in, she lay her head on the desk.

"Care to talk about it? Or do you want me to leave it alone?"

With tears in her eyes, Courtney looked up at him. "Please, don't leave." Then considering further, she said, "Better shut the door."

When they were alone, Courtney took the tissue that Ben offered.

"Thanks."

"You sure you're okay?"

She shook her head and burst into tears. Ben sat quietly, waiting until she could speak.

"I *hate* crying at work," Courtney spit out the words with venom in her voice.

"I know what you mean."

"And I feel like such an idiot—such a fool. He tooled me around, and like a dummy I fell for it."

"Who tooled you around? Travis?"

Courtney nodded.

Ben winced. "Sorry."

"I've been an idiot."

"Sounds like you're being pretty hard on yourself."

"Oh, if you only knew, you'd probably fire me," Courtney sniffed. "And at this point, I hardly care. At least I'd never have to worry about running into *him* again."

Ben waited, so she filled the silence.

"I know you don't approve, but . . . he took me to Williamsburg for a weekend last month."

Ben remained quiet, a look of compassion on his face.

"And I really thought we had something special."

Ben nodded. "And after that he told you he had herpes?"

Courtney gulped. "No. I totally made that up to humiliate him."

Ben tried to suppress a smile, but Courtney didn't notice.

"The thing is, Ben, the revenge was a lot less sweet than I expected it to be." Her eyes met his. "It really hurts. I feel like

I stooped to his level—and that's pretty low. This whole thing has just been awful."

"Matters of the heart can be tough; they can cloud the judgment of even the best of us."

"Both Lisa and Darlene tried to warn me, but I had enough pride to think it was different with him and me. Now I can hardly face them. So I feel really isolated—in addition to being abandoned."

"I'm sorry."

"Thanks for not lecturing me."

"Why should I lecture you?"

"Because I blew it."

Ben shook his head. "You know, you can be forgiven."

Courtney stopped cold. "If you knew all I'd done, you wouldn't be saying that."

"I'll bet I would."

"I'll bet you wouldn't."

"Try me."

Courtney gulped again. "Okay—there's something I need to get off my chest anyway. The night we got back from our weekend together, he told me all about how he'd been a partner in research with your wife's late husband, and . . ."

"He what!?"

"You know, on that stem cell project."

Ben blinked twice and shook his head. To his knowledge, Sudderth had never even talked with Tim.

Courtney continued, "I told him about the cell line, and he told me it would really help if he could have a sample of it."

Ben stared in disbelief. *Why would Travis want anything to do with the cells?* "And you gave it to him?"

She nodded, and a single sob escaped her lips. "I'll have my resignation on your desk in the morning."

Ben leaned back in his chair and sighed. Then he shook his head.

"Courtney, I'm not going to fire you."

"You're not?" The surprise showed in her red eyes.

"No."

She swallowed hard and took a deep breath. "You're not angry with me?"

Ben rubbed his temples and stared at his knees. "I'm grieved." He looked up at her.

"Because I violated clinic policy—and your trust?"

He shook his head. Then, choosing his words deliberately, he spoke in a voice that was barely audible. "Not just that. Tim Sullivan's special cell line—the embryonic cells—produced two very sick little girls. You know that, right?"

Courtney nodded, and Ben continued.

"I know you think an embryo becomes a person when it can function, but I believe an embryo has personhood on the basis of 'being.'"

She looked confused.

"You know, as in 'human being.' The Bible describes each human being as an imagebearer of God. People have inherent dignity simply by being human—not because of anything we do. That means old people, the mentally limited, the comatose—and, yes, embryos—they're all fully human, even if they can't function in some way."

"So you feel like the research violated the innate dignity of the embryos?"

"Yes. Also, at the time Tim developed those embryos, he was breaking the law, although now it would be acceptable for most in the scientific community to do what Dr. Sullivan did. Yet, beyond that, we know there's human life in the cells because two girls living in Mexico came from that cell line. But we also know they're very sick, so we can't discount the enormous potential for illness that resides in those cells."

"I see," said Courtney quietly. "So what are you going to do?"

Ben looked deeply into her eyes, as though he could see her soul. "I'm going to forgive you."

"That's it? You're just going to forgive me?"

"Yes, and I promise never to mention it again." He got up to leave. "I'm so sorry for all you've been through." He extended his hand, and when she took it to shake it, he put his other one on top of hers for a moment.

"Are you going to tell Luc?"

"Yes, I think I need to. But he will agree with my decision."

"How do you know?"

"Trust me. I know."

In disbelief, Courtney said, "So you're not even going to sue me for stealing your biological material?"

He shook his head.

"You're not going to make me pay?"

"Somebody already did, Courtney. Two thousand years ago."

Luc slipped into bed late, assuming Janelle had already fallen asleep. He had stayed up reading journals and considering what Ben had told him about Courtney. He started to plant a cold foot on Janelle's leg, just to watch her jump, but she was too quick. She grabbed it when it got within an inch of her.

"Oh no you don't!" she said playfully.

"Jan! You're awake!"

"Yeah, I waited up for you."

"Something in particular you need?"

"Actually, yes. I resented that you weren't here, but then I figured I should talk to you about it instead of going to sleep upset."

Luc reacted defensively. "I was doing some work."

Janelle spoke gently. "I wanted to connect, but I realized I shouldn't expect you to read my mind."

"What's *on* your mind?"

"Nothing in particular. I just wanted to know about your day."

Luc folded his hands behind his head, relaxed, and considered a moment. "Ben told me something troubling, but also intriguing." He told her about what had happened with Courtney.

"The cells are the property of the clinic, right?" Janelle was trying to understand.

"Right, if you can describe life as property."

"So, technically speaking, they belonged to you and Ben? And there's no agency you have to report her to?"

"Right. It's legal to do research on embryonic stem cells now," he explained. "So it's not like it was an illegal substance. Legally speaking, she stole a biological substance from Ben and me, so it was up to us to decide what to do."

"What were the options?"

"Sue her, fire her, or forgive her."

"Sue her? Not your style—or Ben's either."

"Not even close."

Janelle sat up, hugging her knees pensively as she thought. "Luc?"

"Yeah?"

"Don't you think it's sad—considering all we've been through—how little the world values children before they're born? Like size really matters. I've been thinking a lot about that lately. It's a good thing God doesn't have that attitude about Earth—considering it's just a tiny blue dot in relation to the rest of the universe."

Marnie emerged from the bathroom, decked out for the newswire service's Christmas party at the Omni Shoreham Hotel. When Ben saw her, he uttered a low wolf whistle. He came over and whispered a friendly little growl in her ear. She responded by purring. They exchanged an affectionate kiss then started downstairs.

Will had agreed to entertain Emily for the night. She lay sprawled on the floor in the den ready to play Uno with him. When Ben and Marnie came down, she jumped up and smothered them with hugs and kisses, then insisted that she would go with them. They had to convince her that she would have more fun at home. On their way out, Ben looked at Marnie. "What time do you think we'll be home, hon?"

Marnie shrugged.

Ben looked at Will. "Maybe around eleven."

Marnie winked at her dad.

The couple drove through an elegant D.C. neighborhood to the old-world-style Washington landmark. The valet took their car, and they stepped into a winter wonderland of decorations. The wire service marketing department obviously had a sizable budget for this party.

Marnie introduced Ben to her colleagues, some of whom he had met at the wedding. But that day had been such a blur, he didn't remember them. Ben did know a few people, though, former patients who came over to say hello and meet his new wife. After dining on beef tips and chocolate cheesecake, he and Marnie danced to Top Forty tunes, played by a live band.

More than once they overheard people saying something behind their backs about "newlyweds."

Toward the end of the evening, Ben asked Marnie what time she wanted to head home. She smiled a sly grin and reached in her purse. Holding up a room card, she told him, "Any time. Home is upstairs tonight."

Ben's eyes widened. "If you'd told me that earlier, I'd have insisted we leave sooner!"

Marnie's eyes danced. "Not to worry. The night is young, and so are we."

As they made their way up to the suite, Ben asked, "When did you check in?"

"I called and made reservations a few days ago. Then when you thought I went to the rest room, I picked up the room card."

Ben laughed and shook his head. "Pretty sneaky—and I, for one, like it!"

Chapter Twenty-Nine

COURTNEY LAY IN BED, STARING UP THROUGH her skylight at the stars. She had hardly slept the previous night, and she figured this one would probably drag by, too. She couldn't stop thinking about the wonderful weekend with Travis, the horrible revelation, and the humiliation she felt around the women in the office. But even more than that, she kept coming back to what Ben said about the embryos being fully human. She had heard such sentiments expressed before, but never by anyone with Ben's credentials. And what she found still more amazing was that she still had a job. For as long as she could remember, no one had ever offered her forgiveness—especially not before she asked for it. *I need to be like that. Travis made me angry, and I took revenge; I violated Ben's trust, and he forgave me. We're not the same. . . .*

She wondered what Ben meant about someone paying for it two thousand years ago. She figured it must have something to do with his Christian belief in Jesus.

I'll have to ask him about that.

Marnie opened one eye, feeling disoriented until she saw the large four-poster bed. The drawn shades made the room quite dark, though the clock read eight o'clock. Then she remembered the wonderful night she had just shared with her husband. She turned over to look at him. As he lay sleeping, she offered thanks to God. Ben's health and stamina had improved, their child was growing in her womb, and she felt a love so intense she could hardly bear it at times. Her life had such sweetness, and she prayed it would never end.

Not wanting to disturb Ben, she quietly slid out of bed, pulled the shades open a bit, and slipped into the elegant bathroom. Then she noticed a few small blood spots on her night gown. She checked herself and noticed a little more blood— not a lot. She sat staring and burst into tears. *No cramping, no clots.* She mentally rehearsed the questions she'd heard Ben ask anxious mothers-to-be over the telephone.

In the quiet of the morning, she whispered a prayer for her baby. Then she slipped back into bed and gently shook Ben until he awakened.

"Ummm," Ben responded as he roused. "Good morning, Marnie." He reached over to pull her close.

"Honey, I'm bleeding . . . just a little."

Ben looked at her moist eyes and red nose. "What?" He sat upright, now fully awake. "How much?"

"Just a bit, but I'm scared."

Ben pulled her close and held her. "Cramping at all?" he asked softly, soothing her with his voice yet obviously anxious about her answer.

"No. Just some spots and fresh blood on the toilet tissue."

"Okay. It's probably nothing serious. Perhaps we were a bit 'enthusiastic' with romance last night. Sorry."

"Oh, Ben." She held tightly to him. "Tell me it's gonna be all right."

He put his finger under her chin and raised her face to look into her eyes. "I love you, honey." He stroked her hair. "We'll be fine. I'll give Dr. Dale a call, and we can see what he wants to do, though you know the deal—off your feet, no lifting, no more 'hot dates' with me, and a sono."

"Can we do a sono today?" Marnie pleaded.

"If he can't get to it, we can . . . uh . . . swing by the office." She knew by the way Ben hesitated that, as much as he wanted to know, he didn't want to be the one to make the diagnosis if a miscarriage was inevitable.

"Mommy, we're here!" Emily came bounding into Marnie's bedroom and jumped up on her bed to give her a hug.

"'Nelle, you're awesome. Thanks for picking up Emily from school."

Janelle sat on the edge of Marnie's bed. "How are ya?"

"Bored! Bed rest is driving me nuts."

"Sorry."

"Hey, but compared to what you've been through, I'm grateful."

Janelle smiled and nodded. "You gave us all a good scare. Please take care of yourself."

"I will, don't worry. Where are the boys?"

"Tearing up your backyard."

Emily interrupted their conversation. "Mommy, can I go out and play with them in the snow?"

"Sure, honey, but be sure to bundle up."

Emily tore out of the room.

"So what did Dr. Dale say?"

"He was great. He met us at the office on a Saturday. Said he was gonna be there to make rounds anyway."

"That was nice of him."

"Yeah, it was. He did a sono, and the baby looked fine and

active. We're not sure where the blood came from; I haven't had any more. It was way too early to be sure on the sono. Could have been from the placenta or perhaps a cervical bleed from 'romantic activity.'"

With a dramatic gesture, Janelle held the back of her hand to her forehead and, in her best Cleopatra voice, said, "Alas! No more swinging from chandeliers for the newlyweds."

Marnie feigned a disappointed expression. "We have to stop doing *that*?"

Janelle was the first to break down and smile. "Hey, let me throw together a spaghetti dinner for y'all, and then I'll get out of your hair."

"You don't have to do that."

"Of course I don't have to, . . . but I want to." Janelle jumped up and headed for the kitchen.

"Janelle."

She turned around. "What?"

"You okay with this? You lost your baby, and you're taking care of a pregnant woman."

Janelle looked at the floor. "I know the terror you felt; I wouldn't wish it on anyone. And somehow, it helps me to help you." She looked up and added, "Besides, a wise woman once told me there's not much point in comparing. Pain is pain."

"I believe that's called giving away grace, Janelle, and I'm deeply grateful."

"No problem," Janelle turned to leave again. She walked off adding lightly, "You just take care of yourself, or you'll hear it from me!"

Most of the employees at Novacef had gathered around the table in the break room. One of the drug reps had again sprung for a "Merry Christmas" lunch of Chinese food. Ben and

Courtney arrived late, delayed by a complicated *in vitro* fertilization case. One by one, people drifted back to work, until Ben and Courtney had the room to themselves as they finished their sweet-and-sour chicken.

"That sure was a mess, once you got inside today, wasn't it?" Courtney said with a sigh.

Ben nodded. "I don't like surprises like that."

"The cycle's not looking too good for her, is it?"

"Not great, but I've seen tougher ones where pregnancy resulted."

"Speaking of pregnant," said Courtney, "how's your wife feeling?"

"She'll probably be back on her feet tomorrow. Thanks for asking."

Courtney fell silent. She looked down at her food and finally spoke again. "Ben?"

"Yeah?" He looked at her, seeing that something was on her mind.

"Can I ask you something?"

"Anything. Shoot."

"Remember when we talked, and I asked you why you weren't making me 'pay.'"

Ben nodded.

"You said something I didn't quite understand."

"What's that?"

"You said someone already did . . . two thousand years ago. Shall I assume you were referring to Jesus?"

"Uh-huh."

"Well, I've never read the Bible, so . . . I keep wondering how a man who lived two thousand years ago could have anything to do with paying for what I did."

"Good question, Courtney—really good."

She looked at him, expecting an answer.

"How much do you know about what happened to Jesus?"

"I know he was executed, and . . . um . . . it's said that he rose from the dead."

"So you already know quite a lot."

"Yes?"

"Sure, it's a good start. I'd like to tell you what I believe and show you what a difference that one life and death makes. Since you're not familiar with the Bible, I'll just tell you the story. But I believe that God reveals himself in the Bible. Everything I explain to you can be found there. Later, if you want, I can show you."

"Fair enough," Courtney said.

Ben continued. "I believe that there is a God—an all-powerful, all-knowing personal being who created everything, humans included. And he not only created us, but he cares deeply about us."

"Really? You reject evolution?" Courtney was puzzled, ready to dismiss Ben's logic at the outset.

"Not entirely," Ben replied. "I'm comfortable with 'micro-evolution'—you know—birds evolving into different sizes and shapes of birds. But the human creation?" He shook his head. "We're made in the image of God."

"Hmmm." Courtney listened, still sizing up Ben, face to face. She was sure she had never met a doctor who didn't believe fully in evolution.

"God made us and gave us the ability to make choices. We can choose good or evil. And from the first couple on, humans have chosen badly. God calls those bad choices sin. And sin causes a distance, a separation from God, who is perfect and pure."

Courtney nodded for him to go on.

"So now there's a problem between God and every individual, because a perfectly pure God can't be in the presence of sin."

"I'm with you so far."

"And the penalty for sin is death," Ben continued.

"Everybody dies," she answered with candor.

"True. You mean physical death—and you're correct. We're all headin' that way. But, more importantly, spiritual death is separation of the soul from God."

"Sounds depressing."

"Well, that's the bad news. The good news is that God is also loving. So he came up with a solution that would satisfy the tension between his justice and his love."

Courtney leaned forward. "Is that where Jesus comes in?"

Ben nodded.

"How so?"

"God became a man."

Courtney looked skeptical.

"And he willingly gave his life to satisfy the justice of God."

"What? A willing sacrifice? I thought his own people killed him."

"True, a lot of people were responsible for the act of his death. But he willingly allowed himself to be put to death by people who didn't understand. And he loved and forgave even them," Ben said.

"Interesting."

"Ever heard of John three-sixteen?"

"Yes?"

"Do you know what it says?"

Courtney looked confused. "It can talk?"

"Hmmm, I guess I'm not making much sense here. John, three-sixteen is a verse in the Bible."

"Wait. You mean like 'John three-colon-sixteen'—written on banners at ball games, and I once saw it written on the side of a barn in Pennsylvania."

"That's the one."

"All this time I thought it was an ad for a hair care product or something, like Alberto VO-5."

"Sorry." Ben smiled kindly.

Courtney blushed. "I guess I should've taken Comparative Religions as an elective instead of Biology for Everyday Living!"

"Well, how would you know? Anyway, John three-sixteen says that God loved the world so much that he gave his only son—that anyone who believes in him will not perish but have eternal life."

"So I have to *believe* it."

Ben nodded.

"Well, frankly, I think it's *hard* to believe. Sounds rather simplistic—too good to be true. But anyway, if I understand the point you're making, you believe Jesus paid for your mistakes two thousand years ago . . . and somehow that makes you able to overlook what I did to *you*?"

"Something like that."

"Interesting. Then in your ideal world, no one who wrongs you ever gets punished?"

"It's not exactly like that. But I don't feel like I have to take revenge when somebody does something wrong to me, because I've made my share of 'mistakes,' and someone else paid the big debt for me."

Courtney shook her head. "I still don't get that."

"Jesus told a lot of stories," Ben said. "And he tells one story about two guys who owe a lot of money. The first guy owes someone a boatload—like millions. He begs for the debt to be forgiven, and it is—the entire debt is forgiven by the man to whom he owes it."

Courtney nodded. "That would be lovely. Like the charge card company telling me I don't have to pay what I owe . . . and then some."

"Right. But the same man who has received so much grace turns around and tells someone who owes him a few bucks to 'Pay up.' In fact, he has the debtor thrown in jail, even though the man begs for the debt to be forgiven."

Courtney was incensed. "After what he has been forgiven?"

"Precisely my point, Court. I've been forgiven much. How can I demand that you resign when you've expressed your remorse?"

Courtney shook her head. After pausing, she said, "I cannot say I understand it, but I do appreciate being on the receiving end of forgiveness. And I'm pretty sure I wouldn't do so well on the giving end—dealing with being wronged. I still want to punch Travis."

Ben nodded. "I'm guessing you'd probably have to wait in line."

Marnie, Ben, and Emily sat at the dining room table finishing up a pot of chili. Ben pushed himself away from the table and asked, "Got anything for my sweet tooth?"

"I thought we might make a dessert run a little later," Marnie said.

"Yippee!" Emily exclaimed. "Can we go now?"

Marnie shook her head. "I'm stuffed. Let's wait a few hours."

Emily's face fell. "Oh, all right," she pouted. "Then can I go play on my computer?"

"Sure, honey."

Emily skipped off, and Marnie began to clear the table.

"Great to see you back on your feet," Ben told her. "How are you feeling, sweetheart?"

"Couldn't be better." She looked at him and was touched by the love she saw in his eyes. "The terror of it all hasn't totally subsided, but physically I feel fine."

"Good."

"Tell me about your day," she said.

"Let's go into the living room, where it's more comfortable."

Marnie settled back beside Ben on the love seat. He reached

down, pulled up her feet, and began to massage them as he talked.

"I've been thinking about something," he told her. "And it troubles me."

"What's that?"

"Remember back about the time we went to Mexico—did I tell you about Travis Sudderth?"

"That he got shipped off to Atlanta for detox?"

"Right."

"And then later, you told me he got off easy and was back."

"Right again. Well, I had an interesting conversation with Courtney recently."

"Yeah?"

"She gave him some of Tim's special cell line."

"What? Why?" Marnie was alarmed.

"Apparently Sudderth told her he was Tim's research partner."

Marnie sat up straight. "Either Tim lived even more of a secret life than I knew, or Sudderth lied to her!"

"Sudderth? Lying? No!" Ben said, his tone dripping with sarcasm.

"But why would he want the cells?"

"Precisely what I'd like to know. Harrison is the only other person besides us—to my knowledge—who knows about the cell line. And we know he wants them. So maybe after we refused, he made a deal with Sudds."

"You think so?"

"I don't know. I mean, what would be in it for Sudds? What could have been the connection?"

"Good question." Marnie wore a thoughtful expression. "Good thing you married well."

Ben looked puzzled. "What do you mean?"

"Let me do some investigative reporting. I still have some fine connections myself."

Ben raised his eyebrows. "What are you going to do?"

"I could tell you," she said. Her eyes sparkled, then narrowed, "but then I'd have to kill you."

Chapter Thirty

"CHRIS WINSTON ON LINE TWO," Lisa said to Luc as he walked past her desk, holding a chart. "Want me to take a message or have him hold?"

Luc picked up his step. "I'll take it now, thanks." He walked back to his office, where he shut the door and punched line two. "Hello there!"

"Hey, Luc," Chris said.

"How goes everything in the law world?"

"Pretty well. I'm calling with good news."

"Yeah?"

"I checked out Tim Sullivan's liability policy. And it'll probably cover the difference between your policy limits and what Carlos Rivera is demanding."

"That *is* good news."

"It's a decent malpractice policy and, as you know, the good ones let the docs participate in the settlement discussions within the limits of the policy. Tim was negligent and doing illegal work, so it would cost the insurer more to defend the policy than to pay what you recommend for them to settle it. But having said all that, I have to tell you that I still don't advise you to pay it all. Rivera has been totally bullheaded about negotiating."

"Chris, if there's any way we can do it, I want to try to give him what he's asking."

"You're too generous."

"The man has two sick children—children who require expensive care—and it's not his fault. It's the clinic's."

"A clinic that's no longer in existence."

"Technically, perhaps. But it's the right thing to do if there's any way."

"All right, I figured you'd say that. I'll look into it. Turns out Tim had his own policy—an 'occurrence' not a 'claims made'—as a supplement to the group policy, so we may be able to attach some of the settlement to him."

"Great. This feels like the suit that will never go away, and I'm ready to be done with it," Luc insisted.

"I'm sure you are. I just hate to give in on everything."

"You aren't. I am."

❦

At the noon hour, Ben called home to check on Marnie. "Hi, sweetie. How are you feeling today?"

"I'm great. Don't worry . . . I'm taking it easy. Been sitting at my computer all morning surfing the Net and making a few phone calls."

"Miss me much?"

"Totally. And guess what?"

"What?"

"I made an interesting discovery."

"What's that?"

"What do you know about where Steven Harrison works?"

"Um, last I knew he was supervising special research under the surgeon general's direction."

"Doing government work, right?"

"Right," Ben agreed.

"Wrong."

"Wrong?"

"He got fired a week after Sudds returned to D.C."

"So, where is he now?"

"Running a research facility for Genevex . . . in Dallas."

"Fascinating."

"The same facility where you and I met with Tim in Dallas."

"No way!"

"Genevex bought Tim's old research facility for Harrison. The whole complex! And bet you can't guess what he's doing."

"Bet I can . . ."

"Yeah, you probably can." Marnie said. "On the Genevex web page, they're proudly boasting the accomplishments of their new lead researcher."

"No way!"

"Way! And there's more."

"You're amazing."

"I try," Marnie said, clearly enjoying herself.

"So tell me . . ."

"Guess who signed out Sudds at the Atlanta clinic?"

"Who?"

"Harrison's former assistant—probably just a coincidence."

"Sure."

Marnie's tone changed. "So, Harrison is going to make millions using Tim's research, and we can't bust him. He got the samples legally."

"Yes, but they were developed illegally."

"But there's nothing we can do."

"It would appear that way—right. At least for the moment."

"That's really rotten."

"Yes, it is. I'm sorry, Marnie." Ben felt the pain in her voice. "I never would've dreamed that Courtney's situation would wind up being painful for *you*."

"First it was the lawsuit, then Tim's disappearance, then the cells, now the cells again. Do you think the break-in and Brock's death could be connected with Harrison in any way?"

"Great question."

Courtney spent New Year's day with Ben and Marnie, again eating too much and watching football. This time, she watched their friends closely, wondering how sharp, professional people could have such strange beliefs. That night, she again lay staring at her skylight, only this time she focused on the stars. *I wonder if someone really did create them?*

It seemed impossible. And Ben McKay seemed naïve to believe all that supernatural stuff. *But he's a good person—a man of integrity; so God, if you're there, show me the way. I don't know what to think, and I'm so lonely. Something seems to be missing.*

In late January Dr. Harrison emerged from lunch at the Enclave with a few colleagues. He slid into his car and started to turn the key, then he froze. *Strange. It smells faintly of cigarettes in here.*

He looked around inside the car but found nothing out of place.

Later that week, Dr. Lowell sat in Dr. Harrison's plush office preparing to make his report.

"Can I make you a drink?" Harrison asked, pouring one for himself.

"No, thanks." Dr. Lowell waved off the suggestion. "I'm fine."

Harrison walked over and slid behind his desk. "So, talk to me. Where are we?"

"Looking great."

"Specifically?"

Lowell handed him a written report and launched into his findings. "We're working on several cell lines, as you suggested. Marrow, red cells, white cells, lymphatic cells, and kidney cultures."

"Good, good." Harrison was pleased. "How's it going?"

"We've been successful taking the cells to maturity. They're all growing well, though the renal ones seem to be a bit slower than the rest."

Harrison nodded. "We expected that, didn't we?"

"Yes."

"But we have a clear advantage."

"What's that, sir?" Lowell asked.

Harrison looked at him. "While other companies work with normal stem cells and fight the bureaucracy, we're well on our way. The LG cells do a particularly good job of mimicking the cells we culture them with, right?"

"Ah, I see what you mean. Yes, definitely."

"And we want to be the *first* to offer an effective treatment for bone marrow replacement for the late-stage cancers. We'll make our mark there," Harrison insisted.

"Right. And while other companies are each working on a specific area, we can diversify. We have a shortcut with your special cells, sir. They're clearly a unique, amazing culture," Lowell said. "Your LG cell cultures seem to be able to latch on and grow without the rejection phenomena on our test subjects, so I think we're almost ready to go public."

"Excellent. I expected to be the first with the human trials. Let's call a press conference and announce our success. Perhaps we should rename the culture line H cells."

Lowell smiled but hesitated. "Genevex has not done well

with human studies in the past. Our work with viral vectors seems to be stonewalled. So the government will really watch us."

"That's why Genevex hired me," Harrison said with a grin. "I have government connections. If we have a good product, we should be fine. And I'm counting on you."

Lowell smiled. "Thank you, sir. I'll do my best. This is really an honor—really thrilling stuff."

"One more question."

"What's that?"

"Now that we know the cells can make a nice copy of whatever they're placed with, let's see if we don't have better luck this time getting them to go totipotential—to reproduce themselves."

"I'll see what I can do."

Victor had spent the day tailing Dr. Harrison. Now he crushed a cigarette butt with his heel and got into his rental car. Within moments he had discreetly slid onto McKinney Avenue, keeping a safe distance. A few minutes later, he'd figured it out. *Ah . . . eating at the French Room again tonight. I predicted correctly! Six days a week on the research floor. Sleeps late Saturday. Likes expensive restaurants, usually the French Room or the Mansion. Lives alone on Beverly Drive. Likes hard liquor but doesn't do illegal substances. No steady girlfriend, but a few favorite dates. No new discoveries here tonight. I'm headed home.*

Victor yawned and made his way back to his Dallas hotel.

"Hold still!" Leigh Rivera held up a camera and clicked. "Perfect! Just perfect! Okay, I'm done. You can eat the cookies now!"

Lily and Gaby, now two years old, were dressed in red velvet. The twins grabbed red, heart-shaped cookies off the table and stuffed them in their mouths.

"Wait!" Carlos insisted. "Let me take a photo of you with them." He patted Leigh's stomach. "You are beginning to look like you might have a baby in there. And you are the picture of beauty today."

Leigh smiled at her husband. She wiped the girls' faces and persuaded them to stand still.

Afterward, Gaby spotted two brightly wrapped presents her father had placed on the table, and she toddled over to explore more closely.

"Go ahead," her father told her. "That one is for you."

Lily, not wanting to miss out on the action, walked over and tried to take the box from her sister.

"No, no, *niña!*" her father insisted. "There is one for you, too." He pointed to the other package. Then he nodded eagerly. "You may open them now if you wish."

The girls tore the wrapping and found stuffed white rabbits inside.

"Soft, Mommy." Lily was the first to speak. She had a huge toothy grin.

Gaby plopped down and began to play with hers, twisting its ears. Carlos and Leigh sat down in the two rocking chairs and drank in the scene of their two little blonde wonders. "It is good to have them well," Carlos said.

Leigh nodded. "Yes," she whispered. "Very good . . . the best present I could receive on the *Día del amor y la amistad*— to me, Valentine's Day.

"They are normal, yes?" he asked his wife.

Gaby, having been quickly distracted, climbed into her mother's lap. Leigh shrugged. "They're lagging behind a little in development, small for being two years old. And they should be talking more, but that will come in time. They've been very sick."

Again, not wanting to be outdone by her sister, Lily held out her arms to be picked up by her father.

Ramon appeared in the door of the nursery. "*Señor*, telephone," he told Carlos.

"Later, Ramon. Take a message."

"Yes, sir, but it is your attorney saying he has good news."

Carlos waved him off. "It can wait. I will call him back. I am too busy enjoying other good news." He kissed his daughter's head, then tousled her hair.

Two weeks later, Carlos Rivera logged on to his e-mail account. He had flagged "Genevex" and "Steven Harrison" as options for his search engine to locate whenever they appeared in the news. He smiled when he saw that today his list included a Genevex press release. He read it with interest.

Researchers Close in on Stem Cell Breakthrough

Dallas, February 28—Genevex, Inc., today announced a key breakthrough in human studies with stem cell research.

The company's scientists have been able to produce nerve, renal, and blood cells in the laboratory by using stem cells drawn from both bone marrow and aborted fetuses.

Both Carlos in Mexico and Marnie in Virginia leaned slightly closer to their monitors.

The director of the Dallas operation, Dr. Steven Harrison said that the company had been developing cell lines for months, but that it had only recently begun human trials. While other researchers have tried marrow treatments with moderate success, Harrison's team has already seen very encouraging human results.

The research was conducted at the Genevex research facility in Dallas, Texas, and a complete account of the results appeared Monday in the *Journal of Stem Cell Research*, based in Los Angeles.

"It's really beautiful," Dr. Jason Lowell, the scientist supervising the human studies, told *The New York Times*. "I see this as a truly significant step along the way toward developing new technologies for the treatment of major diseases."

Judith Irvin of Valane University's medical school, co-author of the research, said "Stem cells are found primarily in the bone marrow and can differentiate into each specific cell type, defining every organ in the body. With Dr. Harrison's approach, they can be taken from the patient under treatment, eliminating the concern about adding tissue the immune system might attack."

By the end of the day, Carlos noted that Genevex stock had climbed several points.

Marnie also saw the stock fluctuation and seethed.

Chapter Thirty-One

IN EARLY MARCH, EMILY ROSE EARLY AND padded into Ben and Marnie's bedroom. "Mommy, can I get in bed with you?"

Marnie moaned. "What are you doing up so early, honey?" She opened one eye to read the clock. *Seven-fifteen. Whoa! I stayed up too late.*

Emily's whisper was louder than her normal speaking voice. "You said we're going to make cookies today, remember?"

"Yeah, but not before the sun comes up." Marnie scooted closer to Ben, who was still sleeping soundly. She patted the bed next to her, and Emily climbed up. They all lay together for a few minutes while Marnie dozed off. Emily's loud whisper once again awoke Marnie. "Mama, can I watch a Sesame Street video downstairs?"

"Uh-huh." Marnie said sleepily.

Emily bounded off, and Marnie lay resting, when she felt something wet. *Gross! Emily wet the bed! She hasn't done that in two years.*

Marnie fumbled in the dim light from the window to find a clean nightgown. Then she went into the bathroom to change and quietly shut the door. Turning on the light, she gasped. Bright red blood stained her gown and trickled down her legs. *Emily didn't wet the bed—it's my blood!* "Ben!" she shrieked.

"What?" He awakened with a start.

"Ben! Help me!"

Ben jumped out of bed, banging his shin on the corner. He limped to the bathroom, and asked, "What is it?"

Tears poured down Marnie's face. "Oh, Ben, I'm bleeding! I'm losing our *baby!*"

"Hang on, sweetheart." Ben soothed Marnie with his voice. "You know pregnant women bleed all the time. Let's see." He examined his wife. "No, that's not so much." He carefully picked her up, carried her to his side of the bed, and helped her lie down. As he flipped on the light, he noticed the blood stain on her side of the king-size sheet. "We've got lots of tricks we can use." Ben felt the swollen abdominal fundus with his skilled hands "I don't feel any tenderness, tightness, or contraction. Probably just a placental problem. Though the cervix can bleed like that, too."

"I'll bet you say that to comfort all the women." Marnie forced a smile, but Ben remained focused.

He laid his ear against Marnie's tummy and listened. "We're okay; I can hear the heartbeat—sounds terrific." Just as he finished saying the word, the baby fired off a hearty kick. "Wow!" Ben smiled.

"I felt that. That's good, isn't it?" Marnie implored.

"Yeah, it's real good."

He sat up and looked at her. "What did you do yesterday? Weren't you out walking around a lot? Sometimes that stirs up a little bleeding."

Marnie nodded.

"Then let me call Dr. Dale and tell him what's up. We can meet him down in L&D; we need another sono to check out the baby and the placenta. Then maybe do an exam. We'll see, but I'll bet the baby's fine." Ben wiped her tears and kissed her cheek.

Marnie and Ben sped off to the hospital, leaving Emily with Will. Ben called L&D from his car phone to let them know they were coming. By the time they got there, Marnie's bleeding had slowed to a trickle. Before long she was lying on the table in L&D with monitors strapped on, awaiting a sonogram. Ben sat at her side, stroking her arm.

"Monitor shows no contractions, good fetal heartbeat with accelerations," he told her.

"Ben, why is the heart rate speeding up and then slowing down?" Marnie asked, her voice revealing her nervousness.

"We call that variability. It's a good sign. Whatever is going on, the baby doesn't seem to know about it! Little McKay is looking good."

The nurse wheeled in the sono equipment, and Dr. Dale followed shortly after that. When he entered, the nurse told him, "Minimal active bleeding, a few small old clots, no uterine tenderness or contractions, good fetal activity."

"Great," he responded. "So Marnie—just couldn't keep it simple, could you?"

He grinned at her.

Marnie forced a smile through her fear. She had been slowly gaining confidence because of the words and behavior of the L&D team. Ben had helped, but she also knew he could sound totally calm in the middle of a tornado.

"Let's take a look with the sono," Dr. Dale told them. "See what we can see. . . . Want to know the gender? We might be able to tell at this stage."

"Not really," Marnie said. "But I know Ben will be able to tell, and there's no way *he's* going to know while I'm left in the dark!"

"That's the spirit!" Ben laughed.

Dr. Dale squirted the warm sono gel onto Marnie's stomach

and began scanning. He studied the monitor. "You've got an active baby here! Transverse, good fluid, good variability. A real champ."

Marnie bit her lip as she and Ben peered at the ultrasound screen.

Dr. Dale turned to Ben with a grin. "Do you want to tell your wife or shall I?"

Ben looked at Marnie and burst out with, "It's a boy—a son!" He leaned down and kissed her. "Way to go!"

Dr. Dale smiled and continued. "There's no problem with the baby. Let's focus in on the placenta." He moved the probe gently. "Anterior . . . kinda low . . . yep, that's it . . . we've got a low-lying placenta. Maybe a partial previa. That's why he's transverse . . . can't get into the pelvis."

"Is that serious?" Marnie wanted to know.

"Not usually," Dr. Dale told her. "Most often when we find them at this stage, a little bleeding 'announces' to us to be careful. But as the uterus grows, the place where the placenta is attached kind of grows up out of the pelvis. The placenta doesn't 'migrate,' but the spot where it's attached grows along with the rest of the uterus and gets it up out of the way."

"So, why is it bleeding?"

"Probably a little bit of the placenta is close to the internal opening of the cervix. So with lifting, exercise, or intercourse, you get a little bleeding. It's pretty common. We just need to keep a close eye on things with the sono."

"And avoid the 'aforementioned'?" Marnie asked.

"Yep, afraid so. Any 'romantic nights' will have to stop for a bit. And no exercise. I'll keep you in the hospital for a day or two, but I expect the bleeding to stop right away."

Ben smiled down at her. "But . . . we're having a baby boy. I couldn't be happier!"

By early April temperatures had climbed to over one hundred degrees during the day in Culiacán. But while the sun beat down during the day, the nights were pleasant, and Leigh had been spending the evenings rocking her girls on the porch swing. Even though the Rivera ranch house had air conditioning, Leigh cooled it by letting in the fresh air at night.

Beneath curtains that swayed in the breeze, Leigh lay next to Carlos, dreaming of home in Grass Valley, California. Suddenly she heard a voice.

"*Señora?*"

Leigh awoke with a start. "Ophelia?"

"*Sí.* I am sorry to wake you in the middle of the night, *señora.*"

Leigh squinted to read the digital clock. *Two forty-three.*

"Ophelia! What is it?"

"Please come."

Leigh tore out of bed. "What is it? The girls?" Her voice revealed her panic.

"Only Gabrielle."

Carlos moaned and turned over.

Leigh grabbed Ophelia and walked her briskly out of the bedroom and down the hall to the nursery.

"I took her temperature—it was over one hundred degrees," the children's nurse told her.

Leigh reached down and felt Liliana's forehead, but Ophelia assured her, "That one is fine. No problem."

Leigh nodded.

"It is Gaby . . ."

Leigh laid the back of her hand gently on the face of her other sleeping child. "Yes, she feels too warm."

"Shall I call the doctor, *señora?*"

"Thank you," Leigh nodded, tears forming in her eyes. She hoped it was just a common cold or something, but she also feared the worst.

After a few moments, Leigh heard Ophelia say, "We will meet you there soon."

Not again! They were doing so well!

After Ophelia hung up, she explained to Leigh that the doctor was taking no chances and recommended that they come to the hospital for a blood count—with both girls.

Leigh nodded. "I suspect whatever is wrong with Gaby will soon be wrong with Lily. Perhaps we can prevent things from getting worse for her. Please get them ready while I dress and explain to my husband."

Much to Leigh's surprise, Carlos wanted to come, too.

"But you'll be exhausted at work tomorrow," she told him.

"Leigh, you are seven months pregnant with my child. I will not allow you to go to the hospital alone at three in the morning in your condition."

"Thank you." Leigh let out a little sob and darted into the bathroom.

Three days later, both Gaby and Lily lay in ICU at Culiacán General Hospital. Leigh and Carlos waited in the nearby conference room to meet with their physician. Before long the doctor briskly entered. He set the girls' files on the table, folded his hands, and stared down at his fingers.

"What can you tell us, doctor?" Carlos asked, the stress showing in his voice.

The physician slowly shook his head. "I am sorry," he said. He glanced up at them, then looked down again. "The leukemia has returned. And we have nearly exhausted all of our options. As a last resort, we might have considered Mrs. Rivera as a bone marrow donor again, but she is thirty weeks pregnant. If we had a sibling from whom we could get bone marrow—but it is just a little too early to deliver Mrs. Rivera. I am very sorry. We are still searching for a suitable donor but, as in the past, we have had no successful matches so far."

After he left, Leigh and Carlos went to look at the girls for a moment. They lay in full isolation, with a long list of medical precautions being exercised. The medical staff had instructed Leigh and Carlos not to hold their children. Gaby was asleep, but Lily lay moaning and crying out, "Mama, Mama."

The Riveras stepped back out into the hallway, and Leigh buried her face in her husband's chest. Then she collapsed in his arms in a sobbing torrent.

Everyone who passed by did so solemnly.

When morning came, Carlos slipped into the hospital conference room by himself and punched in some numbers on his cell phone. Dr. Harrison was out of the office, but Carlos left a detailed message. The return call came several hours later, after Carlos was back in his office at the city hall.

"I had a message to call you," Dr. Harrison told him.

"Yes. As I mentioned briefly on the message, it is about our girls. They are very sick again. I have been following your progress on the Internet, and . . ."

"And you want to know if there's anything we might be able to do to help?"

"Yes," Carlos said humbly. "Anything—anything at all. The situation here is very grave."

Harrison paused for a moment, his mind racing through the possibilities. "How fast can you get me some small blood samples from the girls?"

Dr. Harrison burst through the door to the lab and made a beeline for Dr. Lowell.

"We have the blood samples from Culiacán!" he announced. "Let's get to work. How long you figure it'll take us to cook up some marrow?"

"Maybe two weeks."

"The Rivera twins may not have that long. Do everything you can. We have enormous potential here for international exposure. I mean we've got a perfect match—human studies virtually guaranteed to work."

Ten days later the delivery from Genevex arrived by helicopter. Lily and Gaby, looking tiny and pale, lay under the watchful care of an ICU nurse. Their left arms, taped to boards, were each hooked to IVs that dripped new marrow from Genevex. Leigh sat outside, praying, as she waited for her next visitation time. She tried not to think about what would happen if this last option was unsuccessful.

In a conference room at the Dallas Hilton, Dr. Harrison stood before microphones that were clumped together like grapes. During his presentation, he took credit for the incredible success of the therapy on the twins. When he'd finished, reporters took turns asking a steady stream of questions. Another stood when Harrison acknowledged him.

"How long did it take for the therapy to work?"

"We saw results within forty-eight hours, but the entire process took about two weeks to recovery."

"Is it true, doctor, that you sometimes use aborted fetuses for your stem cell research?"

"Yes, and as you can see, we are saving lives with tissue that would otherwise be discarded. But we are also making great strides using umbilical-cord blood. Next?"

Harrison nodded and another reporter stood. "Is it possible that the twins' remarkable recovery was due to some other factor?"

Harrison shook his head. "It was definitely Genevex's cutting-edge bone marrow therapy. Our researchers have done outstanding work. There was really no hope for the Rivera twins otherwise."

Harrison started to look for another reporter, but the same one continued. "But what makes Genevex so different here— what sets you apart?"

"We have a special cell line we've developed that gives us an edge."

Marnie's journalist friend had sat quietly throughout the presentation but now caught Harrison's eye and stood. Having spent the morning on the phone with Marnie, he spoke confidently. "Isn't it true, doctor, that your marvelous treatment of these children was done using their own illegally obtained cells?"

Everyone turned and looked at the journalist in shock.

Harrison fumbled. "Uh . . . sir, I don't know . . . uh . . . where you got your information, but no, that is absolutely incorrect. We used blood samples from the infants as a template for the marrow." He looked around at the remaining hands raised. "Sorry, we're out of time. Thank you. No more questions, please." He walked off the platform, muttering to Lowell, "Get the name of that reporter." Then he lost his footing, regained his composure, and disappeared with his entourage through a side door.

⁓⊱✲⊰⁓

Carlos knocked on the door to his wife's hospital room. "Come in."

He peeked inside and smiled at her. Then he opened the door to reveal a huge bouquet of flowers with a dozen balloons.

Leigh smiled.

He swept into the room and set down his gifts, then came over to his wife and kissed her affectionately. "A son, Leigh, and he is wonderful."

The happy mother glowed. "He looks just like you."

"Yes," Carlos said in an almost hushed tone. "Tomorrow when I take you home, our family will be complete. A healthy boy, two healthy girls, and a beautiful mama."

After Carlos left, one of the bilingual nurses came in to talk with Leigh. She sat down beside her bed and said, "Good morning, *Señora* Rivera. It is an honor to serve you. Do you have any questions I can answer for you?"

Leigh nodded. "Actually, I do have a few."

"Please ask."

"Okay," Leigh said. "Our son, little Carlos, is a preemie . . . uh . . . is premature. . . ."

"You were at thirty-six weeks, no?"

"Thirty-five."

"Okay," the nurse nodded.

"So is he at any special risk? I mean the doctor said everything was just great. But should I watch out for anything unusual?"

"The doctor will see him regularly. He may get a little—how you say, *amarillo*, ah!—jaundiced. And I am afraid his feeding schedule may be every two hours for a while, so you will not get much sleep."

"That's no problem. We have good help."

The nurse smiled. "As long as he is eating well, everything should be just fine. Anything else?"

Leigh shook her head. "Thank you."

The nurse looked at her chart on her way out. "Hmm, interesting."

"What?"

"Your doctor instructed that your placenta, the umbilical cord, and the umbilical cord blood be cryo—"

"Cryopreserved?"

"Yes, that is the word. That is very unusual."

Chapter Thirty-Two

LUC AND BEN SHOWERED AT THE CLUB following an early morning game of racquetball. As Ben was pulling on a T-shirt, Luc told him, "I guess you heard Sudds got busted."

"What?" Ben stared.

Luc looked at Ben, who had surprise written all over his face. "I thought you knew."

Ben shook his head. "What's he in for this time?"

"Stopped for a possible DUI, and they found half a kilo of coke in his car, along with some ludes and rufies—you know, the date rape drug. Doesn't look too good."

Ben shook his head. "Amazing."

"That's what I said. But there's more . . ."

"What?"

"He's out on bail, and he called looking for you on your day off yesterday. He claims the stuff was put there as a plant, and he wants you to vouch for his character—help him prove his innocence."

"He can't be serious!"

"Totally. He thinks the fact that he turned around on his charting should help him."

Ben shook his head. Later, when he got to the clinic, he picked up his messages and sifted through them until he found the one from Sudderth. On the way back to his office, Ben passed Darlene.

"I guess you heard about Sudds!" she gloated.

"Yeah." Ben was solemn. He kept walking.

Darlene called after him. "Serves him right!"

Ben said nothing and walked into his office. He lifted the phone receiver, knowing that talking to Sudderth would get no one anywhere. But before he had finished punching in the numbers, he heard a knock. It was Courtney.

He motioned for her to enter, and he set down the receiver.

"I guess you heard," she said, a huge smile on her face. "Serves him right!"

Ben was silent.

"You don't seem happy."

"Did you expect me to be?"

"Justice was done."

Ben shrugged. "Yeah, but it's still sad when someone with so much potential gets into so much trouble."

"He can rot in jail for all I care!" Courtney stood to leave.

Still having trouble with the idea of forgiveness. Ben sighed deeply and dialed the phone.

The Riveras sat, once again wringing their hands, in the waiting room outside the pediatric ICU ward. Their girls had taken another turn for the worst, and only five days after baby Carlos had come home.

"I just don't know if I can bear the continual roller coaster of hope and despair," Leigh Rivera managed through her sobs. "I feel like I'm going crazy. Just when everything seems to be going great, something always . . ." She lost herself in another wave of tears.

Carlos stroked his wife's hand. "It just does not seem to

make sense. Their new, transplanted marrow was doing so well. But the special cells, it seems, did not work for long."

Carlos had been on the phone to Dr. Harrison for ten minutes, and he wasn't getting anywhere.

"But our babies!" Carlos pleaded. "I cannot understand why it stopped working and why you cannot make more."

"Right. And as I already tried to tell you, the relapse could be for any number of reasons. Perhaps the transport was flawed," Harrison insisted.

"Then we will try again. What will we need to change?" Carlos Rivera was not usually desperate, but he was willing to do anything to save his daughters.

"Or maybe your doctors down there were incompetent and failed to infuse it correctly. Perhaps if they had better training and skills?"

"What?" Carlos demanded.

Harrison sighed impatiently. "Look. I've done what I can. I can't spend any more effort on this one case. I have many pressing projects. We hoped for the best, and it didn't work out. There's really nothing else I can do for you, and if you think about it, I believe you'll see that I went out of my way to cover for—uh—to help you. Good day." The phone went dead.

Carlos interpreted Harrison's words as a veiled reference to the clinic break-in. He hung up and slammed his fist on the desk.

When Ben picked up his messages, he was not surprised to see that Carlos Rivera had called. *I'll bet his wife had her baby, and he's calling to inform us.*

Ben liked to return first those calls that he thought would

be good news. Now, as he sat listening to the tragic story, he could hear the pain of a father in desperation.

Carlos told him, "For a while our girls were doing so well. But the cells they received just stopped working."

That's exactly what the cells did in Tim's Parkinson's patients, Ben thought.

Carlos continued. "Our son is still too small to harvest enough marrow to save both girls, and we cannot bear to have to choose between them."

"I am so very sorry," Ben said quietly, imagining how that would feel.

"But maybe there is still a way. At one time, you or Dr. Morgan told me you had some cells that might help our girls, doctor. And now I am asking you—can you please help us? We have no other hope."

"Mr. Rivera, I can't tell you how sorry I am to hear of your sad news. I assure you I'll do anything I can to help," Ben told him. "Now, from what you told me, Dr. Harrison already tried the special cell therapy, so we need to consider other options."

"But he did not use your special cells, did he?" Carlos insisted.

Oh, if you only knew. "I have concerns about using them," Ben said. "Judging from Dr. Harrison's work, I think they would probably help only temporarily, if at all."

"What can we do?" Carlos asked, almost despairing.

Ben spoke in a soothing voice. "Actually, we may have one more option, though I hate to get your hopes up. When did you say your wife delivered?"

Carlos gave him the date and then added, "But we already tried, and as I told you, he is still too small."

Ben ignored Carlos's last remark, thinking in another direction. "I don't suppose there's any chance that your doctors kept his umbilical cord?"

"Is that the cord that comes out of the mother after birth?" Carlos asked.

"Yes."

"They did keep it—they are most competent. It is frozen along with some other materials."

"Excellent!"

"That is a good thing?"

"Mr. Rivera, I wish you could see the smile on my face," Ben said. "I have a colleague who works for a company called Astor in Portland, Oregon. He's spent the last five years researching the use of umbilical cord blood to help sick children . . . and . . . let me give him a call."

When Ben called Dr. Wagner, he didn't have to hold long. The doctor came on the line, and Ben said, "It's Dr. McKay, hoping you'll remember me."

"How could I forget a doc who'd miss a Cowboys game to deliver my wife?"

"You do remember!"

"Of course. Man, you're a saint. What can I do for you? I don't imagine you're calling to arrange a tee time?"

"Trusting . . . hoping. What I've read about your research with Astor . . . I need your help to get out of a really tough spot."

"Fire away! What can I do? We're making some exciting progress."

"Great. Don't know if you've heard of the work at Genevex and Dr. Harrison."

"Yeah, doing some great stuff with stem cell research—good results with some kids in Mexico."

"Right. But unfortunately, the kids have relapsed as the artificially generated marrow is rapidly dying off. They're left pretty much defenseless."

"And there are no good matches, I assume?"

"Right. That's where you come in."

"Me? Oh, Ben, I don't think so. We're doing some great cultures with cord blood stem cells, but just a random culture—no way it could work. Sorry."

"Hang on. We have some umbilical cord blood from a new sibling, just weeks old, cryopreserved and ready to go. The doc in Mexico really had some foresight. Given the twins' history, he must have banked on needing that material."

"That's amazing! Get it to me, and I can nudge those stem cells into marrow in about a week. If the match is anywhere close, it could work."

"Can't tell you how happy I am to hear you say that. I didn't know how close you were in your research."

"Well, buddy, it's not like you've got a lot of options. Send them up; we'll be ready to go."

"Thanks, man. You're a magician!"

"Glad to help. By the way, rumor has it you got hitched."

"Ah, word travels. I'm about to have a son!"

"Awesome! Congratulations. Boy, you didn't waste any time. Aren't you like, way old for that?" he chuckled.

Ben laughed. "Actually, I couldn't be happier—couldn't be prouder."

"Glad for you, buddy. Well, anyway, I'll get the lab alerted, and you have the folks in Mexico give me a call. This could get a bit pricey, my friend."

"No worries. We've got it covered."

"Okay, I'll do what I can."

Carlos Rivera entered the hospital waiting room, where his wife had spent so many days of her daughters' lives. She looked up when he appeared.

"Leigh?"

"Yeah?"

"I've been making some phone calls."

She looked hopeful.

"I have another possibility."

"What?"

"Dr. McKay is going to help us."

"Dr. McKay? What can *he* do?"

"He knows a researcher who may be able to work with us by using the frozen cord material from baby Carlos."

Leigh stared at him through puffy eyes.

Carlos sat next to her, but a moment later Leigh noticed he was seething. "What's wrong? I thought you said it was good news."

Carlos shook his head. "I called Dr. Harrison first, and he refused to help."

Leigh's face fell.

Carlos continued. "He blames our 'incompetent doctors' and claims he cannot devote anymore time to our case. He uses us to get famous, then discards us."

After Emily was tucked into bed, Marnie and Ben sat together on the love seat watching TV. Marnie, now near the end of her pregnancy, drifted off to sleep. When Ben got up to turn off the TV, she awoke and apologized.

"That's okay. It was boring, anyway," Ben told her.

"But I wanted to stay awake long enough to hear about your day," she pouted.

"No problem. I do have a little news, if you're interested."

"Of course. What?"

He filled her in on what Carlos had told him about his girls and about Harrison. "Carlos Rivera still doesn't know that Harrison used his girls' own cells to treat them and to make a name for himself."

"We can hardly be surprised." Marnie sat quietly for a long time.

"What are you thinking, Marn?"

An odd look—thoughtful yet amused—spread over her face. "Trying to consider the difference between justice and revenge."

"Uh-oh," Ben smiled.

Marnie gave him a sly look. "What do you mean by that?"

"I mean I know you have something brewing in that brain of yours. Care to share it with me?"

Marnie's eyes lit up. "Wouldn't it be more fun to just read it in the news?"

Carlos Rivera summoned Ramon late in the evening. His assistant appeared and received Carlos's brief instructions: "Contact Victor and tell him to take care of 'the problem.'"

The next morning, Marnie called her journalist friend, a medical reporter. "Want another scoop on Genevex?" she asked.

"If it's about that blowhard Harrison, you know it!"

"Yeah, looks like he, uh, stepped deep in it this time. He made that big announcement, but now the patients have relapsed. Genevex stock is taking a nosedive."

"No kiddin'? Tell me more."

"All right, but first you have to promise me something."

"What's that?"

"A lot of researchers who use human embryos for stem cell research justify their work by saying that the embryos would be destroyed anyway. I'll make you a deal. I'll give you the scoop on Harrison if you'll promise to do a piece on couples who are adopting embryos. My husband and his partner have an adoption matching service here at the clinic. You don't have to mention the clinic; I'm not looking for free publicity here. I just want people to know there's another alternative."

"Sure. I owe ya! But why aren't *you* writing this stuff?"

"If you could see me, you'd know why."

"What do you mean?"

"I'm nine months pregnant!"

Two days later, Dr. Harrison sat in his office answering e-mail, drinking his coffee, and wondering how to explain the Rivera twins' deterioration to the Genevex board.

His e-mail news search brought up a story on a Dallas bioresearch firm, so he clicked to open it. Moments later, he realized the company was Genevex, and he was reading about himself.

The newswire story, written by the same cocky journalist who had embarrassed him at the press conference, confirmed that Harrison had achieved his "medical breakthrough" by growing stem cells with illegal origins. The story reported the twins' continuing deterioration, Harrison's refusal to help Carlos—quoting Rivera himself—and that the much-publicized treatment of the twins had been performed using the girls' own cells, which had been obtained unethically. The article raised questions about Harrison's competence in light of the news that his "discovery" was really the illegal work of another researcher, now dead.

By five that evening, Genevex stock, already falling, had dropped again by fifty percent.

Chapter Thirty-Three

BEN WAS AT HOME ON SATURDAY AFTERNOON when Dr. Wagner called from Portland.

"Hey, what a surprise!"

"Hope you don't mind my calling you at home, but I think we have good news."

"No kidding! What can you tell me?"

"I got the sample of the cord blood along with samples of the twins' blood. The preliminary match is good—not perfect—but good. So we'll harvest the stem cells from the cord and culture them with the baby's blood. Then we'll send them to the hospital in Mexico. In the interest of time, do you want me to send them by private plane? It could run you into the thousands."

"Do whatever you have to do."

Because of Marnie's complicated pregnancy, her physician had scheduled an induction. A few days before her "due" date, she heard Ben close the door to the bathroom in the middle of the night. When he walked toward the bed a few minutes later, she asked, "Have to go do a delivery?"

"Naw," he said, crawling into bed. "I just have a bit of a

headache and some general aches so I took some Tylenol. What are you doing awake? Was I too noisy?"

"No, I don't think so," Marnie said. "More like—hey, why did God make women with bladders the size of a nail head?"

Ben sat in the chair beside Marnie's bed in L&D and squeezed her hand. "This is it, babe."

"How you feeling, 'Dad'?" Marnie asked, responding to the look in his eyes.

"An incredible moment. I dunno—joy, anxiety." Ben also felt a touch of sad remembrance, but he wanted to sustain the buoyant mood, so he kept that part to himself. "Maybe I've done a zillion deliveries, but there's something unique about my own—*our* own—baby. You're giving birth to my child today." He rubbed her hand. "Amazing."

Betty, the admission nurse, came in. Though she knew Marnie and Ben from past admissions and also from Ben's work in L&D, it was still necessary to take the medical history. Betty glanced at the clock. "Seven-fifty," she said. "Just about time for scheduled inductions and morning rounds. Dr. Dale should be here in just a minute."

"Can you believe I made it to term after all we went through?" Marnie asked.

"It *is* amazing, Mrs. McKay."

"But now that my blood pressure's creeping up, I guess the doc thinks an old lady like me needs to be controlled as much as possible."

Ben shook his head.

"You disagreeing with the old lady remark, or suggesting it's impossible to control me?" Marnie teased.

"The age remark, *of course*. You don't look a day over twenty-five," Ben insisted.

"Good form." Betty smiled at Marnie. "You have him well trained!" She hooked up the fetal heart and contraction monitors, then wrapped elastic bands around Marnie's waist to hold them in place. "Okay, everything looks great." A check of Marnie's blood pressure showed a slight elevation at 140/90, but Betty just glanced at Ben and nodded. Making small talk, she started the IV while Ben watched.

"All right, Mrs. McKay," her voice sounded pleasant. "Dr. Dale will arrive any minute, and of course, a tech will drop by to draw admission labs. Sounds like Dr. Dale is planning to break your water and off you'll go."

"Thank you," Marnie replied. "I'm ready. . . . Couldn't be more ready! With this July heat—ugh!"

After Betty departed, Ben turned his attention back to his wife. He reached his arm around her middle and laid his head against her belly. "See you soon," he whispered to the tiny life inside.

Marnie wiped a tear and reached down to stroke the hair on the nape of Ben's neck. They remained like that for a minute. Then Ben scooted around, took Marnie's hand, and held it to his chest. He placed his face within inches of hers.

"How's my bride?"

"Okay. A little nervous, I guess. But ready. I don't remember feeling nervous with Emily, but I didn't know then all the things that could go wrong!"

"I know what you mean."

"This has to be a little nerve-wracking for you, sweetheart," Marnie said.

Ben nodded and looked at the floor. "How about if we pray?"

"Great idea."

After breathing a brief request for grace and safety, Ben sniffled. Then he reached over and wiped the tear from Marnie's face with his thumb. "I love you," he whispered. Then he kissed his wife with feeling.

"Hey, hey! Enough of that!" Dr. Dale, a slender, silver-haired physician with square features entered. "That's how you got into this fix." They all chuckled at his remark as he planted himself on the side of the bed. He still had on his suit and tie, as he was headed for rounds and the morning office schedule after he started Marnie's labor.

"Ready to rock and roll?" he asked.

They nodded.

"Okay." He punched the nurse call button.

"During my only other experience at this," Marnie said, "the water broke on its own. We were at a movie theater. What a mess!"

"Well, this will be a bit less dramatic, I'm afraid," Dr. Dale said with a smile.

"Less dramatic is great with me. How long will it take?"

"To deliver? Or for labor to start?"

"For the *pain*. And how long until I can get my epidural?"

"Oh, is that what's worrying you? I'm no good at predicting, but you were about two centimeters yesterday at the office, so I expect you'll start contracting within the hour. You should be 'cooking' before long."

Betty returned and handed a pair of gloves to Dr. Dale, then opened the amnihook—a plastic instrument shaped like a crochet needle.

Ben watched, confident in his colleague's skill.

Dr. Dale performed the vaginal exam gently. He looked at Ben. "Yesterday's sono reaffirmed the placental position—low lying but out of the way."

Betty handed the hook to Dr. Dale. He guided it between his fingers into the vagina, then into the cervix. After he gently scratched the sac, a flow of amniotic fluid trickled out.

"Oh, that's warm," said Marnie. "Feels like I'm wetting myself!"

"Well, you are," said Dr. Dale, "in a grown-up sort of way."

The fluid was clear. Only a small amount of blood stained Dr. Dale's gloved hand. Nothing out of the ordinary.

Ben relaxed back on the bed next to Marnie, knowing they'd now reached the point of no return. In a matter of hours, he would hold his child. *Amazing.*

As Dr. Dale stood to leave, he assured them, "Gotta make rounds; I'll drop back before I head over to the office. Betty will take good care of you, and I'll be handy. Everything's looking good. Baby's heartbeat looks great. Now we just wait and watch."

"Thanks, doc," said Marnie.

After Dr. Dale left the room, Betty rechecked the blood pressure and charted the fetal heart rate.

"All's well," she said. "I'll be back in a few minutes to change your pad."

"Thanks," Marnie said.

"When do you want to call Emily?" Ben asked when they were alone again.

"Better wait until it's all over. She'd drive Dad nuts wanting to come up and look through the window in the nursery—and who can blame her?"

"Good point," Ben said. "So where's the list of everybody else we need to notify, just so I know?" Ben felt fidgety and wanted to keep his mind occupied.

"In my Palm handheld. It's in my purse," Marnie said. "I listed everyone in correct calling order with the numbers next to their names."

"Impressive."

"That's what you get for marrying a publicist—*Announcements 'R Us.*" Marnie motioned to her purse. "Can you get it for me? I just thought of one more person we need to call."

Ben pulled out the handheld computer and handed it to his wife. But when she looked at the list, she got choked up.

"What's wrong?"

"Funny," she said. "I was fine until I read Dad's name. I guess I'm still used to seeing Mom's next to it. It just sort of hit me that Mom was here when Emily was born, but she's gone now. I guess this side of heaven, even happy events have their painful details, huh?"

Ben nodded. He sat silently holding her hand for a minute, staring out the window. Then Marnie swallowed hard and began talking Ben through the list. As she was talking, Ben noticed a slight flattening on the monitor strip that traced the baby's heart rate. It was still in the 120s, but that was down from the 140s where they had started. He stood to examine it further.

Marnie looked up and watched him. "Is everything okay?"

"I think so. I just want to watch this for a minute." Ben concentrated on the monitor, and his own heart rate shot up as the baby's slowed down. He hated what he saw, but he didn't want to scare Marnie. So he reached down and pushed the nurse call button. Just as he did, the baby's heart rate fell below 120 and set off the alarm.

"Ben!" Marnie panicked.

"Let's turn you on your left side, okay, babe?" Ben said calmly, though inside he felt anything but calm. He patted her arm, then rested his left hand on her with his eyes still focused on the monitor. Betty burst into the room. She studied the monitor for a moment, then punched the emergency button on the intercom and opened an oxygen mask.

Ben, watching the baby's heart rate continue to drop, pulled back Marnie's sheet to find a small pool of blood soaking the pad. He noted that Marnie's pulse remained unchanged.

Betty guided the mask over Marnie's face.

"Can I help you?" asked the secretary's voice on the intercom.

"Page Dr. Dale, STAT." Ben spoke firmly. *Gotta be fetal blood.* He looked at Betty. "Got an OR open?" The baby's heart rate was in the 80s now and steadily declining.

"Two C-sections in progress now." She spoke just above a

whisper as she tilted down the bed. "We've got a room, but staffing will be tough."

"Go and open," Ben said.

"Ben! What's happening? Is the baby all right?" Marnie, still lying on her left side, begged from behind the mask. Ben looked at her, trying to hide the fear in his eyes. Nothing was changing the steady slowing of their child's heartbeat.

Dr. Dale swung open the door. "What's up?" He immediately recognized the frenzied activity of a medical emergency.

"Fetal bradycardia," Ben replied. "No variability. No response to conservative change." He pointed to the pad. "And we've got some increased bleeding. Must be fetal. They're opening a room, but they've got two cases going. We're gonna be shorthanded."

"Gotta roll! Get her moving while I get on some scrubs."

"Got it!" said Ben, in full "doctor mode." Betty unhooked monitors and prepared Marnie for the move. The fetal heart now registered in the sixties.

Glancing down from the monitor, Ben caught Marnie's eyes pleading up at him. He leaned down. "We've got some complications. But I'm here, and I'm not going to let anything happen to you or the baby."

As they wheeled Marnie out of the room, Dr. Burris, the anesthesiologist, met them.

"What've we got?" Burris asked, noting the IV in place.

"STAT section for fetal distress," Ben replied. "FHTs in the sixties."

Dr. Burris quickened his pace to keep up with Ben as they made their way down the corridor to the operating room. "Any medical history? Allergies? Risks?"

"No," said Ben. "She's strong and healthy."

Dr. Burris nodded. As they reached the OR, they found nurses scrambling to open the equipment. The scrub nurse had the instruments out and was quickly arranging them on the table.

Ben and Dr. Burris helped Marnie scoot over to the OR table. Then Ben moved the labor bed out of the room while Dr. Burris hooked up the monitors and blood pressure cuff, preparing to put Marnie to sleep.

The circulating nurse, Ann, pulled out the Doppler to check the heart tones while Marnie lay on the table. As Ann guided the instrument, she whispered to Ben, "The residents are tied up in the other sections. We have no one to assist Dr. Dale."

"No problem," said Ben. "I'll scrub in until one of them gets free."

"Oh, Ben," Marnie shuddered.

Just then the nurse found the heart rate. No more than forty beats per minute. Critically low, and everyone knew it except Marnie.

"Ben?" she pleaded, "Is the baby okay? Is our baby going to be all right?"

Ben nodded when he saw the fear in her eyes. "Honey, I need to go scrub, but we'll make it. Hang in there."

He flashed her the sign language for "I love you" as he headed out of the room to grab a mask and hat. He was already wearing scrubs for comfort, having come prepared for a long day in labor and delivery.

A tear ran down the side of Marnie's face and soaked into her surgical cap.

Ben met Dr. Dale at the scrub sink. "Time to go. FHTs in the forties." Their eyes met. Every moment counted. In a little over ten seconds they had soaped and rinsed their hands and trotted into the room where Ann had just begun the abdominal prep.

Cheryl, the scrub nurse, quickly gowned and gloved the doctors. As they moved over to the table, Ann abbreviated the prep. Time was running out.

Dr. Dale and Ben covered Marnie's abdomen—now pinkish from the soap—with sterile drapes. Then they nodded to Dr. Burris.

"I'm going to put some medicine through your IV that will make you go to sleep" the anesthesiologist calmly told Marnie, while already injecting it.

Ben peered over the drapes arranged in tent-like fashion, which separated the surgeons from Marnie's face. He spoke to her gently. "Love you, Marn. We're good to go."

She couldn't form a response, as in those few seconds the medication had circulated. She was asleep.

Is our baby going to be all right? Her last words echoed in Ben's mind, distracting him momentarily.

Dr. Burris nodded at the surgeons as he continued his monitoring.

Dr. Dale, scalpel in hand, made the skin incision. Just below the navel to just above the pubic hairline—no time for an efficient shave. Ben, surgical sponge in hand, blotted behind the stroke of the knife to keep the field clear of blood. Dr. Dale made the second stroke through the fat down to the fascia, the glistening fibrous layer that provides strength to the abdominal wall. He nicked the fascia in the midline as each doctor now elevated the abdominal wall so the incision would pose little danger to the internal organs. Next, he carried the incision through into the abdominal cavity. Only seconds had passed, and they now saw the large, pink uterine wall.

"Russian pick ups." Dr. Dale instructed the nurse, indicating the kind of forceps he needed for elevating the tissue before he made the next incision. The beeping of Marnie's cardiac monitor made the only other sound.

The neonatologist, having received Betty's emergency call, stood ready to receive the baby. The Ohio overhead warmer and other necessary equipment were checked and ready for the infant.

Dr. Dale created a bladder flap. He made a quick nick of the peritoneal covering, bluntly dissected off the lower uterine segment, then again asked for a scalpel. Cheryl had the instruments ready even before he asked.

Now Dr. Dale scored the uterine wall transversely, stroking three times before he encountered fluid. "It's got fresh meconium."

Ben shook his head. He did his best to follow every move with the proper assistance to keep the operative field clean.

Dr. Dale skillfully inserted the index finger from each hand into the incision and extended it transversely with a firm pull. Less than one minute had elapsed—and they were inside the uterus. The surgeon then reached in with his left hand. He slid his hand over the baby's head and cradled it. He guided the head up toward the incision. "Got it. Push!"

Ben responded by applying firm pressure to the fundus, the upper margin of the uterus. And the baby was pushed out through the incision.

The infant delivered easily but lay pale and limp. Dr. Dale couldn't detect a pulse at the umbilical cord, which they quickly clamped. As the baby lay cradled in Dr. Dale's hands, Ben cut the cord. His eyes clouded over, but he said nothing. No one in the OR uttered a word.

Oh Father, not again, Ben prayed. *Please, no!*

Dr. Dale turned and handed the baby off to the neonatologist, Dr. Kindberg. Silently, she began to work. Dr. Dale looked up at Ben, and their eyes met. Then they returned to the operative field. Ben, prayed for some word of encouragement from the neonatal team. Glancing over, he could tell that the neonatologist had already intubated the baby and was breathing for the child.

At one minute, the nurse noted an Apgar score of zero.

Dr. Kindberg, injected 10 cc's of sterile saline to try to get some volume in through the umbilical vein. But no response. She and a nurse breathed for the baby through the tube that extended from the mouth into the trachea. They also did chest compressions with two fingers on the baby's sternum.

"Nothing." She shook her head.

Chapter Thirty-Four

ONCE THE DOCTORS DELIVERED THE AFTERBIRTH, they looked at it closely. They tracked the blood vessels from the placenta, across the membranes that make up the amniotic sac, to the umbilical cord.

"Vasa previa," Dr. Dale noted, then muttered his self-denunciation. "I must've nicked one of these vessels when I broke the water. The baby's been bleeding out."

Unusual complication, Ben thought. *But Marnie's bleeding in early pregnancy and low-lying placenta had already set up some problems.*

Ben watched the lifeless form of his son as the doctor and nurse performed CPR, trying to get a response.

As minutes passed, the chances of success ebbed steadily away. Ben took a deep breath, conscious of his racing heart.

Dr. Dale told Dr. Burris to give the pitocin, to contract down the uterus after the placenta had delivered. Marnie's body responded appropriately. Dr. Dale reached into the abdominal cavity and exteriorized the uterus for easy closure. He clamped the corners and sutured the uterine incision. He began to sew while Ben sponged the field and assisted as well as he could through his tears.

"Anybody here O neg?" Dr. Kindberg asked in desperation. "I've got to get some volume in this baby."

"Marnie is," Ben offered.

Dr. Kindberg looked puzzled.

Ben gestured toward his wife. "The patient. Her name's Marnie."

Kindberg nodded and glanced over at Dr. Burris. "Get me 10 cc's."

Quickly Dr. Burris drew up the maternal blood from Marnie's IV site and took it over to Kindberg.

"Hope there's not too much anesthetic in here," Kindberg mumbled, as she injected the red blood cells slowly through the umbilical vein. Her team continued the chest compressions and oxygen ventilation. So far they had seen no response from the baby.

But then, as the blood circulated, he began to change color.

An eerie stillness enveloped the room, broken only by the beat of Marnie's heart on the cardiac monitor and the sound of the ambu bag ventilating the infant.

Dr. Dale, having closed the uterus, now began to sew up the abdominal wall incision. "Ben, you can scrub out and go over there if you want. I've got this now."

Ben didn't speak as he turned from the table and toward the wall, pulling off his gown and gloves. He felt his legs quivering. *I'm losing it. I failed again.* He covered his face with his hands, and closing his eyes he prayed with all his might. *Please, Lord, if you've got to take somebody, take me. Let my child live this time. Take me instead.*

"I've got a pulse," Dr. Kindberg murmured. Then louder, "I've got a pulse!"

The infant's Apgar score had moved from zero to two at five minutes.

Ben turned and moved toward the child, who was now surrounded by neonatal nurses assisting Dr. Kindberg.

"We got some volume in him, and we're oxygenating him well. He's pinking up!"

"Any respiratory effort?" Ben asked, his hopes rising.

"Not yet."

His shoulders fell.

"But he has some anesthesia onboard from your wife," she replied in a soothing tone—not promising, but hopeful.

Ben watched over the nurse's shoulder while Dr. Kindberg methodically squeezed the ambu bag, moving oxygen into the baby.

"I think we should move your son to the ICU," Dr. Kindberg told Ben at the ten-minute mark. She looked over at the nurse. "Are they ready for us there?"

"You bet."

They gently lifted the baby—now pink, with a steady pulse of his own—and left the operating room with him. She turned to Ben with a sparkle in her eyes. "He's making some respiratory effort. We're lookin' good!" It was a short walk down the hallway to the neonatal intensive care unit.

Ben followed quietly behind. He glanced back at Dr. Dale and told him, "I'll be back soon."

Dr. Dale nodded and flashed the thumbs-up sign with his bloody glove. "We're about done. I'll meet you in recovery."

Ben sat at Marnie's side in the recovery room for about half an hour while she slept off the anesthetic. One of his colleagues, having heard about the mishap from Dr. Dale, came by to see him. He and Ben stepped out of the recovery room into the hallway to talk. About a minute later, the recovery nurse touched his arm and smiled. "Dr. McKay, the patient is asking for you."

He returned to Marnie's side. She still had her eyes closed, but she was calling out his name, panic in her voice.

Ben took her hand and leaned down close to her. Speaking gently, he said, "I'm here, Marnie. I'm here. It's okay."

Her eyes still closed, Marnie exhaled and smiled, then relaxed. She squeezed his hand. Ben was deeply touched by the affect of his presence, even in her semiconscious state.

Then she grew tense again. "Ben, our baby?"

"We have a son."

"All right?"

"He looks beautiful, with a full head of gorgeous brown hair—just like his mother."

"He's all right?"

"Yes. He's fine—healthy. He gave us a bit of a scare, but all is well. Dr. Kindberg was amazing. Wait'll I tell you the whole story. *You* saved his life."

Now almost fully alert, Marnie's eyes filled with tears, and Ben leaned down to kiss her forehead. "Soon as you wake up more, I'll take you down to the ICU nursery to see him."

By the time Ben wheeled Marnie, still in her recovery bed, to the nursery, Dr. Kindberg had removed the baby's breathing tube, and he had perked up.

Ben carefully navigated through the IV and some monitor cords to pick up his son. Then he carefully placed him in Marnie's arms. She looked down at her baby, then dreamily at Ben, then back at her child. She swallowed hard and smiled. "Thank you, heavenly Father," she whispered. She stared at the infant's face then looked up at her husband. "A little bit of you and a little bit of me."

Ben nodded. "How 'bout that?" he said, a look of adoration on his face.

The nurses gathered around and ogled, showering Ben and Marnie with their parent-encouraging compliments: "He's gorgeous." "C-section babies are always cuter." "I love his hair." "You'll make a great dad, Dr. McKay." "What is his name?"

Ben looked at Marnie and smiled. "Robert Edward McKay. Bobby for now."

When everyone had returned to their jobs, Dr. Kindberg came over to congratulate the family.

"So you think he's all right?" Marnie asked, studying the doctor's face for signs of encouragement.

She nodded. "I'd like to keep him just for observation, but I feel good about this. He's a normal baby; just 'volume depleted.'"

After she left, Marnie asked Ben, "What does 'volume depleted' mean?"

Ben hesitated before answering. "He bled from a nick in his umbilical cord and lost probably half his total volume."

Marnie's eyes grew wide.

Ben shook his head and smiled. "Have I got a story for you, babe."

"You must have been terrified."

Ben raised his eyebrows. "Yeah, my heart got a pretty good workout today, but . . ."

"But what?"

He looked down at the baby. "That was then; this is now." Ben reached over and caressed the tiny face of his newborn son.

Once they had admired their son from head to toe, Ben wheeled Marnie toward her room, where the first order of business was a call to Emily and Will.

Ramon and Victor sat behind empty beer bottles at a noisy bar on Greenville Avenue in Dallas. Ramon waited impatiently for Victor to finish his cigarette so they could leave.

"I still do not see why you couldn't have just called me with instructions."

Ramon shrugged. "It is what the mayor wanted." He sat another moment, then said, "Give me your cell phone."

Victor nodded and handed it over.

"I am going out in the parking lot where it is quieter. I will be right back."

Moments later, Ramon returned. Victor extinguished his cigarette and stood to leave with him.

"I must tell you one more thing," Ramon said as they walked out the door.

"What is that?" Victor asked.

"When you have completed your assignment, I want you to call me on your cell phone. I have just programmed in the number, and it will be untraceable. Even you will not know it."

Victor showed his annoyance, but Ramon ignored the reaction.

"Just push this pound sign, then the one. I programmed it for speed dial. Just press those two keys and it will ring me. Call once the work is finished. Our employer wishes to remain removed from this little task." He handed the phone to Victor.

"No problem."

Victor watched as Dr. Harrison emerged from dinner at the Enclave. Genevex had quickly severed all ties with him, but that was not saving the company from sinking into financial ruin. Now he was working his business contacts. He would not likely find anything in the image-conscious world of medical research, but surely someone needed the expertise of a slightly soiled executive.

As Harrison put his hand on the door handle, he turned toward a man in a doctor's lab coat standing nearby in front of a Mercedes with the hood popped. The doctor talked to Harrison and pointed to his car.

They must know each other. Victor cursed.

Harrison drove the man over to Presbyterian Hospital. There the white-coated figure got out and waved Harrison on.

Harrison drove to Highland Park, where he turned onto Beverly Drive. He drove past several sprawling homes in the opulent neighborhood before turning in at his own drive. The garage door opened, Harrison pulled inside, and the door began to shut.

The blast was more spectacular to see than to hear. The force projected metal shrapnel from the automobile, and pieces of wall and roof arced outward in a semicircle of debris. Victor could feel the wave of heat from the fireball in his car at the end of the long driveway and across the street.

By now, the blast into the house had ignited the gas line. Victor knew that by the time firemen reached the scene, the large two-story would be engulfed in flames.

He tossed the transmitter onto the seat beside him and drove away. When he reached Hillcrest, two fire engines screamed by. He wanted to hurry but reminded himself to stay within the speed limit. South on Central Expressway to Washington Street. Left on Live Oak.

He could relax. The scene was far away, and he doubted any of Harrison's neighbors could give more than a vague description of the car had been parked on the street. Pulling into a deserted parking lot, he picked up his cell phone. After punching in the pound and number one, he heard Ramon's voice.

"The job—it is finished," Victor said, then lit a cigarette.

"No complications this time?"

He took a puff. "None."

"Good."

Victor heard a dial tone. He shut off the phone, and then was surprised when it rang—as he still held it in his hand. An instant later, his own car exploded in a blazing inferno.

Leigh Rivera took a walk in the early evening, then went to the nursery to look in on her girls. They had been infused as before, and once again they had improved remarkably. Leigh prayed that the roller coaster would not take them down again. She was encouraged by what the doctor had said—that the umbilical stem cells didn't seem to elicit the feared immune rejection response. So Leigh had guarded hope.

Marnie lay in her hospital bed, watching the national news broadcast. The death of Steven Harrison shocked and saddened but did not surprise her. The spokesperson for the investigation cited a string of possible motives, from Genevex stockholders, who now held worthless shares, to fellow employees who would lose their jobs when the company closed its doors. A physician with whom he had eaten dinner just an hour before his death described him as "depressed" about the loss of his job and the failure of his research project.

Four days after Marnie's delivery, Dr. Dale released her. As Ben and Marnie pulled into their driveway, Emily ran out to meet them, then bounced up and down until Marnie opened the door. She threw her arms around her mother. "Mama, I'm a big sister now!"

"Yes, you are—such a big girl!"

"Let me see! Let me see my brother!"

"Let's go inside, honey," she said. "Then you can sit and hold him."

Emily had taken a sibling's class at the hospital, and she felt very important in her new role.

Will followed with a camera, videotaping everything.

"Where'd that come from?" Marnie asked, a look of delight on her face. She pointed to a huge painted stork, draped in blue ribbon, that stood in the front yard.

Will gave Ben a look. "Tell ya later."

Once they were inside, Will pulled Ben back while Marnie took Emily into the breakfast nook to hold the baby.

"A lady named Patti came by." Will hesitated. "She leads a support group at your hospital for people who've lost babies. They show up with the stork whenever someone in their group has a child again, and they figured you'd earned the right. Hope it's okay."

Ben blinked fast. "Yeah. It's more than okay. It means a lot."

"And Patti's not the only one who came by. Take a look." Will pointed in the direction of Emily and Marnie. Ben followed him into the kitchen. They checked out the refrigerator, which was stocked with meals, and the counters were covered with breads and desserts. "That's some Sunday school class you have. Makes me think I need to start going to church!"

Ben laughed.

"They really are a nice bunch, though it'd probably shake 'em up a bit to have an old codger like me walk in. Until today, I thought that Joan of Arc was married to Noah," Will joked.

"You mean she wasn't?" Ben feigned shock, and Will gave his arm a playful slug.

"No," Will insisted. "Emily read a book about Noah to me, didn't you, honey?" She nodded enthusiastically. "And his wife's name was *Mrs.* Noah."

"Right!" Emily insisted.

Will waved at the kitchen. "I'm sure Emily here is glad for all this food—don't think she likes *my* cooking much."

"Squash, yuck!" Emily said.

"You haven't exactly raised her to appreciate fresh garden

produce," he said, shaking a finger at Marnie in mock accusation.

But Marnie had her eye on Ben. "You okay, hon? You look a little green around the gills."

He shook his head. "It's weird. The sight of all this food makes me a little queasy."

"That's odd," she said.

"Too much excitement around here, perhaps."

"Perhaps." She gave him a sideways glance.

That night, Ben and Marnie lay side by side in bed, holding hands. "It's so great to be home again," Marnie said. "I sure missed you."

"It wasn't any fun sleeping alone again." Ben pulled her close. Marnie moved gingerly, her C-section scar still tender. Then she relaxed. "And now you're here, and I'm here, and we have a daughter and a son. . . ." Feeling deeply loved and secure, Marnie drifted off to catch a little sleep in Ben's arms before the next feeding.

An exhausting week after the baby's arrival, Ben slept through the alarm. Marnie eased out of bed and went around to his nightstand to shut off the buzzer. Ben opened one eye and saw her looking down at him.

"You okay?" she asked.

Ben slowly stirred, then sat up. "Man, I feel lousy."

A wave of anxiety swept over Marnie. "How lousy is lousy?"

"I only got up once to help you with Bobby, but I feel like I didn't get a wink. And I'm a little queasy."

"Oh no—I hope you're not pregnant. Sounds a little like morning sickness," Marnie joked to hide her concern.

Chapter Thirty-Five

MARNIE WOKE EMILY, THEN RETURNED TO FIND Ben lying with his eyes closed. She sat on the bed facing him, and he finally looked at her. Saying nothing, she looked closely at his eyes, and he knew what she was thinking. "It's probably just a bug. Don't worry."

"Tell me more about how you feel."

"Yes, doctor."

She waited for his answer, and he sighed. "A little nausea, worn-out, but otherwise I'm fine."

Marnie looked skeptical but said, "All right. Can I fix you a little breakfast? How about some dry toast?"

Ben nodded.

"I need to get Emily ready for school. The carpool is picking her up. But I'll make you something while she eats."

In a few minutes Marnie returned to the bedroom with a tray of dry toast and orange juice. Then she turned to attend to the baby, who was fussing in his bedroom corner bassinet. Ben frowned in his frustration. "I'd help you with him, but I don't want to give him the flu."

"That's okay, honey," Marnie said.

"In fact, maybe we should move his bed to the nursery for the time being."

Marnie nodded and went to finish helping Emily get ready.

When Marnie came in to get dressed, she heard Ben talking to Luc. He sounded defensive. "I've been *trying* to take care of myself—at least trying to get as much rest as anyone *can* with an newborn . . . eating right . . . my energy's been pretty good . . . doing everything I could to recover my strength."

After a long silence, he spoke again. "I think it's just the flu."

After he hung up, Marnie sat in the armchair across from the bed. "I can't believe he gave you a hard time."

Ben lay back against the pillow. "He's envisioning a long stretch of mega-call. He needs to spend more time with Janelle. Even good folks can say hurtful things when they're tired and stressed, but he really was trying to understand. I wouldn't like it either if I were him."

At midday, after Marnie had nursed the baby and laid him in the nursery, she came into the bedroom to take a nap. Ben had already drifted off—his copy of *Dark Night of the Soul* lay on his face. She gently removed it, marked the page, and set it on the nightstand next to him. She noticed he seemed to be itching a lot. He was scratching his arms in his sleep, and she wondered if that meant anything significant.

Ben rested and read most of the day and into the evening. When he got up to use the bathroom, he shuffled slowly. By the next morning, he was itching all over. It seemed as if he'd aged decades overnight. Marnie glanced up and saw him staring at his eyes in the mirror. As soon as he emerged from the bathroom, he picked up the phone and called Mark McLaughlin.

When he hung up, he told her, "I need to go in for some lab work. I want you to stay here with the baby. I'll see if Bob King can take me."

She didn't argue. *Too tired to drive? Too sick? Knows he'll get admitted and doesn't want his car there?* Marnie wondered.

Dr. McLaughlin immediately knew this wasn't the flu. He only hoped that the hepatitis relapse would be mild. "I'm going to admit you again," he said. "The urinalysis shows up abnormal, and your spleen feels large." He didn't mention that Ben's liver felt smaller—a finding that troubled him.

Within a few hours, Ben lay in the infectious disease ward. He called Marnie and complained.

"My weight's down, lab values are up, and I'm under 'double isolation' with fluid precautions."

"What does that mean?"

"Visitors, even nurses, have to gown and glove before entering. Everything I touch—including my tray—is disposable. They've stuck me on a pretty strict diet. Mostly fluids. And they're measuring all my input and output. If I don't get better fast, I get a catheter."

"You sound depressed."

"Yeah, you could say that."

"When can I come see you?"

"Marnie, I'd really rather you didn't come up here. I'll be fine. I'm sure of it. I just want you to take care of the baby."

"I feel like you don't want to see me."

Ben recognized that the delicate hormonal balance during the postpartum time was making this even harder for his wife, but he felt too tired to remember how to be gentle. "You know better than that," he insisted.

He knew when he hung up that she was probably crying, and he felt he had handled the call with little sensitivity. But he was so tired—and scared.

Luc found Courtney alone in the lab. "Just thought you'd want to know—Ben's back in the hospital."

Courtney looked distressed, so Luc sat on the stool near her.

"How bad is it?" she asked.

"Don't know much yet, but they've got him in double isolation. Looks like the hepatitis has flared up again."

She looked down, shook her head, and cursed.

"We're hoping and praying for the best," Luc added.

Courtney looked up at him. "Anything I can do?"

"We'll all have to pitch in to cover his load around here," Luc said.

"Sure. That's the least we can do," Courtney insisted. She was silent for a moment, then spoke again. "Luc, maybe I could grow liver cells in the lab. You know, take some fetal cells from a newborn."

Luc smiled at her eagerness to help, and he thought a moment. Then he shook his head. "It'd be a long shot. Who knows if it would be a good match, and then there's the potential for latent virus."

"Yeah, I thought so," she sighed. She thought for a long time, then shook her head. "I just can't believe this is happening to him. He's a really special person. I've never met anyone like him."

Luc nodded. "Yeah. . . ."

Courtney looked at Luc. "I really mean that. There are some things about him I just don't understand, though maybe that's part of what makes him so likeable."

Luc looked surprised. "Like what? What don't you get?"

"Like, the whole God thing, and he doesn't even believe in evolution."

"Neither do I."

"Oh?" Courtney digested this bit of information.

Luc nodded. "Yup."

"Okay. Well . . . then . . . he has some funny ideas about forgiveness."

"What funny ideas?"

"Like . . . how could he be a character witness for Travis after what Travis did?"

Luc shook his head. "He never agreed to be a character witness."

"Oh." Courtney realized she'd just assumed Ben would forgive Travis in the same way he'd forgiven her. She looked sheepishly at Luc. "I guess he probably told you about what I did."

Luc nodded.

"Well, he never came out and said it, but I think he believes I should forgive Travis. But if Travis showed up today, there's no way . . ."

Luc looked confused.

"Not after what he did to me."

"Courtney, you may be confusing forgiveness with trust."

"What do you mean?"

"You can forgive people, but that doesn't make them trustworthy. I don't think for a minute that Ben would say you should have even a friendship with Travis."

"You don't think so?"

"No way."

"Well, anyway, since we're talking about it, I want to thank you for giving me another chance," Courtney said. "I was so ashamed, but I appreciate your not holding it against me."

Luc nodded. "Sure."

"Still, if trust is not the same thing as forgiveness, why didn't you change the combination to the safe where you keep the cells?"

"You were deeply sorry. Ben knew you'd never do anything like that again."

"That's true. I was—and I am."

Luc nodded and shrugged. "So, there you have it."

Through the rest of the day, her conversation with Luc replayed again and again in Courtney's mind. There was a lot about Ben and Luc and their view of things that she didn't yet understand, but she liked the way they treated people.

All afternoon a steady stream of doctors came through to see Ben. Fred reported seeing the hooker whose fingernails had wrecked Ben's health. She had shown up again in the ER with symptoms of diseases related to full-blown AIDS. She had refused to take her medications. Bob King came back to pray with Ben late that afternoon, and Ben asked him to see that Marnie got some support.

After rounds, Luc dropped in. He sat next to the bed and smiled when Ben opened his eyes. "Hey, Ben, you didn't have to get this sick for me to believe you."

"You knew I wasn't *faking!*"

"This is just my inept way of saying I shouldn't have given you a hard time. I've been feeling bad about that."

Ben waved it off. "Don't worry about it, Luc."

The next morning, Janelle offered to keep the baby so Marnie could see Ben.

Marnie tiptoed into the room and tried to read a magazine until he woke up, but she couldn't concentrate, so she set it down and stared out the window.

When Ben opened his eyes, they misted over. "I knew you'd come."

"You're not upset?"

"Of course not. Once I got here, I wished I'd had you bring me. I hated being alone. I want you with me whenever you can be here."

On Ben's third day in the hospital, Dr. McLaughlin came to see him, accompanied by his residents. The labs had continued to show deterioration, and the doctor was concerned for his patient. When they arrived, Marnie was with Ben, and he seemed fairly alert. "Hello. How do you feel?" Mark asked.

Ben struggled to focus. "Okay, feeling okay."

"All right then. How about you tell me your full name?"

"Sure. It's Ben."

"Right. And the rest?"

The patient tried to chuckle. "*Doctor* Ben."

"Right. And the date today—and the year?"

Ben tried to concentrate. "I've been in here so long, I've lost track of the days." He looked out the window. "It's summer though, right?"

"Okay, let's try this. Finish the sentence. Absence makes the heart grow . . ."

Ben looked confused. "Heart? Grow?"

Marnie looked at Mark in panic.

"Sorry," Ben said. "I'm sure tired." He spoke with slurred speech.

Mark spoke to Ben in gentle tones. He adjusted the lighting in the room to make it easier on Ben's eyes, and in a few minutes, the patient had drifted off to sleep. Mark guided Marnie into the hall and sent the residents away.

Chapter Thirty-Six

Dr. McLaughlin's expression had a sobering effect on Marnie, who was already visibly upset. "His liver's is simply not recovering," he told her. "It looks like he's still losing liver cells. He doesn't have all the signs of fulminant liver failure, but he sure could get there. I'm going to order a machine that will clean his bloodstream of the stuff that's making his mind fuzzy. It's mostly ammonia and nitrogen byproducts."

"And what's ahead?" Marnie fixed her dark eyes on Mark, looking for clues beyond what he had told her.

"You know we're doing everything we can, and Ben is a strong man."

"I don't understand how this could happen. I mean, he didn't get HIV or anything like that."

"Yes, but it looks like we're dealing with hepatitis C. And that virus in some people can be as bad or worse than HIV, depending on their immune response. Most people get over the initial infection without much trouble, but with a few special people like your husband—it just won't settle down."

"Do many die? Could *he* die?"

"A few. But we aren't talking about dying here. We'll plug him up to the Hepocleanse EC, and he should perk right up.

Give me a few hours here. We'll put him on IV nutrition and watch him like a hawk."

After he finished talking to Marnie, Dr. McLaughlin returned to the group of residents and med students. He spoke in his usual booming voice. Marnie paused to listen to the impromptu lecture down the hall from inside the door to the room.

". . . Two billion infected with hepatitis annually according to the World Health Organization. That's 325 million with chronic hepatitis. About thirty to fifty thousand people die annually from the disease in the U.S. alone, and about nine thousand of those we attribute to hepatitis C. We're going to put him on extracorporeal liver support. It's similar to dialysis, but we extract different things." He quizzed one of the residents. "Dr. Oglesby, what key circulatory changes and metabolic abnormalities do we expect to see with advanced hepatitis?"

Marnie sagged against the wall. As she looked at Ben, her mind was a swirl of confusing questions. *Is he asleep or unconscious? Will he make it? How could I ever find contentment if he doesn't survive, now that I've known what love can be? Why would God allow such a thing to happen to a man like him? Why, after all I've been through—why can't I be allowed to enjoy a life with this man I love? We just had a baby. Why?*

Tears were streaking her face. She walked over to pick up a tissue and blew her nose. Then she splashed water on her eyes and cheeks at the sink. Once she had settled down, she reached for Ben's Bible and opened it to Psalm 91. She read the first two verses three times: "He who dwells in the secret place of the Most High shall abide under the shadow of the Almighty. I will say of the Lord, 'He is my refuge and my fortress; My God, in Him I will trust.'"

Hearing a light tapping on the door, she got up and opened it to find Courtney.

"Come on in." Marnie sounded weary.

"How is he?" Courtney asked.

Marnie shrugged. "Not great." She motioned for Courtney to sit down, and then she pulled up a chair, too. After going over what Mark had told her, she finished with, "I just don't see how it could happen so fast."

Courtney nodded. "Hepatitis can be like that. Once the liver starts to fail, it can be only weeks, even days, before patients get critical. It can go very fast."

Not exactly big on bedside manner, are you? Marnie thought, feeling her tears welling up again.

Courtney shifted awkwardly. She reached over for a tissue and handed it to Marnie. "I wish there was something I could do. He's a good person, and it's obvious that you love each other very much."

Marnie nodded.

Courtney grasped for something to say. "How are you juggling childcare?" she asked. "You must be exhausted with all you've got going right now."

"My dad lives with us, and our church friends—you've met a lot of them—they're helping virtually around the clock with the baby. And they're praying non-stop. I'm living by God's grace, that's for sure."

"You really do have some great friends."

"I really do. Sometimes I wonder how I lived so long without such a terrific support system."

Courtney looked surprised. "What do you mean by 'lived so long'? You're not old!"

"I mean, I've only been a Christian since Tim disappeared. And I've only had friends—really good friends who share a common faith—since then."

"Really? I figured you grew up with it."

"I'll take that as a compliment. Sometimes it all still feels so new."

"So, how did you accept it?"

"Accept what?"

"I don't know exactly what you call it. But how did you, you know, how did you get your faith?"

"When we had the memorial service for Tim, Ben gave a message about heaven. And afterwards, I had a lot of questions. I'd figured that I needed God's forgiveness, and Ben helped me to see that Jesus made that possible. By the end of that night, he had prayed with me, and I believed in Christ. Now I can't imagine how I ever made it without the Lord."

On Courtney's way out, she passed Luc and Janelle on their way in to see Ben.

"How is he?" Luc asked.

Courtney shook her head. "Worse than I thought. I'll let his wife fill you in." Courtney couldn't say anything more, and it showed.

She headed toward the exit, but she paused when she passed the door to the chapel. Peeking inside, she expected to find a lot of people praying, but it was empty. She sat down on one of the padded benches and thought. *God, if you are there, and you are the God that Ben and Luc believe in, what are you doing? Is there anything I can do? Anything at all?*

She walked up to the altar. It was illuminated by a stained glass window with a light behind it. A large Bible lay opened. Having never read it, Courtney didn't know what the numbers meant, but someone had underlined some words. Her attention was drawn to them.

"Trust in the Lord with all your heart, and lean not on your own understanding; In all your ways acknowledge Him, and He shall direct your paths."

The words didn't make sense to Courtney. *How can anyone believe in something that cannot be seen and studied. Can you trust without understanding? I'd like to try. Can you help me, God?*

She looked around the room and suddenly felt very exposed there. So she slipped out the door and started for her car again. But as she walked across the parking lot, the thought occurred to her to go back to the lab and review Tim's research notes.

Three hours later, she let out a deep and hopeless sigh. She had studied the meticulous records and found them incomplete. Then she remembered what Luc had once mentioned. Dr. Harrison had complained that the last week of Tim's notes was missing. *Was he too sick to write? If not, this guy kept records too carefully to let a week go by without notes. What could've happened to them?*

Around noon the next day, Marnie entered Ben's hospital room and found him asleep. But she was glad to see he seemed a little better. She'd been sitting next to him for about fifteen minutes, holding his hand and praying, when he awoke. He smiled sweetly at her. "I was hoping you'd come soon."

She squeezed his hand.

"Marnie, you know, don't you?"

She looked puzzled.

"You know how much I love you?"

She nodded. "Probably about as much as I love you." Her eyes clouded over.

"My life is more than the air that I breathe."

"What do you mean?"

"Remember what I wrote to you on our wedding day? What makes me feel alive is those I love. And if that's true, I'm really quite well."

Marnie got tissues for both of them.

After a long silence, he looked back at her. "We need to talk about some things, in case I can't later."

Marnie gasped. "It can't be *that* bad. . . . You got better last time. And you're better today."

Ben shook his head. "My labs still show steady deterioration. Liver enzymes are climbing. I'm at pretty high risk for bleeding. So they're listing me with chronic subacute hepatitis. I have every intention of making it through this, but just in case . . ."

Marnie swallowed hard.

"I've got my affairs in order. I'm not afraid to die. That doesn't mean I'm in a hurry to do so, mind you," he half smiled. "Anyway, you know my feelings about life support if there's no decent chance that I'll recover to full function, right?"

Marnie nodded, fixing her eyes on him.

"Okay. We do have good insurance coverage." He paused again for a long time, then took a deep breath. "When Juli died, I bought a joint burial plot. That's where I'd like to be buried. There's room for another next to me, if that's what you want."

Hearing Ben talk of his own burial made Marnie's insides twist, but she continued to gaze at him through her tears. "What do *you* want?"

He looked away. "I'd like to think you'd want to be next to me. But who knows what'll happen to you in the future. Yet . . ." he smiled vaguely, "I'd also like to think I'm so unforgettable that you'd want to be near me."

Marnie was sobbing. She nodded. "I hope you know you are."

"Bet you feel sort of ripped off. You marry a sick guy like me—not exactly what you bargained for. In fact, it's what I was trying to avoid."

Marnie moved to the bed and sat near him. She spoke gently. "Ben, you may never understand this, but being married to a sick Ben McKay is far better to me than not being married to you at all." She wiped her eyes and went on. "I want you to be well, to be whole, but I'd go through all this pain and more just to have known the joy of being yours."

"Marnie . . ." Ben whispered her name, but could say no more.

~ ❦ ~

When the evening nurse came in to check on Ben, she caught Marnie in a full yawn. "Go home and get some rest," she insisted. "We'll keep an eye on him."

Marnie hesitated, but she knew she had reached the point of exhaustion. Emily needed her, and she should spend time with Bobby. Pumping and refrigerating her milk at the hospital had proved highly inconvenient, but she felt she had no other option.

As Marnie was leaving, she crossed paths with Courtney in the hospital lobby.

"Hello, Courtney," Marnie greeted her.

Courtney smiled shyly. "Could I speak with you? I have a question, if you have just a minute." Courtney motioned to the chairs.

Marnie shrugged. "Sure."

"I've been studying your late husband's research," Courtney told her.

Marnie grew tense.

"He kept incredible records."

"Yes, Tim was very good with details."

"Which is why I find it puzzling that the notes for his entire last week of research are missing. Do you think he was too ill to keep records?"

"No, he was lucid until the last day," Marnie said.

"Then, do you have any idea where he might have kept any other records?"

Marnie shook her head. *Doesn't she know this is a bad time to bring this up? I have a lot more important things on my mind.*

"Was anything sent to you from the research hospital when they gave you his personal effects?"

"No one sent me anything," Marnie explained. "Ben brought home a box of stuff he emptied from Tim's locker."

"What was in there?"

"Nothing exciting. I didn't look that carefully. Just a shirt and a change of shoes, I think. . . . Why are you interested in Tim's research? The cells he used—we don't want anyone experimenting on them, especially at a time like this."

"I know," Courtney said. "I was hoping, just maybe, that there might be a way to use his discoveries to help us support your husband's liver, while staying within his comfort zone."

"Oh." Marnie was glad she'd kept the impatience out of her voice. "That's really kind."

Courtney sighed. "Not that I've come up with anything. I feel helpless and want to do anything I can."

"Sorry I can't tell you more than I have," Marnie said. "But I never found anything in his computer files . . . nothing like that anywhere."

"Okay. Well, I'm sure you need to get home," Courtney said.

Marnie nodded and stood. "Thank you so much for trying, though. I sure appreciate it, and I know Ben will, too."

Late that evening, unable to shake her conversation with Courtney, Marnie dug around in the guest room closet until she found the box of Tim's personal effects. She had shoved it aside with some of his winter clothes, thinking she'd sort through it all—sometime. She opened the box and found it just as she remembered. She pulled out the flannel shirt and the tennis shoes. *Nothing here.* Folding up the shirt to put it back, she felt something hard. *There's a disk in the pocket!*

Marnie's heart started pounding. Then she reminded herself that, even with Tim's notes, Courtney would not be able to help Ben without destroying embryos, and she knew he would never agree to that.

Still, she slid the disk into her computer and fired it up. *Voilà!* She stared at Tim's diary of research notes dated the last week of his life—excluding the day he actually died. She tried to read them, but the complex terminology made little sense, and she was too tired to sort through it.

Marnie called Luc for Courtney's home phone number. Talking to Courtney a few moments later, Marnie could almost feel the embryologist's intensity through the phone line.

"Can you send the file by e-mail right away?" Courtney asked.

<hr>

As soon as Ben's visitors all left, he drifted off to sleep. But an hour later he woke up, disoriented. He tried to get out of bed and fell, hitting his head on the side of the bed. The jerking action set off an alarm on the monitor. Within seconds nurses swarmed around him. One of them called the house mouse, the intern with the "bad beeper" who dealt with all the calls, everything from sleeping pills and laxatives to pronouncing people dead. Now he came to examine the patient who had slipped and fallen.

By the time he got there, the nurses had Ben back in bed. The intern looked him over and told him, "You've got a small knot on the side of your head, but otherwise it looks okay." Just then his beeper went off with the cardiac code, and the cardiac doctor was paged over the intercom.

"I'll leave you here in the nurses' hands," the intern told Ben before disappearing.

The nurses got Ben hooked up to the monitors again and

snugly situated back in bed. "Don't try anything like that again," one of them warned good-naturedly.

"Sorry," he responded with a sheepish smile. "Musta been dreamin'."

Chapter Thirty-Seven

COURTNEY'S SOFTWARE DIDN'T SUPPORT THE DISK, but she pulled it up in "text only." The formatting was lost, but she could still decode what Tim had written. She read through Tim's meticulous notes, marveling at the mind that wrote them. But when she got through reading the last entry, she read it again just to be sure she hadn't misunderstood. She sat back, shook her head, and smiled. *I need to call Dr. McLaughlin.*

She called his answering service and left an urgent message.

"Thanks so much for calling me back," Courtney said, when he returned her call fifteen minutes later. "I'm the embryologist that works with Ben McKay and his partner."

"Sure, I know who you are, Courtney. What can I do for you?"

"Did you ever get a liver biopsy on Ben McKay?"

"Yeah. Why do you ask?"

"How did you preserve it?"

"Most of it was fixed in formalin . . ."

Courtney sighed hopelessly.

Mark quickly added, "But I froze some because of the HIV concerns. I thought if he did turn positive, I'd already have a sample at a very early stage."

"Fantastic!" Courtney exclaimed. "Can you send me some of his liver cells for something I'm working on?"

"Sure, I suppose. What are you thinking? You know his liver has just about completely shut down."

"Yes. But I have an idea; I just may be able to help. I need what you've got ASAP," she insisted.

Shortly after six-thirty the next morning, the nurse made her rounds. She shook Ben but couldn't rouse him. Grabbing his wrist, she found a slow, steady pulse. She checked his eyes—one pupil was widely dilated and nonreactive, the other reacted sluggishly to light.

She cursed, punched the emergency call button, and shouted to the nurse in the hallway. "Call Dr. McLaughlin and the resident, STAT!"

"You mean the first-year resident—the house mouse, Dr. Levy?"

"No. We need the senior medicine resident—right away!"

Dr. McLaughlin was on his way to the hospital to do rounds when he got the emergency page. When he and the resident got there, Mark took one look at Ben and shook his head. The nurse told him, "They say he bumped his head last night, which for a guy with clotting problems may have led to a big bleed in his head."

Mark spat out orders. "I need a neurology consult to find out the extent of the damage. Looks like a stroke. Page Dr. Davidson right away. See what she thinks about a CT scan. Let's get him transferred to ICU. I'll call over and get us a bed." He called CT and asked for times, but waited for neuro to get the go-ahead.

Once Ben had been transferred, Mark called Marnie. In a cool but firm voice he told her, "I'd like you to come down here as soon as you can make arrangements for your kids."

"Is something wrong?" Obviously he had awakened her. "Is Ben okay?"

"There's been a little accident, but he's stable now." *But then again, death is stable, but not exactly good.*

Marnie could leave Emily with Will, but he felt unable to handle the baby. So Marnie got Bobby ready to go to Janelle's. Seeing her in tears, Emily asked, "Mommy, what's wrong? Why are you crying?" Without waiting for an answer, she asked another question. "Is Daddy going to die like my other daddy did?"

Marnie swallowed hard. She leaned down and touched her daughter's shoulder, looking her in the eye. "Honey, he's very sick. But his doctors are the best, and they're taking good care of him." She grabbed her daughter and held her for a moment.

Marnie got the kids in the car, and Will took her to Janelle's. When Janelle met her at the door, Marnie nearly fell sobbing into her arms. But she wanted to get to the hospital in a hurry, so she handed Bobby to Janelle and left.

Will sped her to the medical complex and dropped her off before returning home with Emily. When Marnie went up to Ben's room, she stood in shock when she discovered Mark had transferred him to ICU. In her dazed state, she made her way to the ICU floor, where the nurse manning the central desk pointed her to Ben's room. An enormous window allowed observation, and the door was actually only a curtain that extended far enough to cover, if necessary, the window. She entered and glanced around the room, noting that Ben now breathed with the aid of a ventilator. She let out a tiny gasp, then steadied herself. "Hello, sweetheart," she said.

He tried to respond, and gave her a half-smile.

"I came as fast as I could. The kids are with Dad and Janelle."

Ben looked confused, as though he couldn't place who she was talking about.

She swallowed her tears and took his hand. "I love you, Ben."

He nodded, then drifted back to sleep. Dr. McLaughlin came in shortly after she arrived and motioned for her to join him in the hall.

"What can you tell me, Mark? How bad is it?"

He shook his head. "It's bad, and it's getting worse. I'm sorry." He looked down.

"What's going on? What happened to his head?" Marnie squeezed hard on her wadded up tissue.

Mark sighed and looked up at her. "Ben became disoriented last night in his sleep and tried to climb over the bed rail. He apparently fell and hit his head. That's why he has that nasty-looking bruise. His liver damage has really fouled up his clotting ability. The resident physician examined him. . . ." Marnie hung on Mark's every word. "He thought it was a simple bruise. But even that little bit of trauma . . . It looks like he's had a small stroke."

Marnie's eyes flashed. "A stroke? He's in the hospital and he had a stroke 'cause he tried to climb out of *bed*? Where were the nurses? When they sent me home, they said they'd watch him. If only I hadn't gone home."

"I'm very, very sorry. He seems to be doing quite all right now. I've got the neurologist on her way over for a consult. But the fact is, I'm actually more concerned about the liver situation. He just keeps getting worse. Basically the relapsing hepatitis is destroying Ben's liver cells so fast that it's overwhelming him."

Marnie blinked.

"And he's not responding to conservative therapy. Not only is his protein way down and the bilirubin way up, but his clotting studies are shot. We can't seem to keep ahead of him with the EC machine."

Marnie worked to pull herself together. "Is there anything you can do?" Mark handed her a fresh tissue, and she blew her nose and wiped her eyes. Then she took a deep breath, struggling to maintain some semblance of composure.

"We're doing all we can," Mark told her. "We're carefully controlling every drop of fluid intake, but Ben's showing signs of tremor. Well, frankly, I expect him to slip into a coma unless we make some headway with the machine, or if the liver destruction slows. And I'm concerned, of course, about further extension of the stroke . . . about clotting and hemorrhaging."

"He barely woke up when I came in today," Marnie whispered, as though saying it more quietly might make the pain less real.

"Each day I've had him write his name, and we've compared the signatures," Mark explained. "But for the last few days, he hasn't been able to write at all."

Marnie slowly shook her head.

"I'm not a really religious person," Mark said. "But I know your husband is. If you've got people who will pray, I'd sure be open to supernatural help." Mark put his hand on Marnie's shoulder. "I'm so very sorry."

She stared at the ground and nodded. After a moment in thought she looked up. "Would you mind calling Luc Morgan and telling him all the medical stuff?"

"I'd be glad to."

That afternoon Courtney was fuming. The lab had misplaced Ben's liver biopsy cells. They assured her they would locate them and do their best to deliver them to her by morning.

Luc and Janelle fell into bed, exhausted physically and emotionally. Luc and Mark McLaughlin had been playing phone tag all day, unable to connect. Finally, Lisa had managed to schedule a time when the physicians could meet at the hospital in the morning with Marnie.

Luc reached over and grabbed his wife's hand. "I'm grateful for you—that you're still around." He choked out the words.

"Scary, isn't it?" she said.

Luc nodded. "I can't imagine having a new baby and facing what Marnie's going through."

"Would you mind telling me how you're feeling about Ben? Not Marnie's stress, but your own losses. He's your best friend, your partner."

"I'd rather not talk about it. . . ." He noticed his wife's sigh. "But I will. I know it's important."

Janelle rolled over and hugged him. As she held him, he began to weep.

By the next day, Ben was bleeding from his gums, bleeding into his GI tract, and bleeding at his IV sites.

His communication with his wife the previous day had been his last sign of consciousness. Marnie sat at his bedside wearing a gown and gloves. The phone rang, and she answered it.

"Hey, Marno, it's Janelle."

"Hello," Marnie said sadly. "How're the kids?"

"Bobby's sleeping, and Emily is out back on the swing set with the boys."

"You're a gem."

"I feel so helpless. It makes me feel better to do something. You okay?"

"Ben's in a coma," Marnie choked out.

"Oh, Marnie. . . . Well, I just wanted to let you know Luc's on his way."

Thirty minutes later, Marnie sat in a conference room with Luc and Mark.

Mark stared at the table. "I'm afraid Ben's fighting a losing battle. His liver's essentially gone functionally, and we have no viable options." He didn't mention his call from Courtney. To his mind, Ben was going downhill too fast to benefit from anything she might come up with.

"Transplant?" Luc asked, knowing what the answer would be.

Mark shook his head. "He's not a candidate for transplant. He's too sick to handle major surgery. Besides, we're talking overwhelming viral infection, and bacterial infections have gotten established because of his weakened immune system. We're using all the available technologies to transfuse what he's lacking, but . . ."—he paused and looked down again—"there isn't much hope."

Marnie let out a little gasp and worked hard to control the sobs welling up inside.

Mark continued. "I'm concerned that we'll be facing a catastrophic event right around the corner."

"What do you mean?" Marnie asked.

"I expect a stroke or cardiac event within a few days. And I need to know from you how we should respond. If Ben arrests, we might be able to bring him back, but without any definitive plan for his liver, he wouldn't wake up. If he has a convulsion, he'll likely suffer another stroke." Mark paused, then pressed on. "My recommendation would be to let him go and not resuscitate. I like Ben a lot. I just don't think he'd want to survive on machines if he's not going to wake up."

Marnie had turned pale. "Isn't there something you can do?"

Mark shook his head. "We've tried everything we know to do, and even stretched a few techniques beyond the proven range."

Luc asked, "What about anticonvulsants?"

"No." Mark insisted. "Any medicine to stop seizures might deepen the coma or kill him outright. As you know, with hepatic coma, treating the seizures can make the coma irreversible. So, do you let him convulse, knowing he could stroke out his brain? Or do you treat him aggressively with anticonvulsants and likely seal him in a persistent vegetative state? We're really at the end of our abilities here."

Marnie bravely asked, "Could he be an organ donor? He believes strongly in it."

Luc dropped his face into his hands.

Mark shook his head again, but spoke in a level voice. "No. I'm sorry. Due to the nature of the infection, Ben isn't a candidate for donating."

Luc moved over to Marnie and put his arm around her shoulders. "I'm so sorry, Marnie, so very, very sorry."

"What should I do?" Marnie squeaked in a voice that came through her weeping.

Mark wisely kept silent while Luc spoke gently. "I'm afraid Mark is right. Ben wouldn't want to be resuscitated if we couldn't get him back. He's told me as much, even as I've told him the same. He knows where he's going. *We* know where he's going. And if it's time . . ."

Mark quietly stood. "We're in agreement then?" He waited for a response from Marnie, knowing she faced one of life's toughest moments—having to say that it's okay to give up and let the one you love die.

With tears streaming down her face, she looked at Luc. His gentle face, moist with tears, nodded slightly. She looked at Mark, closed her eyes, and nodded.

Mark touched her compassionately on the shoulder. "There really isn't another choice. I'm sorry. Ben was one of the finest human beings I've ever known."

Mark's use of the past tense for Ben was more than Marnie could take. She broke down, weeping aloud.

Mark quietly slipped out of the room, carrying Ben's chart. He stopped just long enough to write a DNR order—"Do Not Resuscitate." Then he added his signature. As he passed the nurses' station, he dropped the chart on the desk. He didn't make eye contact nor did he perceptibly alter his pace. In a flat voice he told the charge nurse, "McKay, in bed five, is DNR."

She looked up, a sad expression on her face.

"Yes, doctor," she responded.

Chapter Thirty-Eight

MARNIE SPENT A LONG MORNING IN BEN'S ROOM, leaving only long enough to pick at some food in the cafeteria. She had asked for no visitors other than Ben's colleagues and her pastor, Bob King.

When Bob arrived, Marnie told him of Ben's "no code" status. "We just don't have any good options. I mean, is withholding treatment a good option when it could lead to his death as well?" she asked.

"I'm not sure what you mean," Bob said, motioning for her to join him out in the hall.

Marnie followed. "They say he might start having convulsions soon. If they give him drugs to stop it, it could make the coma irreversible. But if they let him keep convulsing, it could be fatal."

Pastor Bob looked at her, compassion in his eyes. He thought a moment, then responded. "Life is precious. And you have a lot of people praying for you. I don't know what to tell you. I know you want to do what's right."

"I know that Ben will be in heaven. I just don't want to make a decision that will rush it. I can't bear the thought of living without him. The baby—our baby . . ."

"If it's any help," Bob said, "your husband and I have talked at length about these kinds of situations."

Marnie looked up, inviting Bob to continue.

"He once told me that in all the life-and-death decisions he has to make, he has life as his goal as long as there's the slightest evidence of brain function. But the tricky part is to prolong life, not prolong dying."

"And nobody but God really knows if Ben can recover any function from his current state," Marnie said. "None of the medical choices look good. Every choice risks everything. But then, maybe he won't convulse. Maybe the blood cleansing techniques will work."

After Bob left, Marnie walked into the bathroom and let the sobs tear through her body. *We got to be married less than a year. . . . He's in a coma. . . . I have to raise a baby who will never know his father. . . . Not a single positive word from the medical people. My God, why have you forsaken me?*

"Luc! I thought you'd never get here!" Courtney met him at the door to the clinic.

"I was up at the hospital. Ben's a DNR."

Courtney stared at him. "No."

Luc shook his head. "It's the best option."

"I think I may have found a way we can help him," Courtney insisted.

Luc guided her back to his office. He was skeptical but willing to listen.

"I found the notes from Dr. Sullivan's last week of research."

Luc raised his eyebrows, and his eyes grew wide.

"How'd you do that?"

"More on how, later. At any rate, I couldn't believe it when I read his very last entry."

"What did it say?" Luc asked, clearly engaged.

"He took the whole cell line he'd developed—the totipotential cells, or what you refer to as 'embryonic'—and he progressed them beyond the stage where they could develop into humans. They're at the pluripotent stage. He left a note to Ben. He knew that Ben had problems using anything that he considered a life. Dr. Sullivan didn't see it that way, but he didn't want such a precious pure cell line wasted, so he solved the ethical quandary."

Luc stared in stunned silence.

"I suspect that the LG cells—being a perfect line—could produce cells resistant to Ben's virus. So, we may have a solution for Ben that falls within his belief system. We can do a 'transplant' with an 'artificial liver' derived from LG cells and his own liver. We just have to keep him alive long enough for it to work."

"But you'd need a biopsy, and with his clotting studies, he'd never make it."

"I'm a jump ahead of you," Courtney smiled. "I finally got Ben's liver biopsy cells from the lab this morning."

Luc's eyes grew wide again. "How?"

"Mark McLaughlin did a liver biopsy back when Ben went into the hospital the first time."

"Amazing," Luc said, shaking his head, a huge smile coming over his face.

"So, with your permission," Courtney said, "I'd like to use the LG line to try to grow him some good liver cells."

With hope rising in his heart, Luc exclaimed, "That may be exactly what he needs. If Tim told the truth, and we have no reason to think he didn't . . ." Luc had a revelation. "That's why Harrison couldn't get the cells to reproduce themselves! Courtney, you're right! The cells no longer represent the ethical quandary of embryo experimentation." But then the smile disappeared, and Luc's shoulders fell. "Now that I think about it, the cells don't last very long. When they were used to develop bone marrow for the Rivera twins, the cells all died out within weeks."

"That was with marrow cells. Liver cells grow faster. The twins had no marrow cells of their own. Here we have Ben's liver biopsy cells and what remains of his liver structure. So, we just want to develop a patch to give Ben's own liver cells time to regenerate. Three weeks may be all it would take."

"This could work." Luc was fighting his own unrealistic expectations."

"I certainly hope so. To give him the best possible chance—to generate enough cells to make a difference—I'd need to use everything we have."

"Do it," Luc agreed.

"It'll take at least three or four days to grow a good sample, even if we convert it all."

Luc said. "And Ben's DNR."

"Guess you'd better get it changed—fast!"

Marnie pulled the chair close to Ben's bed, sat down, and slipped her hand into his.

She studied his face, realizing that unless a miracle happened, she would only see it on this earth for a few more days. She prayed for such a miracle but then released him to God, not wanting Ben to remain and suffer indefinitely. She studied his hand, slowly running her fingertips over his. Then she held it again and lay her head on the bed. When Ben squeezed her hand tightly, a thrill ran through her. *He's waking up!*

She looked up with hope in her eyes. But when she followed the contracted hand up a tight arm, shoulder, and neck, reality dawned—*He's having a full-blown grand mal.*

Alarmed, she threw open the curtain and called, "Nurse! He's having a seizure!"

The nurse moved quickly but calmly into the room. Dr. Solomon Levy, the house mouse, sat writing notes on his patients, and the nurse called out to him for help.

Seeing Ben convulse, even for a moment, had terrified Marnie. She knew better than to watch, so she stood outside.

Leigh Rivera sat on the long porch at her hacienda in Culiacán, rocking on the hanging swing as she nursed little Carlos. Her girls played in the shade of some trees.

Carlos called to find out how her day was going with their son, and she had told him the girls were having their best day ever. So he told her he'd come home for siesta—something he rarely did—and see for himself.

His car wound up the drive, and soon he sat down beside her on the swing. He took the baby from her and held him. Looking up, he watched the girls playing for a few moments, then looked down again to admire his son's perfect face. Leigh had never seen him act so paternal, and she smiled as she watched her husband with their child.

Carlos glanced over at her. "Before he is even able to speak, our boy has saved his sisters. He will be great. You will see."

"He already is, Carlos."

"Ah, you are quite right, Leigh. He already is."

Dr. Levy and the nurse watched Ben's pulse rate decrease. The doctor then increased the oxygen concentration on the ventilator. But the machine wouldn't breathe into Ben because the pressure was too high.

"Ambu bag," he told the nurse. "His pulse is falling. Get me some IV diazepam—10 mg. I'll push it until this stops."

The nurse gave him what he asked for but studied him with a critical look as he manually breathed for Ben. "Doctor, he's a no code."

Dr. Levy asked the nurse to squeeze the ambu bag, giving Ben oxygen while he slowly pushed the medication into Ben's IV line. In a matter of seconds, the seizure stopped. Ben finally lay relaxed, and both doctor and nurse breathed sighs of relief. But suddenly, in response to the big dose of anticonvulsant, Ben's heart rate became irregular. The doctor gave Ben oxygen, but that only made the heart problem worse.

"PVCs," the doctor said. "We need Lidocaine here."

Again the nurse gave him the eye.

"Gotta settle this rhythm."

She obliged, and the doctor injected some of the medication. "No real response," he said softly, not really intending to be heard. Then he cursed. "V fib."

The premature ventricular contractions had triggered ventricular fibrillation—so no blood was pushing through, rendering the heartbeat ineffective.

"Charge up the paddles," the doctor said, his anxiety building.

"Doctor," the nurse grew more brave. "The patient is a DNR. We have orders."

"Charge up the paddles, Nurse Brantley. Give me three hundred. I'm not letting him go on an OD of anticonvulsants."

She glared at him, then turned to one of the other nurses, "Page Dr. McLaughlin again." Reluctantly she charged the paddles.

Dr. Levy popped Ben with the electric shock. The jolt lifted him partway off the bed. Then he did it again. Having had time to work, the Lidocaine smoothed out the rhythm, which returned to normal.

Marnie continued to stand outside the door. She heard the order for paddles and knew. *He's going. I'm not ready yet. Thought I had a few more days at least. . . .*

Moments later, Dr. McLaughlin hurried into the ICU. He spotted Marnie and asked, "What's up?"

"He had a seizure," she said numbly. "Just like you said. They've been working on him for quite a while. Nobody's told me anything. I don't know if he's . . . I just don't know."

"Okay," he said, laying a hand on her shoulder. "Let me check." He disappeared behind the curtain. Nurse Brantley motioned to Dr. Levy. "I *told* him the patient was a DNR. But he went on anyway."

Defending himself, Dr. Levy jumped in. "Caught him in status epilepticus—tried to break the seizure with reasonable dose diazepam. Then he got multifocal PVCs and V fib. Only took twice to get him back to normal rhythm."

Mark studied the young doctor with displeasure. "Considering his liver function, that dose was way too high. And now you've brought him back just to lose him again."

Dr. McLaughlin's beeper interrupted. He looked down and read it: "Cancel DNR on McKay." The message included his own office number, followed by "STAT."

When he identified himself, his office receptionist connected Dr. McLaughlin to a nurse. "You have an urgent message from Dr. Morgan," she told him. "He and Dr. Pak have a plan, and they need you to take Dr. McKay off DNR. They want to keep him going."

When all the data was in a few hours later, Ben's physicians met around a conference table. Mark McLaughlin had called in Dr. Patterson—a gastroenterologist—and the neurologist Dr. Davidson to discuss the results of the brain scan and consider options for his GI bleeding.

"I see significant damage," the neurologist reported. "We have no way of knowing how much function he could recover, assuming that he survives. Many areas are affected."

Dr. Patterson added, "That big load of blood cells in his gut will definitely throw the numbers off the chart as they're absorbed."

Mark shook his head. "It doesn't seem to matter what we do. It doesn't look good. We can't keep his blood levels normal enough to prevent more seizures. And we'll likely reactivate the bleeding, destroying more brain function. If we load him up with anticonvulsants, he probably won't wake up either. It really seems best to let him go."

"Why are Drs. Morgan and Pak so set on keeping him alive?" asked Dr. Davidson.

"Dr. Pak is working on a stem cell line using a liver biopsy I had done on Ben over a year ago," said Dr. McLaughlin. "Sort of an experiment. I think the chances are zilch."

"Is there anything else experimental we could try?" Dr. Patterson asked.

Mark thought for a moment. "Well, we could try the Japanese "artificial liver." They've used pig liver cells cultured into a machine that runs the blood through them. It could buy Dr. Pak a few days to establish her stem cell line."

"What have we got to lose?"

In the ICU waiting area, Luc joined Marnie.

"This was his worst fear," Marnie said, looking at him with hollow eyes.

"Ben wasn't afraid of dying."

Marnie shook her head. "That's not what I meant. I meant having me watch him die. He tried to spare me—those months when we could have been together, but he was too concerned about putting me through this."

"Regrets?" Luc asked.

Marnie shook her head again. "It wouldn't have changed my decision to marry him—not for a minute. Even if I'd known we'd only have a year. I just hate that he's having to live his worst fear."

"He doesn't know, Marnie. In the mercy of God, he doesn't know."

Luc started to tell Marnie about Courtney's plan, but it occurred to him that if it didn't work, she'd get her hopes up only to have them dashed again. So, he decided to wait at least another day to evaluate the success of Courtney's efforts.

Chapter Thirty-Nine

BEN REMAINED IN CRITICAL CONDITION WITH no change for the next twenty-four hours. The labs didn't improve, but they didn't continue to worsen, either. Marnie spent long hours waiting, eating hospital food, and waiting some more.

The following morning, Luc checked with Courtney in the lab. She gave him the thumbs-up. "By midnight tonight, we may be good to go."

He smiled. "How about if we go over and explain it to Marnie together. At this point, she knows nothing about this."

"You didn't tell her?"

Luc shook his head. "Don't think I question your ability, Courtney. I just . . ."

"I know. It's a long shot."

Luc shrugged.

A few hours later, Marnie followed Courtney and Luc into the ICU conference room.

"I know it's critical," Marnie said, thinking they probably wanted to nudge her out of denial.

"Actually, there's a tiny glimmer of hope, "Luc said. "That's what we wanted to talk to you about."

Marnie looked astonished.

Luc motioned to Courtney to take the floor. She nodded and began. "After you e-mailed the file on the disk, I was able to open and read your late husband's records. Do you know who Dr. Harrison was?"

Marnie nodded. "Yes. I know all about the Rivera twins, too."

"Okay," Courtney smiled. "Well, Dr. Harrison had two different chances to reproduce the LG cells, but he couldn't get them to replicate themselves. They could develop organs and they could treat certain cancers in clinical trials."

"Yes," Marnie said.

Courtney continued. "I know Ben would never want anything to do with cloning or experimenting on embryos."

"Right."

"So don't worry. That's not where I'm going with this."

"Okay," Marnie looked relieved. "Because Ben would have been very against using the LG cells to help him. And I want to respect his wishes. Besides, I agree with him."

"All right," Courtney said, "but that's assuming they're still embryonic cells."

Marnie looked puzzled.

"It seemed too coincidental that, when Dr. Harrison tried to use the cell line, he couldn't get them to act like embryos. But when researchers put the cell line with different cell types, they would generate whatever organ matched the cells."

"Not sure I follow," Marnie said.

"When researchers put the LG line with blood cells, they developed into blood cells. When they put the cells with skin cells, they made skin. But if they tried to reverse the cell line back to embryonic, to make more cells precisely like themselves, they would be totally unsuccessful. We call the embryo stage 'totipotential,' and the organ-making stage is called 'pluripotential.'"

Marnie nodded.

"Well, it would appear that, whereas at one time the cell line was totipotential, it has begun acting pluripotential."

"Okay, I follow so far," Marnie said.

"When I read Dr. Sullivan's notes, I found out why."

"And?" Marnie was still not sure where all this was leading.

"Knowing the concerns Ben had, but wanting the cell line to be useful, Dr. Sullivan figured out how to take the line from toti- to pluripotential. He determined the number of divisions required for cells to pass from the human 'life' stage to the human 'organ' stage. In his last act, he took all the LG cells through that required number of divisions, and then he re-froze them. Now all the cells are in the organ stage—the mul-tipotential stage. Tim wanted to assure that his wonderful cells might someday be of some use to someone."

Luc jumped in. "Marnie, she's saying that Tim did what we would never do—he caused the cell line to progress be-yond the point of no return. He pushed them to mature one step farther. It's really incredible that he figured that all out. And the good news is that he made sure that he re-tained the organ potential. So, if we use the cells now to help Ben, we're not messing with life. We may have a solu-tion for Ben that falls within our belief system—a transplant with an 'artificial liver' derived from LG cells and some of Ben's own liver cells."

"But his liver is too sick for you to culture. And that could take so long . . ."

Courtney interrupted. "I got some cells a few days ago from the lab. Dr. McLaughlin had cells from a liver culture he ran on Ben over a year ago, so I used those cells. His liver was pretty healthy then."

Marnie's eyes got big. "But still, it took two weeks to get a cell line working for the Rivera twins. We don't have that much time."

"Liver cell lines develop far more quickly than marrow," Courtney explained. "In fact, they're about the fastest growing cells."

"When could they be ready?"

"I think we could attempt an injection as early as midnight."

"Tonight?"

Courtney nodded.

"Answer to prayer?" Luc asked, with a faint smile.

"We can certainly hope so!" Marnie exclaimed. "But the stroke . . . who knows how much brain function he's lost."

"One crisis at a time, Marnie," Luc said gently.

"I know. I'm sorry. This is really great news." She looked Courtney straight in the eye. "Of course I hope it works. But even if it doesn't . . ." She waited a moment to be able to continue. "Even if it doesn't, thank you so much for trying."

As Marnie walked from the conference room to Ben's bed, it hit her with full force. *Tim's work, which ruined our lives, could end up saving Ben's. Wouldn't that be just like the Lord— to once again make beauty from ashes?*

When Marnie got home that night, a woman from church had the kids tucked snugly in bed.

"Thanks so much for your help, Mary."

"How did it go today?" her friend asked tentatively.

Marnie gave her a tired smile. "Actually, for the first time since Ben's been in a coma, we have reason to hope."

"Really?!"

"Yeah. One of his colleagues plans to try a very experimental procedure tonight. So we need to pray for him as never before."

"What kind of procedure?"

Marnie motioned toward the den, and they sat together on the couch. Marnie tried to explain, but the technical details baffled Mary.

"Never mind," Mary said with a chuckle. "I'll just pray. And I'll spread the word. We'll get everybody praying."

At 2 A.M., Courtney entered the hospital carrying a vial. She had coordinated a time when Ben's GI physician could be present, knowing that injecting the cells into the liver would pose additional risk for someone with minimal clotting ability.

The doctor applied local anesthesia to the skin, although Ben's comatose condition probably kept him from feeling pain. Dr. Patterson couldn't risk Ben suddenly moving with the needle in his liver. Guided by ultrasound, he carefully inserted a thin needle with multiple side ports that were designed to distribute, over the broadest possible area, the 10 ccs of red slurry. He aimed for the right lobe of the liver, away from major blood vessels and the gall bladder—knowing that if he shot them into the wrong location, it would be like pouring liquid gold down the drain.

Courtney stood by and watched, ready to help. If all went as planned, the new cells would line up along the old scar lines within Ben's liver and rebuild it, without stirring up any major hemorrhage within the organ.

When finished, they stood for a moment, hoping—as though their hope might somehow speed the process.

And the long wait began.

A few hours later, the lab ran the daily tests, but it was too early to see any change. The only news was that the blood count had remained stable, confirming that the doctors had avoided a new hemorrhage. All the levels were virtually unchanged. Ben remained in a deep coma for the next twenty-four hours, totally unresponsive to stimulation. The following day, his labs improved a bit, but there were no other reasons for optimism. When Marnie went to get a drink from the water fountain, she overheard some of the medical personnel talking.

"Even if it works—which I doubt—he's stroked out at least part of his brain. Who knows what's left?"

"I don't see why they took him off DNR. It's obvious the man is in a vegetative state—he's gorked. He's not going to wake up."

She ran into the bathroom.

When Luc showed up that afternoon, he read the chart while Marnie watched his face for a reaction. Mark had told her virtually nothing, and she craved information.

"Looks like a slight improvement," Luc said.

"How slight?" Marnie asked.

"Liver cells regenerate quickly—but not *that* quickly. It's too soon to tell."

"But we'll take any little sign we can get," Marnie said.

The day dragged. Even with a slight improvement in the labs, Ben remained unresponsive.

Marnie arrived in Ben's room around eight the following morning, and took her place by his side. It seemed like an eternity waiting on labs for some small glimmer of hope. When Mark came in, he announced, "It looks like those new liver cells have begun to function. We've got an increase in liver size and, based on ultrasound evidence, several areas look much better."

Marnie's hands flew to her mouth.

Mark opened Ben's eyes to shine light into them. He moved the beam, then nodded. "Don't get your hopes up," he told Marnie, "but his eyes focused and reacted to the light. So he's responding reflexively to stimuli. It's just a lower brain function, so there's still no way to tell how much of Ben will come back. But it's certainly an encouraging sign."

That afternoon, Courtney dropped in for her daily visit. Marnie gave her no sign of hope, but Courtney looked up after reading Ben's chart. Then Marnie smiled.

"Excellent!" Courtney exclaimed.

Marnie nodded.

"I can't believe it!" Dr. Pak's eyes misted in a rare show of emotion.

Marnie couldn't suppress her delight. "Courtney, you're amazing."

"This is thrilling—just thrilling!" Courtney said. "I know better than to get hopes up but—how can we help it?"

She and Marnie laughed and cried together.

Later, Courtney got into her car in the doctors' parking lot. She fastened her seat belt and put the key in the ignition. Then she stopped. Resting her head against her hands on the steering wheel, she prayed with all her heart for Ben McKay.

At nine that night, Marnie sat by Ben's bed, singing softly to him. He opened his eyes.

"Ben!" she whispered.

He couldn't speak because of the ventilator, and he couldn't move his right arm because of the stroke. So he moved his left hand in the restraints. Marnie grabbed it and held on.

He pulled it away to flash the sign language for "I love you" before taking her hand again.

He knows what he's saying. His brain still works! Marnie hugged him, kissed his face, and called for the nurse. "Ben, you're back! I can't believe it! Thank God! Thank you, God! I can't believe it! I already said that, didn't I? But I can't!"

The nurse hurried in, then stopped short. Quickly surveying

the scene, she checked the monitors, then asked Ben to blink twice for yes and once for no. "Are you in pain?" she asked.

He blinked once.

"Great. Do you know where you are?"

He blinked twice.

"Recognize anyone?"

Ben nodded, then winked at Marnie.

The nurse squeezed Marnie's shoulder. "Lookin' good!" she said as she exited.

For the next hour, Marnie stumbled over her own words, chattering giddily in a bundle of nervous energy.

Chapter Forty

Luc and Janelle came by, as did Courtney. Each stayed with Ben for only a few minutes, not wanting to tire out the patient, but they had to see for themselves his remarkable progress. He opened his eyes each time a new person spoke to him, then drifted back to sleep. Afterward, they were all too keyed up to go home. The three of them sat in the waiting area and visited for a few minutes.

Luc looked at Courtney. "I do have one serious concern."

"What's that?"

"The cell line helped the Rivera twins for only a few weeks. So, while I hate to put a damper on our great joy here, I'm nervous about Ben's remarkable progress."

"I've thought of that, and I share your concern," Courtney said. "My hope is that, as I said before, liver cells grow fast. The only question is whether they can grow fast enough. So we have to pray that the boost he got from the special cells will help his own liver to be rejuvenated before the cells die out."

They started to leave the hospital a few minutes later, but Courtney stopped when she got near the exit. "I have something I need to do here before I go. See you in the morning," she said.

Luc looked at her. "Okay. Listen, Courtney, what you did was beyond amazing."

The doctor smiled and looked at her feet. When they left, she turned down a hallway toward the chapel. She flicked on the light switch. The stained glass window was illuminated, as was the Bible, which still lay open at the marked-up page. She read it again. "Trust in the Lord with all your heart, and lean not on your own understanding; In all your ways acknowledge Him, and He shall direct your paths."

She looked up at the stained glass window. In the scene depicted, a simple path led to a cross, behind which stood the resurrected Christ.

Courtney stared at it for a long time, then nodded to the image of the risen Savior.

The next morning, Ben woke up hungry and fully alert. He still couldn't speak because of the respirator, so Marnie got him a writing pad. He awkwardly wrote with his left hand, "Bobby & E?"

So Marnie brought her husband up to date about their children. "You know I can't bring them up here because they don't let kids in ICU."

Ben nodded.

"But I did bring a get well card Emily made for you." She showed him the card—with a crayon drawing of Emily's family that now included baby brother.

Ben smiled as best he could. Next he wrote, "How?"

Marnie looked confused. Ben pointed to his surroundings, but Marnie still didn't comprehend what he wanted to know.

At that moment, Luc arrived, and he moved to the bedside. Ben showed him the note then pointed to his own chart.

"You mean . . . how did you get well?"

Ben nodded.

Luc smiled broadly. "Good thing you didn't fire Courtney."

Three weeks later, as the cell line began dying out, Ben's liver was producing enough healthy, rejuvenated cells to assure recovery. He lay in a private room, disconnected from all his tubes. Only the IV drip gave any evidence of the crisis that had passed. The right side of his body remained sluggish from the stroke, so he had been assigned to a physical therapist. He had trouble remembering some events in his long-term memory, but he promised Marnie he wouldn't use it as an excuse to forget their anniversary.

Late one afternoon, he lay holding Marnie's hand. When she looked at him, he gave a sideways smile.

"I know you didn't want me to see you like this," Marnie whispered. "It was your worst fear."

Ben had lost feeling in half of his face, so he spoke with difficulty. "I guess God gives us grace to make it through what we thought we could never endure, huh?"

Marnie nodded.

"And you know how much I hate to need help. Guess that has to change. God had to knock me out to teach me."

It felt good to laugh.

"Know what else?" Ben asked her.

"What?"

"Tim's goal was to keep people from losing a loved one who could be helped with cell therapy. He was wrong in violating ethical guidelines and breaking the law—and wrong in sacrificing his family, but . . ."

"But it also saved your life," Marnie said.

Ben nodded. "That doesn't make what he did right. But it

does mean God is bigger than our mistakes. And he can re-
deem them."

The following May, Leigh Rivera walked from her bedroom
to the nursery, leaving a trail of perfume. She stopped at the
entryway to check her reflection in the mirror. After blotting
her lipstick, she continued to the nursery to help dress her
three children in party clothes. With Ophelia's help, she secured them all in their car seats, then drove down to the park
by the lake where Culiacán citizens held grand celebrations.

She opened the car door to jubilant cheering. She stepped
out, smiled broadly, and waved to the crowd of Culiacán city
employees. They had gathered to celebrate the twins' first public
appearance since infancy and to honor the physician team who
had made the city proud. Carlos strolled over to the car. He
usually didn't help much with the children, but now he aided
Leigh, eager to show off his lovely, healthy family.

"Be right there—I'm getting the picnic basket," Marnie called
to Ben.

With the aid of his cane, Ben walked over to the Explorer,
where the kids were already buckled in.

Moments later, Marnie emerged with the basket and a
blanket.

Four hours later, they arrived in Westfield, New Jersey, at
the home of Tim's mom. Emily yelled, "Grandma!" even before they pulled in the driveway. Mavis Beth, eager for them to
arrive, had been waiting on her long porch.

After everyone exchanged hugs, Mavis Beth looked at her

granddaughter. "I've got a stack of chocolate chip cookies with your name on them, Em." Then she took Bobby, now barely toddling, from Marnie's arms. "Why don't y'all head on up to the cemetery now," she said to Ben and Marnie. "We can have lunch later. The kids and I will find you over at Mindowaskin Park in about an hour. Meet you right across from the library."

Marnie nodded. "Sounds great."

"I'll bring some bread so Emily can feed the ducks," Mavis Beth added and was rewarded by Emily's cheers.

Marnie gave Mavis Beth a peck on the cheek and, with Ben, got back into the car.

When they arrived at the cemetery, Ben offered to stay in the car, but Marnie came around to his side. Quietly she told him, "I know I need to make peace by myself, but I'd love for you to be nearby."

Ben nodded. They made their way to Tim's grave, and Ben found a bench where he sat and prayed for her, knowing this was not an easy moment.

Marnie walked to Tim's headstone and stood for a long time. Although she knew that Tim could not hear her words, it helped to be able to say them.

"I forgive you, Tim. You were wrong, and you weren't sorry for the choices you made, . . . but I still forgive you."

She stood silently for another minute. Then she motioned for Ben to join her. He slowly made his way over and took her hand in his. They stood there together for a long time. Then Ben said, "Thank you, heavenly Father. Thank you for somehow always bringing good out of bad."

"Amen." Marnie nodded solemnly. Then she looked up at him. "I'm ready now." She entwined her fingers in his, and they slowly walked away.

When they got to the park, there were no other cars in the lot. Marnie pulled the car into a spot that faced the lake. Then she reached around and pulled the sparkling grape juice from the cooler. "I've been saving this for a special occasion," she told him.

"Isn't that the stuff we were going to drink the day you told me you were pregnant?"

"You remember."

"A lot has happened since you bought that."

"And I think it's time we celebrated."

"Time, indeed."

Marnie got two glasses, and they toasted each other. No words were necessary.

When they'd finished, Ben set his glass on the dashboard and said, "I have a surprise for you, too."

Marnie gave him a curious look.

He slipped a Rachmaninoff CD into the car's stereo player, lowered the windows in the car, and turned up the volume. He motioned for her to get out and then walked around the car to join her.

"Did you know you can dance even when you're lame?" he asked.

"I'm counting on it." Marnie held up her arms. So Ben took her in his left arm, supporting his right side with the cane, and they danced.

After a minute she said, "Funny. It's even better."

Ben gave her a skeptical look.

"I almost lost you. Now I have you back. So I'd say you've never danced more beautifully in all your life."

Unable to hold the emotion in his heart, Ben's eyes welled with tears. He smiled tenderly and held Marnie in a momentary gaze. Then he leaned down and gave her a kiss.

For more information on topics covered in this book:

www.aspire2.com The authors' Web site provides information about our publications. In addition, we provide articles on bio-ethical topics such as infertility, end-of-life issues, abortion recovery, stem cell research, the Human Genome Project, and cloning.

www.cmds.org The Christian Medical and Dental Associations (CMDA) serve as a voice and ministry for Christian doctors. Its mission is to "change hearts in healthcare." One of CMDA's many goals is to address policies on health care issues.

www.cbhd.org The Center for Bioethics and Human Dignity exists to help individuals and organizations address the pressing bioethical challenges of our day, including managed care, end-of-life treatment, genetic intervention, euthanasia and suicide, and reproductive technologies.

www.stemcellresearch.org is the Web site of Do No Harm: The Coalition of Americans for Research Ethics. This national coalition of researchers, health care professionals, bioethicists, legal professionals, and others is dedicated to the promotion of scientific research and health care that does no harm to human life.

www.hannah.org The Hannah's Prayer Web site provides information and support for couples facing infertility and pregnancy loss.